Praise for Cornis

'Delicious and del
Fforde and Jenny Colga
Highlands is not to be m

'I loved Clem, she's a human tornado whose heart is in the right place....most of the time!'

' It was great that this book wasn't just a regular romance story, it had layers, laughter, looting and love. What more could you ask for?'

'Fabulous. Couldn't put it down. More please.'

'It was great that this book wasn't just a regular romance story, it had layers, laughter, looting and love. Clem is absolutely FABULOUS!'

By Liz Hurley

The Hiverton Sisters Series

Dear Diary (novella)
A New Life for Arianna Byrne
High Heels in the Highlands
Cornish Dreams at Cockleshell Cottage
From Ireland with Love
Aster's Story

Writing as Anna Penrose

The Golden Mystery Series

The Body in the Wall
Dead Winter Bones
Death at Castle Wolf

HIVERTON

Cornish Dreams at Cockleshell Cottage

LIZ HURLEY

First published 2024 by Mudlark's Press
(Previously issued 2021, Hera Press)

ISBN 9781913628147

http://www.lizhurleywrites.com/

DEDICATION

For Anna, this one isn't about you either

Chapter One

The morning sun flooded into the room filling it with light. The frost outside added to the sparkle of the champagne that was being poured into glasses. A bed was covered with a pile of dresses and gowns and a cat slept unperturbed on a pillow of cashmere and satin.

Ariana, Countess of Hiverton, sat at her dressing table, picking up various necklaces and earrings as she tried to decide what to wear. She smiled back at her reflection and laughed up at her three sisters.

'I think it's the ruby necklaces and the diamond tiaras that I find the most ridiculous. You know what I mean?'

Clem laughed. 'For me, it's when they call me Lady Clementine. I keep wondering if some bigwig has just arrived.'

'It's the bank balance for me, all that money and I didn't earn any of it.'

'There are lots of ways to earn money, Aster,' said Nick. 'Although, yes, you have a point,' she broke off laughing, 'the bank balances are rather incredible.'

Ari joined in the laughter as the girls discussed their recent change in fortunes. It had been almost a year now since their uncle David, their mother's brother, had died and Ari, as eldest sister, had inherited the estate and title. They had always been a very small family but today they were about to add another member. Ari was getting married to Sir Sebastian Flint-Hyssop and the sisters all very excited. After her first disastrous marriage their big sister deserved a fresh start and

Seb doted on Ari and her two sons. He was a very welcome addition to the clan.

'Clem, don't you think I should get dressed now? We're cutting it fine.'

Clem had designed and made everyone's gowns. As this was Ari's second wedding and the twins would be present, she hadn't wanted a full-on white wedding dress. Clem had raised her eyebrow at Ari's resistance and had started sketching some ideas. In the end she had fallen in love with a simple cream, full-length duchesse satin dress with a slim skirt, falling to the floor. Over the top of the dress, Clem had drawn a large single cowl that sat on her shoulders like a cape. It was in white organza, trimmed at the top and bottom in a white satin band. Ari had gasped when she saw it.

'Seriously, Clem, that is the most bridal dress I have ever seen. It's almost religious.'

Her sister had protested with a huge grin on her face. 'But there's no veil, as requested, and no train and no lace and no frills and…'

'… and I love it. Will you be able to make it in time?'

Despite having said that he would take time to woo Ari, Seb had not been able to wait. He wanted to marry her as quickly as possible, she felt the same, why wait? However, Ari had been worried that the speed might be too much to handle. Clem had dismissed her concerns, explaining that because the design was so simple she'd have no time issues. She would also be able to do the four bridesmaid dresses as well. 'We'll have our dresses in caramel and our capes in cream.'

With that decided, Clem had then flown to her sewing machine and barely came up for air as she rushed to deliver what she had promised her sister.

'Do you know it's incredible to think this is the sort of wedding that our grandfather must have wanted for Mummy. A big fancy do, marrying someone with a title. And he was prepared to throw her out because she chose someone who brought her nothing but happiness. Imagine how different things would have been if he had only been more forgiving. I almost feel sorry for him.'

Clem stared at her big sister in disbelief. 'He was an arsehole.'

'Clementine!'

'What? He was. How can you defend him?' Clem was used to being chastised by her sisters for speaking her mind, but she was surprised that any of them would disagree with her on this point. 'We grew up wearing hand-me-down clothes. Eating meals that our neighbours shared with us. We didn't have a single holiday, and when Mum and Da died, we were left to fend for ourselves!'

'I'm not defending him, but could you remember not to swear in front of the boys?'

Clem looked in embarrassment at her nephews, who were now standing grinning in the doorway.

'Little tinkers, I thought Paddy was taking care of them?'

'I was,' said Paddy, who walked in behind them. Despite gracing the top catwalks around the world and being on the want list of the top fashion designers, Paddy currently looked as mischievous as her two nephews. Her long red locks were

3

tied up into two side pigtails and she had splatters of mud mixing in with her freckles. Now she was shaking her head in mock condemnation of Clem's choice of language. 'How was I to know when we came back from our snack, that you'd be swearing?'

'It's Clem,' drawled Aster, 'it would have been a pretty safe bet.'

Clem gave her a mock growl but was glad that the mood had lifted. She still couldn't come to terms with a mother and father who could abandon their daughter for the sole crime of falling in love with the 'wrong' man.

'Who were we talking about anyway?' asked Paddy. She smiled at her sisters; between them and her two nephews there was no one she loved more in the world.

'Grandfather.'

'Oh yes.' Her face fell a little. Her grandfather was the root of her mother's banishment. 'It's so sad, isn't it, that they weren't able to see how happy their grandchildren are and meet their gorgeous great-grandsons.'

'Is that us?' piped up Leo.

'Are you gorgeous?' asked Paddy, tickling them.

'Yes!' shouted William laughing.

'Well, I guess it must be you two, then. Now just play with your tractors whilst I sort out Mummy's hair and face. Spit spot.'

'About time! No one is putting their dresses on until you've finished with the make-up,' said Clem, 'plus you need to wash your own face. Honestly!'

4

'Don't worry, Clem,' said Paddy hugging her sister, 'I can do this with my eyes closed and then we can all get dressed in your gorgeous creations.'

Nick nudged Aster. 'Shall I do your hair and you can do my face?'

'Clown cheeks and pigtails?'

'Like Paddy? Absolutely!'

Paddy swatted the pair of them with her hand. 'Behave! Nick, don't lead Aster astray.' Which made everyone laugh. At twenty, Aster was the youngest of the five girls, but the idea of her being led anywhere was preposterous.

'I'll do your make-up in a minute. Let me sort out Ari, then Clem can dress her. And we can get this wedding day production line underway.'

Unrolling her make-up brushes, she started to apply a light base of colours on her sister's face. Having been a professional model since sixteen, Paddy was a dab hand at applying the perfect make-up for any occasion and sorting out hairstyles with a flick of the wrist.

'Do you know, I don't care about our grandfather? I just wish Mum and Dad were here,' said Ari, as she watched her sisters chatting.

'I think they are. I think they are looking down on you right now, Ari, and are sending you all their love,' said Paddy.

'Oh damn, I think you're going to have to do my mascara again.'

Paddy dabbed at her own eyes. 'It's okay, I'm using waterproof on all of us. I know you'll think this is daft, but when I'm with you four, it feels like they are here with me anyway.'

Ari nodded in agreement. 'I'm the same when I see the things you do or say and I catch a glimpse of them. I don't think they could be prouder than I am, at how we've all turned out.'

Half an hour later, there was a gentle knock on the door and Mary, Sebastian's mother, leant around it and the girls all greeted her enthusiastically. They liked Ari's soon to be mother-in-law and despite her being Lady Flint-Hyssop, she was down to earth and welcoming to all the sisters. In turn Mary enjoyed the company of these vivacious girls; individually they were either quiet or calm or boisterous but together they were like a flock of birds and lifted the spirits of the entire room. Once more, Mary thought her son was very lucky indeed. Now she cleared her throat.

'I think we're ready when you are. Can I help with anything?'

Eventually, in a flurry of chiffon and diamonds, the girls slipped on their shoes and prepared to leave. They were heading to the local parish church that lay between the two estates. Having got ready at Hiverton Manor, the actual wedding reception would take place at Hyssop Hall, Seb's ancestral home.

***

As Lord Flint-Hyssop waited in the church foyer with Ari he gave her a very soft kiss on her forehead. 'Do you know, I am honoured to walk you down the aisle. My only regret is that I never met your father; he must have been an incredible man, for little Lily to run off with him and for them to bring up five amazing girls. He would be so proud of you today.' He patted her hand. 'As proud as I am to welcome you into my family. Now shall we go and entertain the crowd?'

As the music from the organ swelled to fill the church, Ari, Tony Flint-Hyssop, her four sisters and her two sons started to walk down the aisle. In the simplicity and elegance of their outfits they almost floated, the little boys solemnly carrying the ring cushions. As Ari walked towards Sebastian he stood and watched as she moved in beauty towards him and he knew he was finally complete.

***

The ballroom pulsed with laughter and music. Champagne flowed and the wedding guests danced and drank their fill. Small children crawled under tables gathering up fallen shoes until the occasional adult leant down and waved them away. Women returning to the dance floor either did so barefoot or in shoes too small or too large. Whether they noticed or not was unclear.

Groups of friends poured each other drinks, some balanced glasses on top of each other, bow ties hung loose around necks as cigars were puffed on. The tables had been cleared by teams of waiting staff and moved to the edges of the ballroom in readiness for the dancing. Despite the wintry conditions, the ballroom glass doors were open to the wide stone patio and a few brave souls stood outside to escape the heat of the room. Those inside were glad of the cool air; girls shivered delicately as opportunistic chaps swung their jackets over the girls' shoulders. More than one pair caught each other's eye either for the evening ahead, or for years to come. Garlands hung from the chandeliers and party poppers lay strewn over the floor. Dancers kicked the debris to the edge of the floor and would clap and cheer as a couple would swing into a waltz or a tango, regardless of the music playing. Fathers danced with their children standing on their feet whilst their mothers watched on, chatting with family and friends as they swapped stories of previous weddings, and agreeing this was one of the jolliest in a long time.

The four sisters sat lounging back on their chairs; they had eaten enough, drunk maybe a glass too much and danced their stockings off. Now they watched Ari dance and laugh with their new brother-in-law. The Ladies Clementine, Nicoletta, Patricia and Aster had been delighted to stand behind Ariana and Sebastian and now relaxed, their duties done. More usually they were known as Clem, Nick, Paddy and Aster. Aster alone was not one for nicknames.

'He'll do, won't he?' Aster was rarely the first to comment on anything, but in this marriage, she had been quite attentive. Probably because she had had to live with her previous brother-in-law whilst she waited to escape to university.

'I suppose so,' drawled Clem. 'I mean he does have a title, Sir Sebastian, so it's not like she's marrying too far beneath her?' At which point all the sisters burst into laughter, causing heads to turn and people raised their glasses to the happy group.

'I hope the Countess of Hiverton remembers her dignity,' said Nick, as the DJ loaded up an Abba medley. 'Remember the last time she danced to Abba?'

'I warned her those hot pants didn't have much give in them when I made them for her,' protested Clem but joined in with the other girls laughing at the memory of their big sister dashing off the dance floor at the local tower block's community rooms, her hands firmly clasper over her derriere.

Paddy hiccupped. 'I think she looks wonderful. I don't ever think I've seen her look happier.' A loose balloon bounced over and she patted it back to a group of teenagers who were currently playing volleyball with them. 'And I love the fact that Seb couldn't wait any longer to marry her.'

'Maybe she's pregnant?'

The other girls considered it but Paddy protested, saying it was because Seb loved her so much. Despite the family's problems, her natural setting was blind optimism in the face of anything. She was a born romantic. Nick leant over and squeezed her twin's hand. 'Of course he loves her. Look at them.'

Despite the long tails of his morning coat, Seb was now strutting his disco stuff with Ari waving her arms in the air and trying to keep her tiara in place, until the two of them fell into each other's arms laughing. As they watched, Seb pulled Ari closer towards him and started to whisper in her ear. She looked up at him smiling and then looked around the room until she spotted her sisters in a corner of the ballroom. Giving them a little wave goodnight the pair left the dance floor and headed out one of the side doors without fuss or fanfare.

Paddy looked around the room and smiled as she watched Bhupi Aunty pick up one of the canapes and pop it in her mouth. Her lips pursed and she shook her head disappointedly at Mama Vy, who withdrew her hand from the

9

buffet. The two ladies wandered along the table surreptitiously shaking their heads until Aunty spied something and both ladies started laughing. A moment later their husbands joined them, they appeared to admonish them and then whisked them onto the dancefloor, the gold thread in Bhupi Aunty's sari catching the light as her husband spun her around.

'What do you suppose that was about,' said Clem as she nudged Paddy.

'No doubt they were unimpressed with the catering. I'm surprised they didn't try to smuggle in a tray bake.'

'What do you suppose they found at the back?'

'Ari rustled up some golgappa using Bhupi Aunty's recipe. More chillies than can be found in all of Brick Lane. Seb put a little warning flag on the plate. I've been watching some of the teenagers daring each other. Even Aleesha winced!'

Clem slapped her hands on the table 'Right. Ari's gone, it's time for the mice to play. Let's show everyone how ladies of the twenty-first century party!'

Laughing, the four girls hitched up their bridesmaid dresses and headed for the dance floor, even Aster who as a rule would prefer to sit and watch, joined her sisters laughing and whooping. As they began to dance, they attracted the attention of curious eyes. The ballroom was filled with people from Ari's old life as well as her new one, but all were united in wishing Ari and Seb a wonderful future together. Some in the room had watched this group grow from happy little girls, through the tragedy of their parents' and into confident young women. To others, Ari's sisters were an unknown quantity.

Now they dominated the dance floor; Paddy's and Clem's trademark long red hair was unpinned and flowing out, Aster and Nick laughing at their exuberant sisters. As a group they sparkled like the diamonds around their throats. Dancing and spinning, they were the perfect reflection of the bride's happiness.

Still whooping, Clem went up and had a word with the DJ and soon had drum and bass blaring out of the speakers. The teenagers in the corner finally left their balloons and surged onto the floor to join in the throng.

Gradually the older guests waved goodnight as the lights turned down and the music turned up.

'About Cornwall,' shouted Paddy to Nick.

'Tomorrow,' yelled Nick. 'Let's talk about Cornwall tomorrow!'

Chapter Two

The sisters spilled out of the large front door of Hiverton House and down the steps to say goodbye to the newlyweds. Everyone was waving as Ari, Seb and the boys drove off on their honeymoon. Sebastian had found the perfect accommodation in Crete, where the family would explore the island and uncover Greek myths together. As the staff had been given a fortnight's holiday, Aster had taken a week off uni to house sit and take care of the animals but the others needed to get back to their jobs. Paddy had gone back upstairs to shower having fallen out of bed to say goodbye, but the other three were still running on nervous energy.

Heading into the large kitchen, Aster popped the kettle on the Aga and began to pull out various items from the fridge. Soon the room was sizzling and the dogs sat expectantly whilst the cats had to be shooed off the work surface.

'About Cornwall,' said Clem, her expression worried.

'I know,' replied Nick, her tone matching her sister's.

Aster banged a tray of sausages and bacon down in front of Clem and Nick. 'You two need to stop treating Paddy like a baby. Do you ever think she might be insecure and uncertain because she knows you are always waiting for her to collapse?'

'Ah, come on, Aster,' protested Nick, 'that's not fair. You don't remember what she was like when Mum and Dad died.'

'Sure I do. She was an unholy mess. But she was fourteen and that was ten years ago. When the hell are you going to let her let that go? Even now you're whispering about her behind her back. Cornwall is an easy gig. It's not like what you are trying to sort out up in Scotland.'

When Ari first learned the extent of her inheritance, she had been overwhelmed by the amount of properties that she now owned. The major buildings were Hiverton Manor, a large Tudor mansion in Norfolk, the ancestral home of the de Foix family, a castle in Scotland that was causing Clem constant headaches, and an entire village in Cornwall. Beyond these, there were various other smaller properties and developments that were still being sorted out. She had asked her sisters for help and together the family were gradually working together to run the entire Hiverton Estate.

Tregiskey, the Cornish village, had originally been built centuries ago for the local workers at Kensey House. The little hamlet grew as the fishing industry expanded and the Hiverton Estate capitalised on their excellent location and bountiful harvest. Today the Hiverton estate still owned Kensey House and the village, collecting the peppercorn rents. But times had changed and now the villagers had little to do with the big house up on the hill. Sitting in the woods behind the village, Kensey was now mainly used as the de Foix summer retreat. There was a land agent based in Truro who was responsible for the running of Tregiskey and Kensey House, but it all seemed fairly stable as far as Ari could tell. She just needed someone to go down, make her face known and find out the lie of the land. It still seemed incredible to her that an entire village could be owned by a single family but she had been assured by her solicitor that there were several examples of this in Cornwall.

Spearing a sausage, Aster waved it at her sisters. 'It's not as if Paddy has to do anything, and yet you are still fussing over her. Give her a break. Besides, she wants to stop modelling. This is the perfect opportunity for her to think about what she does next.'

'Yes but…'

'No Nick, there are no buts. You have always been ridiculously overprotective of her, even when you didn't want to be her twin. Ari thinks Paddy can do this and that should be enough.'

Alerted to something, she called out, 'We're in the kitchen, kettle's on, bacon's cooked.'

Paddy walked into the room in a full-length pashmina kimono, her long hair damp against her back, and promptly headed towards the bacon. 'Oh God I know I shouldn't, but how do they make their bacon taste so good?'

'I think being wildly hungover improves the taste,' said Clem quickly hoping that Paddy hadn't overheard their conversation, 'or at least that's my theory. And don't share it with the bloody dogs!' she cried as Paddy dropped some bits in their food bowl.

'What? They deserve a treat too!' Looking at her three sisters glaring at her she came and sat down at the table, whispering to the dogs that she'd smuggle them some later.

'About Cornwall,' she began and was surprised when all three looked at her warily. 'It's just, do you think it will be okay if I drive down tomorrow rather than today? Not sure that today is a driving day?'

She hugged her coffee cup and drank deeply. Last night's wedding party had gone on into the small hours and Paddy was feeling a little soft. The last thing she wanted was to go on a road trip.

'Good call, told you those espresso martinis were going to kill you,' said Nick, 'but look, I still need to return to London today. Do you want to walk the dogs with me before I go? That way you can smuggle them more scraps without us noticing.'

Nick and Paddy both lived in London and had rented a small flat together. Both worked erratic hours, so the situation worked well. When Ari inherited, they moved into the family townhouse an embarrassingly large pile in the west of the city. Nick's daily commute had increased and she was looking for a new place to live. Plus she just wasn't comfortable in West London; unlike Paddy, who was happy anywhere, Nick was an East End girl through and through.

Paddy laughed at her twin. 'I suppose we should be amazed you lasted as long as you have out here in the sticks. Let me get dressed and we'll head straight out.'

***

As Paddy and Nick headed up towards the wood, the dogs bounded around them and then rushed off to investigate all the small movements and curious smells. Their tails were wagging and tongues lolling as they jumped in and out of the undergrowth. There was a fierceness to the air, the land was rock hard and the grass was white from a heavy ground frost.

With each cloudy breath, Paddy felt the sleep and booze being actively forced out of her system.

'Do you think it will snow?' asked Nick.

'God knows.' Paddy looked up at the sky. 'I bet if we'd grown up here, we'd have been able to read the berries and the clouds like proper country girls.'

'Read the berries?'

'Well, you know,' shrugged Paddy, 'I think there's something about, if there's lots of berries it's going to be a cold winter.'

'Doesn't sound plausible.'

'You read the stock market on just as implausible hunches.'

'Fair enough.'

For a while Nick's career faltered as she was unable to convince anyone to take her forecasts seriously. The days of risky gambles were over and no one was prepared to let a new kid loose on their portfolio. She tried to make her way into the inner circles but with the wrong accent, gender and upbringing she couldn't work out how to get her foot in the door.

Instead, she set up her own small business and decided to target new entrepreneurs; little people like herself, who couldn't break into the exclusive clubs. It had been hard work and she'd had no set-up capital but eventually she'd got into a position she was proud of and was helping to grow the money of self-starters like herself. When her sister had inherited the family estate last year, she'd been finally in a position to manage a very large portfolio, although now she had a client of one, the Hiverton Estate. She was still something of a workaholic though, simply because she enjoyed it so much and was already itching to get back to her screens.

The girls walked on in an easy silence, their scarves wrapped around their faces and their hands plunged deep into their pockets. Nick picked up some pinecones and threw them for the dogs.

'It's odd to think that Mum grew up here, isn't it?' said Nick again, working out how to broach the subject of Cornwall. 'That she had all this and gave it all up for Dad?'

'I think it's wonderful. I mean we knew how much they loved each other but when you see all this, it makes you realise just how much she loved him.'

'Do you think it bothered him? Do you think he felt guilty?'

'I don't know.' Paddy kicked some dry leaves ahead of her before replying. 'I don't think he'd have felt guilty, though, it's not like he let her down the way I let you all down.'

Nick stopped and looked at her sister as she walked on. 'What are you talking about? You've never let anyone down.'

'It's okay, Nick, I know I did, you even told me at the time. My grieving was too indulgent. I nearly tore the family apart by allowing the social workers and doctors to say Ari wasn't coping with me.'

'I never said that!'

'You did. And it was true.'

'But I didn't mean you were letting us down.'

'But you were right. My grief was a monster. I had lost control of it and it was a selfish thing to do to all of you.'

Nick grabbed her sister's sleeve. 'No one ever thought that, Paddy. We were all so desperately worried that we were going to lose you too. Those social workers were waiting for any excuse to split us up.'

Paddy shrugged, thinking back to a time she could only remember with pain. 'It had the desired effect. I was so horrified that I had let you all down that it was the only thing that got through to me. I am honestly grateful.' She sighed deeply and headed towards a fallen tree trunk. 'That's why I threw myself into the modelling business so hard. In my own way I tried to make amends and support the family as best I could.'

'I thought you did it to distract yourself?'

As they reached the top of the woods, they sat on a tree stump and looked out over the fields below.

'Well, it helped. And it was a lot of fun at times. But primarily, I did it to bring home the bacon. Oh, that reminds me…' Delving into another pocket she pulled out some rashers and called to the dogs.

'Ari's going to murder you if she finds out you're spoiling them.'

'Well, I'm not going to tell her?' she grinned conspiratorially at her sister as the dogs raced across the field back to them. As she fed the dogs she carried on, avoiding Nick's eyes.

'So, that's why Cornwall is so important to me. I want to take stock of my life and decide what to do next. I also want to prove to Ari that I'm a safe pair of hands. Not some emotional wreck.'

The sisters watched the dogs run around. Nick was silent and staring off into the distance. Paddy knew that she had upset her. That wasn't what she had meant to do at all.

She was trying to reassure Nick that she was going to be okay down in Cornwall. Instead, she had dragged up old memories.

As a child, Paddy had leant on Nick too much, to Nick's total exasperation. Despite their genuine closeness, as a little girl, Paddy suffocated her sister, who wasn't in the slightest bit interested in being a twin. On one occasion Nick cut off all her hair in a desperate attempt to not look like her sister. Paddy promptly followed suit. Within seconds though, she was bawling her head off. Her beautiful red hair had gone, her neck felt cold and she looked like a strange scarecrow. And worst of all Nick hated her for copying. Since then she'd begun to be more independent.

But independence only took her so far: she was happiest amongst her family. Even as a young teenager, she still preferred playing at home and being with her family. Pop stars and pin-ups held no appeal. The best parties were always at home, where their front door was open and neighbours piled in and out. Clem would be playing on the piano, her mum and pa singing along.

When her parents died, her grief had been insurmountable and no one could get through to her. One stupid, out-of-control lorry and her parents had been gone in the blink of an eye. It had felt like months of darkness. Then one day, Nick hissed at her that if she didn't stop blubbing the Social would say that Ari was failing and come and take her away. What would Mum and Pa say if she was the cause of the family being split up even more? This resulted in a fresh round of hysteria, but the following morning Paddy woke up, stopped crying and went to school. With the support of her teachers and friends, she gradually caught up on her work and occasionally began to smile, now and then.

At night, she and Nick would read stories to each other and to Aster, whilst their big sisters sat downstairs going through paperwork. Eventually the centre held and the little family prevailed.

Now she just wanted Nick to know that she was fine.

'I know Cornwall's a long way away but I'm going to be all right. I promise. Besides, the whole thing is running like clockwork. I've got this.' She grabbed Nick's hand and gave it a little squeeze. 'Trust me.'

The truth was, she was bloody petrified, she was completely out of her comfort zone. She was a brilliant model and she was great at following instructions, with an instinctive ability to find the light and create great poses. She was also a consummate grafter and had a fabulous agent that handled all her bookings. But she had never been truly independent and she didn't have the first clue about how to take charge of something. This was daunting but she was determined to make a success of it. After all, how hard could it be? All she had to do was drive to Cornwall, check out the paperwork, see that everything was running smoothly and report back to Ari. Compared to opening the show for McQueen, this should be child's play.

Chapter Three

The next day, after a late breakfast Paddy was finally on the road. Clem had flown back up to Scotland shortly after Nick had returned to London, so there was just Aster to say goodbye to. Hugging each other, Paddy had asked what Aster was going to do all by herself in the house and had to be satisfied with Aster's raised eyebrow and one word answer. Indeed, what else would Aster do but study? But over the years, the sisters had all discovered that Aster studying meant a lot more than just reading books. God knows what she was going to discover.

Paddy hadn't been to Cornwall before and was looking forward to it. Once her school had gone on a week to Devon but the family couldn't afford it so her folks had taken them on a day trip to Brighton instead. She remembered jumping over the waves on the stony beach and screaming with delight. When her school friends came back full of gossip and tall tales, she was a little envious, but kept it hidden, focussing on how much fun she'd had with her family.

Smiling, Paddy had settled into her car and set off. Her MGB was her pride and joy and her sole extravagance. It was British racing green and she had taken it to a local garage to have lots of modern comforts fitted, including a system whereby she could hook her phone in and bring the vintage sports car right up to the twenty-first century. She had set up the satnav and had been surprised by her late arrival time; dismissing that as ridiculously overcautious, she dialled up some Vivaldi and hit the open roads.

As she joined the M25 two hours later, her phone rang and she tapped the clever talk pad that had been added to her steering wheel.

'Hi Paddy, where are you?'

'M25 – just got on.' In the background Paddy could hear Ari relaying this information to Seb.

'Were you delayed? Is the traffic bad?'

'No, it's all good. Aster and I had a late breakfast is all.'

'You won't get there till late. Shall I call the land agent for you?'

Paddy rolled her eyes. 'Stop fussing and enjoy your honeymoon. I'm quite capable of calling the agent myself. Send my love to everyone. Got to go, roadworks.'

Hanging up, she felt a bit put out. The drive was boring and it would have been nice to have had someone to chat to for a bit, but not if they were going to fuss over her. The phone rang again and Paddy was immediately suspicious: had Ari hung up and called one of the others?

'Clem! How lovely, how's Scotland?'

'Oh you know, same old nightmare. Look Paddy,' said Clem, straight to the point. 'Ari says you set off late. Seriously you don't want to arrive at the house in the dark, it will be tough to find your way around.'

'Stop it. This is ridiculous. When my flight to the Milan fashion show was cancelled, I had to catch trains all across Europe to get there on time; I arrived in the early hours and managed to get to the hotel, and then get to the morning rehearsals on time.'

'But you speak Italian.'

'Jesus, Mary and Joseph, Clem! I speak bloody English. So what if I arrive late? The world won't end, and if I can't find the house I'll sleep in the car.'

Clem swore down the line. 'You're five feet ten, how the hell will you sleep in the car? Plus you'll freeze to death. You should break up the journey. Book into a Travelodge or something. Where are you now, I can find some—'

'Seriously, Clem, I'm fine. Tell Ari I'm fine and leave me alone.'

Tapping the phone with more energy than was necessary she ended the conversation. This was ridiculous, they were dampening her mood. She was half expecting Nick to call next, it was no good, this was ruining her concentration. She switched on Radio 2 for a bit of company and distracted herself listening to a spirited conversation on whether the Royals were good for the country. Checking the satnav, she noticed that it hadn't recalibrated much and it did indeed look like she was going to arrive after office hours. She pulled into the services and grabbed some fruit and water and then called their land agent in Cornwall. When she explained where she was, the agent agreed that she wouldn't be there for hours. He suggested that he wait at the house for her, but she wouldn't hear a word of it.

'You leave the key under the mat, or wherever. Then in the morning, come over for coffee. You might need to bring the coffee though.'

She could tell that the agent wasn't happy with that suggestion as he tried to push the point.

'Lady Patricia, it won't be too much trouble at all. We have taken care of the estate for your family for decades. It doesn't feel right leaving the new heir to stumble around in the dark.'

'Ah but I'm not the new heir, Mr Chadwell, I'm just her kid sister. Honestly, at the end of today go home, then tomorrow you can show me around properly.'

It took a bit more wrangling but finally she got him to give her detailed instructions regarding the last few miles of the journey. He told her he would leave the gates open and the front door key would be tucked behind the left-hand lion in front of the main door. It all sounded rather grand but then she was beginning to get used to that. Her mother's family seemed to relish being grand. Driving on, the discussion had given way to the news and she switched over to Radio 3 and began directing the orchestra as the car sped on along the M4. She began to run through her head all the things that needed doing and tutted when she remembered that she hadn't called Duncan back. Her agent had needed her forwarding address and she had promised to send it straightaway, but then Leo and Wills had come in with a beetle they had discovered, and she had become completely engrossed in playing with them. She loved her little nephews and was going to miss them terribly, stuck down in the wilds of Cornwall.

Calling Duncan up, she smiled as she heard his enthusiastic voice fill the car.

'Have you changed your mind? Are you coming back? Please say you are coming back?'

As always, she felt a bit guilty that he was hungrier for her success than she was. He had convinced himself that she was just burnt out and that she would soon return to the industry, but since her change in fortunes he knew he was probably flogging a dead horse. He had never once questioned her work ethic but her heart just wasn't in it; he knew she was working for her sisters, to support the family. To be a supermodel you needed to be doing it for yourself.

'No, no and no.' She laughed, happy to be chatting. Unlike her sisters, Duncan didn't treat her as a child; he treated her as a serious professional. 'Sorry Duncan, I'm still running off to the *godforsaken ends of the universe*, but you wanted the address? I think the Royal Mail extends to Cornwall?'

Like a lot of Londoners, Duncan couldn't perceive an existence outside of his beloved city. Milan, New York, Tokyo were nothing but tolerable shadows. He had a house in Hampstead, which he considered the countryside. Or at least the only bit of countryside that he was interested in.

'Very well, I'll send them forward, I hope you have a letterbox large enough to go with that fancy address. There are a few contracts, and a couple of gorgeous photos for your model book but it's mostly just presents. Bon Voyage gifts and the like. Stella has sent you a blanket and some sheepskin slippers, says you're to find a rock on a beach to sit on and stare out to sea looking like a stranded mermaid, your hair dancing in the wind. John sent you a blouse from his Forbidden collection; not sure where the hell you will be able to wear that in public. Don't they still stone witches down there?'

'Duncan! Don't be so rude, you think Hampshire is still in the dark ages.'

'Hampshire *is* still in the dark ages. We went out to a weekend house party, last month, not a single parking meter accepted contactless!'

'Shocking. I advise you never return,' said Paddy with a twist to her lips.

'I shan't. Anyway, there's lots of other bits and bobs. The divine Victoria sent you some trousers, and Carlotto sent you a framed photograph of himself. You know the one, where he's staring into the lens like a raptor.'

'Good grief, why on earth does he like that so much?'

'I think he thinks it makes him look mean and manly.'

'But he's a teddy bear!'

'Yes,' Duncan drawled, 'I rather think that's the image he's trying to distance himself from. Anyway, he said he wanted him to be the first person you think of when you decide to come back.'

Paddy frowned. If she hadn't been driving, she'd have thrown her hands in the air in exasperation.

'You have made it clear to everyone that I'm retiring, haven't you?'

'Be fair, you haven't categorically said that. You said you were going to the country for a few months to consider your future options.'

Paddy could picture Duncan looking down the phone with a raised eyebrow. If she listened closely, she could probably hear his finger tapping on the desk.

'Hmm. I suppose you're right.'

'Of course I'm right, plus it makes you even more attractive. That and the title.'

Now it was Paddy's turn to raise her eyebrow.

'Ah, come on now, Duncan, I don't want anyone to be led on; I don't want anyone to think I'm pulling a stunt to raise my profile.'

'No one who knows you would ever think that. Trust me, you are straight as the day is long. That's why everyone likes working with you so much.'

Changing the subject, they chatted for a while and caught up on some of the recent gossip. She was delighted to hear how everyone was doing but didn't feel the slightest bit tempted to get back on the horse. They then discussed a few of her contracts and how they had been settled. Paddy had worked out every last contract preferring not to let anyone down and had a few ongoing campaigns that would still feature her. She may have stepped back for a bit but it was important to wind her brand down carefully, just in case she wanted to come back. Finally, the call came to an end as Duncan regretfully had to answer his other phone that had rung at least twice during their conversation.

The motorway continued and Paddy wondered if her day would ever end. The traffic was slow and tiresome. It was only four o'clock but she felt like she had been driving forever. Pulling in at Bristol services she was thrilled to arrive in what was considered to be the West Country. Surely it wouldn't be much further now. Calling the land agent she told him where she was and was surprised when he laughed. Apparently, she was still several hours away. Sighing, she decided to stop for a bit to stretch her legs.

As she headed towards the services she was caught out by a squally shower and she pulled her bomber jacket over her head, sprinting along with others towards the front door. In an explosion of laughs and exclamations the crowd poured into the services shaking the water off their clothes, grinning at each other. For a moment they were all united in the need to escape the weather and then they separated back into their little groups in search of food, a quick coffee or simply a loo break. Paddy headed off towards the little shop, unaware or immune to the looks and double takes as she walked past people. She was wearing trainers, jeans and a sweatshirt, her hair was scrapped back and she had no make-up on but there was no mistaking the fact that she simply caught the eye. She was tall, striking and always smiling, it was a rare day when Paddy didn't turn heads.

Grabbing some salads, snacks and a large coffee, she was distracted by her phone buzzing and she saw a text from Aster. It was a video clip of Lori, a model who had always caused Paddy trouble. In fairness, Lori caused all models trouble; she was vain, capricious and unkind and was incapable of playing nicely with others. Now, in the video, she was walking along the catwalk and appeared to upstage another model but got caught in her own outfit and stumbled, falling into the audience. Paddy tried not to laugh, but it was impossible, especially when the video stopped on her snarling face and exposed backside.

She tapped an emoji laugh back to Aster and decided to head off again. Her phone rang and expecting Aster, was delighted to see Nick's details instead.

'Hello, you, how's it going? Conquered the Nikkei yet? Is the Dow Jones playing to your tune?'

'Give them time.' Nick was clearly calling from work; her voice had that brisk tone that meant her mind was whirring away on several problems at the same time. 'Now look, Clem told me you set off late and won't get to the house in the daylight. Where are you now?'

'Bristol, but I—'

'Jesus, is that all? You are definitely going to arrive in the dark. Make sure you call the land agent and tell him to wait on.'

'I've already contacted him and told him to go home. He's leaving the key for me and we will sort things in the morning.'

'That's outrageous. I'm going to call him. What the hell does he think he's playing at?'

'Nicki! Stop it. Stop overreacting. I'm quite capable of sorting things out. All I've had the whole drive is you three picking holes. Look I'm going to hang up. I love you all but you are doing my head in.'

The next ten minutes were a flurry of phone calls from various sisters and a deeply apologetic land agent. Having made him swear on his life that he was not to wait for her, she then sent out a group text to Ari, Clem and Nick telling them in no uncertain terms that they were to stop treating her like a child and to get off her back. Within a second her phone beeped and Aster had been added to the conversation. Followed by a text from Nick.

-You forgot to add Aster to the conversation so I've done it for you.

Paddy looked at her phone with incredulity. No one could make her as mad as her sisters. No one else in the world treated her like a child except for those three; she understood they were doing it out of love and they fully respected her as a model, never interfering in that, but in her everyday life, in her basic ability to function as a human being? They were all over that. She started to type and hit send.

-*I* didn't forget her. I didn't include her because she hasn't been a total bear's arse. I am going to arrive in the dark, in the Cornish countryside ffs. Not Colombia. There are no drug lords, no terrorists, no volcanoes, no poisonous insects. I am twenty-four and have been working for the past eight years. I am not a baby, GET OFF MY SODDING BACK!'

Chapter Four

She had been about to set off but driving angry wasn't smart so she took a quick turn around the car park. Her phone pinged and, ready for round two, she saw with relief it was another GIF from Aster. This time Leonardo Di Caprio was raising a champagne glass to her. Aster was the queen of the perfect GIFs and knowing exactly what was needed and when. Laughing, Paddy's bad mood had passed as quickly as it had arrived and she got in her car heading towards Cornwall.

The phone rang again and just as she was preparing to throw it out the window, she saw it was Billee BB. Wilhemena Barbara Bains had been a model who had successfully transitioned over in the film and TV work. A wicked gossip, with no filter and bags of ego she was always good for a fun time, even if she couldn't be relied on when things went south.

'Hey BB,' said Paddy smiling.

'Girl. Is it true? Are you really going to Cornwall?'

'Driving there as we speak.'

There was a squark down the line.

'Oh my God. You'll love it! Didn't I always says that you and Cornwall were made for each other?'

Paddy remembered no such thing but she didn't contradict her friend as she ploughed on.

'Cornwall is a dream. I mean they have no shops but other than that it's amazing.'

'I'm pretty sure they have shops.'

'Not real ones.'

By real ones, Billee meant shops that sold handbags for thousands of pounds.

'And you'll have total anonymity. It's incredible. The Cornish are so cool, they totally ignore you. I was saying to Tom the other day, Cruise, not Hanks, how incredible it is. He'd been on holiday and he was only asked for his autograph once and that was by a tourist. Isn't that incredible?'

'Incredible.' Paddy wasn't required to add much to the conversation. She just smiled and nodded along, agreeing or disagreeing at the right time.

'Even I found the same thing when I was on holiday last year.'

Paddy smiled to think that Billee considered herself more famous than Tom Cruise but no one would ever accuse Billee, *The Nation's Sweetheart* ™ as having a small ego.

'I swear I was out walking Buster, and the only things people said to me was to ask if I had poo bags, where the car park was, and could I hold the gate! Incredible!'

'Incredible.'

'I mean, obviously they knew who I was but they were so chilled. They even ignore the Prime Minister when he comes down here. They just understand that we need a rest.'

Paddy wondered if the Cornish were that caring or whether living in a media bubble you just get used to being surrounded by fans, sycophants and trolls.

'You're going to love it. I bet they don't even recognise you.'

Paddy rolled her eyes. Billee didn't mean to sound insulting, she just simply didn't have a conversation where she wasn't the most important person in the chat. As they carried on chatting Billee told her all about her new role in a remark of Casablanca and Paddy said she was going to be a huge success.

'I know, right? But honestly, I watched the old version the other day. Tell me babes, am I making a mistake? Ingmar Bergman was so cool. I'll never compare.'

And here was the other side of her monstrous ego, Wilhemena Bains was a colossal bag of insecurities. Paddy suspected that this was the true reason for her call and she began to reassure her friend.

'Why would you want to compare yourself? You're Billee effing BB. You bloody rock girl! You are going to walk on that film set and do it your way and that way will be epic. Who are you?'

'Billee effing BB,' laughed Billee nervously down the phone.

Who?' shouted Paddy, laughing.

'Billee effing BB,' roared Billee and as the two girls started laughed their conversation returned to matters mundane before Billee had to leave for a press junket. Hanging up, Paddy was once again reassured that she was making the right call by leaving the modelling industry and she knew that acting would be the wrong choice for her. But what was she going to do?

Whilst they had been talking the sun had just set and to her left, she saw a lone group of trees clustered around the top of a hill. They were striking and there seemed something very romantic in their beauty and isolation. Ten minutes later she drove past the county sign for Cornwall and breathed a sigh of relief. *Nearly there*, she thought. An hour later she wondered just how big Cornwall was, as she still seemed to be driving. However, the phone was beginning to give instructions more and more frequently. It was now fully dark and she had long since left the wide-open moors that the A30 had cut across, and she seemed to be driving along lots of impossibly small roads, her headlamps carving out tunnels through the tall hedgerows looming over the little car.

She turned down a road that was signposted to Tregiskey and also labelled as a dead-end. It appeared that she had driven to the ends of the earth. At least a no-through road meant she had to be very close. Just as the phone told her she had arrived she drove past a large driveway and reversed back. It was just as the agent had described: there was a lay-by to the side of the road and then two large white painted gates. The gates were solid, allowing no view from the road, but tonight they were wide open and Paddy drove through, following the drive around to the front of the house.

In the dark she was aware of it looming over her, her headlamps illuminating a perfect lawn hedged by bushes swaying in the wind. It was only eight o'clock but she was shattered. The porch light was on and, finding the key, she unlocked the front door and walked in. Mr Chadwell had also left the hall light on and she was grateful for the kind thought. Heading back to the car, she unloaded her overnight bag, locked it and then locked the front door behind her. The front hall was comfortably wide and long and took her past a couple of doorways and then opened up into a crossroad of passageways and an elegant Georgian staircase. She could easily picture a photoshoot here with some models leaning against the wall, others sitting holding onto the spindles of the balustrade.

The lights continued up the stairs and into the first bedroom, where the light was on; further down the corridor was another pool of light and so Paddy found the bathroom and her bed for the night. Brushing her teeth she mentally thanked the land agent for turning the heating and lights on. It was a thoughtful gesture. She was prepared to bet there would also be milk in the fridge but for now she just wanted to sleep.

She set her alarm clock and opened the curtains, an old trick that she employed to make sure she woke early; the last thing she wanted to do was oversleep. Pushing up the large sash window to let some of the heat out of her room, she decided that Cornwall was definitely warmer than London or Norfolk. A cool breeze passed across her skin and she slid into bed. In the dark room she lay under the heavy duvet and listened to the wind in the trees outside. As the wind lulled, she thought she could hear the sea and wondered if she had already fallen asleep. Was it possible that she could hear the waves from here? Imagine being able to live this close to the sea? Smiling hopefully, she fell asleep.

***

Paddy heard the gravel crunch outside and she went to open the front door. She was dressed in a smart pair of flat leather boots, indigo jeans and an oversized linen blouse. It was the only change of clothes she had as she waited for the rest of her luggage that would be arriving today. She wanted to impress the land agent and show him that she was going to be a safe pair of hands. First impressions were everything and she was already concerned that her sisters had unintentionally undermined her with their phone calls yesterday.

Standing on the doorstep was a smartly suited man in his fifties. He was tall and skinny and his suit fitted him like an afterthought; looking at it she thought it might have been at least twenty years old. As much a part of him as his shrubby eyebrows. He smiled and stuck out his hand.

'Lady Patricia? Malcom Chadwell. Pleased to meet you.'

Paddy welcomed him into the house and settled down for a second brew. Thanking him for his thoughtful gestures with the milk, heating and lights she then apologised again for her sisters.

'They just get a bit overprotective.'

'Big sisters are like that. I have two of my own and they still phone me up to check I've done things. *Have I seen the forecast, did I remember Rosie's birthday, did I get a flu jab?* I'm afraid it's just a burden we have to bear.'

Paddy nodded and listened to this man chatter on as she drank her coffee in silence. She wasn't sure how to start so she thought she would let him take the lead.

'Right then, enough of my going on. Have you had a chance to explore yet?'

Paddy shook her head. 'Honestly, I'm not long up. Yesterday's drive was quite a long one. I feel like quite a slugabed. Why don't you show me around?'

Built in the 1800s Kensey House was designed to be a summer home for the de Foix family. *Most people settled for a caravan*, thought Paddy, as Mr Chadwell closed the door on yet another bathroom.

When Paddy had first seen the house from the outside she wondered if there was a latch on the side where she could open it up and look inside. The house was built like the prettiest doll's house. It was a large Queen Anne design, five windows wide, three windows tall in perfect symmetry. Decorative brickwork ran in two columns on either side of the front portico, up to the slate roof which housed the third row of dormer windows. A pair of simple chimneys sat at either end of the property, again in perfect symmetry.

The pair of them wandered down elegant hallways, through tall gracious rooms, and Paddy felt completely out of place. Nothing about it was homely. It felt like some perfect film set or holiday let, which is exactly how it had been used for the past few years. Every room had wall-to-wall carpets but instead of making the rooms feel cosy, they felt claustrophobic, despite the tall ceilings and large windows. Many of the rooms at Hiverton Manor were even larger but somehow, they felt honest and lived in.

After their tour of the house, including a surprise chapel tacked on to the back of the building and accessed via a private door, from the house, or an outside porch on the other side, they headed back inside for a discussion of the village itself and what responsibilities were involved.

It wasn't onerous; each house or cottage had been well maintained over the decades. Tenants took care of their properties, enjoying the peppercorn rents and the idyllic location. Tregiskey was more a hamlet than a village; it led down to a sheltered cove and a popular pub, sitting just above the beach. Kensey House sat on the hill overlooking the small cluster of cottages.

'Sounds like it runs like clockwork then?' said Paddy, as Malcolm explained how the rents were managed.

'Pretty much. Did you plan to introduce yourself to the villagers? I could send out a letter to them. They already know that a new heir inherited last year.'

'To be honest I'd rather stay on the down-low. The QT?' She paused, looking at his blank face. 'I'd rather be here incognito for a bit, just whilst I find my feet. Is that acceptable? It all seems to be running fine so I don't want to come swinging in, throwing my weight around.' She stopped talking and plumped up a few cushions before continuing. 'If I'm honest, I'm a little bit nervous about them. Plus they aren't really my tenants, they're Ari's.' She drew breath feeling a little foolish. 'Is that okay?'

Malcolm smiled at her. 'Of course it is. You find your feet first and then say hello. Mind you, in a place like this everyone will already know someone is staying up in the big house. But no one's likely to come and knock on the door. You'll find the Cornish are friendly but not forward.'

'Sounds like heaven. But while I'm getting into the swing of it, I'll start reading through all this paperwork.'

Nick had already received all the financial details for the property and the village and had found it to be one of the more profitable arms of the Hiverton Estate. Now Paddy and Mr Chadwell continued to look through some of the bookings that were in place for the house, including some film shoots.

'Will I live here whilst they are filming, or do they need all the space?'

'Ah, now that's something else. There is a smaller property that I thought you might like to stay in whilst they are here. Let me show you.'

They got into his car, and he drove down a steep driveway hidden behind the main house. She hadn't noticed it before as it was tucked to the side behind some towering shrubs. As they drove down Paddy was delighted to see that the drive ended at a small beach. Sitting alongside the cove and just up from the gently lapping waves, sat a perfect cottage. They were about to head off and explore the property, when Mr Chadwell received a call. His son had fallen off a swing and had been taken to casualty. He had to go. Paddy agreed but was also surprised: she was used to a more business-oriented world where family concerns were second place. Malcolm offered her a lift back up to the house but she waved him on saying she would explore by herself.

As he left, he leant out of the window, calling out to her. 'The Grotto is up the steps behind the cottage. Well worth exploring!' and with that he was gone.

Smiling, she waved him off and turned back to the sea. How lovely this place was, where the family, not the job, came first. She did hope his lad was going to be okay and made a note to send him a card and a bar of chocolate. She thought a boy would prefer that to grapes or flowers.

A slight breeze caught her hair and rustled the trees behind her. Nudged out of her thoughts she headed towards the cottage. She'd go and see what he meant by a grotto after she had explored her temporary home.

The porch of the little cottage was lined in cockleshells pressed into plaster. All three walls of the porch were covered in the pretty white shells although in patches some had broken or fallen off. Paddy made a note to start collecting shells from the beach to repair it. Turning the key in the lock she smiled at the idea of it being little. It had three bedrooms for heaven's sake! Walking in through the door she found a small room on her right overlooking the garage/boat shed. Paddy thought that this room might work as a study. Ahead of the front door was the staircase and to the left, the rest of the house had been knocked through to offer one large living space. The kitchen sat closest to the staircase and its windows looked back towards a small garden before the land rose steeply, covered in rough-looking shrubs, as the cottage was tucked into the hillside. She opened the window to let some fresh air in and was suddenly engulfed in childhood memories as the scent of coconut filled the room.

Like all the kitchens on the terraced street where Paddy grew up, Bhupi Aunty's kitchen was small and made smaller by all the neighbourhood children crowding around Aunty's feet waiting for a chance to scrape out the bowl, whenever she made Coconut Ice. Growing up, Paddy was used to spending as much time in her friends' kitchens as her own. The London terraces where she grew up were busily being gentrified, but as a kid they were full of large families all spilling out on the streets and into each other's houses. Sharing a room with one or more sibling was so commonplace that having a room to yourself was considered an oddity. Now she had a whole house. She smiled again.

Leaning out of the window, Paddy discovered the smell of coconut was coming from the yellow flowers covering the hillside. She would go and cut some in a minute and put them in a vase, although the smell was so strong she probably didn't need to.

The rest of the lower floor was a large open plan living room with a big fireplace to the right and an end wall that had sliding patio doors leading onto a wide slate lined terrace. Heading onto the patio, she looked over the sand and water and thought she had found heaven. Taking in a deep breath she laughed. The unexpected noise caused a flock of birds to fly up, keening as they went. With a grin she looked around and discovered a second lower patio. This led out onto the rocks and at high tide she assumed that the small ladder would take her straight into the water. Looking back at the house she knew right down to the marrow in her bones that this was going to be her home. Not the big house on the hill.

Smiling, she returned inside and ran upstairs. The three bedrooms were of a similar size and there was a single bathroom. It was very gloomy and as she investigated, she realised that she would need to open all the external storm shutters. Plus, she needed to find some dusters and then sweep the seaweed off the patio, as she walked around the cottage, she was making a list of all the things she needed to do and felt an excitement begin to bubble up.

From the back bedroom she saw some steps and remembered the grotto. She dashed back downstairs and headed outside. Behind the garage she found a small gate leading to a flight of heavily overgrown, slate-lined steps, winding up on the right-hand side of the hill. Leaning over to pick some of the yellow flowers she was quickly defeated by an intense array of thorns. Her fingers were covered in scratched and her notion to fill the house with these sweet, scented blooms was quickly vanquished.

Climbing up, licking the blood off her fingertips, she was soon looking down on the roof of the cottage and out to sea. The path turned and she came to a small flat area, and built into the hillside was a small stone building. All she could see was a door and two wooden shutters on either side. Underneath these stood two stone benches looking out to sea. She unlatched the metal bars on the window shutters to reveal two un-glazed apertures. Opening the wooden door with a bit of a push, she blinked waiting for her eyes to get used to the gloom. As the light filled the room, she could see it was larger than she expected. It was about seven-foot square and utterly festooned in shells and decorative stones. Unlike the little simple cockleshells on her cottage porch, the shells in here were large and elaborate. Clam shells were overlapped in the shapes of flowers with little periwinkles in the gaps between, long razor clams fanned out under a ceiling dotted with large conch shells. Wherever she looked she could see beautiful shapes and motifs made out of shells. The ceiling was lined with what looked like icicles made out of long pointed shells, the floor was a swirling pattern of cobbles laid in intricate patterns. All along the edge of the walls ran a bench, presumably so that when it was raining you could sit inside in your magical little grotto and look out to sea.

Again, some patches of the walls were bare and shells and rubble lay broken on the bench. Here, like the cockleshells around her porch, was another project she could get her teeth into. Although the shells in this grotto seemed to come from around the world and some of the shiny yellow and blue stones looked semi-precious.

Making everything secure she walked back down to the cottage. Grinning to herself she headed up the drive to Kensey House just in time to direct the delivery driver down the lane to offload the rest of her suitcases. She didn't know what else she was going to do but at least for now she had found where she was going to live. Her own little cockleshell cove.

Chapter Five

Henry Ferguson sat looking at his feet. The grandfather clock softly chimed the quarter hour from the downstairs hall, and he became aware that he must have been sitting looking at his feet for fifteen minutes. The rest of the house was quiet and empty; his father and stepmother were out for the evening. He was now dressing for this evening's charity event where he was giving a keynote speech on the importance of clean wells in war-torn countries.

The clock chimed another quarter and he was amazed that he had now wasted thirty minutes looking at a pair of black socks. His life was a mess and he had no idea how to jump start it. A year ago he had been fighting in the Middle East for King and country. A violent and terrifying existence surrounded by friends and enemies. Life was black and white; save people, kill people, avoid getting killed, watch others die. His hair constantly thick with sweat and sand. Now as he ran his fingers through his blond hair it was smooth and glossy. Like everything else in his life.

An honourable discharge had brought him home where he floundered.

A stupid, banal accident during a football game with some local kids had snapped his cruciate ligament and sent him home to England with an honourable discharge after only a few years of active service. An anterior cruciate ligament injury was repairable but it left a permanent weakness. He'd been offered a desk job but he felt it was time to come home and help his father run the family estate. Following the death of his mother, Hal's father had married again, a lovely lady, but following a minor health scare, Hal didn't want to miss any more time away from the people he loved. Life simply was too short and gone in a heartbeat.

Between one heartbeat and the one that never came.

He helped his father run the estate, he began to attend parties and events and yet his life seemed shallow. There seemed to be no purpose to it. Initially, he had struggled to come to terms with his ACL injury and then he began to party hard, finding nothing else to do. He felt out of control; he needed a purpose but he didn't know what that was. It was at times like this that he missed that calm voice of his mother. He felt foolish that at twenty-eight he was still turning to his mother. He just wished she were still around to help him. Instead, now here he sat staring at his socks.

Lacing up his shoes, he stood up, checked his bow tie in the mirror and then headed downstairs and did a tour of the house and the grounds. Maybe he should move out. Who still lived at home at his age, but it seemed the easiest option. Normally he wouldn't be so meticulous but no one else was home tonight so he liked to be certain of the security. He headed into the small library that was known as his mother's. It was rarely used these days but when he felt flat, he found her presence buoyed him up. Recently he had made the biggest decision of his life and it was bringing him nothing but misery, and in his despair he was behaving badly. As he left, he touched the little jewelled snowdrops on the bookshelf. The flowers had been made by Fabergé and had been in his mother's family since they had been first purchased as a birthday present from the London branch of Fabergé in the early 1900s.

Every time he saw them, they raised his spirits; he would remember his mother telling him that these tiny delicate blooms would emerge through the ice and snow. Whenever a task seemed insurmountable, she would say, he was to remember the first flowers of the year. As a little boy he had nodded solemnly at his mother's words and tried to take them to heart. Smiling now he realised that, as ever, her words cheered him up. He had made his decision, now he needed to live with it.

Having checked all the house doors were locked, Hal switched his torch on and made his way over to the kennels. He wasn't going to bother with the lower pens, Brian always had those in hand; besides, you'd have to be a very determined burglar or vandal to go and find those sheds in the pitch black. The kennels and estate offices, however, were an easier target. He wondered if security lighting might be an idea; he would mention it to his father. Who would no doubt scoff at the idea and add it to Hal's other suggestions to drag the estate into the twenty-first century. Some days Hal wondered if the estate had even left the eighteenth century, in which it was first built.

It was important to him that he ran the estate properly, to show his father that when the time came, he could hand the reins over to Hal, with complete peace of mind. Since his mother's death, he and his father had grown distant. For the thousandth time Hal regretted joining the Army and leaving his father to cope alone. At the time all he could think of was his own grief. Everything about Cornwall, and indeed

England, reminded him of her. There was no escape from his pain.

Only under the hail of gunfire and explosions were his memories quashed. The harsh sun and arid landscapes offered no soil for his misery to take root. He watched his colleagues die or sustain injuries, he took part in rescue missions where babies screamed for their mothers lying bloodied across the floor. It seemed a world made mad with men wailing in pain, women silent in horror. Whole populations seemed to be on foot trying to find a place of refuge from the enemy, from their own side, from the soldiers that were here to help. Everyone desperate for food and shelter or simply a night without attack. This was the sort of life that placed his own grief in proportion and whilst it didn't lessen it, Hal learnt to deal with it. And as he learnt, he felt his mother's presence alongside him, nodding her approval and offering her protection.

Vollen was a beautiful Georgian house built in a soft warm brick more commonly associated with the Cotswolds and indeed that was where the stone had been quarried. When Hal's ancestor had made his money in the mining industry, he wanted to display his wealth as visibly as he could; so rather than build in the local granite he had the warm Cotswold stone brought by cart to Cornwall at colossal expense. It was his idea of a little joke and whilst not everyone found it as funny as he did, every time he rode home and saw the sun warmly reflecting on the walls of his house, he smiled in pleasure at what he had achieved.

Now his grandson, many times removed, walked across the cobbled yard and looked in at the dogs. All four of them looked up as he shone the torch on them. There was a lazy wag of a tail and a yawn and then three of them went back to sleep. This was a voice and smell they knew well. No need for alarm. Hal smiled to himself as Nimrod padded over to see if he was okay. When his mother was dying, he would come out to the kennels and cry himself to sleep, curled up amongst the dogs. Only Nimrod now remembered those times, little more than a pup herself. In the morning his father would berate him for his weakness; he was sixteen not six. His mother, though, would hug him as tightly as she was able and then gently suggest he shower before school.

How nice it would be to just stay here, he thought, bring the dogs into the house, and all sprawl out in front of the fire.

Sighing, he returned to the house and waited for his taxi to arrive. These past few weeks, though, he had preferred drinking to thinking, and had fallen asleep in a stupor most nights. His life seemed to be turning in a direction that was not of his making. He knew this maudlin behaviour also had to stop but he had no idea how. He just wanted to be happy again instead of just pretending to be. He should focus on the snowdrops.

Folding his tall frame into the taxi he thought about the week ahead. He had a few social engagements and there was the estate to take care of, when his father didn't disrupt his plans that was, but other than that there was nothing interesting on the horizon at all. Maybe the party would be fun. Something had to happen. He'd better go and be the life and soul of the party. Again.

Chapter Six

The young bride knelt at the altar of her family chapel. Her hair was hidden by a long white veil that flowed down her back, covering a large shiny wedding dress. She looked up solemnly at the priest, her small face framed by heavy make-up.

'Do you, Patricia Byrne, take Henry Ferguson, to be your lawful husband to have and to hold?'

Patricia took a deep breath to steady her nerves. 'I do,' her voice was quiet and husky, and there were appreciative nods from the people standing around. The priest turned to the bridegroom, a tall man with a bored expression wearing almost as much make-up as Patricia.

'And do you, Henry, take Patricia…'

All eyes turned to the handsome groom, who opened his mouth and promptly gave a massive yawn and stretched his arms. The bride tried not to giggle. In the corner of the chapel, the director yelled, 'Cut!'

Paddy stood up and stretched. The stone floor of the chapel was freezer and she waved for the heater to be brought over so she could stop her teeth from chattering. She had been at this all day and was turning into a popsicle.

The German film crew had arrived at Kensey House yesterday, a few days after Paddy had settled in and she was enjoying watching them bring the big house to life. When the director had offered her a bit part, she was even more excited. Normally when a camera was rolling, she was the main attraction. For once she was just a face in the background and she was loving the anonymity. She had been even more delighted when she met her acting partner. Initially she had mistaken him for a model; he certainly had the looks and height, and the way he grinned at her suggested that, for once, he wasn't gay. However, it was quickly apparent that he wasn't an actor or a model. He had none of their nervous energy. He was so confident that she wondered if he might be a producer but after five minutes of his company it was clear that he wasn't that either. He was relaxed, had a great sense of humour and took the mickey out of himself. A confident and powerful man with no need to prove anything. He had introduced himself as Henry but promptly invited her to call him Hal, saying that's what his close friends called him. Now he was making a mess of their small scene.

'Come on, Klaus! Have pity. I'm nursing the most colossal hangover.' He yawned again. 'See! Why don't you just dub over the yawn? No need to cut.'

'Because the camera is pointing at you, everyone would see you yawning.' The director was growing increasingly frustrated. This tiny scene was being totally ruined by some jumped-up amateur. The role had been won in a charity auction so Pieter had no choice but to put up with him. He was about to shout action again when the man spoke over him.

'Look Fritz, I've an idea. When I'm speaking, point the camera at the bride. She's easily the prettiest thing in the room. Why would anyone want to look anywhere else?'

Pieter groaned. He knew having amateurs on set was going to be a problem. 'Because that would look ridiculous. Okay, is everyone ready? From 'Do you, Patricia Byrne, take'.'

Now Paddy was blushing furiously and if anything her smile was even sweeter than before. Obviously, people were always commenting on her looks but no one had ever made her blush like this before. Hal really was something, but at the moment a lot of that something was rudeness.

They knelt at the altar rail and started again. The actor they had got in to play the role of priest seemed confused and flustered and Paddy wondered if he had also won his role. All the professional actors were currently engaged at the church porch. Apparently, that was the big dramatic scene. During a village wedding, the heroine is revealed to be the daughter of the local mayor. Or something like that. Paddy's German was a bit sporadic but she thought that was the rough gist.

The director finally convinced Hal to toe the line and whilst Paddy found him amusing, she also thought his behaviour was a bit poor. Everyone was on a tight timetable. As a model herself she fully understood how time meant money; too many takes made for a particularly unpleasant atmosphere.

When she and Hal had gone to sign the register, the priest kept getting annoyed with the cameraman, insisting that he didn't get so close. When she asked what name to use the priest looked at her as though she was deranged, telling her to use her name. She and Hal had a non-speaking role so hadn't been assigned names. The priest was right, so long as she could be seen writing something, that was all the camera man needed. She had had to explain to Hal that even though they were speaking for the camera, their voices would be cut from the final show.

'We're just fancy extras,' said Paddy with a grin.

The cameraman's English wasn't great so Paddy kept trying to act as go-between, although both priest and cameraman seemed to be getting exasperated. The groom wasn't exactly helping as he had started to yawn again and at one point had wandered off to see if he could find some communion wine. 'Hair of the dog,' he winked at Paddy. The cameraman went ballistic and started shouting to the director, who came back and started generally shouting at the priest, Hal and Paddy, as though they were all equally to blame.

'If we could just finish this final scene and then we won't need your services anymore. Just stand at the altar, the priest will pronounce you man and wife, the groom will go to kiss the bride and just before he does, Ignetta will smack Johan across the face and the whole congregation will turn around to look at the drama unfolding by the main door. Okay!' The director glared at the three of them and the rest of the crew to ensure that everyone understood.

It was a well-known feature of life in Cornwall that there would always be a German film crew filming episodes for its wonderful Rosamunde Pilcher series. Jobbing actors enjoyed the opportunity to get some paid work, even if it was only as an extra. However, the congregation had been playing up; chilled by the cold February air and the unheated chapel pews, they had started to fidget and play on their phones. The smack scene was their only chance to be properly featured on camera. Up until now they had just been backs of heads as the camera had been fixed on the bride and groom, but now the director would want some reaction shots and they were beginning to mug up their roles. It was his third take and poor Johan now had to have the make-up artist rush in each time to try and hide the growing red mark on his face. She seemed to be slapping him with enthusiasm and he wondered about the prudence of commenting on her weight gain just before filming.

'Okay, for the fourth and final time…'

'Klaus!' The groom had been lounging on the steps and now sprang up. 'Look, don't you think this is all a bit boring? I don't get to kiss the bride? That's what everyone wants, isn't it? I know I do!' He laughed and was joined by a few men in the congregation.

Paddy hissed at him. 'Shut up! I'm not kissing you! And stop calling him Klaus, for God's sake. His name is Pieter.'

Hal looked over at the director, who was now diverted by a concerned lighting engineer. 'Don't think so. Pretty sure it's Klaus or Fritz or something like that.'

'Maybe Gunther?' Paddy rolled her eyes.

'Could be. I honestly can't remember. My head is absolutely thumping.'

Now Paddy groaned. What was it with public school boys and their confidence, that everything they thought was right? 'And I think you'll find it's Pieter.'

'Really?' Hal yawned again. 'Not convinced.'

'Hey Pieter?' Paddy called over to the director, who by now was trying to reassure his leading lady that she hadn't put on weight and she wouldn't be upstaged by the bride at the other end of the chapel. 'What's your name?'

'Pieter.'

'Cheers!' Paddy grinned at Hal.

'Well I never. Why on earth didn't he say?'

Paddy raised an eyebrow. She didn't want to be rude. 'Maybe he did and you weren't listening?'

Pieter cleared his throat loudly enough for even Hal to get the point.

'Right! There will be no kissing! Last time. ACTION!' And as the groom leant down to kiss the bride for the fourth time, a slap rang out, the congregation turned, and the director cried cut. As he did Hal leant forward and gave Paddy a very chaste little peck on the cheek and winked at her. 'Can't leave a bride unkissed at the altar. Bad luck or something.'

She laughed. 'Well, if it's to ward off bad luck I suppose that's fine.'

Paddy had resolved to give him the benefit of the doubt. It had been a long day and for someone unused to it, it could be bewildering how long it took to shoot a couple of minutes. It didn't help that some directors were known for doing a thing twenty times, only to go with the first take.

'Tell you what,' he said, 'after we get out of these costumes what say we make an evening of it? Dinner over at Cliff House? They've just got their third Michelin star?'

Paddy thought it was a great idea but was unconvinced that he'd get a table at short notice. Nevertheless, she agreed and headed off to change, smiling to herself. Despite his momentary lapses, he had been run company throughout the day and when he wasn't yawning or getting his cues wrong, he had entertained her with stories and ran to get her hot drinks every time she had begun to shiver. Now, the promise of warm food was more than she could resist. Today was shaping up very well indeed.

Chapter Seven

As she quickly wiped off her make-up, she tried to analyse her feelings. Something about this stranger appealed. When he smiled at her he gave her his full attention, not just because she was good-looking but because he was interested in her for who she was as a person. As she stepped down from the make-up trailer, he was already waiting by a large Range Rover. She had swapped into a big, padded bomber jacket that Zac Posen had gifted to her and a pair of high-waisted denim jeans. On her feet she wore sheepskin lined boots that were finally returning some warmth to her frozen toes.

Leaning forward he kissed her again on the cheek. 'You look even prettier! How is that possible?'

Paddy laughed. 'Well, I was wearing a polyester wedding dress and had almost as much slap on my face as you did. In fact, I think we even had the same colour foundation.' Leaning forward, Paddy rubbed her thumb along Hal's jawline causing him to raise his eyes.

'Here, they missed a bit.'

'Bloody hell, they'll think it's panto season again.' Opening the door of the car for her, he told her the restaurant had managed to squeeze them in. 'Although I suspect we're probably by the kitchen doors!'

Paddy laughed. 'Just what every bride dreams of. So, who else is joining us?'

Hal got into the car and looked across at her. 'On our honeymoon? Just boring old me I'm afraid.' He paused, uncertain by the concern clouding her face. 'Sorry. I was just joking about the honeymoon thing. I just thought it would be nice to go for a meal?'

Paddy felt foolish. And then felt foolish for feeling foolish. Jumping into some random stranger's car seemed pretty high on the list of things she was not supposed to do. But he did seem lovely, if a bit roguish, and she really wanted to eat at Cliff House.

***

Paddy settled into the car as Hal nipped around the country lanes. She was finding driving in Cornwall a bit challenging. Hal's car sat quite high and gave a better view of the road ahead and she wondered if she would do better to swap for something bigger. She adored her MGB, but she did find driving it around here a little alarming. It was definitely a city car. 'So how did you get us a table at such short notice?'

Hal slowed the car for a tight bend before replying.

'We sometimes supply Toby with his game meats, and I know he tends to keep a table free for friends and family, so I chanced it. Rather glad you got rid of that make-up off me or I wouldn't have heard the end of it.'

Paddy watched as Hal smiled but kept his eyes on the road. Even if he was sitting higher up than other cars, he obviously wasn't ignorant of the issues of driving down single-track lanes with giant hedges on either side. 'We won't get a sea view but the food more than makes up for it. Have you eaten there before?'

'No, I've only just moved down.' She still felt out of sync with her new title and family wealth and decided not to say anymore. She hadn't even mentioned that her family owned the chapel they had spent the day in and decided to change the subject. 'When you say, 'We supply' who is we?'

'My estate. It's mostly mixed, arable and livestock. You'll have to come for a tour of it.'

Paddy confessed that she didn't know where the Vollen estate was and he explained he lived about thirty miles away near the north coast.

'You'll discover that a Cornish thirty miles can seem a very long way away. It can take forever to get anywhere and that's in the quiet months. Wait until summer. The county fills up with holidaymakers and you can't move a muscle!'

Paddy smiled inwardly; it was kind of him to try and introduce her to some of the foibles of her new home, but really, having grown up in London she knew all about congestion. Deciding to change the subject she asked instead how he had ended up playing the role of a groom and was treated to a lively tale that included a charity fundraising evening, a spirited auction to go deep sea fishing and being a tad worse for wear. Finally, he worked out he'd been bidding most vigorously on the wrong item. 'Even worse, I had to do it today! Headache and all. I had considered cancelling but I didn't want to let them down or give the charity a bad name. If I knew just what a small part I had, I might have stayed in bed.'

Paddy laughed. The idea that he thought everyone would be waiting on him, a role that until the night before hadn't even been allocated, was amusing but she didn't want to puncture his ego.

'Sorry, that wasn't very gallant of me, was it. If I'd stayed in bed, I'd have never met you. Will you forgive me? So tell me a bit about yourself. Where do you live? What do you do? When can I see you again?'

Paddy grinned, a second date before the first one was even over. Even so, she was still trying to settle in, and didn't want to talk about herself.

'I'm in between jobs at the moment and staying near Tregiskey.'

'What line of work are you in?'

'Modelling.'

'Ah,' Hal nodded his head sympathetically, 'that's a pretty competitive industry I hear. Still, look at you. I bet you'll find something else again soon, and Tregiskey is a lovely village. Are you looking for work down here?'

Paddy said she was currently taking a break and was relieved by how quickly they had arrived at the restaurant. Hal hadn't been driving fast but the time had flown, and she was finding the conversation too close to home. Tonight, she was simply Paddy, starting afresh with a clean slate. He had no pre-conceived ideas about her and she was revelling in his attention and ignorance of her title and her history.

The headlights from the car illuminated the exterior of the restaurant as they swung around to the car park, and as she stepped down from the Range Rover, she could hear the North Atlantic rollers crashing onto the shore below. The air was chilly and she quickly headed towards the reception with Hal holding the door open for her.

Walking in, it was clear he was well-known and there was some friendly banter with some of the chefs in the open kitchen. Once again, the fact that she was in everyday clothing and no make-up meant that she was generally unrecognised, even if her hair was something of a trademark. She did notice that some diners were turning their heads to see who had arrived, given that the volume level had risen as various people greeted Hal. From their expressions, a few had clearly recognised her. This was a restaurant that attracted a certain crowd, the leisured wealthy, and amongst them would be ladies that attended fashion shows, or read *Vogue* and *Harper's* or followed certain brands.

Happily though, Paddy discovered that Cornwall was a county where, as Billee predicted no one cared who she was and she loved it.

Now, looking across at the gorgeous man in front of her, she was beginning to see that it might hold other charms. She couldn't make up her mind about him. He was certainly easy on the eye, but that was hardly a draw for her. His lazy confident manner was attractive but also not something she was unused to. But every now and then though, a vein of genuine kindness shone through. They had just sat down when a waitress walked past, laden with too many dishes. Her table had obviously tried to be helpful, adding small plates to the dishes she was removing. Spotting her dilemma, Hal had jumped up and lightened her load, following her into the kitchens. As he returned, he apologised to Paddy for abandoning her, and continued chatting as though he had done nothing remarkable. She liked the way he paid attention to minor details and the fact that he seemed utterly interested in her. Well, who wouldn't like that?

'So, tell me,' said Paddy, 'was that your dream wedding?'

Hal pretended to take the question seriously. 'I think that in nearly every aspect my dream wedding would be different. For a start, I wouldn't be wearing make-up and the congregation would be better behaved.'

Paddy stopped poking the olives. 'I'd settle for a better-behaved groom!'

Hal winced. 'Was I dreadful? I'm afraid I was very hung-over, aren't grooms supposed to be hungover from the stag do?'

'If you a real groom you can do as you please but jobbing actors have to toe the line.'

He winced again making Paddy laugh.

'I'll send them an apology. And an offer of any help they may need.'

'So long as you also promise not to appear in front of the camera ever again.'

Hal groaned and put his hand in his head.

'Alright, banged to rights. Next time I shall be the perfect groom.'

Deciding to take pity on him she returned to the beginning of the conversation. 'So you said you would change nearly every aspect, which aspects did you like?' Paddy was fishing for compliments and Hal knew it. 'Well, the bride was tolerably fair…'

'Tolerably!' Paddy wondered if throwing an olive at Hal would be considered out of order. Instead, she gave him a mock scowl and waited whilst their next course was laid out. 'So, besides the tolerable bride, were there any other highlights?'

'The chapel was pretty special, although there wouldn't be much room for all the trees.'

'Trees?'

She leant forward curiously, surely he couldn't be thinking of the same thing she was.

'Yes,' he refilled her wine glass and then took a sip from his own. 'Do you remember when William and Kate got married, they lined the aisle of the abbey with giant trees? I thought that was stunning.'

'Why Hal, are you a romantic?' Paddy asked delightedly. She had watched that wedding and all the royal weddings, with hearts in her eyes. Everything was so dreamy and she had soaked it all up. She had almost swooned when she had seen the trees; it was like a fairy tale. Now here was a man who looked like a fairy tale prince telling her that he had also loved the trees.

'Guilty! What about you then, any trees in your church?'

'Oh I wish. But I could never imagine getting married in a church that big. Yesterday's chapel would be just fine, but lit by candles and I'd have all my sisters as bridesmaids. My dress wouldn't be nylon and I wouldn't have a heater under my skirts to try and keep me warm.'

She laughed remembering the electric blower that Hal had kept dragging backwards and forwards to keep her warm. 'But the wedding wouldn't be the big deal for me, it would be the marriage. I'd live in a perfect home…'

'What would make it perfect?'

'It would have a thatched roof, some deer in the garden and birds singing around the window.' Paddy looked at Hal. 'Are you sniggering? We'd also have lots of children.'

'How many?'

'Undetermined at this stage but at least two sets of twins.'

Hal started laughing. 'Good grief woman, how would you keep on top of the housework?'

'Silly. There wouldn't be any housework. This is my perfect life remember. I'd see the children off to school…'

Hal interrupted her, surely in this Mary Poppins daydream she'd be walking her children to school. 'Don't you take them?'

Paddy's lips twitched, that sounded far too much like real life and she shook her head. 'Hush, you're spoiling it. I'd then potter around and make their beds,' she paused reflectively, 'there, see, there will be housework. Then I'll read for a bit. Afterwards, I'll go into the garden and pick flowers for the house. Come back in and take the cake out of the oven.'

'Wait, when did you make a cake?'

'I didn't, weren't you paying attention? But there will always be something baking, ready for when I come in from the garden with the flowers.'

'What about winter?'

'There will always be flowers. Stop trying to derail my dream. Anyway, while the cake is cooling,' she gave him a fake scowl, 'I will go out and ride my horse all afternoon and then I'll be home just in time for when the children walk back through the door. My darling husband will come home from work calling out 'Honey, I'm home'.'

She scowled again. 'You have quite a loud laugh, don't you?'

'I think Walt Disney and the 1950s want their daydream back.'

'Well, they can't have it,' pouted Paddy, 'it's mine. Anyway, I'll take his coat and hat and we'll all sit down and discuss our day.'

Hal topped up his glass and smiled across at her. The candlelight catching the lights in his eyes. 'So what does your perfect husband do? Is he a crime fighting hero, a spy, a top shot money man?'

Paddy sipped her wine. 'No idea, but he loves me and he thinks I am the most wonderful person in the world along with the children. He is always there for us and that's the only detail I care about.'

A strand from Paddy's fringe fell forward across her face and Hal stretched across the table to tuck it back behind her ear. As he did, his finger lightly traced her skin and Paddy was astounded by her reaction. Heat ran across her face were his finger had been and her throat tightened as she struggled to catch her breath. Flustered, she stopped talking and looked down at the table. Things suddenly felt serious and Paddy blushed. What had started out as a light-hearted game had become very revealing. After a pause, she was grateful that Hal continued with the conversation.

'Well, when I marry the seventh Mrs Ferguson, it will be absolutely the final time. We'll be in Vegas and I'll have just blown this month's pension on an Elvis impersonator to tie the knot.'

Paddy was hugely relieved that Hal hadn't noticed her embarrassment and had switched the subject to himself. She couldn't decide if she was more mortified by how much of her daydream she had revealed or how much her body had surged when he touched her. She was still struggling to get her heartbeat under control and was more than happy to play along with his Las Vegas scenario.

'Will you be wearing rhinestones?' she asked, relieved that her voice wasn't shaking.

'We both will. Although she'll be in a bikini so there won't be much room for rhinestones on her outfit.'

'A bikini!'

'It has a fringe. It will be a very tasteful bikini.'

Paddy laughed as he protected the taste levels of his future wife. 'Well, indeed, if it has a fringe…'

'Exactly, Tiffany is nothing if not tasteful. Besides, if you've got it, flaunt it.'

'Indeed! And does Tiffany have a career?'

'No, but she did win the lottery.' He waggled his eyebrows wolfishly causing Paddy to laugh out loud.

'So, why will she want to marry some six-times-married old letch then?'

Hal grinned back at Paddy, laughing at her insults. 'The accent. American girls love the accent. Plus I told her I own a castle.'

'Poor old Tiffany when she discovers a lack of castle.'

'Who says I don't have a castle?'

'Oh God! Do you have a castle?'

'No, no castle.'

'Poor Tiffany.'

Now Hal roared with laughter and ordered another bottle of wine. Paddy was almost giddy with how much freedom she was experiencing. She couldn't remember when she had laughed so much and let her defences down with anyone outside of her family. Hal made her relax; she didn't need to be on her guard; she could be silly and just act without care. Life was exciting and full of possibilities. Right now, she felt like a blank canvas, the world was her oyster and anything was possible. To hell with it. What could possibly go wrong?

Chapter Eight

Paddy slowly woke up. There was a languid torpor in her limbs and a lazy smile on her face. She stretched under the cool cotton sheets, dozy and utterly relaxed. Just before she worked out where she was, her foot touched a warm naked leg and, jack-knifing upright, she pulled the sheets around her. To her left, looking utterly angelic, lay Hal. A soft curl of hair framed his still face, dark eyelashes lay closed against his cheek. Paddy blinked and very quickly tried to process the previous evening. The food had been spectacular, the drinks divine, the company, oh God, the company. Hal had kept her entertained all evening; he had chatted and made her laugh the whole time. She couldn't remember the last time she had enjoyed an evening so much. Then they'd crossed to the neighbouring hotel for more drinks and when he suggested a room she just agreed. Last night it had seemed like the most natural thing in the world. And this morning? This morning, she just grinned to herself. This morning was wonderful. He had suggested last night that they go surfing, if she could brace the cold water? She had never tried it before and was looking forward to spending more time with Hal. She had told him she had been swimming every day and had been pleased when he looked at her in admiration.

She wasn't in the habit of one-night stands; in fact she had never had one before, just a few doomed relationships, which was fairly typical for a model. As she'd entered the modelling profession her sisters and the agency guardians helped to take care of their younger models. At sixteen it would have been easy for her to be taken advantage of, but her agency was scrupulous about protecting their workforce. By the time she was eighteen, she had picked up good habits and was better attuned to certain tactics. Nick was even more sharply attuned as she wasn't directly involved, and between the two of them they quickly filtered out the sleaze bags. However, after the creeps and the guys who just weren't interested in her, there weren't many men left and as she became a rising star, her beauty put other suitors off.

But not Hal.

Smiling, she slipped out of bed and ran herself a shower. Enjoying the hot water she wondered how the rest of the day would unfold. Humming softly, she wandered into the bedroom and switched the kettle on. Hal was awake and gave her a lazy smile.

'Are you one of those obscene early risers? Why don't you get back into bed and I'll make the coffee?'

He patted the duvet and beckoned her towards him. Paddy blushed, she felt like a teenager. She didn't want to seem forward, which made her laugh, but she was also shy about getting back into bed with him. As much as she wanted to.

Her phone rang from the sideboard and looking for a way to distract herself, she answered it. A very shrill voice squawked at the other end and Paddy saw that she had picked up the wrong phone. Sitting upright, Hal's face collapsed in horror.

The voice down the line continued. 'Who the hell are you?'

Paddy tried to stutter a reply but the woman continued over the top of her. 'For God's sake. Put my fiancé on the phone right now.'

The word fiancé exploded in Paddy's brain. Mortified, she held the phone out towards Hal. She stood mutely whilst he tried to placate the woman at the other end of the phone.

'A receptionist... Of course not... Honestly, I don't even know her name.' He looked over at Paddy and cringed, then returned to the call. 'No, I'm looking forward to it... Yes, I'll bring them with me. Alright, see you later and stop being silly. Yes, love you too.'

As he hung up, he looked across at Paddy, who had collapsed into the armchair. Her huge eyes welled with tears, and she looked utterly bereft. He wasn't sure if he had ever seen anyone look more miserable in his life. He was overcome with the desire to wrap his arms around her and promise her that everything was going to be all right. Even more ridiculously, he felt a surge of anger that someone had hurt her. The hypocrisy of wanting to blame his fiancée for calling so early did not escape his notice. He knew he was to blame but, damn it, why did she have to look so heartbroken?

She continued to look at him mutely. What was she waiting for? A denial? God, he wished he could tell her it was a complete misunderstanding. That what he had planned was for them to spend the rest of the morning in bed and then maybe hire some surf boards. Afterwards he could take her back to his house and show her around, introduce her to his friends.

'Your fiancée?' Her small voice broke his daydream and he scowled at her.

'Yes. Look, sorry about that. Bit awkward but we're all grown-ups, aren't we? These things happen. You know the score.'

He was talking bollocks and trailed off. He was utterly ashamed of himself but couldn't think how to resolve the situation. 'Look, can I give you a lift home? Or wherever?'

Despite all their time together, he hadn't found out very much about her. He had avoided any conversation about his own private life and now he discovered that she may have done the same.

Paddy looked at him in horror. 'A lift?' She angrily started retrieving her clothes from around the room, pulling them on. 'You think I want to spend another second with you?'

Sniffing, she rubbed her eyes with the back of her hand and pulled on her heels. Grabbing her handbag she opened the bedroom door. She turned, and Hal was ready for her to start screaming at him, instead her breath hitched in a sob and she fled out of the room, slamming the door behind her.

***

The taxi dropped Paddy back at Kensey House. Another scene was currently being shot on the croquet lawn but the filming had lost all of its sparkle. Giving some of the crew a quick wave, she headed to the beach house. She was still grinding her teeth, a bad childhood habit, when she got to the

69

bottom of the drive, but looking out over the sea she felt her jaw relax.

The cove was strewn with seaweed at the moment but she didn't care, as far as she was concerned this was the most beautiful beach in the whole world. She'd bought a little kayak and had begun to explore her coastline. She was also swimming daily but until she was more confident, she stuck to the cove. Swimming in the sea was more fun than a pool but it was also more challenging and she was mindful of all the local horror stories of holidaymakers coming down and getting into troubles.

Now, still angry at herself for sleeping with a jerk on a first date, she stripped down to her knickers, the wind chilled her body. Her beach was completely secluded but she wasn't particularly body conscious. For years she had stood naked but for a G-string, surrounded by strangers as she was manoeuvred in and out of dresses for runways or photoshoots. She'd been zipped in, buttoned up, stitched into or cut out of a bizarre variety of outfits. On one occasion she'd been buck naked the whole time painted to look like a jaguar.

The sea was still too nippy for a bikini, though, and so she'd investigated wetsuits until she found the perfect one for her. Back home she was used to swimming in the Thames and nearby lakes and waterways which were also known for their less than favourable conditions. What she discovered about sea swimming, though, was the greater level of buoyancy caused by the salt levels; added to the suit, sometimes she felt like she was almost on top of the water instead of in it. Now she pulled on her winter wetsuit that was still hanging on the line from two days ago, she walked into the sea.

God, some of the stuff she'd done had been fun, especially some of the catwalks, but mostly the photoshoots were tedious. She had briefly toyed with the idea of an acting career, but after yesterday, she could see it was just more of the same, '*Once more, with feeling.*'

The cold water snapped her into alertness and she grinned as she duck-dived in, gasping for breath as she broke the surface. How's that for feeling? This was the joy of sea swimming; out here everything became more manageable; you just couldn't fixate on a problem, you needed to pay attention to your surroundings. It was the perfect way to sort through issues without dwelling on them.

Heading off, she turned right, swimming along the base of the coastline. There wasn't another accessible beach in this direction for a few miles. She'd gradually been swimming a bit further each day, staying close to the safety of the shoreline. Paddy hadn't gone far when she spotted something on the rocks. A large seal was lying out in the sun watching her. She paused bobbing up and down in the water, watching the seal watching her. What was on his mind, she wondered? Was he trying to decide what to do in his career? Was he still mortified by his behaviour from the night before? Did he want to explain himself? Justify his actions? Curl up in a ball of misery? Paddy continued to bob. No, he probably was just enjoying the warmth of the sun and wondering when he would next eat some fish. Deciding that that sounded like excellent advice, Paddy gave him a quick salute and headed back to her cottage. Her new mantra was to be more seal. Live in the moment and eat fish.

By the time she made it back to the shore, she felt silly and energised. She bent down to pick up a few shells and added them to the bucket by the front doorstep. She was beginning to build up quite a collection and was looking forwards to when she could start repairs on her porch. Today was also a good day to start weeding the steps up to the grotto, she needed to attack something.

Sleeping with Hal had been incredible. And stupid. He had a fiancée so he wasn't exactly what she'd consider a good sort, so why waste any time over his opinion of her? Be more seal! Heading back into the house, she left little wet footprints on the slate floor as she walked into the kitchen. She wrapped a blanket around her, flicked on the kettle and popped some mackerel fillets under the grill. She wasn't going to spend another minute thinking about Hal. Not one. No siree.

Chapter Nine

A week had passed since Hal had met Paddy and he hadn't had a day's peace since. He knew he had almost upended everything and had to silence a little voice that said upending everything would be a good thing.

He'd met Bianca shortly after he'd been discharged. She always seemed to be at the same events that he was, and was good for a laugh. They'd dated for a bit but it hadn't been working out. Just as he was about to call it a day, she announced she was pregnant and his world crashed. He had always assumed he would get married and start a family. Just not with Bianca. It seemed, however, that fate had different ideas and he rushed to get an engagement ring and she had said yes, just as quickly. Two weeks after that she told him she had lost the baby. That was two months ago but it hadn't stopped Bianca's astonishing efforts at getting the wedding underway.

Bianca had apparently been devastated and Hal had been at a loss as to how to console her. His own pain was surprisingly raw but he knew better than to voice it. Eventually, she had suggested some retail therapy might help and he readily agreed. He had been surprised just how effective it had been. A week later it was as though nothing had happened to her, and yet Hal still felt a yawning hole. What was worse was that he knew his feelings for Bianca had changed. He admonished himself; of course he was still going to marry her. What would that say about him if he called the engagement off now? Surely it would suggest he had only proposed because she was pregnant. And yet, that was, of course, the case.

For a change, the winter skies were bright blue and whilst that meant the air was colder than normal, it was at least dry. After a mild and damp Christmas, Hal felt his county had forgotten how to do festive weather. Now crunching through the leaves and twigs, his dogs bounding in and out of the fields, Hal felt a hollow sham. The haunting call of the curlews drifted up from a nearby river and Hal was surprised by how far the sound had carried; he was several miles from any estuary, maybe they were just flying through. He however, had made his bed and now had to lie in it.

His thoughts drifted as he walked down to the livestock pens. He had managed to reassure Bianca nothing was wrong but he was racked with guilt.

'So why would a hotel receptionist be answering your phone?' her voice had been hard when he had dashed up to London to reassure her.

'Because my hands were full.'

'Of what? Her?'

Hal had taken a deep breath; it was probably best to make a clean break of it but just as he was about to speak, she rushed to interrupt him.

'Ignore me. I'm sorry,' she wiped a tear away and continued, 'my damn emotions are such a mess since I lost the baby. Forgive me?' As she cuddled into him, Hal had felt his heart sink further.

She deserved a lot better and he was determined to live up to the man his mother would have expected him to be. Just because Bianca had lost the baby didn't mean they couldn't have another one. He needed to grow up and start behaving responsibly. He had asked her to be his wife and she deserved his respect and his fidelity. He decided Paddy had been a test. A test he had failed woefully but one he was determined to improve on. He was never going to see Paddy again and he needed to get on with his life. Get married, settle down, help run the estate. Sorted. Dismissing thoughts of pale skin and red hair draped over a freckled shoulder, he tried to focus on the job in hand. Her green eyes flashing with laughter under her auburn lashes. It was hard though. Everywhere he looked he saw her smile, out of the corner of his eye. Every conversation he had, he wanted to ask her opinion on it. He had revelled in how he felt in her company. Nothing seemed complicated or burdened; he felt he was with someone he had known all his life. Like a sister or a best friend, and yet he imagined he would be facing a very long jail sentence if he thought about a sister the way he did Paddy.

Coughing, he tried to banish her again from his mind and turned his thoughts instead to the new estate developments he was putting in place. Try as he might, though, he couldn't hear any sounds of work from the new livestock pens. He had walked from the house enjoying the chance to stretch his legs in the dry and had taken the longer route to the lower meadows. Checking his watch he saw it was already nine. Surely everyone should be at work. It seemed a bit early for a crib break.

As he walked into the yard, he could see Brian hauling some of the feed sacks from the back of a pickup but the new buildings were an abandoned outline of half started breeze blocks.

'These feed sacks never seem to get any lighter, do they?' puffed Hal as he threw one up onto his shoulder. Walking towards one of the old pens, Hal nodded towards the breeze blocks. 'Problems? I thought we'd be done by now. I did ask for this project to be given priority.'

Brian paused and put his sack down turning to look Hal square in the face. 'The thing is, Henry, your father asked me to shelve this.'

Hal was astounded. He had discussed this very project with his father, who had said it sounded like a good idea. In fact, he had nodded through all his suggestions. The new pens were one of many changes Hal was implementing around the estate. When he returned from the Army, he'd spent a few weeks looking at his home with fresh adult eyes and then started visiting a few other working farms and estates. As he had feared, his own was falling behind. He had talked it through with Brian who made a few of his own suggestion and Hal appreciated the older man's advice.

When he was eighteen his mother had finally died from the cancer that had been chasing her for years. Hal could find no solace at home and had thrown himself into his studies at university. His father had thrown himself into the bottle. When James Ferguson met his new wife, he had started to pay attention to the estate again. Certainly the farm seemed to be making more money but Hal couldn't see how. Their machinery was tired, although well-tended, and he had no criticism of Brian's work. But the fact of the matter was that their tenants' properties seemed a tad scruffy, the yields on some of the fields seemed to have stalled and the livestock were just ticking over, their birth rate last year had been the lowest on record.

'Did he say why? What about the new plantation?'

Brian shook his head. In truth, he thought Henry's plans were good ones, but Henry wasn't his boss, his father was, and if James Ferguson said no, then no it was.

'Right.' Hal prepared to head back to the house but then noticed the trailer was still full of sacks. 'Where are the other men?'

'Friday, isn't it? Your father said there was no need for them on Fridays and that everyone could enjoy a long weekend.'

Hal looked perplexed, what was Brian on about. 'Every Friday? Or just today. Have I missed something?'

'No, it's every Friday.' Brian didn't say any more.

'But that's crazy, there's always work!' Hal caught himself. Criticising his father in public, even to someone he had known all his life, seemed disloyal. It seemed like he had lots to talk to his father about, but first he threw his coat over the gate and rolled up his sleeves. Those bags weren't going to shift themselves.

***

Odette heard a clatter from the backyard as Hal returned from his morning walk. The dogs were all jumping up around his legs as steam rose off their coats in the morning sunlight. It was a lovely sight and Odette was very proud to have such a handsome stepson. However, right now an angry frown spoilt his countenance and he strode into the kitchen in muddy boots, kissing her on the cheek and asking where his father was. She winced as she watched the muddy footprints head off towards the study and made a note to ask their cleaner to address those when she arrived. She returned to her needlework but looked up as she heard James shouting and a hand being slammed on the table. Her husband had such a temper but she'd never heard him shout at his son before. Deciding that she would ask Angela to clean the other end of the house today she went off in search of a vacuum.

***

'Don't bloody tell me how to run my business!' James slammed his hand on the table. 'I've been running this estate ever since I married your mother and we've gone from strength to strength.'

'Yes but…' Hal tried to get a word in edgeways but his father was just building up steam.

'What about that physio pool I had built for you! Hey? Not complaining about that, are you?' Hal thought that was a particularly low blow. He hadn't asked to be injured, he hadn't asked his father to build him a pool and yes, he was incredibly grateful for it. It had sped up his recovery enormously. But that was not what this was about, his father was dodging the issue.

Hal went and sat in one of his father's leather armchairs: towering over his father's desk wasn't helpful. At Sandhurst they had been taught how to negotiate, how to intimidate and how to listen. It amused him to think that tactics he had learnt to placate enemy combatants should now be used against the old man.

78

Realising his son had stopped engaging and was just waiting for him to run out of steam James glared at him. 'Well!?'

'Okay, Father, maybe I was trying to do too much?' Personally Hal thought he was doing less than half that needed doing. If only they could work together. He didn't know why his father was fighting him on this. 'But updating the estate is essential. We fall below modern ethical standards and with the new government regulations…'

'Dammit, Henry. I said no. The Government is always bringing in some new fandangled idea. It's bloody nonsense if you ask me.'

'It's not nonsense, it's the future. We need efficient game crops, sound bio-diverse corridors—'

'At the cost of bloody yield, where's the sense in not ploughing a field right up to the edge? All this bloody plough to plate rubbish you keep spouting on about. If we want to make a profit we have to plant more, not less!'

Hal sighed, this was only the basics that the estate needed to address. The new government initiatives were also addressing the physical properties of estates. Including the tenanted residences and he knew for a fact that they were nowhere near compliance.

'The days of EU grants are behind us and if we're going to survive, we need to adapt.'

'We'll be fine, the government knows how beneficial estates and farms like ours are. And if they don't, we'll soon teach them a thing or two.' James laughed knowingly, as if the Government would change their mind in light of his stance.

Hal stared at his father. Nothing he said seemed to be getting through to him. Every time James conceded a point, Hal thought he could get started on fixing a thing, only to discover that James had changed his mind again.

'I was talking to Giles the other day…'

Oh God, groaned Hal, Father and the old boys' network; anything new was met with mistrust and rebuttal. Why couldn't he see a large section of their livelihood was at risk if he didn't modernise?

'Look, tell you what,' he said cutting across his father, 'why don't we pop up to Humphrey's?'

Humphrey Blackstott had a large sporting estate in Hampshire that mixed shooting in winter and fishing in summer, as well as having a good mixture of arable and livestock. It was a very successful venture and Hal knew that the two men were old acquaintances; Humphrey might be able to change James's mind. 'Now that the season's finished why don't we do a spot of fishing and see if we can't pick up some tips.'

James perked up. A day's fishing was always a pleasurable event and if it meant he could get his son off his back for a while then why not? Whilst they were there, James could inspect Humphrey's business and show young Hal where they were pulling the wool over his eyes. He leant back and puffed on his cigar. 'Now that is the first sensible thing you've said since you came in here. Set it up.'

Going to the window, Hal slid the panes down. 'You know Odette will only complain if she smells that.'

James grumbled at the cold air and then pointed out that Henry had stormed in still wearing his muddy boots.

Father and son looked at each other and shared a joint grimace. 'Right, well I'll go and organise things but first I'd better find the vacuum.'

As he got up to leave he remembered Brian working on his own. 'By the way, Father, Brian said you've taken to giving the men long weekends? It's a bit tough on him?'

'Has he been complaining?' growled James, and Hal rushed to head him off.

'Brian? Complain? Sun will rise in the West before that happens. No, I just thought it was nice of you to give the men a shorter working week, just that maybe Brian would like it as well? Or some more staff?'

'He's still getting paid, isn't he?'

'Well yes.' Hal paused at the door. 'Hang on, do you mean the others aren't being paid?'

He stared at his father in horror.

'Good God boy, of course they aren't being paid.' James roared with laughter. 'Imagine paying people not to work. Don't think you are quite ready to take over the running of this estate if that's how you plan to do things.'

Hal stood at the door. What was his father thinking? There was loads of work to be done. Whilst he had admired his father's generosity in giving the staff long weekends, he had worried about his inability to see the workload. Now he feared his parsimony. The last thing this estate needed was fewer man hours and Hal wondered if the old boy wasn't losing his senses.

Chapter Ten

'Beryl, are you in?'

Of course I'm in thought Beryl, *the front door is open and I said I would be waiting for you.*

A young woman walked into the kitchen. 'There you are!'

Where on earth else would I be, she thought. Honestly, Paul's eldest didn't have the brains she was born with. She was always wittering on about clouds being ways for the government to kill people and dream catchers being a way to repel bad energy. She had tried to get her to explain it once but she'd faltered after a few words. Still her mother had been fairly vacant as well. Maybe it was hereditary. In the past, Beryl would have muttered something sarcastic but these days she had learnt a little bit of peace and ignored the stupidity around her.

'Are you ready?'

'Aye. I'm ready,' she got her coat, 'and I'm still not deaf,' she muttered.

'What's that?' Ella asked brightly. She liked Beryl, she should be in a home really, but she had no family to make her, dear of her. Still, she had started mumbling a lot. Just the other day, Ella had been explaining how the elite were trying to poison the atmosphere with chemicals, and Beryl's eyes had started to twitch and she didn't seem to understand what Ella had been telling her. She'd told her dad about it but he said simply that Beryl would outlast the lot of them and to stop bothering her with scare stories. Now the pair of them were walking down to her dad's pub to meet their new village landlord. Beryl had said she could manage just fine but Ella was worried that at her age she might forget. Ella was glad she'd asked because Beryl had started to mumble and twitch again.

'Have you ever met Lady Patricia de Foix? You know seeing as how you've been here the longest and all.'

Ella tried to sound relaxed but in reality, she was terrified. She'd lived in one of the houses since moving out of the pub and had one of the short tenancies. People like her dad and Beryl were fine, they had generational tenancies, but other people, like her, only had rolling short hold ones and at a peppercorn rent. She and Sam both worked and they wanted to start a family. The cheap rent meant she'd be able to stop working for a while but if it went up, they might not be able to afford a family or even to stay in the village. She knew she wasn't alone in worrying. The Hiverton Estate had not been very involved in the village for the past decade. Why the sudden interest?

'Truth told, I never paid them much attention. It's not as though we mixed in the same circles.' She patted Ella on the hand. 'Don't you worry yourself none. All the lawyers in the world can't kick you out of your home. You and Sam have done a lovely job there. And if all else fails, bribe them with some of your jams.'

'It is good jam, isn't it?' said Ella smiling. 'I don't like to boast but I haven't been beaten on the WI stall now these past five years. Do you remember when that woman from Tregarron tried to sneak a shop jam past the judges. The nerve of her. The trick is in the pectin, I've always said so. Shop bought can't touch a proper homemade jam.'

Ella carried on and Beryl was glad to have diverted her for a few minutes. The girl was truly a colossal ninny but that was no reason to not care about her and her worries. Tregiskey village had been a small friendly community for well over two hundred years and hopefully would continue to be so. But as the old families had died out or moved away, generational tenancies lapsed and the properties had reverted to the estate and stood vacant; in fact at her last reckoning around twenty properties lay empty. It might not sound a lot but it was pretty much half the hamlet.

She didn't want to alarm Ella, but everyone knew they were living in prime real estate. Their little hamlet led down to a sheltered bay with a small harbour protecting them from the worst of the winter storms. Each cottage had a decent sized garden with fruit trees, as well as flowers and vegetable beds. When the properties had been built, Hiverton Estate had decreed that each householder needed to be self-sufficient and gave them the space to achieve it.

The cottages weren't overly large but they were more than hovels. There were also some properties that had been built with shared responsibilities. Honey Cottage had a row of bee boles built into the back garden wall. Net Cottage housed a long drying gallery for fishing nets. Apple Cottage had the village cider press and backed onto the pub. It was fair to say that whilst the original builders had been practical, they hadn't wasted any time on thinking of names for the cottages.

As they arrived at the pub, they greeted others coming in. Not everyone could make it due to work commitments but the new owner had said it was purely informal. Despite that, as many as could had taken the time off work. Ella wasn't the only one worried.

***

Paul looked up and saw his daughter leading Beryl in. Poor Beryl, he'd send her a couple of bottles of stout later, by way of an apology. Smiling at the pair he waved them to some seats, almost a full house. Turning around he saw a striking young lass come in. It was only ten o'clock so he hadn't thought to put up a closed sign but he'd better let her know. She seemed a nice sort, bit too tall and skinny for his taste but it took all sorts to make the world go around. It was a bother to turn away a paying customer in February but people needed to speak their mind and they might be reluctant in front of holidaymakers. Passing Bill, he told him to grab a chair and then headed to the bar where the girl was waiting.

'Sorry, maid. We're not open yet. We've a private meeting on, see. We'll be open at twelve if you want to come back then?'

She looked a bit embarrassed and then apologised. 'I'm sorry, I spoke to you on the phone the other day. About arranging a meeting with the villagers?'

'No, that was Lady de Foix.'

She shrugged. 'Me.' Seeing his confusion she was quick to apologise. 'I am so sorry. I thought you realised. But how could you when I didn't say anything? My fault. God, I'm so sorry. I didn't mean to make you embarrassed.'

'No, it's just I expected…'

'Someone older? Posher?'

Paul laughed, agreeing it was pretty much exactly what he had thought. Inside he was dying. Nice way to greet his new landlady, trying to evict her. A move worthy of Del Boy. What a plonker.

'Maybe you could you do me a favour?' she asked.

Whipping out of his daydreaming, and adding 'no dreaming in front of new landlord' to the list of things not to do, he agreed to anything.

'It's just, I'm a bit nervous. I've never done this before and I don't want to cock it up. If I say something stupid, could you jump in and help?' She raced on spotting his hesitation. 'Sorry, was that wrong of me to ask? Ignore me. Come on let's do it.'

And as Paul led her through, promising to help her if she needed it, she could have sworn she heard him whisper, 'Nice and cool, son, nice and cool.'

Facing the villagers, Paddy thought she had never seen such a hostile sea of faces. There wasn't a smile shared amongst them and she wondered what she had done wrong. She smiled nervously and cleared her throat.

'Good morning, my name's Paddy Byrne, or rather Lady Patricia de Foix,' she mumbled and then coughed, 'sorry, you'll have to excuse me. I'm just getting used to the new title.'

'I don't care what you're called, love,' a voice cut across her. A man had stood up and was pointing at her. He was all but bald except for an eccentric fringe that Paddy thought made him look like a monk. His belly hung over a straining belt and for some reason he was wearing a tie over his jumper. 'I just want to know, are you planning to kick me out of my home? Because I'm telling you now, maid, you won't get me out without a fight.'

A low mutter seemed to back him up and Paddy looked at the crowd in dismay. Why on earth did they think she was going to evict them?

'I'm not planning on evicting anyone. At least my sister isn't. It's her that actually owns the freeholds. But she isn't evicting anyone either.'

'That's what they all say,' he said running his fingers through his fringe and patting it down over the crown of his head. 'Pass the buck, blame someone else, wring their hands, but so long as they still get to go on their la-di-dah holidays and drink champagne for breakfast, they don't care what happens.'

Paddy could feel her face was burning up. Who was this horrible man? She looked to Paul for support, but he'd already got to his feet.

'Now look, Bill. What's the point in her coming here to talk, if you're going to tell her what she's going to say, hey? Keep your peace and let's hear her out. Don't want her going away thinking we're all as rude as you.'

The muttering from the pub was stronger now and Paddy thought maybe they weren't all in agreement with Bill's bluster. She wished her sisters were here; any one of them would handle this better than she could. Ari had given her a few tips but the problem was that Paddy was nothing like Ari, she had far more in common with Clem, the other overly emotional sister in the family. In fact, Clem would have made the situation worse, but at least she wouldn't be quivering in front of them. That was what she loved about Clem, of the five sisters she and Clem were the most openly emotional. Like Paddy, Clem wore her heart on her sleeve. Paddy knew her own inner personality was sunny and calm, a spring butterfly. Clem's inner personality was a volcano.

This wasn't helping her current predicament though. Maybe she should pretend the villagers were like the paparazzi, just give them what they wanted, but she didn't want to think of them like that. She wanted to be liked for who she was. Not because she manipulated them into it.

She cleared her throat again and noticed one or two of the crowd seemed to be smiling at her, or at least not scowling, so she focussed on them instead. Nick told her that the trick to public speaking was to catch a few friendly eyes and direct your speech to them.

'We've been studying the finances of the village and see no need to make any drastic changes. Our policy is to watch and see how things work. There are a lot of empty properties, and that's just not on. People need homes so we'll be looking to bring in new tenants.'

'What about us? What about our tenancies?' called out a woman's voice from near the window.

'They stay as they are. Nick, that's my sister and the financial brains says why fix what isn't broke.'

'You going to sell any the properties? Could I buy my place?'

Paddy shook her head.

'That isn't on the cards but if we were to consider selling anything, existing tenants would get first refusal and if the tenant didn't want to buy that would be the end of that.'

'Seems as how you've put a lot of thought into this,' sneered Bill, 'which is funny as how you said you hadn't any plans yet.'

Paddy took a deep breath and gave Bill a tight smile, her cheeks burning.

'We don't have any plans but that doesn't mean we haven't been studying the situation for months and thinking about the options. That's why I'm here. To check that what we have been told, and what the finances say, tally with what I find out.'

'Snooping on us?'

Paddy could feel her neck beginning to flush but as she was about to reply she was saved by an old woman sitting near the barn who slowly got to her feet.

'Bill Hunkin, you're a damned fool. This girl's family owns all these properties. She ain't snooping, she's getting herself acquainted. Leave her be and let her get on with her job. She's told you, you ain't losing your house, so accept it. But if I was you, I'd be inclined to tidy up my garden a bot. Don't want to give her any grounds for eviction now do you?'

There was a lot of laughter at this and Bill sat down quickly. Paddy had wandered into the village twice now and on both occasions had thought what a shame it was that one of the houses had a broken washing machine in the front garden and a lawn full of weeds.

As the meeting broke up Paddy was relieved that it seemed to have gone well. The villagers appeared reassured that the estate had no plans to do anything to the village in the first year and whatever it did do, it would honour every tenancy. Some of the villagers pointed out they didn't have a tenancy but a generational understanding, and whilst Paddy had never heard of such a thing, she promised that those too would be honoured. She then asked the villagers what they wanted and, relieved they weren't about to be evicted, she was quickly overwhelmed with requests for better parking for tourists, internet connection, mooring rights (or removal of) for holidaymakers, a bus stop. The list went on and whilst she smiled and nodded and said she'd investigate everything, she could hear Nick asking how any of them thought it was going to be paid for.

The chief issue was with people parking in the lane during summer. Sometimes the place became grid locked as locals and tourists alike came to visit the pretty little beach. Paul was a little more reticent than some of the others as the pub landlord, his business relied on these visitors. He had a small car park but could only accommodate twenty cars. Apparently, there had been plans once for a car park to be built further up, and steps leading down to the beach. It seemed like a good idea but she could already see Nick throwing her hands up in despair. Plus, if they did build a car park more people would visit. Was that what the villagers really wanted? Paul was unsurprisingly in support of this idea.

Paddy was surprised the villagers didn't seem to understand just how lucky they were. She would have given her front teeth to come somewhere like this when she was young, and thinking back to her old neighbours where she grew up, she knew they would love this place too. Ari had had a fabulous party at her place last year, maybe she could do the same? Invite everyone for a holiday. But then they would be adding to the villagers' overcrowding problem. Hmm, maybe they had a point? There had to be a way of sharing all this though and she was determined to phone Nick and then Ari to discuss her findings.

Chapter Eleven

As she left, she told Paul to put everyone's drink on her tab. That, at least, she could afford. As she got to the door the old woman who had spoken up for her, came up and introduced herself as Beryl Hunkin, *a distant relation unfortunately*, and invited her back to her house for a cup of tea. At the door, a young woman came to see if Beryl was okay; she smiled warily at Paddy but couldn't quite meet her eye. 'Help your father tidy up, dear, Lady Patricia will see me home just fine.'

Paddy watched as the girl turned back into the pub and couldn't tell if she was relieved or put off. Paddy hadn't seen any ice on the road and the woman seemed quite steady on her feet but maybe she liked company?

'Are you okay walking? I mean, do you need me to go slower?'

Beryl craned her neck up and chuckled.

'Ha! When I was your age, I'd have outrun you over three fields. These days I'm not quite so fast but no, I don't need help. Young Ella there seems to have put me in my coffin before my time. She exhausts me, with her speaking slowly and loudly and bringing me catalogues for infirmity aids. I'm not having her put all that rubbish negativity on me. No, you were my excuse. Come on then, I'm this way.' And she started to move off at a decent pace. She turned around to tell Paddy to watch out for the seaweed, 'It's slippery, m'lady.'

Paddy moved to catch up. The pub sat at the bottom of the lane overlooking the small beach. Instead of walking back up the lane Beryl headed across the mouth of the beach, where the tarmac ended and the sand began, and up a stone path leading to a few cottages perched on the hillside, overlooking the sea.

'By the way, please call me Patricia, the lady stuff is a bit formal.'

'Right you are, miss.'

'Patricia. Miss also sounds wrong.'

'Very well, m'lady.'

'No, I…'

'The thing is,' said the old lady, 'I was never brought up to believe that all men are equal. Even though we are. So I'd as soon call you Patricia as I'd call Ella, Miss Trewalla. I'm afraid that's just not going to happen, miss.'

The two walked on whilst Paddy thought about it. The girls had all warned her not to become over pally with the locals. It was important she tried to keep some sort of distance in case there were problems. Paddy had a habit of seeing the good in everyone and whilst she didn't see an issue in it, Nick had been adamant she should try to create some space.

Imagine if you get down there, make best friends left, right and centre and then need to evict someone or something horrible like that. How on earth would you manage? Paddy had thought that was totally unfair but also completely valid.

'I think I can cope with miss.'

'Right you are, miss,' and Beryl gave her a big smile.

As they walked along the cottages, Paddy peered in the windows. 'These are empty, aren't they?' As the occupants had died or handed back their tenancy the estate hadn't renewed the leases and now the properties lay vacant.

'They are. All but me. I'm the last one and I'm not leaving!'

Paddy looked at her in alarm. 'Of course not. Who would leave this, it's magical? Who's making you leave? Can I help?'

Beryl paused in front of her door. Around the front of the house lay various interesting rocks and shells, blue and green glass balls tied up in rope, a boot scraper and a small bench where the path ended. As the last cottage, she looked down over the beach. The path on the seaward side was protected by a slate stone wall studded with small green plants. As they'd arrived a black cat had slid off the wall and over the other side on to the rough brambles on top of the cliff.

'God it's a bit narrow up here. How do you get stuff up here? Is there a road behind the cottages?'

'No, miss. Everything has to be carried or pulled up and I guess when I die, they'll have to drag me down like they did with old Mrs Cloke. She died when she was seventy and everyone said that was a great age.' As Beryl chatted she pottered around the kitchen pulling out some china cups and saucers from the back of a high cupboard. 'Now here I am in my nineties and everyone seems to think that's normal. I tell you, when I was a girl, ninety would have been a miracle. Mind you, I bet you think I'm ancient?'

'Well ninety is a tiny bit ancient, isn't it? But it's not like you even look seventy. Must be all this healthy sea air.'

'Aye. That and the NHS, a decent wage and a single life. Old Mrs Cloke had fourteen children, and her husband died at sea. Leaving her with nothing but hard work and grief.

That'll make anyone look old. Now, you look like you need some fattening up. Have you had Thunder and Lightning?'

Paddy wasn't sure how any of that last sentence connected so she waited for Beryl to explain, until it became clear from Beryl's look that she had nothing further to say and Paddy had to confess that she didn't understand. The weather had been drizzly but sure she only lived across the way herself. Wouldn't she and Beryl have the same weather?

Beryl hooted with laughter and then apologised for making fun of her. 'It's what we've always called it so you tend to, I don't know, forget the other meaning. If that makes sense. No, miss, Thunder and Lightning is a Cornish treat.'

'Oh, a cream tea?'

Beryl tutted from the fridge. 'No, Thunder and Lightning is a proper Cornish treat. Scones is for the tourists.'

A few minutes later Paddy was tucking into a concoction of clotted cream and golden syrup in a soft sliced bun that Beryl called a split. Paddy wasn't sure if it was going to be the carbs, the fat or the sugar rush that was going to kill her first, but at least she'd die happy.

'So tell me,' Paddy mumbled through a full mouth, 'why do you think you have to leave? These are bloody gorgeous by the way.'

'Well, I've got eyes, I know I'm sitting on a lot of money here. You could tear these cottages down and build some fancy monstrosity full of glass, like that chap on the telly with the scarf and the alarmed expression.'

'Bloody hell, Beryl, we would never do that. In the first place we would never get planning.'

'The rich always get planning.'

'Okay, let's say we got planning, why would we want to? It would ruin the village. It would be a complete waste of perfectly good houses. It would, oh I don't know, it would be a blasphemy.' Wiping cream off her lips, Paddy looked at Beryl earnestly. 'We will never ever tear these houses down. Even when you are long gone and when I am long gone these houses will still be here.'

Beryl smiled at Paddy and nodded. 'Well then, what are your plans for them? If you don't mind me asking.' She sipped her tea and looked at Paddy keenly. 'If you want my advice, you'll turn them into holiday lets.'

'As it happens, I think I agree. We could make loads out of these, if we did them up posh like. But the lack of road is a bit tricky.'

'Oh, that's part of the charm. You know these up-country folks have more money than sense. They'll say it's charming or sweet or Lord preserve us, quaint.'

'But what about you?' Paddy stretched her legs out in front of the fire that Beryl had re-stoked when they came into the house. 'Won't you mind them?'

'No dear, it will be nice to have a bit of company and, of course, if they're awful, there'll be a fresh set a week later. I rarely see anyone up here. Your grandfather saw to it that the coast path loops around the back of the village.'

Paddy already knew about this as she and Nick had looked at the maps and property details for Tregiskey. 'Yes, we spotted that, although it seems like we have to pay for the upkeep of this section?'

'Price your grandfather was prepared to pay for the privacy of the village and the house. And of course because the path is inland there's less maintenance. Smart chap your grandfather.'

Wanting to change the subject from a man who threw her mother out on her ear and left his grandchildren to grow up in poverty she asked Beryl how she managed without a car and was surprised to learn that Beryl had never had one and didn't even know how to drive.

'Anywhere I want to go I can walk or catch a bus.'

'What about holidays?'

'When I was young, we'd take the train to St Ives and that was wonderful. Not like we had the money to go anywhere else. I went up to your London once, but I didn't care for it. Smelt wrong. Never been abroad.'

Paddy was astonished; in her career she had been all around the globe. Admittedly she rarely saw anything beyond a catwalk or a hotel room, but still.

'Besides what do I need with travelling when everything I have is here?'

'Oh you mean like the fresh air and the Cornish skies?'

Beryl looked at Paddy like she was a simpleton and then nodded. 'Well yes, that too as well, but I meant my books, my music and the internet. Come and have a look.'

Pushing herself out of her chair she waved Paddy to follow her as she slowly climbed the stairs. Both back bedrooms were floor to ceiling covered in books. Wherever Paddy looked there was something else that caught her eye and as she wandered into the front bedroom she saw a neat little single bed pushed into the corner. Once more the room was full of books as well as a chair and a small table by the window looking out to sea. Sitting on her bed, Beryl gestured Paddy to the window seat.

'As a girl I would stand here and watch the sea and when I saw a shoal of fish in the bay I would holler down the lane and wave a white flag on a stick to the men in the village. They would rush out in their boats and we'd all come down to the beach to help them haul the nets in. All the children would be stood in the water, their skirts and trousers soaked by the waves as we rushed to haul on the nets. Our mothers would be behind us filling the baskets as fast as they could before the next boat would land its catch.' Her face had softened with the memory and Paddy could almost see the scene unfolding on the beach below. 'Oh, they were fabulous days. But then the fish left and the village dwindled. The young men had died in the wars and those that came back needed a more reliable trade than fishing. The big house no longer needed so many staff either. By the seventies, there wasn't a single person in the village that relied on the fish to put food in their bellies and only a handful were employed to work up at Kensey.

Beryl paused and Paddy looked at her, the old woman's face lost in memories. She looked back out to sea, not wishing to intrude, and waited quietly for Beryl to continue. This village was as pretty as any Paddy had ever seen, but poverty was no respecter of location. She knew what it was to be poor and exhausted.

'Those were tough times. I worked in the nearby school and made my money that way. Eventually they retired me, and me and my books have been exploring ever since. And I still watch the sea. Although these days I send my observations to the local conservation groups. I am what they call a citizen scientist.'

Paddy grinned back at her.

'Recently, I've noticed we have a new mermaid in the bay.'

'I may be from 'up-county' but I'm not a total idiot,' said Paddy. 'There's no mermaids in these parts.' And then with a twitch of her lips, 'they're further west.'

Beryl slid a CD into the player and tones of Wagner began to softly seep out of the speaker. 'This particular mermaid likes to swim to a soundtrack.'

Paddy's head spun away from the window, her hair flicking out, and she looked at Beryl in dismay. 'You can hear my music from over here?'

'Don't worry, it's only from up here. You can't hear it at all down by the pub or the lane, but stuck out here, high on a limb, the sound travels across the water.'

Paddy was mortified. In London she had always been mindful of neighbours, it was truly the only way to live in a city. Keep to your own space, don't intrude, don't spread. But in her little cove she had thought herself utterly isolated and had lived as a wild woman, free of care and not thinking of anyone else. And all the time she had been disturbing this lovely woman's peace.

'Wipe that look from your face, girl. Don't you dare dream of turning it down. New pleasures are few and far between for me but hearing Mozart or Mussorgsky float across the water is one of them.'

Paddy stole a quick grin at her.

'I know it's crazy, but it's like I'm swimming back into the arms of someone noble and wonderful.'

Beryl laughed. 'I was never much for romantic fancies but it certainly is wonderful swimming out there. Have you discovered the seals yet?'

'Oh aren't they wonderful? I sing to them, and I sincerely hope you can't hear that because that is not one of my talents.'

'Well, we can't be good at everything, girl. What do you expect?'

Paddy grinned quietly; as the pair of them had relaxed into each other's company, Paddy had spotted her being call Girl and Maid, which was a slight softening on Miss, and suited her fine.

'If you swim across this bay here, and carry on there's a lovely arch you can swim through plus a few caves, but you'll need a high tide. Maybe, I'll even join you in summer? But now look, you see those clouds?' Beryl pointed to a collection of small dots of clouds covering the western horizon. 'Those are called mackerel clouds; it means there'll be no swimming tomorrow.'

Paddy looked dubious, and Beryl went on to explain how clouds could be read to foretell the weather and then went on to discuss tides and waves, until Paddy's head was spinning. Eventually Beryl got up from the bed and walked to the back bedroom calling Paddy to follow her. She scoured the shelves until she found what she was looking for and handed it to Paddy. 'Here, take this, then you won't need to try and learn it all at once.' Paddy took the book and thought the title *The Cloud Collector's Handbook*, sounded just the ticket.

Plus it looked really pretty. 'Now,' said Beryl as she started to walk back downstairs, her finger tightly gripping the banister, 'I'm tired after entertaining my betters and I need a nap.' Seeing Paddy's worried frown she dropped a quick curtsy and laughed. 'Go on, girl, I always have a lunchtime nap and unless you want to see if my snoring sounds worse than your singing, I suggest you go home.'

Reassured, Paddy headed out the door, promising to return the book as soon as possible. Just as she went to leave, she noticed the addition of two beer bottles to the collection of flotsam by the doorway. Handing them to Beryl she wondered what sort of milkman the village employed and whether he could be encouraged to add her to the round.

Chapter Twelve

Beryl hadn't been kidding about the weather. The next day the wind and rain started to pick up and Paddy began to wonder about how safe she was in a house by the sea. This was her first storm and she was unprepared for how her little bay could be swept up into a maelstrom. She lit the fire having first watched a video on YouTube on how to do it, and was thrilled with her efforts. A modern-day Prometheus. She laughed and watched something soporific on TV until she yawned and headed to bed. With the fire banked down and the TV off, the noise of the storm grew louder. Switching her light off she snuggled down under the heavy eiderdown and listened to the wind blowing around the house and the waves crashing on the shore, she gradually fell asleep.

A loud bang jerked her out of her slumber and for a second Paddy didn't know where she was. In a rush it all came back and she leant over to switch on her bedside light. She tried again and decided the power must be out. She'd never experienced a power cut before but that was all she could think of. The bedroom door was banging and she got up searching around for her dressing gown. She switched on the torch on her phone and felt a breeze on her face, surely she hadn't left a window open?

Heading downstairs, she felt the odd spot of rain and saw in the small pool of light that one of the windows looking over the beach was broken. There was glass on the floor and Paddy headed into the porch for her boots. The sound from outside was terrifying, the tide must have come in while the storm was still raging. Grabbing a load of towels she stuffed them in the broken pane and retreated to the study and tried to decide what to do. She was terrified the house was going to be swept away but she was also terrified that if she tried to walk up to the big house, a tree might fall on her. Something smacked against the side of the house making the windows shake. With a small yelp of terror she grabbed the house keys and flung open the side door. The wind tried to rip it out of her hands and she was terrified by the white waves she could just make out in the darkness, tearing away at the beach. She screamed at the waves but they just roared back. Dragging the door closed she stumbled up the drive to the big house. Her phone torch gave her a small pool of light as she stepped over branches and seaweed, strewn along the drive. Leaves and rain hit her face and she was convinced the waves were racing up the driveway ready to pull her back into the sea. She tripped and fell twice on loose branches, scuffing her palms as she fell. In her panic she didn't even feel it and finally stumbled into the house, closing the front door behind her. Shaking, she headed for the first bedroom. She wasn't sure what to do for the best; there was no point in calling anyone until the day broke. Nothing could be done in the dark.

Now she lay shivering under the covers, she found herself wanting to call Hal. He would know what to do. She had tried to avoid the big house ever since the filming. Each time she wandered into the chapel she thought of Hal. Despite her best efforts she hadn't been able to get him out of her mind. He wasn't her type; she normally avoided upper class spoilt types but as she had got to know him over dinner, she had begun to discover a man with the same sense of humour as her own and a depth of kindness and attentiveness that surprised her. She wanted to call him now, knowing that just hearing his voice would calm her down. Instead, she shivered under the covers feeling miserable, until she finally fell asleep.

A few hours later she woke up to blue skies and sunlight pouring in. For a few seconds she was disoriented, this wasn't her bedroom. And then it came back to her, her bedroom was down the drive. Once again, she found herself thinking about this large empty house. She felt guilty that a house this big didn't have people in it. She would have to do more about getting some more holiday bookings or film locations booked in.

It was only seven but she got up and walked back down the drive in her dressing gown to survey the damage. She was mocking herself as a terrified city girl running from a bit of noise when she stepped over a plant pot, halfway up the drive. Coming around the corner she could see her poor little home had taken quite a beating. The small table that normally sat on the lower patio was around the back by her car. There was no sign of the chairs. The big wooden table and benches on the top patio were roughly in place but tipped over and now she understood why they were chained down. The worst of the damage, though, was the broken porch window and two wooden shutters, hanging loose off their hinges. Her bucket of cockleshells was nowhere to be seen.

Paddy groaned. When she had first told Mr Chadwell she was going to move down to the cottage, he had told her how to use the shutters and to always pay attention to any storm warnings. Especially easterlies. She was lucky she hadn't lost more windows. In the kitchen the cooker timer was flashing. At least she had electricity again so she put the kettle on, and headed upstairs for a shower. She got dressed into some practical clothes and shoved her filthy nightdress and dressing gown into the washing machine. She would also have to strip last night's bed. Looking at the state of her body and clothes she was prepared to bet the sheets up in the big house were covered in mud. For now, though, she went and found a broom. Currently her patio was covered in stones and seaweed but at least she wouldn't have to sweep them far.

At nine she called the land agent and explained she needed a few repairs. Applauding her bravery he told her someone would be with her later that day. Apparently, it had been quite a big storm and he'd get the workmen to check the roof as well. She hadn't even thought to check the roof. Looking after property was a bit of a revelation.

'Any damage on any of the other properties?' his voice interrupted her thoughts.

'God, that hadn't even crossed my mind! I'll get over there straightaway and find out.' Damn, her first actual event and she hadn't thought beyond her own windows, let alone the roof, let alone anyone else's.

'Don't worry.' Mr Chadwell sounded distracted, she imagined he was dealing with many similar calls this morning. 'If there was any damage they would have been in touch. We have a good system of repairs and renovations. Your insurance will pick up any major problems, but we generally fix things from your contingency funds.'

Only slightly mollified, Paddy thanked him and then walked over to the village to check anyway. Everything seemed fine but she was determined not to make any assumptions and knocked on the pub door. Beyond a fresh layer of seaweed in the beer garden, Paul told her there was nothing to worry about. He offered her a drink, but she wanted to get home and ask Nick to explain the finer points of insurance and contingency funds.

Chapter Thirteen

For the next few days Paddy continued to settle into a Cornish rhythm. She still wasn't sure what to do about the big house. The German film crew had left and the grounds were quiet again. It just seemed like a colossal waste. The village needed no interference from its owner; when she had held the small meeting in the pub the general tone was cautiously welcoming once they were happy that eviction wasn't imminent. Paddy could see there were some concerns about rent increases but Ari had said that was not going to happen in the first year and was unlikely to be anything other than the general inflationary rise in the following year.

One morning she drove into Truro. She was getting a bit braver about driving, and following a tip from Paul, she had switched the satnav to make sure it picked the main roads not the interesting and terrifying lanes that seemed to comprise most of the Cornish road network. When she first arrived, she'd visited a local fishing village and had been appalled to discover the tiny road she was on was actually two way, despite it only being one car wide. A caravan was heading towards her and they were looking even more alarmed than she was. Behind them was a string of cars all snaking down from a steep hill that must have been terrifying for the caravan owner to drive down. The cars behind her were reversing back and around the corner of the shops and houses, and try as she might, she was making a total pig's ear of the same manoeuvre. Eventually, a pedestrian tapped on her window and with a large smile offered to reverse her car for her. She was certain her insurance would have had something to say about that but she couldn't get out of her car quickly enough. As she got out, she could see there was quite a crowd of jammed traffic and curious passers-by. She was fully expecting scornful glances but instead people seemed mostly sympathetic. She did hear some woman muttering that people who couldn't reverse their cars should stay up-country. She wanted to point out that she'd learnt to drive in London; she'd like to see that woman manage Tower Hamlets at rush hour. Deciding a smile would work better, she gave the crowd a little grimace and followed her car as it was swiftly reversed around the corner and promptly parked up in a tiny lay-by. Seconds later the caravan drove past her and she gave them an encouraging thumbs up. She wasn't sure if they noticed, their eyes seemed wide and fixed. Oh dear, she thought, welcome to Cornwall. Remembering what Hal had said about the Cornish roads in summer she began to get some understanding of what he meant. Lots of caravans on these tiny roads would be a nightmare.

Retrieving her keys, she thanked everyone profusely and then decided she had had enough excitement for one day and had driven home rather than exploring any further. She absolutely didn't like people glaring at her.

Driving into Truro, though, was a doddle. This was the county's only city although she found the description didn't quite match what she had in mind. To her a city had shopping malls, and congestion, beggars and high rises. This one had streams running along the pavements and wide-open spaces. Making light work of its peculiar roundabouts, Paddy parked up and went off for an explore. The past week had been incredibly sunny and surprisingly warm for the beginning of March and Paddy was looking forward to long sunny days stretching out ahead of her. The hedgerows were turning yellow with primroses and she felt herself falling in love with Cornwall again. How pretty it was, as each month arrived with the promise of soft winds and a new colour.

Today, however, she had woken up to a wet and chilly sea mist and despite it not being freezing it was cold enough for her to wrap up in a large coat and a pair of heavy leather boots. She had watched on the news how farmers up north were pulling their livestock out of snowdrifts and she marvelled at how different the weather was in this little tip of Britain. Speaking to Ari in Norfolk and Clem in Scotland, she was aware they were both still very much in the grip of winter, Clem in particular. The Cornish drizzle, however, didn't seem to be hampering anyone's moods and she decided that wet skies were just a way of life here in Cornwall. Which reminded her to pick up some hair serum. The sea water and damp air were killing her curls.

As she reached a large plaza, she could see other people were also braving the rather dismal weather. There was a busy farmers' market going on, as well as a small protest group and a children's merry-go-round. Whilst small, the market seemed to have just enough of everything she could want and she wandered between each stall, adding to her shopping as she went. Each stand seemed more tempting than the last and she was beginning to wish she had more arms as her purchases began to pile up. Just as she was juggling some mackerel with a bunch of daffodils the stallholder offered to keep her bags behind the counter for her, saying she could collect them when she'd finished with the rest of her shopping. Paddy looked at her amazed. Who did that? Every time she thought she was getting used to life outside of London, it threw her another curve ball. Thanking the lady profusely she headed towards Waterstones. However, she kept looking back over her shoulder, wondering if she wasn't being a total idiot. Not looking where she was going, she bumped into someone and started apologising. It was one of a small group of protestors that had been calling out to passing shoppers. As she spoke, Paddy bent down to pick up some of the leaflets from the wet pavement and was horrified by the brutal images of animal cruelty covering the pamphlets.

'Oh my god. This is awful!' She shoved the leaflets back to the girl, desperate to get the images away from her. Tears instantly began to well up in her eyes, those poor rabbits.

Thanking her for helping, the girl asked Paddy if she wanted to sign their petition banning hunting in the county. Paddy agreed instantly and the protestor looked her up and down.

Mandz was always on the lookout for opportunities; as cunning as the fox she protected, she was always quick to exploit a new angle. Now, looking at this well-groomed girl, head to toe in casually expensive clothing, Mandz spotted a photo opportunity. She'd look great at a protest or a rally. It was a look she herself scorned, preferring her long blonde dreadlocks, patchwork trousers and rainbow DMs, but she knew the media liked to negatively portray her and her fellow activists. This girl could be a model and Mandz knew that the papers would print any picture with someone this striking in it.

Taking the clipboard back she thanked her for her signature. 'You know, it's just nice to see someone caring. It breaks my heart how people walk past us and walk past these poor tortured animals.' She gave an exaggerated shudder. 'How can they sleep at night knowing badgers are being ripped out of their beds, foxes are being torn apart by dogs, that rabbits are trapped in cages, poisons being dripped into their eyes.'

Paddy felt quite sick just thinking about it. She always tried to buy ethically and eat as little meat as possible but maybe she should be doing more.

'If only people would do more,' the girl went on. 'We have an event next weekend and we can't get anyone to sign up. They'd rather sit at home, watching TV or getting drunk. No one cares.'

Paddy had always shied away from protestors and petitions but if she was no longer going to be a model then this was fine. Wasn't it?

'What's the event?'

Paddy listened as the earnest young woman introduced herself and explained there was a landholders annual meeting and they were going to be discussing new routes for the dogs to ride.

'What we will be doing is having a discussion and seeing what can be done to find a solution everyone can agree on.'

In fact it was no such thing, but Mandz knew the sort of people would be there that they wanted to target, and because it wasn't a hunt meeting, they would be off their guard and there'd be no security. But she didn't need to explain the finer details to this girl.

111

When Paddy said she thought fox hunting was banned, Mandz snorted. 'Oh yeah. That's what they want you to think. And then their dogs, who are supposed to be running after a liquorish scent for fun, get the scent of a fox and there's no controlling them, they're off. They should all be put down.' Seeing Paddy's alarm she changed tack, 'Or re-housed, obviously, if they can be trained not to attack cats or children. Which they do you know.'

Paddy didn't know this at all. It was terrible. Why weren't more people doing something about this?

'That's the trouble with the elite, they just do what they want, riding around destroying the countryside, shooting at anything that moves. Don't get me started on pheasant shooting or the badger cull.'

Paddy was horrified; she didn't know any of this. Of course she knew about laboratory testing and the fur trade. It would be hard not to in her line of work but she had no idea about badger culls or dogs attacking children or birds being bred just to be shot at. When Hal had talked about shoots on his estate, she thought he just meant they got lucky with birds that flew past. She was appalled at how naïve she had been, living in the city. Thank God there were people in the countryside trying to fix things. Promising she would join them, she gave the girl her phone number and then headed off to continue her shopping. She felt encouraged that she had just taken a positive step to get involved in the local community. The girl had seemed so earnest and Paddy felt that she could finally contribute in a positive way.

Heading home she decided to call Ari that evening and ask if she was aware of the issues in Norfolk. It would help to know both sides of the argument. The more information she had, the more she'd be able to get involved and try and help.

Chapter Fourteen

Paddy was sitting outside wrapped up in a blanket and enjoying a cup of soup as she watched the waves gently lap back and forth across the shore. The sea and sky reached out towards the horizon in a wall of blue as large white clouds swept overhead. Contemplating how lovely life was, Paddy was shaken out of her daydreams by her phone ringing and she struggled to dig it out of her pocket.

'Holly, darling. I know you've said you want to take a break but Ginger has only gone and broken her ankle. Could you walk this weekend? For me? Darling, please? It's Giovanni's show?'

Paddy smiled. It had been a while since anyone had called her Holly. When she had started modelling, the agency felt she needed a bit of privacy and they had suggested a working name. Her sisters had agreed it made sense and so Holly McDonald had been born. It went perfectly with her pale freckled skin and curly red hair. Everyone expected a Scottish burr when they first met her and were surprised by the East End accent. Of course her colouring came from her Irish father but in keeping her family life private, the modelling agency had suggested a bit of misdirection with a Scottish name.

Now she thought about Duncan's request. She wanted to say no; however, she genuinely liked her agent and he had done loads for her over the years.

Yesterday, the German film company had been in touch asking if she could come up to town, as they had something they wanted to discuss. Now Duncan was calling. It seemed the universe wanted her to go to London, no matter how much she wanted to stay in her cottage. She wondered what the company wanted. They had been rather insistent. Maybe she needed to sign another release form. She had requested she remain uncredited, to Duncan's annoyance. No credit meant no fee, so she felt she owed him this.

Agreeing to Duncan's request she asked him to send her the details and then, hanging up, she got on the phone to the production company to arrange an appointment. It was Tuesday now, she'd catch the night train on Thursday, be in London for the show on Friday, meet the production company on Saturday and maybe get back to Cornwall on Sunday. She had called Nick to see if she was free, but she was in the Far East for the next few weeks so there was no point in staying any longer.

Paddy was looking forward to a few days catching up with the old crowd though. See if she knew any of the models in the show. She had walked for Zac Posen a few years back and he had introduced her to Giovanni Zousa, a daring Italian designer she hadn't worked with before. They had hit it off immediately and he made a point of always booking her. Typical Zac, he was always so supportive to the industry. Always introducing people and forging new connections.

***

As the night train pulled into London she prepared for a busy day; as usual, she had a full diary. Today, she had a fashion show; hopefully she'd be able to skip out of the after-show party, although it seemed unlikely. Tomorrow, she had a meeting with the producer from the film shoot the previous month; whatever it was shouldn't take long. She had plans to have lunch with Aster. She had wanted to catch up with the others as well, but Nick was away, Clem was in Scotland and Ari was in Norfolk. Besides, Aster shone one on one; she tended to watch when she was in a larger group, but when there was just two of you, she was a riot. Hailing a taxi, Paddy shivered in the cold spring air. Was she already acclimatising to the warmer Cornish climate? She didn't remember London being quite so bone chillingly cold. As she headed straight to the show she saw the paparazzi were already in place even at this ridiculous time of the morning. Slipping on her large sunglasses she pulled down her beanie and brought her coffee cup up to her face. Who the hell wanted to have their photo taken having just slept on a train for six hours?

With a sigh she discovered she wasn't going to miss this life at all. Heading into the dressing room she was greeted with a barrage of hugs and kisses. She recognised lots of faces, mainly the dressers and make-up artists. She was laden down with pots of clotted cream and as she handed them out some of the models groaned at her and she ducked as a hair roller was thrown at her. She headed over to the hair section and asked Billy to have a look at her tresses. After a bit of hissing and tutting he loaded her up with some serums and masks and told her to try and avoid going anywhere near the sea. Promising him she would, she gave him a kiss and left, hoping he never found out her new daily routine. The backroom was filling up now as more of the models arrived and the volume lifted. There was always a great buzz before a show.

116

The industry was so lovely. Despite the media slant that everyone was a gossipy bitch, it was actually an incredibly hardworking, creative community.

'Oh look, now she's got a title she gets the first spot.'

Well, nearly everyone was lovely, thought Paddy. There were a few exceptions and God knows, Lori excelled at being a bitch.

Another voice called out over the throng, 'She got the front spot because *she* doesn't walk like a camel with the shits.'

The room broke out into laughter as Paddy's make-up girl told her to keep her face still.

When news of the sisters' change in circumstances was revealed they had all kept it low-key. No one gave any interviews and soon the papers and magazines had to accept that, whilst it was a great story, there wasn't much they could do if no one was going to talk. *Tatler* and *Harper's* had loved the fact that Holly McDonald, a regular face in their magazine, was actually Lady Patricia de Foix. The copy editors who knew her, pleaded for an exclusive, but she just smiled and carried on turning up for work as if nothing had happened. Gradually the fuss died down and the news cycle moved on.

Now Giovanni came through the throng and gave her a huge hug, thanking her for stepping in and demanded a pot of clotted cream.

'And how is your clever sister doing up there in bonny Scotland? I have seen some of her designs and she scares me. She is too good and she has my favourite model!' He held Paddy's hands and gestured widely. 'Why do you turn your back on us? You are too selfish!' He smiled warmly, taking the sting out of his words. 'Now, I have given you the opening

117

position. Knock 'em dead. I want everyone talking about this collection.'

She was wearing a stunning bone crinoline over leather trousers with a stitched pinstripe detail. They were going to be tricky to walk in without looking like a knock-kneed foal. But she'd walked in much worse. As the dresser, Emile, put her into her boned waistcoat there was a little bit of huffing and he called out for Giovanni.

'Baby girl, have you put on weight!?' All three of them looked at Paddy's bust line straining over the top of the corset. 'Hmm.' Emile tapped his teeth and then loosened the front buckles. 'Voila! Superb. But Paddy? Less of that clotted cream for you, yes?'

Paddy laughed and apologised. Really, she wouldn't miss this aspect of the job at all. She was surprised though, her diet had actually been healthier since she got to Cornwall and she was swimming and walking daily. Maybe all the sea air was fattening as well as being a hair wrecker?

***

'For heaven's sake, Henry, what are you wearing?'

Hal looked down at his Loakes; admittedly they were a bit scruffy but damn they were comfortable. 'Is that mud? God darling, we're in London, not the sticks, surely you're not going to the meeting dressed as Farmer Gump. What if they want you for more scenes? Won't that be exciting?' Bianca started rummaging through his wardrobe and pulled out his evening jacket from last night's theatre show. 'Here you go. You look so smart in this outfit.'

Hal sighed. He much preferred his rugby top and chinos. He wasn't interested in impressing some film producer. It had been a laugh but the idea of doing that every day filled him with horror. Plus, if he was honest, he didn't care much for someone shouting at him all day long. He'd had enough of that in basic training. If he was in a room, he was used to being the one in charge. Except, of course, for when his fiancée was present.

He was already regretting having told Bianca about the meeting. Between that and the wedding they'd talked of nothing else for the past few days. Hal stifled a yawn and slipped into his Savile Row suit and polished Oxfords. Bianca was going to go shopping whilst he had his meeting, then they would meet up for lunch and carry on talking about the wedding. He wasn't put off by wedding talk, it's just he had very little input into it. There was no sense of excitement at all. He wasn't sure who to talk to about it. Most of his acquaintances thought he and Bianca were a fabulous match, but his father and stepmother had seemed a bit cooler and his oldest friends had straight out told him he was a fool. If he had a best friend, it was probably Jamie or Hugo: one was still on active service, the other deep in a jungle somewhere, filming for the BBC. Both were heading back for the wedding but he could really do with them here now. Hal was concerned that neither cared much for Bianca either. And now on top of all that, there was Paddy. Paddy, who he had probably thought about every single day since he had first laid eyes on her.

'Henry! Henry, stop daydreaming. You'll be late.'

Straightening his cuffs, Hal kissed her on the cheek and then opened the door for her as they headed out of the hotel.

The day was blustery and a sharp wind was whipping empty crisp packets and leaves along the pavements. At least the blue skies meant they would be spared getting wet as well as cold. The roads were still wet from last night's rain, though, and buses and taxis were throwing up plumes of water as they drove through puddles, the regular shouts of protest from pedestrians and cyclists adding to the general London soundtrack. Hal stood on Bianca's right, shielding her from the traffic and steering the pair of them through the morning crowds. The producer's offices were just off Leicester Square, which meant they were trying to navigate probably the busiest section that London had to offer. Ahead of them, a homeless man, sitting on the pavement, was creating a pinch point as the crowds tried to navigate around him and a delivery truck.

'Really. Look at him,' tutted Bianca, 'he's in everyone's way.' She gingerly stepped over his cardboard sheets. 'Ugh. I mean look at how much space he's taking up. What's wrong with these people? The mayor should do something about them.' Realising he wasn't answering her she turned back to look at her fiancé. 'What are you doing?'

Hal stopped, patting his pockets for change, realising his loose change was in his other trousers.

'You can't give him money! It will only encourage him and his sort. They're all on drugs you know.'

Hal paused frowning at Biana. She was probably right but the chap was right in front of them, he could hear everything he said. Realising that he had no change, he mumbled an embarrassed apology to the hunched over figure, who hadn't even looked up.

Side-stepping a group of tourists, Hal moved to the left of the man and continued along the street until they arrived at the production company's offices. Giving Bianca a quick kiss goodbye he headed in towards the main reception, thoughts of the homeless community already gone from his mind as he wondered how quickly he could get out of the meeting and get back to Cornwall. He visited Tregiskey several times in the past few weeks in the hope of bumping into Paddy and apologising again for his behaviour. Maybe he could get the producers to tell him where she was staying, they were bound to have her contact details. If he was being honest this was the only reason he had bothered with the meeting at all. Bounding up the steps he hoped that he would soon be closer to meeting Paddy again.

Chapter Fifteen

Paddy was led through into the producer's office and saw biscuits and coffee laid out on the small table and was directed towards one of the sofas. *Great*, she thought, *bad news*. Sofas and biscuits always preceded, 'I am afraid to say—, there's been a problem—, a delay—, something's come up—, the thing is—, it's not you—, it is you—, if only—.'

Oh well. She'd been paid well for yesterday's show and despite wanting to avoid the after-show party, it had been fun to catch up with friends. When she told them she had been sunbathing the previous week most of them thought she was teasing. They only relented when she showed them her social media feed and she had the grace to point out it had rained nearly every day since that photo!

She looked around her, the room was a particularly fine example of overstated opulence. Everything, from the framed awards and showcased prizes to the photos with the great and the famous, smacked of overachieving. It was typically revolting and gave Paddy an idea of the sort of producer she was about to meet. She sighed. The German director hadn't known who she was but it was unlikely she could strike out twice. Any producer worth his salt would know an asset when they were looking at one. The air freshener was also giving her a headache; she had noticed ever since arriving in London that her tolerance for the city smells had dwindled. Everything seemed overpowering and she'd already had to take some headache tablets just to try and deal with it. Now a sickly artificial vanilla scent was making her feel ill. She was wondering just how quickly she could get out of here. If she only knew what the problem was, she might have a better idea.

The door opened and her gorgeous co-actor walked into the room. Well, now she knew what the problem was. No doubt their scene was going to be cut or altered after all his ridiculous yawning and grinning at the camera. Inwardly she died, no wonder she'd gone to bed with him, he was a God. That easy smile, his lovely hands, those broad shoulders, that lazy confident demeanour. The receptionist clearly saw him in the same light as Paddy did, as she simpered and flirted with him. For a woman who probably dealt with film stars all day long this was impressive. Paddy was determined not to be seduced again, but her resolve nearly fractured when he saw her and his whole face changed from polite friendliness to unalloyed joy.

***

Hal was shown into a meeting room by a pretty receptionist. The room itself was frankly overwhelming. It looked like this production company was clearly a big deal within the industry. Bianca would be impressed; the corridor had been lined with photos of famous film stars, some even he recognised. As he walked into the room, he saw that Paddy was there and was delighted to see her. A second or two later he noticed she was scowling at him, and he felt crushed.

'Oh, it's you again.' Disdain dripped from her beautiful mouth and he saw with a jolt that she was even more good-looking than he remembered. Last time he had seen her she had looked so upset; now she looked cross.

'Yes, bit of a bad penny I suppose. Well, this looks like good news, doesn't it? Sofa and biscuits. Always the sign of good news I've found.'

He was waffling but he found himself thrown by her presence. Once again, he was overwhelmed with feelings of shame and embarrassment and was finding it hard to balance that with how happy he was to simply see her. Her eyebrows arched and Hal felt that he'd said something stupid but again he was uncertain what that could be. He knew he should have started with an apology but he didn't want to discuss their private matters in a public situation. Maybe after the meeting he could take her out for a coffee and apologise properly. Before he could try to dig into the issue, a small man in a golfing jumper with another jumper tied over his shoulders walked in. He appeared to be going for a country look but his Cuban heels seemed ludicrous and designer jeans just made him look, frankly, a bit flashy.

As he walked in, he confused Hal by approaching Paddy and getting her name wrong. 'Holly McDonald. Can I just say, what a total pleasure it is to meet you?'

Holly stood up smiling, and bent down to kiss him on the cheek. Hal thought the scene looked ridiculous; at five ten she towered over this little man, even in his heels. Her slim frame accentuating her height whilst his flabby midriff emphasised his width. It was like a giraffe greeting a warthog. Embarrassed on Paddy's behalf, Hal could see she was too well-mannered to correct the producer, but he felt it was important that this man should at least get her name right.

'Actually the lady's name is Paddy…' and he faltered. He had forgotten her surname and, even worse, it dawned on him that Paddy was probably a nickname not her real name. He was aware both parties were now looking at him with amused pity and his hackles rose. He was about to speak again when Paddy came to his rescue.

'Holly McDonald is my working name.' And when he looked confused, she continued. 'I'm a model; for privacy reasons, I use a separate, professional name.'

'Oh, that explains it.'

Paddy's cheeks burnt. That explained what? Did he think the reason she had gone to bed with him so easily was because she was a model? Was he one of those creeps who thought models basically slept around and had no morals or virtues? Trust her to sleep with someone who thought she was a tramp.

'And what are you then? What do you do? Other than shoot defenceless creatures.'

'Do?' Hal was startled. Where had killing animals come from?

'Yes. What do you do for a living?'

Hal was nonplussed, he'd never thought of what he did as a job.

'Well I guess you'd call it Estate Management.'

Paddy looked at him blankly. 'What does that mean?' She settled back into her chair and pulled a magazine towards her. It was a trick she had learnt years ago. It was rude, she knew, but it often put people off their game, and she was still smarting from the way he had dismissed her as a model. She had never known someone bring out the worst in her so quickly. Her behaviour was dreadful but she was still dying from the shame of sleeping with a man who had a fiancée.

125

Hal stumbled, the girl was pulling a magazine towards her. Was he boring her, had she just blanked him? He was furious and decided to try and impress her, let her know who she was dealing with. On their dinner date they hadn't discussed their private lives so maybe she was genuinely curious? 'Actually, I look after our estate, the main house, 1,000 plus hectares, the tenant houses and the farm.'

'Wow!' she drawled, cleaning imaginary dirt out from under her fingernails. 'Who owns all that then?'

'We do. The family that is.' As he watched her eyebrow arch up he felt uncomfortable. She didn't seem impressed at all.

'Your folks? So it's not a real job? I mean, it's not like they'll sack you?'

She and the producer shared a knowing grin. Both of them had always worked for a living but regularly met people that had it handed to them on a plate.

'So, you're a part-time housekeeper? What else do you do?' Paddy was aware she was now being incredibly rude but she finally had a glimpse into this man's life. After her eldest sister, Ariana, had inherited the Hiverton Estate over in Norfolk, Paddy had a far better idea of this sort of lifestyle. Children were born into massive privilege and wealth; they went to boarding schools surrounded by other children just like them. They grew up and spent weekends playing in the countryside and jetting off to fabulous locations to watch models walk up and down catwalks, or tenors singing in open-air theatres, and polo ponies thundering down pitches. Then they returned to the dining rooms and champagne marquees and would repeat until they had children who would then pick up the baton and continue the cycle.

Hal could see he had been summed up and dismissed and he was furious. He wanted to answer but every response would invite further scorn. What the hell did some girl from the East End of London know about his life? He glared at the producer and cleared his throat.

'You asked us here this morning for a reason?'

Tony jumped. He'd been buttering Holly up in the hope he might be able to get on her good side before he broke the bad news. Inadvertently, he'd managed to annoy Henry Ferguson. Whilst the man had no influence in the showbiz world he was probably armed to the teeth with lawyers and that was exactly what Tony was trying to avoid.

'Yes, right. And how generous of you to put up with our teasing.' He simpered at Henry, who scowled back. 'The reason I asked you both here was because I have some rather tricky news.'

***

Bianca sipped at her espresso and tried to control her heartbeat. It was beyond stupid meeting Raoul today whilst Henry was in his meeting, but she just couldn't resist the thrill of it. They'd only be having a drink, she told herself. If anyone saw them together she could just say he was an old family friend. As Raoul made his way through the tables she watched as heads turned to follow his progression. He was easily the most beautiful person in the room, and she sat preening in the knowledge that he was making a beeline for her. As he got to the table he kissed her warmly on both cheeks, clicking his manicured fingers for a waitress. Bianca loved the way people jumped to attention around him.

He wasn't as tall as Henry nor as broad, but then she didn't imagine that Raoul had ever got himself dirty on a rugby field, scrambling around in the mud with a bunch of other men. He would look beautiful riding on his pony, his lean frame leaning forward over the horse's neck, as he swiped at a polo ball. Sadly, because of a current injury Bianca hadn't actually seen him play yet but she could imagine it. Henry had a much more masculine presence but it was all rather obvious. They'd gone out on a yacht once. Bianca had been expecting a crew to bring her and Henry drinks whilst they lounged on the deck admiring the view. Instead, he had jumped up and mucked in, pulling on bits of rope and swapping rude jokes with the sailors. You'd never catch Raoul messing about like that. He knew exactly how to treat staff. Besides which, it was wrong of Henry to fraternise with the hired help. Her friend, Ginny, had told her that it only encouraged them to overstep the line. Ginny was the real deal; her dad was worth millions.

Holding her hand across the table, Raoul looked mournfully into her eyes. 'Darling, I miss you so much. Why are you so cruel to me?'

Reluctantly Bianca pulled her hand back. 'You know why. I'm due to be married in a couple of months. We can't be together.' God, she loved how dramatic that sounded.

'But what is my life without you in it? It is only you that makes me come alive. Without you I shall have to return to Chile.' He sighed deeply.

Bianca had first met Raoul at a polo tournament. He'd secretly confided in her that his father was a billionaire and that Raoul was in England scouting out ponies and teams for his father to invest in. Bianca was transfixed but annoyingly also dating Henry. He was the only son of a very wealthy landowner in Cornwall with a dodgy ticker. Admittedly Cornwall was out in the sticks but the house was fabulous and everyone treated him like the lord of the manor.

For a birthday present Henry had flown them first class to the Turks and Caicos Islands, where they'd stayed on a friend's private island. She had enjoyed that very much. Every time they went shopping he would pick up the bill and she'd been able to expand her wardrobe dramatically. And she'd enjoyed that very much as well. But then she met Raoul. He always picked up the hotel restaurant bar bill and promised to shower her in jewels. When she had pointed out some earrings she liked, he had sighed melodramatically and said he couldn't buy jewellery for another man's woman. He was too proud. Not too proud about having sex with me though, she thought ungenerously. If he would only propose, but he hadn't, so Bianca decided to call it a day and stick with Hal.

Only then she noticed that Hal was beginning to lose interest in her. Deciding which of the two men was more of a sucker for a sob story she told Hal she was pregnant and just as she had gambled, he proposed then and there. A while later she tragically 'lost' the baby. And again, as she had gambled, Hal didn't cancel or postpone the wedding. She had fleetingly considered trying it on with Raoul but she was certain he was too smart to fall for it.

Temptation, though, was a terrible thing and she couldn't resist meeting with him for a quick coffee. She thought she might be more in love with the excitement than with either of the two men, but she had to be careful not to spoil things. Maybe after she was married, she could bump into Raoul now and then when she was up in London. There was no way she was going to spend all her time cooped up in Cornwall. Looking at her watch she saw with a tingle that she had at least another half an hour. If only there was somewhere a bit more private.

Chapter Sixteen

The producer cleared his throat. 'You see. The fact of the matter is. Well...' Tony was stumbling for words and put his coffee cup on the table. Dear lord but this was a mess. 'Well, I don't know quite how to say this, but the thing is, we think the pair of you might be married.'

Paddy and Hal stared at him in disbelief.

'Did you say 'married'?'

'What the hell!?'

Tony Harper sighed inwardly. It was too much to hope that both parties would be thrilled or amused, but he wasn't expecting such fury.

'I know this is unexpected but please let me explain. It seems there was some confusion between the local church authorities and the German film crew and they accidentally hired a genuine priest. The priest seemed to be a rather confused gentleman and thought the wedding was genuine...'

'How could he possibly think that?' snapped Hal. 'The director was jumping around all the time yelling cut!'

'Well yes but it seems that he'd had a few weddings recently where the couple have had it filmed as well and he just thought it was along those lines. Plus he may be suffering a bit from memory problems. Then you both signed the register, which it turns out was the actual civil register, not a film prop and so you are in fact, we believe, legally married.' He paused. Maybe now they would laugh and be all forgiving?

'I'm sorry but this is bloody ridiculous. I'm due to get married. Everything is booked!'

131

Paddy looked appalled. He was that close to being married when he had slept with her? She wanted to burst into tears.

'Sod his marriage, what about my reputation?'

Hal coughed. Obviously, it was difficult discussing his upcoming wedding in the presence of the woman he had slept with, but he was incensed she had tossed aside his dilemma so arrogantly. It's not like news of this leaking out would harm her. 'What reputation. You're a model?'

Paddy stared at him in amazement; he was sitting there looking like some jumped-up Lord Snooty in his shiny suit, acting like he was the only one to have a problem. 'What the hell do you mean by that? I work bloody hard at remaining private. I stay out of the tabloids, I don't do celebrity guest appearances, I don't do interviews and I don't have a 'reputation'. Now I've got married to a total stranger on a film shoot. It will get plastered all across the magazines. The fact you are about to actually get married makes it even worse.'

Honestly, she could scream. This was appalling.

Hal shrugged; inwardly he was rather offended by her apparent horror. 'I don't see the problem.' He laughed. 'Am I that awful?'

'What! Why?! You…' Paddy could no longer contain herself and jumped up and started pointing at Tony. 'What the hell is the meaning of this? If a word of this escapes I will sue your production company out of business!'

Tony groaned inwardly. So much for them seeing the funny side. His company was up for a round of capital investments; a scandal like this could blow them out of the water for at least a quarter, and in his business, a quarter was enough time to sink beneath the waves. Clearly the groom needed to be pacified but Holly McDonald was a much bigger problem. She was well loved both by the public and within the industry. She was always first to help in any charity gigs, she never pulled rank, she never stabbed anyone in the back and Tony was certain that if she called for help amongst her colleagues, she would be a very sympathetic figure. Models knew the power of maintaining their persona, whatever it was, that they had created. Making her look like someone who would cheat with someone else's fiancé could destroy her future bookings. She wasn't making a false threat when she threatened to sue him and they both knew she would almost certainly win. He was also aware of her recent change in status. She hadn't brought it up so neither would he but she now had a lot of power behind her. Before he could try to reassure her, Henry broke in again.

'Look, Holly or Paddy or whatever her name is, is obviously getting a bit carried away, but seriously this does need resolving. I know we can't stop people talking…'

Tony groaned, *carried away*? nice attempt to diffuse the situation.

He tried to step in but sure enough, Holly was now even more incensed.

'Carried away? Now who's being ridiculous? And of course we can stop people talking. Every person on set will have signed a non-disclosure agreement.' Whipping back from Hal she turned to Tony. 'How many know about this marriage? Bloody hell, what's Duncan going to say?' Pulling herself out of her reverie she snapped again at Tony, 'Well, what are you going to do?'

Hal was a bit startled by her appalled reaction. If he hadn't been in such a bind himself he might have found this funny. As it was this lovely girl, or what he had thought was a lovely girl, was enraged and each time he spoke, she seemed to be getting worse. He tried again.

'Look, Tony, she does have a point. Like I said, I'm getting married soon and I rather think my fiancée would object if she discovered I was already married.' He smiled at Paddy, trying to show her he was on her side in this mess and almost recoiled from the look of fury she gave him.

Tony, realising he was about to have a full-on fight on his hands jumped in to intervene.

'Please. We are hiring lawyers at the moment to establish if this marriage is legally binding. And if it is, we have a few options. We could appeal the validity of the marriage but that could take a few months, we could request a divorce, which would take a year or we could have it annulled which we just might be able to do in a few weeks. Obviously if you are actually married, we will put all our resources behind it. So what is your preference?'

'Annulled!' Two voices finally united.

Tony sighed and waved at Holly to take her seat again. Honestly, he had never met her before but everything he had heard about her hadn't prepared him for this reaction. He had thought Ferguson was going to be the problem. And indeed, when he had entered the offices, Tony had pegged him immediately as someone who was used to getting his own way and having the world revolve around him. For a man who had just discovered his wedding might be cancelled he seemed remarkably relaxed. Once Holly was settled, he continued.

'Excellent, an annulment should be fairly easy to obtain as the marriage wasn't actually consummated.'

There was a pause and a silence as both parties picked up their coffee cups. 'It wasn't consummated, was it?'

'No. Of course not!'

'As if!'

'Right,' Tony paused, smirking inwardly. So much for Holly's golden girl reputation. He should have known it was a front, models and actresses were all the same, jumping in and out of any one's bed to get ahead. However, she was right, she could sue him to hell and back and now he saw that she probably would. A leak like this could destroy her, especially if people discovered that she had been sleeping around. The repercussions would affect his company as well though. It also wasn't worth him losing his reputation as a safe pair of hands for people to invest in.

'Leave it with me. If you can give me your lawyers' details, we will be in touch with them today and get the ball rolling.'

***

As they left the building, Hal held back as Paddy stormed out of the building. He knew Bianca was probably waiting for him and he was reluctant for the two women to meet. Fixing his tie he looked in the mirror and was surprised to see how concerned he looked. The past hour had been bruising. He had totally misread Paddy. He had thought she was a total poppet; the last time he saw her he thought she was genuinely upset but after the performance in there, he wasn't sure who she was at all. Apart from being a ball-busting career girl. That much was clear. God, he couldn't remember the last time anyone had made him feel so insignificant. The two of them smirking over him being a *part-time housekeeper*, who the hell did they think they were anyway? And more importantly who the hell was Duncan? And why the hell did he care? Hal knew he shouldn't be surprised that Paddy or Holly or whatever she was called had a man in her life but it made him feel deeply unsettled.

As he walked into the atrium, Bianca jumped up to join him. She'd just seen some of the cast of *Strictly Wonderful* go by as well as some TV hosts and Holly McDonald. Hal nodded glumly and, when asked, told her that the company just needed him to sign some filming waivers. There was no way he could tell her he was actually married; it would devastate her. For a second, Bianca seemed crestfallen that it wasn't a job offer but then suggested they go for lunch at a new place she had just read about. Hal just wanted to head back home, but instead he gave her a small squeeze and hailed a cab. How in the name of God could he be married?

Bianca continued to prattle on. She seemed particularly high-spirited today, but Hal was lost in thought, nodding occasionally in agreement and then looking out of the window. The traffic was typically snarled up and they sat stationary whilst the lights went from green to red to green again, with no one moving. As he sat watching the street outside, his heart sped up as he saw Paddy walking along the pavement, carrying a large Burger King bag. He didn't think models ate junk food but then she stopped by the same homeless chap he and Bianca had passed earlier that day, and sat down. It was impossible to tell what was being said but both Paddy and the man seemed to be laughing about something.

Paddy offered some chips to the dog before handing the rest of the bag to him. She just sipped from a cup whilst he started to eat. Clearly, as she sat on the floor drinking and chatting with him she seemed utterly unfazed by his appearance. And in fact, as Hal looked at him the chap seemed to come alive. Had he been asked to describe him earlier, Hal was embarrassed to admit he wouldn't have been able to suggest more than white, dirty and middle-aged. Now Hal could see that he was actually quite young. He had a broad face, and a pleasant smile. His laugh looked genuine and he gestured wildly as he told Paddy some story. She was laughing in return waving her cup around and feeding more chips to the dog. As the taxi pulled away Hal craned his body to look back and received a sharp nudge.

'Henry, I don't think you've been listening to a word I said. The caterer has suggested we should alter the menu to include caviar on the canapes. He said they will be perfect. What do you think?'

'I suppose Burger King is out of the question?'

Bianca frowned and changed the subject. Recently, Henry had been increasingly distracted and Bianca knew when not to rock the boat. She was so close to landing her golden goose; he hadn't even mentioned a pre-nup. All she needed to do was play the next few weeks as carefully as possible.

The cab dropped them just beyond the restaurant and there was a small crowd waiting at a pelican crossing. Hal was happy to wait for them to cross, but Bianca was fed up with his lack of attention and tried to push her way through. Maybe if she could get him some food and drink inside him, he might be less distracted. A glass of wine, a nice piece of steak, the old adage of winning a man's heart through his stomach came to mind. A teenager stood in her way and was about to say something to her but Bianca wasn't in the mood. Scowling at her, she shoved her out of the way. The girl stumbled and Hal threw his hand out to steady her. She was tiny, maybe only five foot and Bianca had shoved her towards the traffic without so much as a thought for her safety. The girl looked up at him and then looked back at Bianca.

'You need to ditch her, mate. That is not a good life choice.'

The way she spoke Hal realised she was probably older than she looked and not a child at all, but still no one deserved to be pushed into the traffic. Laughing, she shook her head and slipped away into the crowd as he looked thoughtfully after Bianca.

Everything seemed to be shifting around him and he felt uncomfortable. He was not making good life choices at all. He couldn't get the image of Paddy and that young beggar out of his mind. What the hell was wrong with him? He had always prided himself on doing the right thing, of taking care of people, of being accountable, but that was a lie. That very morning he had stepped over a human being in need. He had summed him up and discarded him, forgetting him within minutes. At the time he could see nothing wrong with his behaviour, but a few hours later as he watched Paddy, he knew that what she was doing was the correct thing and he felt distinctly ashamed of himself. Now he was following in the wake of a woman who was shoving strangers out of her way not caring if they fell. Something was very wrong with his life.

Chapter Seventeen

How the hell could she be married? She had spent all her daydreams on the perfect dress, the perfect pieces of music, and the perfect menu and it turned out that for her wedding she was dressed in nylon, listening to Radio 2 and eating sarnies from the catering trailers. That was her special day? Where was all the rose petal confetti? Where was the horse drawn cart, where were her sisters? She liked foreigners but she hadn't expected there to be so many Germans on her special day. She wiped a tear away, this was ridiculous, she was overwhelmed with self-pity. Her emotions were all over the place recently. *Well what did she expect?* she thought with a laugh, new brides were bound to be emotional. Pinching the bridge of her nose, she took a steadying breath and looked around her.

She was sitting in the National Gallery cafe waiting for Aster. She loved this space and had often sat here as a child with her parents. Trips to the free museums and art galleries were all they could afford but her parents would always insist on buying a drink and a packet of crisps from the cafe as a way of saying thanks to the institutions. Raising five girls on basic wages was always going to be a struggle but Paddy rarely felt they did without. Instead of going to stadiums to watch the latest pop star, her folks had started to take the girls to the local band nights at the nearby social club. That had been fun and some of the bands were really decent. Her overwhelming memory, though, was that adults could be quite stupid and were rubbish dancers. It made her stop and grin to think she was probably older now than some of those 'adults' she had so blithely dismissed. To be so young and certain. But on one thing she could agree with her younger self: adults could be very stupid. Pulling out her phone she hit favourites and was gratified when her agent answered straightaway.

'Hello, Duncan. I need your help, I've screwed up.' She could just picture Duncan rolling his eyes and waving at his secretary to pour him a coffee. He had begged Paddy not to do the film shoot without a proper contract; now he was settling down for his favourite pastime: being proved right.

'It's that German film show thing, isn't it? I knew you should have been properly signed up.'

Paddy moved her phone to the other ear as a young family squeezed past her table and started to settle down behind her.

'So, what's gone wrong? Tell me all about it and I'll tell you how we'll fix it.'

'Hmm, well it's tricky.' Paddy squeezed her tea bag and looked around the room. Deciding no one nearby would be remotely interested in her conversation she took a deep breath, but Duncan rolled on.

'Holly, dear, there is nothing you can do that I can't fix. Besides you don't do anything. You are my golden girl. How can you screw that up? I had Coco in here the other day and, well I can't tell you what she did, confidentiality clauses and all that, but trust me, nothing you say is going to outshine that.'

Confident that no one could overhear her Paddy continued, 'Did she accidentally get herself married? No? Then I win.'

Paddy could just picture Duncan's face.

'Wait, are you joking?' Duncan switched from gossip queen into the ruthless agent she knew and loved. 'Of course you're not. Right. Give me all the details. Leave nothing out.'

By the end of the call Paddy was exhausted. Duncan had asked her to go over every scene and exchange and finally had chided her for going to the meeting without him. 'It's what you pay me for. Now are you certain that I know everything?' Deciding he didn't need to know absolutely everything, she told a tiny lie and then hung up. Finally, she relaxed as he reassured her that not a word of this would get out.

'Hello Ugly!' Paddy jumped.

'Aster! Stop doing that! Do you like bloody float or something?' Leaping up she gave her little sister a huge hug. It had been almost two months since Ari's wedding and she missed her very much, tucked away down in Cornwall.

'Sorry I'm late. You know, London.' They both shrugged; despite growing up there they had mostly avoided the centre. Like all Londoners, they did all they could to avoid the tourist hot spots.

Aster began to tell Paddy about her day, making her laugh at all her observations. 'There was this one woman that had totally smudged her lipstick and I was about to tell her when she shoved me out of her way.'

Paddy rolled her eyes. 'God some people are so rude. Why do they have to be like that?'

'Ah don't worry, it gets better. The man she was with, helped catch me as I fell, and he didn't have a single trace of lipstick anywhere on him!'

'No!'

142

'Yep. Cheating baggage. I hope he spots it and kicks her to the kerb.'

Paddy laughed. Aster was so incredibly observant and so black and white. The woman had been rude to her and now deserved everything that was about to rain down on her.

'So, tell me all about that phone call. Why did Duncan want to know the ins and outs of your meeting? Wasn't he there, and how can you possibly be married?'

Paddy groaned and once again she related the sorry mess, and as ever Aster's grilling was even more thorough than Duncan's. At the end of it she just looked at Paddy and pursed her lips. 'You're protesting quite a lot about all this?'

'Damn right I am. It's my reputation at stake.'

Aster dipped her finger into the crisp packet for the final crumbs. 'The reputation relating to the career that you are leaving?'

'Yes. Oh don't say it like that, you always try to twist everything! If I leave now under a cloud people will think I was driven out.'

Aster raised her eyebrow and asked Paddy if she was finished with her packet. Cleaning that one out as well she leant back on her chair. 'Fair enough. That makes sense I suppose. Now shall we go and have a look at the new exhibition and see if we can spot any of Otto's work.'

Paddy laughed, pleased the moment of tension had passed. Aster was always the most astute of any of her sisters and she hadn't wanted her to see just how upset she was by Hal. She knew she didn't have to ask Aster not to tell the others about the wedding. It wasn't that Aster was discreet it was more that she hoarded, only releasing her treasure when she felt it benefited the family and for no other reason.

As they left the café, Paddy wondered what she was going to do about her feelings for Hal. When he had walked into the producer's office her heart had somersaulted and she could still see the marks in her skin where she had dug her nails into her palms to keep the smile of her face. The fact of the matter was, that was had fallen for the charms of a scoundrel and the less her sisters knew, the better.

Chapter Eighteen

Paddy came in from her morning swim and towelled her hair. It had become chilly and the promise of a long early summer seemed to be receding into a distant desire. Even spring seemed to be properly freezing. Slicing a grapefruit she settled down to her puzzles. She liked doing the harder ones first thing and the general knowledge later in the day when her mind wasn't as sharp. Tutting to herself she was aware she was falling into rather a lazy routine. Plus she needed to make some friends down here. She liked her own company, which was a good thing, but since returning from London her most challenging conversation had been with the seals.

She wasn't naturally gregarious but in certain circumstances she was extremely confident. Around her friends and family, where she felt safe and loved, she would shine. At work, where she was good at what she did and was appreciated for it, she would excel. For the rest of the time she would be happy to just fade into the background. Give her a good book or a box set, a horse to ride or water to swim in and she was content. Sometimes if she was feeling particularly rock and roll, she'd even do a jigsaw puzzle. Paddy didn't need to be clever or talented like her sisters. She was happy and that was enough. It had taken her a long time to be happy again and she knew how precious it was. She had developed an unexpected pleasure in collecting shells and in weeding. She wouldn't go so far as to call it gardening, but she had begun to clear the path up to the grotto. Everywhere around her the hedgerows were bursting into colour. She had recognised the primroses but had learnt about wild garlic and was delighted to see bluebells growing in swathes under the trees. When the weather permitted, she was constantly photographing the countryside, and every day at six am and six pm if she was home, she would nip up to the grotto and take a photo of the sea and sky. She wasn't sure about a written diary, but she thought this was a nice way to mark her stay here.

Her phone buzzed and she frowned at the unfamiliar number. Answering it, it took a while for her to work out who she was talking to. She had almost forgotten about Mandz, the protestor from Truro, but now here she was asking Paddy to come along and help join the debate on animal welfare. Arranging a date and time, Paddy hung up reinvigorated.

She had come to Cornwall to reassess her life. It seemed silly to be thinking about ending her career at just twenty-four, she enjoyed modelling but it didn't drive her. Now, her family's inheritance had given her the opportunity to pause.

Whilst she wasn't bored or lonely down here, she was beginning to feel cut adrift. Without a tight schedule and constantly being in the media's eye, the freedom was going to her head. Her stupid one-night stand with Hal being the perfect example. Meeting him in London had hurt. She had almost managed to convince herself that he wasn't really into his fiancée, but in reality, he was actually due to walk down the aisle with her. The fact Paddy was now currently married to him seemed the irony of the century. She had spent weeks daydreaming about what being his wife would be like only to discover she had been all along. And now that same marriage was about to be annulled. What a whirlwind romance that was. Her disappointment had been intense and surprised her. She hadn't realised how much he had got under her skin. It probably explained why she kept bursting into tears.

***

A couple of hours later she was driving down the lanes towards a large country hotel by the sea. Mandz had told her they were hosting the event there because it was isolated and deliberately hard to get to. That didn't make much sense to Paddy but she trusted Mandz knew what she was talking about. As she arrived a marshal waved her into a field. She wasn't certain about driving on grass but everyone else seemed to be doing it. Getting out of the car she debated pulling on her wellies but the grass didn't look muddy. She hadn't been sure what to wear – what does one wear to a debate? – but she grabbed her mucking out jacket and figured it looked suitably scruffy and country.

'Oh hello. New face! Are you here for the horse trials meeting? I can spot a pony club girl a mile off!'

Paddy turned to see a lovely older woman in smart leather boots, a dress, jacket and a silk scarf at her neck. 'The horse trials? Yes, I think so, but I haven't been here before, so I'm not really sure what to do?'

The woman smiled and stretched out her hand. 'New to the area then? Londoner? Always good to have some new blood. What do you ride?' Soon both women were chatting enthusiastically about their favourite horses, and Paddy was delighted to find out there were apparently loads of riding opportunities in the area. Having introduced herself as

Caroline, she ushered Paddy into the hotel and was soon being warmly greeted by lots of friendly people.

'Let me find you some young people to chat to, you don't want to be stuck with us fuddy-duddies all afternoon or we'll never see you again. My daughter's around somewhere and she's about your age. I won't introduce you to my son, he'll be boring and just stare at you. Wait here and I'll be right back, I promise.'

Paddy watched Caroline weave her way through the crowd laughing and chatting with various people and headed out on to the balcony. Sitting at the bar she felt a little self-conscious. This wasn't exactly what she thought a debate was like but at least everyone was friendly. She had never actually been part of a pony club, but she loved horses and that seemed to be good enough for Caroline. Her mother had always said manners cost nothing and also, if you can't say something nice don't say anything at all. She had tried to live up to her mother's mantra and was probably the most successful of all her sisters at that skill. Thinking of them made her smile. Aware of someone standing at her shoulder she turned, expecting to see Caroline and her children. Instead she was staring straight into Hal's lovely blue eyes. Damn. Had they got bluer, or was he just more tanned?

'Well hello. Fancy seeing you here.' He looked around uncertainly and then refocussed on her. 'I thought you were just on holiday. Or are you with someone?'

Paddy just stared at him. What the hell was he doing here?

Hal tried again, running his hands through his hair. 'Look, shall we call pax?'

Paddy tried to regain her wits. The way his fingers ran through his hair had sent her thoughts careering out of control and she tried to gather her senses. Who the hell was Pax, was he Hal's solicitor? She didn't want a scene. This was her trying to settle into Cornish life. Not have a discussion about her marital status with her husband. And if he could just stop being so bloody attractive. She was like a bloody teenager.

'I don't know Pax?'

'Sorry, I meant peace. Shall we call a truce? I know it's bloody difficult what with, well, everything. But shall we behave like we've just met and pretend there isn't any horrible situation between us?' His lips twitched in a small grin and Paddy found herself smiling stupidly in return.

She thrust her hand out. 'Paddy Byrne. Pleased to meet you.' As her mother had said, good manners cost nothing.

Hal clicked his heels and bowed. 'Henry Ferguson. Enchanted.'

Laughing he poured her a glass of ice water and sat down at the bar beside her.

'Tell me all about yourself.'

Not a hope she thought. 'You first. I understand you're a housekeeper?'

Hal coughed and gave her a friendly glare.

'Not quite.'

'Okay. Let me see. Are you married?' Now Paddy decided to take pity on him as he coughed into his glass. 'Okay then. How many brothers and sisters do you have?'

With a visible sigh of relief Hal poured himself a glass of water, 'Ah, there I can't help you. I'm an only child. And no I wasn't spoilt before you say it.'

149

Paddy smiled. 'You probably were. I mean look at you, you're gorgeous, you must have wrapped everyone round your finger as a little boy. But no, what I was going to say was that must have been lonely?'

Hal paused. 'I think occasionally I probably was, but my mother and father were aware of it. Mother had always wanted more children but wasn't well enough, so they had to make do with just me. I went to a local prep and every weekend there would be sleepovers; the more the merrier as far as she was concerned. After rugby or sailing we'd all troop into the house, covered in mud or sand and then spend the weekend falling out of trees and eating biscuits until it was time for school again. Then I went to boarding school and it was more of the same. Honestly, I loved it. At Christmas and Easter, the cousins would invariably come over, so more noise and mayhem. In fact there were times when I just wanted the peace and quiet of being on my own. Does that sound mad?'

Paddy laughed, his childhood sounded idyllic. 'I grew up with four other sisters, Mum and Pa all living in a three-bed terrace. A bit of peace and quiet doesn't sound mad at all!'

'Seven of you! Dear God, what was that like?'

'Wonderful! Chaotic! Too much hairspray. But I tell you it gave us a perfect view of the best marriage ever. And then when Ari grew up, she's my oldest sister, she married an arsehole and it gave us a view of the worst marriage ever. Just to balance things out.'

Hal grimaced; in light of his recent behaviour he should probably steer clear of this conversation, but once again he was falling under Paddy's spell.

'Was he that bad?'

'It's like she put her hand in the shitty bucket and pulled out the biggest turd in it.'

Hal roared with laughter and several people in the room turned to look over. 'God I'm sorry. That was just so descriptive. Please tell me they're not still together?'

'No, she got married again and her new husband is wonderful.'

Hal watched as Paddy's face lit up talking about her sister. Her hair was tied back and little earrings swung and caught the light as she chatted and pulled faces.

'Phew! Glad to hear it, pretty women should be married.'

Paddy recoiled with a groan. He really was lovely to look at and he made her laugh loads, but good grief!

'Seriously? Did you just say that out loud! That is so sexist!'

'What, that she's pretty or should be married?'

'Both. And anyway, how do you know she's pretty?'

'There's no way someone as beautiful as you has ugly sisters.'

Paddy laughed. That was such a corny line, but what the hell, who could resist such a compliment. 'Oh please! But fair enough, my sisters are all gorgeous.'

'Are they models as well?'

'No. I mean Nick could be. She used to do the odd catwalk. God, you should see her walk. She gets on that runway and it's like she owns the whole bloody world and everyone looking at her knows it. But she doesn't enjoy it as much as I used to.'

'Used to?'

'Yeah. It's hard work, but that's not the issue. It's the lack of privacy. It's the assumptions.' She arched her eyebrows and stared at Hal pointedly before carrying-on. 'After a while it got tiring. Nick hated it pretty much straightaway. There was just something about my face that photographed just that little bit better than the others. To the untrained eye it's not noticeable but a talent scout spotted me and the rest as they say…'

'Were your sisters jealous at all? Especially if as you say they are also pretty.'

Paddy laughed. 'I don't think so but they certainly didn't let me get big headed about it. I remember one day they pinned me down and drew a moustache and glasses on my face with felt tip.' She saw him look concerned, and hurried to defend her sisters. 'Totally standard brother or sister behaviour. Anyway I arrived at the photoshoot with Nick, she came with me to all of them in the early days, and my face was red raw from scrubbing off the felt tip and the photographer absolutely lost it. He screamed at me and called me every name under the sun. He was a big name so everyone just stood there. Nick tried to explain it was a joke and he screamed at her too. You could hear a pin drop. No one knew what to do and then just like that, he shouted at the crew to get the shoot ready and get me dressed. I was a bloody wreck by the time he took the photos; my skin was still scrubbed and blotchy and you could just about make out the moustache marks.'

Hal looked horrified, saying he sounded like a total bastard.

'Oh a total one, but ironically, that photoshoot launched my career. Years later I read an interview with him claiming credit for the whole thing. As you say, a total bastard.'

'What did your parents say? Did they report him?'

Paddy had been enjoying their chat. She had worried about what might happen if she should bump into him again. However, he was expertly dealing with the situation. This light-hearted bantering was avoiding all the genuine issues that lay between them. The difficulties of their unexpected marriage and on-going annulment were all in the hands of the lawyers. The fact that they had actually consummated the marriage was not something either of them was going to admit to.

For now, she was simply enjoying getting to spend some time with him. She hoped to God that his fiancée wasn't here. That was certainly one person she didn't want to get to know. However, as much as she was enjoying chatting to Hal she wasn't prepared to start discussing the more painful sides of her life.

'No, it's your turn Farmer Hal. What did you do after your wonderful childhood?'

Hal paused and for a moment he looked incredibly sad and then smiled at her. 'Yes, it was wonderful. Anyway, I came home for a while and did my A levels locally and then went off to uni. Normal route more or less, from there I went straight into Sandhurst. And from there out to Kandahar.'

'Sorry, you've lost me.' Even A levels weren't the normal route for her. As soon as she'd got her GCSEs, she left school and started earning. 'Isn't Kandahar in

Afghanistan? That sounds exciting. Was Sandhurst who you worked for?'

Hal poured her another glass of water and asked for some olives.

'My fault. You tend to take things for granted and then assume everyone knows what you are talking about. Sandhurst is the Army training college. From there we went out to help fight the Taliban in Afghanistan.'

Paddy grimaced, talk about sounding ignorant. *Going to a war zone – what fun.* Just when she thought she was beginning to come across as reasonable and interesting she went and put her foot in it. 'Oh. Not exciting at all then. God, I bet your mother was a wreck waiting for you to come home.'

'She died when I was sixteen.'

His words fell into a distressed silence as Paddy stared at him in horror. She had been so quick to assume he had had a gilded perfect life. Paddy knew exactly what losing a mother was like, she herself had been fourteen, but what must it have been like to not have any siblings to turn to? Without thinking she leant forward and held his hand, her eyes glistening as he looked down at her, his face awash with an old pain. She could sense he was about to say something but instead he looked over her shoulder and gently removed his hand.

'Henry, darling!' Caroline joined them at the bar along with two others. Clearly from their looks, her son and daughter.

'Hey Hal! Trust you to find the prettiest girl in the room!' Turning to Paddy the girl introduced herself, 'Hi I'm Jemima, Mummy said you needed rescuing from the oldies.

Instead, I see Hal has been boring you about bloody rights of way, if I know Hal?' Laughing, she punched his arm.

Her brother then leant forward. 'Hi, I'm Malcolm, excuse my sister. I can only take her anywhere twice.'

The siblings chimed together. 'The second time to apologise!'

'Sorry, twin thing!' said Jemima.

Paddy laughed. The change in mood was dramatic. For a moment she had felt a complete connection with Hal. She had wanted to stand by him, and let him know that she would always be there for him. That with her, he need never pretend to hide his grief. Instead she was swept up in the exuberance of these two excitable siblings.

'Oh, tell me about it. I'm a twin as well. Non-identical. And no, we don't know which of us is first. Mum didn't want to know.'

'Oh I wish I'd had your mother's brains,' said Caroline. 'All I ever heard as they grew up was that Jemima was more assertive because she was born first.'

'Or because I'm such a gentleman and let her go first!'

'In your dreams, face ache.'

For a second, Paddy thought Jemima might actually try to put her brother into a headlock until their mother intervened. 'For heaven's sake, children!'

Bashfully, they apologised to their mother and Malcolm winked at Paddy. 'Sorry about that but I've been working over in New York for the past few months and we're always a bit high-spirited when we get back together. We promise to behave like grown-ups like Hal here.'

'I seem to remember it was you who called the prefects when we tried to climb out the dorm windows that time, not me,' protested Hal.

Paddy sat smiling, listening to these people laugh and chat. She loved the genuine banter of friends and family and was glad Hal had good people around him. Listening to them she felt homesick and wished she was back with her sisters. Taking a deep breath, Hal nudged her knee with his and raised an eyebrow, mouthing 'okay?' at her. She was surprised he had noticed and gave him a bright grin in return. She was about to join the conversation when someone called out across the busy room that the meeting was about to start.

Jolted, Paddy remembered she still hadn't met Mandz or asked anyone what the strategy was supposed to be. Excusing herself she headed to the bathroom and quickly texted Mandz.

-Where are you? Are you in the meeting room already? Met some of the others, really lovely. Caroline? Should I stay with her?

-We're outside. We got delayed. Where are you? Don't know Caroline. Glad there are others there already.

-I'm in the loos. Can meet you in lobby?

-OK. Coming in now.

Paddy put her phone away and checked her hair. She had spoken to Ari about it but it hadn't gone well. Ari had ranted for at least ten minutes about hunt saboteurs and people that claimed to be helping animals but were actually hurting them. Not to mention damaging properties, tearing down fences and gates. It seemed there were angles that Paddy hadn't considered and it was clear she didn't know enough about the subject. The next few days she had spent a lot of time online reading about various countryside issues and she felt confident enough to ask some questions and hopefully debate some of the answers. Having met Caroline and Hal she was confident she wouldn't make a fool of herself and if she did dry up, she was certain they had lots of great questions as well.

Standing in the foyer, Paddy was pleased to see Hal coming back from the meeting room and heading straight towards her. Muttering to herself, she had to remember he was engaged. Smiling at him, she heard a large angry bang from the hotel lobby doors and she turned her head to see a group of about eight badly dressed people holding banners, shouting loudly and storming towards her. To her horror she saw they were being led by Mandz.

'Hi Pat. You look great. Clive can you get a photo?' she shouted over the other protestors, thrusting a sign into Paddy's hand.

Paddy was instantly alarmed. This wasn't right. Why were they shouting? What on earth was going on? This was like the time a militant group had thrown red paint over her and a bunch of other models. The irony had been that the fashion shoot had been to promote fake fur but the protestors hadn't got the message right. Seeing a camera being pointed at her she twisted her face away, dropping the placard as she did so. 'What are you doing? Don't take my photo!'

'Come on, Pat, it will be great for publicity,' jeered Mandz. 'We'll get right onto the front cover.'

Having shouted for help, Hal turned, snarling at Paddy. 'My God. Are you with these ruddy sabs!'

Paddy recoiled. 'Of course not. They aren't sabs. We're all here to discuss hunting, aren't we?'

'No, we're bloody not,' Hal's face was twisted in anger and Paddy felt genuinely frightened by his expression. 'This is the annual general meeting of the Cornish horse trials and which courses we are going to run.'

'Yeah, that's what you say,' shouted a skinny looking man, covered in a bizarre collection of piercings and blue tattoos. 'It's all the same to you lot. You get on your horses and trample all across the countryside, destroying it as you go.'

'Paddy, seriously.' Hal grabbed her by the arm. 'What is the meaning of this?'

'That's right, ignore me.' The man continued to heckle. 'You've got nothing to say. You and your dogs destroy everything the common labourer tries to achieve.'

'There are no sodding dogs. And what labouring have you ever done?' Rounding on Paddy, Hal looked at her in disgust. 'My god, what a nasty piece of work you are!'

Paddy looked up at him in alarm. The blood drained out of her face accentuating her freckles and her red hair. She was standing so close to him and was incredibly aware of his body as he held her arm but this was all wrong. He was looking at her in anger and great disappointment and she wanted to tell him he had got it all wrong.

'Oi!' shouted one of the women. 'What are you going to do, get out your hunting whip and beat her?'

'That's all you can think about, isn't it? Violence.' He turned from the woman and looked at Paddy again. 'What about the time they threw paint over Caroline's car? That lovely lady you were trying to ingratiate yourself with. Do you know she slept in her stables for the next few weeks. She was so scared. Have you any idea what she went through? Were you with them when they tipped Brian's horse box over with a horse in it?' He was shouting over the volume of the chanting protestors. 'They had to put the horse down; it had broken two legs, it screamed the whole time!'

Paddy was now openly crying. The image of that poor horse was horrible and the hostility from both sides was beginning to get physical. More men had now joined Hal and the voices had raised on both sides. Paddy wanted to die. This was not what she had had in mind at all. She broke free from Hal's grip and dashed to the front door, legging it up the driveway and back to her car. Sobbing, her car skidded on the grass as she sped away. As she drove off, she cursed her stupidity in trying to get involved in country life. They were all monsters. Hal most of all.

Chapter Nineteen

'I think 'fart pants' was the worst one I knew.'

'Bog breath was my favourite.'

'Oh killer. How far did that get you?'

'All the way to the second bell, where my vocabulary was rapidly expanded by sharing litter duty with Year Nine.'

Jemima laughed. 'That's the third year, isn't it?'

Paddy and Jemima were sitting in Jemima's kitchen, enjoying a bowl of soup for lunch and sharing tales of school. The day before Paddy had been all but ready to leave Cornwall. She had been here almost three months and thought it had been working out. The scene at the hotel though had shaken her and she felt completely alone and out of her depth, when her phone rang. She didn't recognise the number, but very few people had it so she answered cautiously. An unfamiliar voice started chatting with great familiarity and it took a few minutes before Paddy worked out it was Jemima, Caroline's daughter, who she had met very briefly at the bar.

'Anyway, Mum said you were new to the area and keen to go riding so I thought I'd give you a call and say hi. It's rotten being the new girl and everything and I just wanted to reassure you we aren't all placard waving thugs. So, do you want to come over?'

Paddy had put the phone down, relieved that the girl hadn't associated her with the protestors. Clearly Hal hadn't stuck the knife in. She shivered again at how angry he had been at her. It seemed wholly out of order. What right did he have to judge her? Even if she had been a protestor, he was

160

way angrier at her than he had been at any of the other actual protestors. Just when she was beginning to forgive him for being a philandering git and an arrogant hooray Henry, he again revealed his true colours.

. Uncertain what sort of ride Jemima had in mind when she called, Paddy placed both sets of boots in the car and headed off in jeans and a tweed jacket over a silk blouse; thin layers were always best when riding. She also tied her hair back into a long plait and headed off.

Arriving at Spinney Barton, Paddy wondered if Cornwall had any normal roads. She had become a lot more comfortable driving around her local lanes; she had learnt where the nearest passing spaces were and had become quite proficient at reversing. As the year began to warm up, she was noticing the roads were becoming busier with visitors. On one occasion she had been happily driving along when she came nose to nose with a bus. She was astonished, given the size of the road, but the driver seemed relaxed and gave her a small toot and a wave after she reversed 100 yards back into a lay-by. She was so delighted that she had managed this by herself she spent the rest of the drive smiling to herself.

The drive down to Jemima's house was bumpy and full of potholes. Murmuring encouragement to her car, she hoped she wasn't ripping the undercarriage apart. Imagine arriving somewhere new and having to explain your car was dead and blocking the drive.

As she drove into the yard a pair of geese came running over, honking and hissing. She wondered if these were the nipping sort. The ones at the city farm used to make a lot of noise and occasionally would nip you as well. But they usually only went for the boys that would run after them and try and catch them. Just as she decided to brave it, the front door of the house opened and Jemima came out waving at the geese and driving them back to the side of the house.

'Sorry about that,' she called out, 'they won't hurt. Angus wanted to install a security system, which I thought was ridiculous, what with the dogs and all, but he's away so much that we compromised on geese. Not sure that it was that good an idea though. They crap everywhere, look at it. Come on in and mind where you step.'

As Paddy made her way to the front door she agreed that Jemima had a point; the whole of the front drive was littered in droppings. Spinney Barton was a lovely low-slung farmhouse that seemed to spread across several levels. It sat on a ridge and looked down over miles of fields and woods and, in the far distance, Paddy could just about spot the sea. Smiling at Jemima, she told her how lovely her home was.

Jemima beamed. 'It sure is, but currently the view is the best thing about it. We bought it last year, when John, the previous owner, died. I think he was born here and honestly that was about the last time anyone had done any work on it. I grew up nearby and knew the place; when it came up on the market, I dragged Angus along and thankfully he fell in love with it as well.'

As she chatted, she led Paddy in through a small corridor with slate flagstones on the floor and into a small kitchen with battered Formica units. The slate floors were nothing like her manicured tiles in the beach house. These were massive slabs the size of gravestones. They were laid where they fell, and the floor was uneven and mismatched because of it. There was a freestanding white stone sink with chips in it and some massive cast iron contraption that took up half the wall. A gentle heat radiated from it and Paddy guessed it was some sort of ancient cooker.

She looked around for somewhere to sit down but the chairs seemed covered in paperwork or cats. Shooing the cats out of the kitchen, Jemima grabbed a tea towel and wiped the chair down and then threw her arms out. 'Ta-dah. Home sweet home. Isn't it a pit?'

Making a coffee she apologised that it was just instant, but Paddy smiled. Instant was fine. If anything Jemima was putting her at her ease. She wasn't sure what to expect. When Paddy had met them, she had been struck by how incredibly posh they all were. They all sounded like the Queen or something, and seemed unaware of their easy elegance and authority. To her they had felt like a solid pack and she had stood as an outsider wondering how to engage with them. All she had was her glamour, and in her eyes that was a superficial construct. She also had a title but that meant even less to her. Basically she was an East End girl who had grown up poor, in a little terrace. Now here she was wining and dining in homes that had larger hallways than her entire childhood home. God knows, she didn't have an inferiority complex, she made friends wherever she went, but she just felt a little out of place. Maybe that was why she liked Jemima's rambling farmhouse. It might be large but it wasn't intimidating in the least.

'I like it. Feels like a home.'

Jemima smiled and waved a packet of biscuits in her direction. 'Sorry they're not home baked; the oven beats me every time so I've given up.'

Paddy listened in silence as she continued to explain how the house was a work in progress. 'The problem is we're now on a bit of a deadline on account of me getting pregnant! It's a bit unexpected but we're thrilled. Just, well the house is barely habitable. God knows how we'll manage with a baby. Angus has taken on extra work in London so we can speed up the renovations of this property. Kitchen first clearly. But that's why we have the geese. Angus came over all protective and hates the idea of my being here on my own. It seemed like a good idea but Mapp and Lucia are proving to be more hassle than they're worth.'

'Mapp and Lucia?' exclaimed Paddy, thinking of the noisy geese outside. 'That's perfect! I love those books. Oh they would be so cross to have geese named after them!'

Both girls laughed and began to swap other favourite books, quickly finding they had lots in common and sharing suggestions the other hadn't heard of. Jemima stood up and, telling Paddy to follow her, wandered down another dark little corridor until they reached a room full of bookshelves. Looking around she found the book she was looking for and handed it to Paddy. 'He's a brilliant writer, properly funny, and the book's set in London so you can tell me if he's got those details right or not.'

Jemima continued the tour of the house and Paddy agreed there was still a hell of a lot to do. 'Will you just lock these rooms off until the floorboards are put in?'

Jemima groaned. 'Honestly, I think we'll have to seal up this end of the building until we have a new roof. Thank God we don't have bats.'

'Do they bite?'

'No.' Jem looked at Paddy in alarm. 'At least I don't think so. Well I suppose vampire bats do, but no, if you have bats roosting in your buildings, you're not allowed to do any renovations. It's a real issue. St Withy's church has bats and every morning the pews are covered in droppings. They've had to raise funds to buy special nets to catch the droppings, rather than remove the bats. Ridiculous, isn't it? But happily no bats here.'

Laughing, Paddy ducked under a beam as they continued their tour along the twisting corridors and tiny little rooms. 'So what does Angus do in the city to be able to fund your money pit?'

'He's a broker for a yachting company. His father used to sail so it helped get his toe in the door. That's when I first met him, at a local sailing regatta. We spent the whole day racing each other and then all through supper we swapped film quotes. The following day I flew out to Kenya to work on a volunteer project, building schools. I was gutted. There I was thinking I had just met the love of my life and then I had to leave him. Anyway,' she held back a piece of peeling wallpaper as they continued their inspection of the house, 'there I was lumping bricks across this courtyard in Nairobi, sweating like an elephant, when someone shouted out *Humperdink*! and I turned round and saw Angus all gleaming and fresh off the plane, and I shouted Humperdink back, and that was that. *Twoo love.*'

Both girls were laughing openly at *The Princess Bride* quotes and Paddy said how romantic it all was.

'I know,' said Jemima, 'it was like we were in a movie. He'd gone to my folks to find out where I was working and arranged everything to come out and join me. Apparently, he had fallen in love with me on our first night as well.' A huge smile was plastered on her face and Paddy couldn't help but smile back. What a gorgeous story. 'So we continued working abroad for a few months and when our placement was over, we came home and he proposed. And now here we are living the dream, surrounded in goose shit, collapsed ceilings, dodgy water and separated for most of the week.'

Paddy was concerned; imagine having to deal with all this and be pregnant as well?

'Honestly, it's not all bad. Come and let me show you the best bit. Do you have wellies?'

As the girls passed Paddy's car, she pulled out her regular boots. Definitely more a slobbies occasion. As she did Jemima looked over her shoulder and exclaimed when she saw her riding boots. 'Are they Königs? God, they are seriously lovely. Mind you, it's a bit too muddy for them here. Stick to your Aigles.'

As they walked beyond the farmhouse Paddy noted the mess and chaos of the house began to be replaced with neat edges. Walking through a well-oiled gate they entered a stable block that was as spick and span as the house was scruffy. Buckets were neatly stacked, tools were hung up under gutters that were free of weeds. The concrete floor was clean and devoid of mud or leaves and looked like it was probably swept daily.

Up until now Paddy had simply liked Jemima, now she felt a huge surge of affection for the girl. Here was where all her time and efforts were spent, making sure her horses were properly looked after. As they headed into the tack room, Paddy pulled out a few bridles and sniffed the leather.

'Been a while?' asked Jemima. 'I get like that when I go on holiday. I can't wait to get home again.'

It had been months since Paddy had last been on a horse and she did indeed miss the saddle. 'Are you okay to ride though, what with the baby and everything?'

'God yes, Mummy practically had me on the saddle but I'll probably stop when I get too large for it to be comfortable. Besides, I bet the baby will love the rocking motion. Come on then, let's introduce you to the horses.'

Already Paddy had spotted the whickering faces of two horses leaning out over their gate. Jemima introduced Paddy to Max, a tall black stallion. 'Angus usually rides him, he's not tricky, just big.' As she watched Paddy make her way around the horse inspecting his feet and flanks, she was happy that she knew her priorities. She then put on and adjusted his harness and saddle, each step to Jemima's satisfaction. 'How long have you been riding?'

'Since I was eleven at a local city farm. Although they were mostly retired ponies. Wonderful creatures but not as noble as you.' Paddy nuzzled Max's ears. 'Then, when I began to earn a bit of money, I joined a local riding school and started to head out on horses with more than one speed setting.'

The girls chatted as Jemima led the pair of them out to a ring just so she had the measure of Paddy as a rider. She certainly talked the talk, and knew her way around a horse and harness, but Jemima wanted to examine Paddy's riding abilities before they went out for a hack.

167

'Are you okay at jumping? Max tends to launch up like he's at the Grand National, even for a ditch.' As he jumped the one-foot fence by a clean four-foot, Paddy landed with an oof and a laugh. 'Bloody hell. He's on springs!'

Pleased that Paddy was as good as her word, Jemima opened the gate and they headed off across the fields. For a while they just cantered until they came to a bridleway which led up onto open moorland then they were off again, the horses enjoying the run as much as the girls. They paused when they came to a small stream and the horses stopped for a drink. There was a bird singing prettily overhead and Jemima identified it as a skylark. 'They have such a happy song, don't they? Blue skies, skylark and a horse. It's not a bad life, is it?'

No, thought Paddy, *not a bad life at all*. Maybe she should find a way to run Kensey herself and live in Cornwall. Between this and her swims with the seals she could be very happy. Maybe she could tolerate more modelling if it meant she came home to this; that way she'd still be contributing financially to the family.

'No, it's not. Although I'm still trying to settle in, yesterday was a bit unnerving.'

'Those protestors? God that was terrible, wasn't it? Hal said you'd legged it and I don't blame you at all. Honestly that was one of the reasons I called. I hated the idea that someone new to the area would think that that was typical of Cornish life.'

'The thing is, and I'm really embarrassed by this,' Paddy blushed, 'but I was there under false pretences. I had met one of those protestors a few weeks back and she invited me to what she had said was going to be a discussion on country issues. So I turned up and, well, I can't tell you how sorry I am.'

'You poor thing. But that's awful. I can't believe they would do that. Well, yes, I can actually but you must have felt dreadful.'

'I felt terrified actually. They were so loud and violent. And then Hal got so angry at me.'

'Hal? Angry at you? That doesn't sound right, he was really concerned you had dashed off. He wanted Mummy to give him your number, but she's very old school. She wouldn't do that without your permission.'

'Good. I mean not good, but well, it's just I was so embarrassed. Can you ask your mum not to pass my details on?' Paddy paused, she couldn't see any good would come of meeting Hal again. They were getting divorced, he was getting married. It was complicated enough. The less she knew of him the better.

'Okay, let's put yesterday's sorry mess behind us; although at least one good thing came out of it.'

Paddy looked over at her enquiringly.

'I have a new friend!' Laughing Jem carried on. 'So, if I'm not being rude, what do you do? And tell me I'm being nosy if you want.'

Paddy had been enjoying listening to Jemima talk and knew she had been rude in not opening up about herself in return. She just felt a bit awkward. Her life had changed so many times over the last year that she didn't know where to start.

'I guess you could say I'm on a bit of a career break. Trying to work out what to do next.'

'What did you do before?'

The girls were riding slowly back down the hill now, chatting and giving their horses a bit of a rest. Paddy patted Max on his flanks, happy he was such an easy-going horse. 'I'm a model but I think I've had enough of that. We had a change of fortunes recently so I can stop now if I want to.'

'Oh no, are you famous?! Should I know you?'

'God no,' Paddy was quick to reassure her new friend, 'I'm not A-list like Cara Delevingne and Gigi Hadid; I mean I walk with them and will do shoots with them, but they are always the stars on set. I'm just the glamorous prop.'

Jemima snorted. 'I can't imagine anyone outshining you. You are embarrassingly beautiful.'

It was Paddy's turn to snort. 'I should put that on my CV! But no, my heart isn't in it the way theirs is and it shows.'

'So what changed?'

Paddy wondered how she could lessen the impact of her words. To her, her new circumstances were still odd and uncomfortable and she felt uneasy working out how to explain them.

'I'm being nosy, ignore me.' Jemima interrupted her thoughts. 'Come on, let's clean the horses down and then, do you fancy some soup? I've got Stilton and broccoli on the hob?'

As they brushed the horses down and cleaned the tack, Paddy felt stupid that she hadn't said anything. It probably wasn't even a big deal to this girl surrounded by her own horses and farmhouse, with a voice like royalty.

'The thing is, my sister inherited our uncle's estate and it's quite a big one, so we've all been sort of roped into it, to help out. Plus, it turns out we all have titles.'

Jemima stopped brushing Dolly's mane and looked at her friend in astonishment. 'Amazeballs! How did that happen? I mean how did you not know?'

As they finished the horses and headed back to the kitchen, Paddy explained how their mother had been blackballed by the family, to the extent that none of her daughters knew anything about their mother's titles and family connections.

Jemima was full of compassion when Paddy told her how her parents had died; no wonder she had been reluctant to talk about it. What a rollercoaster that family had been on.

***

'Here, do you think it needs salt? It's not too school soupy, is it?'

Paddy sipped the soup carefully and declared it perfect. In fact it was delicious. She hadn't had high expectations, shuddering in reflection of school soup in all its watery blandness, but this was rich and very moreish. Not a powdered lump in sight.

Jemima tutted. 'No one can claim to have been to a worse school than me. Our lunches were so disgusting that everyone lost weight in the first term.'

'Ours were so stodgy that we all put weight on!'

Both girls laughed. 'Hmm, you might have me there,' said Jem, 'but I will brook no argument, our games were the

171

worst. Cross-country for five miles through the mud and cows and then we all had to shower together, buck naked in cold water.'

Paddy was going to say that they had to run past the red-light district near the school, but cold showers definitely had the edge.

'But boarding school must have been exciting?'

'Like Hogwarts or Malory Towers? I wish. What it actually was, was lots of homesick first formers, cold showers and freezing dormitories full of farting, sobbing and snoring schoolgirls.'

Well, thought Paddy, that sounded less appealing than she had imagined. As a schoolgirl she had regularly dodged gangs and fights, and dreamt of hockey sticks and adventures. Maybe the grass was never quite so green.

Finally lunch came to an end and Jemima yawned loudly and then stammered an apology. The pregnancy was making her tired at the oddest of moments. Paddy found herself yawning as well and the two of them laughed; at least it was only yawning that was contagious. She couldn't wait to have children of her own but first she needed a husband. A real one.

As Paddy drove away her face was almost aching from her smile. She had had a wonderful day and finally felt that she had made a proper friend.

Chapter Twenty

The days passed and Paddy stayed close to home; she read through her books, swam with the seals and generally hid from the rest of the world. She had loved meeting Jemima but something she had said had rung alarm bells in Paddy's head and she discovered she had a whole new problem to deal with. One morning she looked at herself in the bathroom mirror and laughed weakly, then burst into tears. How had she ignored the signs? A minute later her phone rang and she saw it was Nick. Typical twin energy. Knowing she wouldn't be able to hide anything from her she sent a quick text saying she was in a beauty salon and would call later. And then she started crying again.

So far all she had done in Cornwall was screw things up. And now she had a text from the production company forcing her to wake up. Her presence was requested at the London offices. No doubt they had managed to get the annulment papers drawn up, obviously they would require her signature. It had been less than three months since she had first met Hal and he had changed her world completely.

Paddy took a deep breath and picked up the phone. Some things were best not handled via texts. She may have been prepared to lie but it was time she faced the music and stopped trying to please everyone else.

'Duncan. When I said I'd told you everything and not kept a thing back? I may have kept something back.'

***

The conference room featured a large round table and sitting around it were Hal, Tony Harper and at least six unnamed functionaries. Hal figured that at least some of them were lawyers. Hal hadn't instructed a solicitor yet, he decided he would wait to see how the land lay. The situation was uncomfortable enough as it was and he wanted as few people as possible to be party to his stupidity. As yet there was no sign of Paddy and he wondered how he would feel about her when he saw her again. He felt ashamed of the way he had treated her when they last met and he was beginning to see this was something of a trend. It was just he had been having such a lovely time chatting with her at the bar and all along she had just been trying to get some intel for the bloody hunt sabs. He found it hard to believe he had got her so wrong.

Tony Harper seemed particularly buoyant and Hal assumed the man's lawyers had managed to find a simple way to get them out of this mess. He was a little surprised to discover this made him feel sad. He tried to work out why, when the door opened and two men walked in. Both were sombre in demeanour and had a watchful air; he assumed they were solicitors or agents but their attitude made him think of private security. As Paddy walked in behind them, they gravitated to her side, flanking her as the three of them sat down. None of them spoke. Hal wasn't sure why, but his instincts told him that something was wrong. Looking at her now he was shocked by how pale she was; her freckles were very obvious today and she looked exhausted. Her hair looked greasy and there were bags under her eyes. She was clearly ill and was wrapped in a large coat.

Both parties were tense and Hal could see the production company was not fooling around. Their reputation rested on protecting Paddy's reputation.

One of the lawyers for Harper Productions welcomed everyone, smiling expansively and then passed around the forms for everyone to have a look. Before anyone had a chance to look at the documents Paddy muttered quietly to the man to her left, and then a little louder she said to Hal, 'I'm sorry. I can't do this.'

Hal was thunderstruck. What couldn't she do? He was getting married in just over a month. She had to do this. What the hell was she playing at? He groaned, was this a bargaining ploy for a financial settlement? He hadn't expected her to behave like this. Every time he thought he knew her she confounded him. Presumably, the paperwork in front of them was details of their annulment. Why wasn't she delighted?

The man sitting next to Paddy stood up and addressed the room. 'Gentlemen, could we give my client and Mr Ferguson some privacy?' Everyone looked confused but Hal shrugged his shoulders and gave his assent.

As soon as the door was closed Hal looked at Paddy. The ball was in her court but as he watched her, he could see whatever the problem was, it was causing her genuine concern. He didn't think this was a shake down. Taking pity, he stood up and poured her a glass of water, making light of their situation and then, because it was bugging him so much, he apologised for his behaviour when they last met.

Paddy looked up and gave him a tired smile. 'God, that was horrible but it seems so distant now. I don't blame you for being angry. I've read about what some of those people do and it's terrible. If it helps, I genuinely wasn't with them. Or at least I was, but I thought we were all attending a meeting to discuss land access rights. I'm just so sorry you thought I was one of them.' She drank the water, her mouth was dry with nerves and her fingers kept picking at imaginary bits of fluff.

Hal looked bashful. He was a first-class idiot and should learn to trust his instincts; everything about her felt right and yet here they were again on opposite sides. Why on earth didn't she just sign the papers?

'Now look. About these forms, if it's about money just name your price. I'm getting married soon and I think Bianca might have kittens if she found out I was technically already wed.' He tried a smile to make light of it but Paddy's face had hardened.

'Wow. Is that what you think of me? You think this is a hustle? I'd sign the forms in a heartbeat. Christ, I was even prepared to lie about the consummation, in order to speed things along for you, but I'm afraid that lie won't hold any water now.'

Hal put his glass down. 'What the hell are you on about? It's a simple white lie; it's hardly Go To Jail stuff.'

She looked up at him, her eyes brimming with tears.

'I'm pregnant.'

Chapter Twenty-One

'You're what?'

'Pregnant, up the duff, in the family way. You know, with child, that sort of thing. I could go on?'

Paddy sat braced, her eyes not leaving Hal's incredulous face for a second.

'Well congratulations, I suppose, but what's this got to do with me? '

Paddy watched as he stood up and walked over to the drinks table and poured a glass of water. She wasn't quite sure what to say, the penny didn't seem to have dropped and she wasn't sure how to proceed as he continued on, refilling her glass of water.

'I should have thought you'd want to get this silly marriage annulled as fast as possible. Duncan will obviously want to get married. Or are you both terribly modern?'

Paddy listened to his garbled ramblings and cut him off.

'Duncan is my agent. The baby is yours.'

The silence extended and Hal picked up her glass of water and finished it in one go. Realising he had poured it for her, he got up and poured another glass. He stood and looked out the window and Paddy wished desperately that she could see his face.

'I said—'

'I heard what you said but it's quite ridiculous. How can I possibly be the father? I'm engaged.'

Paddy tilted her head, rubbing away her unshed tears. 'I'm not convinced being engaged is a very practical sort of contraception.'

Hal grimaced. 'No, of course, that was a stupid thing to say. I meant to say we used contraception. I mean you are on the pill, aren't you?'

Paddy pulled at a hang nail on her empty ring finger. What was the point of being on the pill? She so rarely had sex and wasn't in a stable relationship. Why flood her body with unnecessary hormones? At least that had been what she had told herself. In hindsight it seemed like the most stupid decision of her life.

'You are on the pill, surely?'

Paddy shook her head, not trusting her voice.

'But condoms aren't one hundred per cent effective. How incredibly irresponsible of you!' His voice was now rising in disbelief.

'Of me! Why didn't you ask? Why is this my fault?'

'Well, you're the one who's pregnant. And anyway,' he said, something dawning on him, 'how do you know it's mine? We only slept together once and it was months ago. I can't be the father.'

A wave of rage swept over her. She so rarely got angry; she knew he was unlikely to be thrilled by the news but this instant denial made her feel sick.

'Of course you're the sodding father. What sort of girl do you think I am? The only person I have had sex with in the past year is you. Do you think I sleep around or something?'

Paddy watched as he recoiled, and her temper ignited. Grabbing the plate of biscuits in front of her she threw them

178

at him. Not waiting to see his reaction, she shoved her chair back and ran out of the room. She didn't want to see Duncan or the solicitors; she was so ashamed and felt horribly rejected. Flinging open the front door she ran out onto the street.

'Look out!' a voice yelled above the noise of the traffic.

The next thing she knew she was wrapped up in Hal's firm embrace. He had rushed out after her and pulled her back from the path of a furious cyclist. She'd been so upset by his taunts that the baby could be anyone's that her vision was blinded by tears. She had tried to run across the road but hadn't spotted the cyclist speeding in and out of the traffic.

Now, standing in the middle of a busy pavement, she stood shaking, as Hal wrapped his arms around her. The two stood silent, breathing heavily. The noise of the London traffic died away until all Paddy could hear was Hal's heart beating rapidly. This was what she wanted. All that she wanted.

'Come on,' said Hal, his voice hoarse with emotion. 'Let's find somewhere to sit down and I'll start by apologising for the umpteenth time.'

'Henry! Henry! My god. Put that woman down!'

Paddy turned and looked at a beautiful blonde, dressed head to toe in this season's fashions. She could have walked straight out of a display. Even her bag and shoes were this year's model.

As the woman looked at Paddy she did a double take.

'Oh. My. God! Henry, do you know who you just saved? This is Holly McDonald!' Taking Hal's pole-axed expression as ignorance, she laughed. 'She was the model wearing the dress you were thinking of buying me the other day. You know in last month's *Vogue*?' Seeing that she was getting no response from Hal she turned to Paddy. 'Oh wow, Holly, are you alright? This is my fiancé, Henry Ferguson; he just saved your life. This is incredible. Quick Henry, take a photo!'

Gushing, she thrust her phone at Henry urging him to take a photo of the pair of them. Snatching it out of his hand she looked at the photo he had taken and mocked him. 'You've cut Holly out completely.'

Showing it to Holly, she laughed. 'Honestly, men. He only has eyes for me, isn't he terrible? Here, let's have a selfie.' And she flung her arm around Paddy squeezing up to her and snapping a few images as Paddy looked bleakly at Hal.

'Perfect. Gosh, this is so exciting. We were just going to have lunch. Will you join us? Do say yes. You must be so shaken. Are you shaken? You look ever so pale. Henry, why are you just standing there? Hail a cab. No, do it properly. Honestly.'

The idea of spending another single second in this woman's company filled Paddy with horror. What was Hal doing with such an awful person? Paddy was well used to her type. At fashion week, these women would sit on the front row and pay more attention to the clothes than the human. Even at parties they would be quick to point out that a model was just a working girl, whereas they could buy out the whole of Harrods with just the flick of their husband's credit card. Never theirs. Obvs. Their smiles would flick on and off as they searched for a more important person to talk to. Always they would be scanning the crowd over your shoulder, looking for the next rung on the ladder. And Hal was marrying one of them.

A taxi pulled up alongside them.

'I'm afraid I have another appointment,' she interrupted the woman's prattle and before either of them could react, Paddy jumped into the cab that Hal had hailed, telling the driver to leave immediately.

From the back of the cab she fired off a few apologetic texts to Duncan. She had to reassure him that she was absolutely fine but she wouldn't be returning to the meeting and she wouldn't be signing any paperwork. In turn he told her he had threatened the entire company if so much as a whisper of a meeting got out, their names would be mud. He would deal with the paperwork and leave it with him. His final text to her made her laugh, which, knowing Duncan, had been the intention.

-Btw – baby is going to be so beautiful. At least you screwed up with a total dreamboat!

Chapter Twenty-Two

The following day Paddy began packing. She loved her little house by the sea and she was beginning to feel a little more settled, but the discovery of her pregnancy had bowled her sideways. She had never been particularly regular and with her move to Cornwall she had paid little attention to her periods. Their absence was more a blessing than a concern. How could she have been so stupid? Now, after her initial shock she was both delighted and terrified…and remained in a perpetual state of swinging between the two states. She spent half her time staring in the mirror but despite a slightly enlarged chest, her body hadn't changed shape at all. What would she look like as she started to change? Her face and her body were her place of work, despite having chosen to step away from modelling, she found this new development terrifying. How would she cope?

Obviously, she would have wished things were different. For a start, she'd like the baby's father to be in love with her but that clearly wasn't on the cards. She wasn't even sure if he would want to be involved in the baby's life. What would his fiancée say? His reaction had been one of horror but she understood it was a lot to take on. He sleeps with a girl just the once and just like that he's married to her and about to become a father. That was some heavy piece of news to deal with. She hadn't ever imagined being pregnant on her own, but she had her sisters, they would be there for her and gradually she'd work things out.

Duncan had asked her if she was certain she wanted to keep it and the thought hadn't even crossed her mind. In this Hal had no say. And because she wasn't prepared to even discuss it with him, she had some sympathy with the position he found himself in. She wouldn't even approach him regarding child maintenance. But when she had stood there with his arms around her, she had a sense of everything settling into place. When he had suggested that they go and sit down and chat, the way he had looked at her had overwhelmed her. She felt as though he would always be by her side or standing in front of her, protecting her. And then the fiancée turned up.

At least now Paddy understood her sudden bouts of tiredness; she thought she might have had flu. Calling Ari, she had mentioned she was planning to visit but hadn't said why. This wasn't a conversation she wanted to have over the phone. She'd probably just end up bawling her head off. But more than anything right now she wanted to go home, she loved Cornwall but it wasn't home yet and there was no one here to turn to.

The phone rang and she wondered if it was one of the girls doing their sisterly voodoo thing, but she saw with pleasure it was Jemima and answered eagerly. It would be great to have a simple conversation and she was thrilled to hear Jem invite her to a charity bash the following evening. It was short notice and she was probably already booked. As Jem trailed off, Paddy jumped in eagerly. God knows she needed to get out of her own head. Some company would be a good diversion.

'What should I wear? I don't think I've ever been to a charity fundraiser before. Well, not one in the countryside, anyway.' The truth was, she was usually employed to attend these things, often modelling the clothes or jewels that were up for auction. Paddy was excited. A night out with a friend was exactly what she needed. Her mind was too full of things she didn't want to think about, a party would be perfect.

'Oh, you know, the usual.' Paddy rolled her eyes so hard that Jemima must have heard as she laughed. 'Sorry. That wasn't very helpful. It's not formal. Trousers will be fine.'

'What about the men?'

'Oh yes, they can wear trousers as well if they want.' Both girls giggled as Paddy felt more relaxed than she had in weeks. Having established it wasn't black tie, she then hit Google and various society pages and by the end of the afternoon she had a clear idea of what to wear. Her sister was an up-and-coming fashion designer but there was no point in calling her. Clem would only have fabulous suggestions for next year's look. Paddy wanted to blend in, not stand out. Last year's look would suit her just fine.

***

Pulling up outside a beautiful sandstone manor, she switched off her engine and sent Jem a text telling her she'd arrived.

Paddy clicked send and waited. She felt extremely nervous sitting out here in a dark car park in the middle of nowhere. She'd seen lots of cars arriving and groups of people heading into a very large country house. It had been a good thirty miles away and closer to Jem's neck of the wood.

Judging from what she could see of what others were wearing, she had judged her outfit correctly. Working on a country house weekend party she reined it back a bit to take in the Art Auction and felt she had hit a happy blend with one of Clemmie's knee-length shift dresses. It was camel satin with a pretty cream cropped cashmere cardigan. She kept her heels to an inch, patent coffee-coloured sling backs. All in all she thought she looked great. Her bump was non-existent and she felt happy that no one would be able to tell she was actually pregnant.

Fingers crossed she blended in. As usual there was nothing she could do about her hair, but she pulled it back into a low plaited chignon. The damp air had been playing havoc with her curls so she didn't expect the rigid hairstyle to stay in place too long. But once she felt comfortable, she could either let it down, or tie it back into a discreet ponytail.

-Do you want me to come out and find you?

Paddy wanted to say yes but was determined not to be a baby.

-No worries. Where are you?

-I'll be at the front door. I have a carnation.

-Will you be waiting under a clock?

-If I hold my phone above my head will that count?

-Well I suspect I'd notice that!

-Are you going to type all night or get in here? Malc is hovering around the champagne stand and at this rate there'll be none left!

Paddy laughed and put her phone in her bag. Tonight looked like it was going to be fun. As promised, Jemima was waiting for her by the pillars in front of the house, and as soon as she saw Paddy she promptly put her phone on her head, making both girls laugh.

'Where's the carnation? You promised me carnations?'

Jemima looked her new friend up and down and snorted. 'Like I'm going to give you flowers, poor things would wilt in comparison. You look amazing! We aren't going to get a sensible word out of Malc all evening. Right shall we do this?'

Linking her arm through Paddy's, both girls headed into the building and towards a noisy room where people were coming and going.

'You have no idea how pleased I am that you said yes. These things can be such a drag if you don't have a good group of friends.'

Paddy had thought a fundraising event for an art gallery would be a quiet and thoughtful event, but looking around she saw it was just an opportunity for friends to get together and catch up, whilst donating money to a cause.

The girls made a beeline for Malc, who promptly did a double take and then made a goofy bow. 'Ladies', and he presented them both with a glass.

Looking at him Paddy thought he was utterly endearing. If she had a brother this is what he'd be like she decided.

Moving away from the champagne, Paddy and Malc headed towards a large unlit fireplace, whilst Jem went off in search of Angus.

'I'm going to monopolise you now,' said Malc, grinning, 'before all the other chaps spot you and you'll be gone.'

Paddy scoffed ungracefully. 'As if. I bloody hate that. You know, when you're talking to someone and they keep looking around the room to see if there's anyone better to talk to.'

It was then Malc's turn to laugh ungracefully. 'Like that's ever happened to you.'

Grinning, Paddy waved her glass at him. 'All the bloody time, mate.' She wanted a soft drink but was enjoying her chat with Malc too much. It was so refreshing to have a conversation where there were no charged undertones.

'Now I know you are pitying me.' He gave a sad dog face and, spotting that she wasn't drinking, asked if he could get her an orange juice instead.

Paddy declined. Not only was she enjoying her conversation but she had also gone off orange juice. In fact her entire palate at the moment seemed upside down. 'Honestly, in my line of work being overlooked happens all the time. Seriously, being good-looking is just the entrance fee. Influence and money are what's important.'

'Oh dear, I don't think I'd do very well in your world.'

'Why, what do you do?'

'Art restorer. I was in New York last week trying to track down arsenic. Can you imagine? I kept telling people I was Sherlock Holmes but I don't think we quite understood each other as they kept talking about my tattoos.'

Paddy explained the current TV show, featuring a heavily tattooed actor playing Holmes, and then asked about the old paints. She had a feeling he would love Otto, or maybe not, in fact the more she thought about the irascible art forger, the more she decided he probably wouldn't. As the two of them got chatting Jemima returned and told Malc off for hogging her.

'At least let her meet the others; honestly Malc, where are your manners?'

Paddy laughed and assured Jemima that she could happily chat to Malcolm all night long. However, she did need to find the loo before she met the others. As she headed off, Malc turned to his sister.

'She's a bit fabulous, isn't she? Completely out of my league. I'd love to go out with her but I think I'd spend the whole time being miserable, wondering when she would get bored or when someone would swoop in and try and take her away. I think I'm going to aim for friend. She has a wicked sense of humour and I like that in a friend.'

***

Hal's knee was throbbing. Every now and then his knee injury would twinge. The Army surgeons had done the best they could, but had warned him that it wasn't a guarantee and it might snap again. Two years of on and off pain; Hal was certain that the off periods were getting fewer. He was worried that he might be facing another round of surgery.

He'd been putting it off for months but thoughts of becoming a father had changed his thinking. He didn't want to be acting like an old man. He dreamt of showing his children how to ride and swim, how to build a fire, ride a bike. Hal shook his head laughing. At the moment he hadn't even established if Paddy was going to keep the baby. When Bianca had said she was pregnant his heart sank at the thought of being linked to her for the rest of his life, even if the thought of becoming a father had filled him with joy. When Paddy broke the same news, he was shattered. He was elated but he was in the very worst position. Tied to a woman he didn't love, dreaming of a woman who didn't love him.

When she'd disappeared into the taxi on Wednesday, he realised he didn't even have her address. The first time he had met her had been at a film shoot, the following morning she had scarpered. He then met her in London to find out they were married, and he had insulted her. The next time he met her at been at the race meet and again following his dreadful behaviour she had legged it again. When they next met in London, the ending had been predictable. He had lost control of his emotions and she had run away. He terrified the mother of his child and for that alone, he felt deeply ashamed of his recent conduct.

Paddy's news had sent him reeling. That day, he was supposed to be going for lunch with Bianca followed by some new exhibition. Apparently, it was a sound installation on the death of consumerism. He'd have rather pulled his eyelashes out, it sounded like just the sort of tedious virtue-signalling show that was currently so popular in London. Hal found the total absence of irony excruciating; he imagined that Bianca would find at least one thing she couldn't live without in the exhibition gift shop.

He found these events turgid at the best of times but that day he couldn't face it. He had no idea how to explain his predicament to Bianca without her having a complete meltdown. He wanted to spend some time trying to think it all through and have a solution in hand before he sat down with her. He needed to break off their engagement and work out how to do it with the least amount of pain for her.

When Paddy dashed off in the taxi, he had told Bianca to go on ahead of him as he had a few more details to sort out with the production company. What he discovered had knocked him for six, and he drove back to Cornwall in a dream, completely forgetting to meet her. For the past three days she had ignored all his texts and phone calls and now she was due at his home. This was the worst possible timing.

His family were hosting a fundraiser for the Johnston Art Institute. Another one. Why couldn't the Institute just sell one of their wretched paintings, instead of always asking for money from the patrons? Fed up, he made his way downstairs to greet his guests. His father and stepmother were already downstairs making everyone welcome. Bianca was late, as usual, so he still hadn't had a chance to speak to her. But time was running out. How could he tell her the wedding was off. This was the worst possible moment for her to throw a massive sulk.

As he came downstairs, he saw the back of a tall redhead who was wandering down the corridor, her long hair flowing loosely down her back. His heart leapt and then slumped; he was going to have to stop reacting every time he saw auburn locks.

James Ferguson watched as his son came downstairs. He looked on edge and James wondered if it was his knee or his fiancée playing him up. Earlier in the day Hal had explained the wedding was off but that he hadn't told Bianca yet. James didn't know what had happened but the fact that Bianca was no longer going to be his daughter-in-law brought him joy. She'd arrived earlier; too late to be useful and had even brought a friend from London, an Argentine polo player of all things. Odette, James's second wife, had been about as impressed as he was, but if the man had deep pockets, then it was all to the good of the charity. Even so, he was surprised that Bianca hadn't gone straight up to join Hal. Maybe Hal had already had a chance to speak with her and it hadn't gone well? James felt a storm building around him and he felt edgy and alert. He didn't think the evening was going to end well. As he reached the foot of the stairs, James watched fondly as Odette kissed Hal on the cheeks and told him he was even more dashing than his father.

Gallantly, his son pointed out that, once more, his father had the prettiest girl in the room on his arm. As he bantered with his stepmother the tension began to unwind from his face.

Odette enjoyed watching these two together. After the grief they had both suffered when Eleanor had died, James could never imagine another woman even being able to hold a candle to her flame. And yet Odette with her quiet calm way, fell in love with both the father and the son and had helped them through their grieving. As the three of them broke off to start mingling with their guests Odette spotted a stranger following one of the waiting staff back to the kitchens and, excusing herself, she followed to make sure everything was all right.

'Hello, can I help you with anything?'

Paddy smiled as she heard the unmistakable tones of a native French speaker. Turning she looked at an older French lady and instantly relaxed. She loved the French, they never judged her and they always sounded so elegant and in control. Plus this one was wearing vintage Chanel and she knew Clem would be asking to look at the seams.

'Oh hi. It's a bit of a cliché, isn't it, ending up in kitchens at parties? I was looking for a drink.'

The lady tilted her head slightly, smiling as she looked pointedly at Paddy's full glass of champagne.

'Oh I know. I'm just holding this so I don't fiddle. I'm driving so I can't drink alcohol.'

The woman looked concerned and beckoned one of the staff. 'This lovely young lady says we've run out of non-alcoholic options. Please could you rectify that?' The man nodded his head and turned to go, but Paddy stopped him, aware she may have got him in trouble.

'No, no, I'm so sorry. That wasn't what I meant. I simply had a hankering for tomato juice, so I just popped in to see if there was any?'

The waiter turned to her and smiled. 'I'll pour you a glass straightaway.'

'Make it a Virgin Mary, would you? My recipe please.' Turning to Paddy the lady introduced herself as the host and went on, 'I hope you'll excuse the liberty but I think a Virgin Mary will hit the spot.'

Paddy was embarrassed; she hadn't wanted to slight her host. 'I'm so sorry. I hope you don't think I was being rude. Your home is beautiful and there is everything I needed. I was just,' she paused, 'oh, I don't know, I just suddenly had an overwhelming hankering for something less sweet.'

Thanking the waiter as he handed her a tall glass, she took a sip and then her eyes widened in delight. 'This! Is delicious.'

Smiling, Odette turned to the waiter. 'Peter, could you make sure our guest has a Virgin Mary whenever she wants one. Now,' she said, turning to Paddy, 'let's join the others. Who are you with this evening?'

As the pair of them wandered through the corridors back to the party, Odette wondered when this lovely girl's pregnancy would begin to show. She also hoped that she would have a ring on her finger by then. She was all for a modern life but raising a child by yourself was never easy. No matter which decade you were in.

Paddy was about to explain she was here with Jemima when Jem bounded up.

'Found you! I thought you might have got lost. Hello, Odette,' she said giving her a small hug, 'what a fabulous evening. You always make Vollen so inviting. I was just going to introduce Paddy here to some of the others.'

'Go on the pair of you, and Paddy, I shall let the waiters know you have gone outside.' With a smile she wandered off to greet her other guests.

The corridor was getting quite crowded and the two girls squeezed their way through to some side doors that had been opened to a large outdoor terrace. A group of twenty-somethings were all lounging around on tables and benches, arranged around a large fire pit. Everyone was chatting and laughing, their faces animated by the flames. As Jemima and her guest walked towards them, they turned and smiled. One peeled away from the group and walked towards them with her head tilted curiously.

'Hello! Jem you never mentioned you were friends with Holly McDonald.'

'What, who?' Jemima looked between Paddy and the girl in confusion. 'Are you famous? You said you weren't famous! Should I know you?'

The tall blonde laughed. 'Good one, Jem. Of course she's famous, this is Holly McDonald. The model Holly McDonald?'

Jemima looked her new friend up and down. 'Are you ever in *Horse & Hound*?'

Paddy smiled. 'Honestly, I have no idea but I don't think so. Although I did once do a photoshoot with Ackle's Revenge, if that helps?' She could see that Jem was going to say something and she cut her off, turning to the newcomer. 'Seriously though, I'm really enjoying being at a party where no one knows who I am. And it's Paddy,' she said shaking the girl's hand, 'Holly's my professional name.'

'Fair enough. Well look, come and meet the others. I'm sure some will recognise you but they'll be cool about it.'

Paddy wondered what Jemima had been about to say. She hadn't deliberately deceived her but she supposed different people saw things differently. She watched nervously as Jem took a deep breath. 'Look before we meet the others I just have to know.'

Paddy braced herself.

'Is Ackle as sweet as he seems? My friend trains over at his yard and she says he's a total softy but she might have just been humouring me.'

194

Paddy released her breath. She had been worried she might have spoilt her new friendship by being evasive about her background. Pausing, she made a play of looking around and leant in confidentially. 'He is a sweetie but he's also really, really naughty. When I was there, he ate an apple I had in my pocket for him. The trouble was he ate the pocket as well and the jacket had been worth three grand! The designer went ballistic.'

'No!' Jemima exclaimed. 'What a beast!'

Laughing as they joined the others, Jem waved her arm in their direction. 'Paddy, may I introduce you to the honourables and the disgracefuls. I'll leave it to you to discover who is who.' Turning to the others, she introduced Paddy. 'Paddy's new to the area and likes her privacy. I don't know if she's single but if she is, we're all screwed.' Everyone laughed and invited her to join them.

At that moment the blonde piped up, introducing herself as Vix and said, 'I knew there was something else about you I'd forgotten. You need to go sit with the honourables, unless you think sitting with us disgracefuls would be more fun?'

Sipping on her divine tomato juice Paddy looked around the group. 'What did she mean by disgracefuls?'

'Well some of us here are Right Honourables or Ladies, so they are the Honourables but the rest of us thought it would be more fun to be Disgracefuls. Lucy over there is both an Honourable and a Disgraceful at the same time.'

A short girl holding two glasses waved one of them at Paddy saying, 'I resemble that remark!'

Vix went on, 'Our host, Hal, is a disgraceful rather than an honourable, which I think disappoints his fiancée, Bianca, no end!'

'Oh God, is she here?' Paddy was appalled. This was Hal's house? She was having a lovely evening; the last thing she wanted to do was bump into the fiancée of her child's father. Or indeed her child's father. It was such a daytime TV scenario. Besides, she was struggling with her feelings towards the woman. She knew she should be apologetic and sympathetic, the trouble was she just didn't like her.

'Oh ho,' called out one of the girls, waving a bottle at the rest of the group, 'so you've met her then!'

'Where is our host anyway?' asked one of the men, who introduced himself as Angus. He'd been chatting to Malc about the currency exchange but was looking forward to Hal's arrival. Things always livened up when he was around.

'Probably being told to go and change his clothes.'

Paddy tried gamely to say something nice. 'I'm sure she's lovely.'

'Deep down,' said Jem.

'Very deep down,' muttered Lucy. 'The other day she told me she didn't like dogs.'

This proclamation was met by a stunned silence as the group contemplated a life without dogs.

Chapter Twenty-Three

The party had only just started but Hal had already had enough. After the third comment about the impending wedding he knew he couldn't delay things any longer. He went off in search of Bianca who was laughing in the company of some overdressed actor. Excusing themselves from the man who was apparently Argentinian, and not an actor, Hal steered her off to the kitchens and found an empty room. It was hardly a comfortable choice but Hal was desperate that Bianca should receive the news in private.

Bianca followed Hal in alarm. Was bringing Raoul here sailing too close to the wind? Hal had been acting odd for weeks now and she was just trying to remind him of what he would be missing out on if he got cold feet. She had also been ignoring him all week in an attempt to make him feel guilty and apologetic for heading off to Cornwall without saying goodbye. Stupidly, she had thought having Raoul here might make Henry jealous, a good-looking man flirting with his fiancée. Wake him up a bit just in case cold feet were an issue. Instead, Henry had mumbled about seeing him on the television and that he'd been very good. That was the trouble with Henry, he could never see what was standing right in front of him. Now he was pacing back and forth, in front of a chest freezer, talking nonsense about doing the right thing. Realising she might have missed something she asked him to repeat himself.

'The wedding is off.'

'What!'

Bianca stared at him in horror. 'We are getting married next month. What the fuck are you talking about?'

'No, we're not. That's what I've been trying to say. The production company thought I had become accidentally married during the wedding scene, but it turns out that even though we signed the register and it was a real wedding, it wasn't official. There were no banns and no intention to wed. It wasn't real. That's what the meeting this week was about.'

When Hal had returned to the production company's offices after Paddy had sped off in the taxi, they informed him that there was no marriage and nothing to sign except for a promise not to sue them. And a large pile of paperwork and non-disclosure agreements. Instead of being overjoyed, he was filled with a deep painful sadness. In the space of half an hour he had discovered he wasn't actually married but he was in fact, due to become a father. He had been numb for the past few days but the one thing he was certain about was that he couldn't marry Bianca.

'But it was a mistake, why didn't you just get it annulled?'

Hal closed his eyes, then opened them again. Not looking Bianca in the face was cowardly. 'Because I slept with her after the filming.'

'You did what?!'

Hal motioned to take her hand but she brushed him off.

'No wait, I'm thinking.' From the hallway beyond the muted voices chattered on, champagne glasses were chinking. The violin quartet were playing beautifully, their music weaving throughout the large rooms and out over the

198

decorative lawns. Bianca took a deep breath to try and steady her temper.

'So what's the problem. I don't understand. You thought you were married, but you're not, so you don't need an annulment or a divorce, but you still can't marry me?'

'I can't marry you because you deserve better. Not someone that cheated on you.'

Bianca paused, her eyes blinking rapidly as she scrambled to catch up.

'I don't care about that,' she crooned. 'I forgive you. What man doesn't have last-minute jitters?'

Hal looked suspiciously at Bianca, this was completely out of character. Maybe she planned to use this indiscretion to beat him with for their whole married life. The more he thought of it the more he realised that that was probably the case. Why on earth had he ever proposed?

'No, Bianca,' Hal said softly, 'it just wouldn't work. I slept with her and that meant something to me. Even if it doesn't to you.'

'So, have there been a string of them, or something? Is that what you're saying. Because I won't put up with that!'

Bianca's voice was beginning to get a bit shrill and Hal was aware that this was going about as badly as he had anticipated. Hal took a swig of whisky and wished he'd thought to bring a glass for Bianca.

'Christ, no, Bianca, it just happened the once. But look, Paddy is totally blameless in all of this. She had no idea I was engaged. This is completely my fault.'

'Paddy?' Bianca said, her eyes narrowing. 'Where the hell have I heard that name before? Hang on, do you mean

Holly McDonald? Dear God!' Bianca started to quickly recalibrate. She doubted a one-night fling meant anything to Holly, but she sure as hell wouldn't want it to be public knowledge. Maybe she could pull this back. Then it hit her.

'Is that why she's here? You brought your fling to the party?'

'What? She's not here.' Hal was appalled by his second reaction. His first reaction was denial, but then he had wanted to break off this conversation and go off and try to find Paddy.

'Yes, she is, she's out on the patio laughing with those stuck-up school friends of yours. Look, I'll show you,' and she stormed off and out the side door heading towards the fire pit.

***

Paddy was laughing with Lucy, listening to Jemima doing impersonations of everyone from the rich and famous to the local vicar. She clearly had a talent for it and was holding court whilst people were crying with laughter. Paddy didn't know half the people Jem was lampooning but she was a born entertainer and Paddy was having a fabulous time laughing along with the others. She'd been laughing at one of Jem's stories and Angus had asked if she knew the vicar? Wiping her eyes, she said no and everyone laughed even harder. It had been a while since she had relaxed in company and she was so grateful that Jem had suggested a night out. Maybe she didn't need to go to Norfolk after all. Cornwall was lovely and she was beginning to settle in.

She looked around the group and noticed a door open at the far end of the house, light spilling out onto the grass.

Across the darkened end of the lawn, a woman was storming towards them and she saw with horror that it was Bianca. She was angrily brushing Hal's arm off her shoulder, and Paddy knew the game was up.

'Hello, slut!'

Everyone fell silent. Paddy looked around; the majority of the partygoers were inside. At least her humiliation was going to be minor. She knew she deserved it but she'd just started to make friends and she didn't want their first impressions of her to be 'slut'.

Bianca advanced towards her and shoved her. Malc jumped up from the chair and Jemima took a step closer to her. The situation was tense and Paddy tried to think of the best way to diffuse it.

'For Christ's sake, Bianca, she's pregnant!' shouted Hal.

Oh hell, thought Paddy, as she watched realisation wash over the other woman's face.

Baring her teeth Bianca threw herself at Paddy. Trying to step back, Paddy's heels caught in the grass and she stumbled, pinwheeling backwards and fell awkwardly on the grass between the table and chairs. Scrambling, the group brought Paddy to her feet. Malc stood in front of her.

'Hal,' said Malcolm, 'I don't know what's going on, but I think Bianca would like to go inside?'

'Piss off, Malcolm. I know exactly what I want to do.'

'Bianca!' snapped Hal.

'Fuck off, Henry. There's no way she's pregnant. That's just what her sort says when they want to get married. Three weeks later she'll have a tragic miscarriage and your ring on her finger!'

'Is that what you did?' asked Hal quietly. 'Did you fake your pregnancy?'

There was a horrible silence as the group looked at Hal and Bianca. Not waiting for an answer, he turned towards Paddy.

'Are you alright?'

As he stepped towards her Bianca grabbed him. 'Henry, I…'

Hal spun around, his entire world seeming to come unhinged; he knew there were a thousand things he should say or do right now but his only concern was Paddy, the woman carrying his child.

'Enough. Get out of my sight.' His voice was cold, final.

Bianca looked like she was going to say something else but having taken in the sea of hostile faces, she stormed off towards the main house. Paddy watched her go with regret, her heart heavy. She wouldn't have wished that embarrassment on a mortal enemy, let alone a total stranger.

'Paddy…'

Hal was still trying to talk to her, his voice pleading. She just wanted him to leave her alone so she could escape as quickly as possible, to hide from the pitying looks and whispered gossip. Bianca wasn't the only one utterly embarrassed. Struggling to remain dignified, she took a deep breath, fighting back the tears that threatened to fall.

'Hal, I'm sorry. I'm afraid I'm a bit tired. Would you excuse me if I left early?' Giving him no time to reply, she turned to Malcom, her voice trembling slightly. 'Malc, could you show me to the cars, avoiding the house.'

Hal tried again, his voice breaking. 'Please. Paddy.'

'No.' Enough of this. She knew he was simply trying to spare everyone's feelings but it would be easiest if she just left, if she could just escape this nightmare. 'You need to sort things out with your fiancée. I'm just incredibly sorry for spoiling everything for you. Malc?'

Malcolm looked at his friend, who nodded, and the pair moved off towards the other side of the house, Paddy's heart breaking with every step.

Behind him, his friends looked worried, their faces etched with concern. Jem stepped forwards and placed her hand on his arm, her touch gentle.

'Go after her.'

Hal shook his head, his eyes glistening with unshed tears. 'You heard her. She wants nothing to do with me.'

Angus cleared his throat, his voice gruff but kind. 'Jem's right. Go after her.'

As Paddy disappeared into the night, Hal watched her leave and wondered why he was always screwing things up, why he couldn't seem to hold onto anything good in his life. Turning, he tried to smile at his friends, to pretend everything was fine, that his life wasn't falling apart in front of him, but found himself dangerously close to tears, the lump in his throat making it hard to breathe.

'Hal, are you okay?' said Vix, her voice worried, her eyes full of compassion. 'Can we do anything for you?' Looking at them, lit by the flickering lights of the fire, he thanked his lucky stars that he had such incredible mates, friends who would stand by him through anything. He knew he wouldn't even need to ask them to keep this quiet. All he saw was grave concern on their faces, the love and support that only comes from a lifetime of shared experiences and unbreakable bonds. 'No, I'm fine. I'll just, well. Christ, what a mess. Oh and it probably goes without saying, the wedding is off.'

Jemima wanted to make a quip and make everyone laugh, to ease the tension and take away some of Hal's pain, but the anguish on his face was simply too raw, too real. Instead she just mumbled an assent along with the others, her heart aching for her friend.

Turning, he headed back towards the laughter spilling out from the house, each step feeling like a monumental effort, the weight of his mistakes pressing down on him like a physical burden. He didn't know how he was going to face the future, how he was going to pick up the pieces of his shattered life, but he knew one thing for certain - he had to find a way to make things right with Paddy, to be there for her and their child, no matter what it took.

***

As Bianca swept up the lawn, she was fuelled by rage. How had this happened? She had ruthlessly pursued Hal without once letting him know he was being hunted. She had been slowly reeling him in; ever since she had discovered how much he was going to inherit she decided he was the husband for her. She had found out his favourite books and music, she had learnt all about land management and even the politics of the Middle East for heaven's sake. She had ensured there was no domineering mother or a long-lost secret sweetheart from school, poised to snatch him away. She had done her research and he was perfect.

It had all been going so well and then out of the blue someone else had gone and snatched him from under her nose.

Bianca stormed into the house looking for Raoul. There was no way she could stay a moment longer and her mind was racing trying to think how to handle this. As she passed the little library she had an idea. She slipped in and out of the room, her clutch bag a little fatter than it had been a moment earlier. God knows she deserved it. Raoul was laughing with a group of women drinking champagne and, catching his eye, she headed for the front door. By the time he had caught up with her she was crying prettily.

She turned and stepped into his embrace.

'We have to go. I can't stand it anymore.' She sobbed and pressed herself against him. 'I've called the wedding off. I just can't stand it. Seeing you together, I can't stand it. He's not even half the man you are. How can I possibly marry him when it's you I love. Don't make me marry him.'

Raoul was dumbfounded. This was unexpected. He wrapped his arms around her and stroked her hair as she wept against him.

'Come on, let's go back to my hotel. No one's going to make you marry him.'

Bianca leant into him as they walked towards the car.

'You must think I'm horrible but all I wanted to do was marry you. And now there's a church all booked and waiting for a bride and groom.' She trailed off into silence. She paused but the silence continued. 'Of course, now you don't want to marry me. Why would you? I'm such an awful person.' She cried a bit louder, careful not to smudge her mascara on his shirt. She wished she could remember if her eyeliner was waterproof or not, a little dark trickle would look very fetching.

'Oh, *mi cariño*,' Raoul crooned tipping her face up to his. 'Of course I love you. Why wouldn't I want to marry you? What the hell. Let's do it. Come on let's head back to the hotel and celebrate.'

Sobbing and giggling Bianca slid into the Jaguar and thanked her lucky stars she had been born clever as well as pretty.

Chapter Twenty-Four

'PADDY!!!'

Paddy knelt down in delight as her two nephews threw themselves at her. There was no point in being knocked over twice in two days. This morning she had thrown her bags in the car and headed back to Ari. Now, too many hours later, she felt like she was home. As she had driven down the long drive, Hiverton Manor glowed in the last of the day's light. Dusk had leant a softening beauty to the Tudor manor house and Paddy was once again struck by the thought that her mother had grown up here. Despite its splendour, she had run away from it, to live with Paddy's father. Now, that was a love story. She felt so sad she wanted to cry; all she had wanted was to be swept off her feet and fall in love. And when she had met Hal, it had been instantaneous. She had looked at him smiling at her and her heart had stopped. Falling in love had been simple. Everything since was messed up. She had screwed it all up, falling in love with someone who wasn't available, who was always annoyed with her, who thought she was a slut.

Clearly, her nephews had been keeping watch, because as she'd drawn her car to a stop, the front door had been thrown open and light spilt out of the house, followed by the two little terrors, whooping and waving, bouncing around with two dogs, followed by Ari and Sebastian. The boys were in their pyjamas and dressing gowns and had clearly been given leave to stay up until she had arrived. Seb stood with his arm lightly around Ari's waist, and Paddy thought what a lovely image they all made in front of their home, waving at her as she drove up. Pulling herself together she got out of the car to give her gorgeous nephews the biggest hug in the world.

As Paddy had slowly got out of the car, Ari took one look at her little sister and saw the exhaustion in her face and body. Giving her a hug and shooing the dogs away, she suggested Paddy turn in straightaway. They had all the time in the world to catch up.

Paddy slumped upstairs, as Ari and Seb followed behind placing her bags on her bedroom floor. Ditching her coat on top of the bags she climbed into bed, fully clothed, pulling the sheets over her and mumbled good night. Ari and Seb looked at each other and then softly closed the door. They tucked the boys in and headed back downstairs.

***

'Well, that doesn't look good?' Ari had been concerned the minute she saw her sister get out of the car. Her skin was sallow, she had bags under her eyes, she was still clearly wearing yesterday's make-up, and her hair was unbrushed. Ari couldn't even remember seeing her sister so unkempt. Even when she came back from the city farm having spent the day grooming and mucking out and then walking a mile to the bus stop, she looked better than she did sitting in that car.

'Maybe she's just shattered after the drive.' Seb was also concerned; he didn't know his sisters-in-law terribly well yet, but Clem and Paddy were the two energy bombs in the family. Clem was like a whirlwind; Paddy was like the best day at the beach. Full of laughter and energy and attention. She just went out of her way to make people happy. Now he simply saw a young woman who appeared broken. However, he didn't want to alarm Ari further by agreeing with her. 'It is a very long drive remember. I bet the M25 was hell.'

Ari pursed her lips. It was true that Cornwall to Norfolk was a massive drive, it was just there seemed something more fundamental. 'Not convinced. I think something else is up. The other day she rang to ask if she could visit and then this morning, she calls from the road to say she's on her way.'

'What does Nick say?'

'She said Paddy has been avoiding her calls. Aster saw her last month in London and said everything was fine.' Ari paused and turned to Seb. 'Hang on, bloody hell. We have Fig Rolls in the kitchen, don't we?'

'You've lost me.'

'Dickie bought Fig Rolls last month. And I remember wondering at the time why, when none of us particularly like them. But growing up they were Paddy's comfort food of choice.'

'Do you think Aster called Dickie to stock up because she thought Paddy might be heading home?'

'Yes. Which means she knew back then that something was up.'

'Your little sister would put Machiavelli to shame.' Of all the sisters, Aster was the one he couldn't pin down. He liked her, but she was very quiet and always watching. He knew part of the issue was that he wasn't certain if she approved of him yet. It was a slightly disconcerting feeling. Especially because he wondered what might happen if she eventually decided he didn't actually pass muster. 'Why couldn't she just tell you?'

Ari gave him an old-fashioned look. 'Privacy? Secrets? Aster.'

'Not helpful though.'

'That's not fair.' Ari hated disagreeing with Seb but she knew he was seeing things from an outsider's point of view. 'She was helping in the way that she knows how. She guessed that whatever she found out, might mean Paddy would be coming here. Probably before Paddy had even thought about it. So she planned ahead ready to have something nice in the cupboard for her when she arrived.'

Seb kissed Ari on the forehead. 'Remind me again never to play chess against Aster.'

Heading back into the drawing room, Seb tidied the boys' toys off the sofa and Ari poured him a drink and returned to her cooling hot chocolate. The fire crackled in the hearth and the dogs settled back down, happy that the humans were back with them.

Ari wiggled her toes in front of the fire. 'Do you know, it's silly but I love it when my sisters are here. I just feel a little bit more complete.'

Seb looked across at his wife, her face glowing in the warmth of the fire. Even when her sisters brought troubles, they lightened Ari's world. He was perpetually amazed by how she had coped at eighteen, taking on all she had. 'Why don't we invite them all over for Christmas? I don't think Clem can cope with it a second year running. Or will it be too much for you? Are you going to tell Paddy our news?'

'Not yet. I want to see what's wrong with her first. But I think Christmas altogether is a wonderful idea.'

Ari smiled back at him and quietly she hoped to herself that whatever was troubling Paddy would be done and dusted by then.

Chapter Twenty-Five

Ari was sitting on her own in the kitchen. Breakfast was slowly frying on the Aga and she was on her second tea, wondering for the umpteenth time if she had mice or twins in the larder. Or maybe it was the dogs? She seemed to be constantly writing new shopping lists. Flicking through a magazine she looked lovingly at some of the new wallpapers and wondered if it was too soon to start remodelling the house. Since she'd moved in, she'd pretty much left it how it was, and how it was, was dated. She'd started to bring the gardens back to work and Seb had implemented designs for some long flower borders and an arboretum. Now it was time to start thinking about breathing new life into the house as well. Just as she was wondering if Paddy was ever going to get up, she heard her calling out.

'Morning. I'm in here! The boys have all gone over to their grandparents for the morning to give us time to catch up. I'm doing you a full English and we've got some Fig Rolls as well…'

Ari's voice trailed off as Paddy who had wandered into the kitchen, suddenly held her hand over her mouth and ran out to the downstairs loo. Ari ran after her to find her in a familiar state of distress. Kneeling on the flagstones, Ari held her sister's hair back and made soothing noises until Paddy stumbled back onto her feet, pushing herself up off the toilet bowl. Tearing off some loo roll, she wiped Paddy's eyes and mouth and passed her a glass of water. At least one mystery had been solved.

'Come on. Let's fix you some warm lemon water and ginger biscuits. They were all I could manage in the morning when I was pregnant.'

Paddy came back into the kitchen and sat down gingerly, while Ari took the frying pan out of the kitchen and placed the contents in the dog bowls to their unalloyed joy.

Putting the biscuits on a plate, Ari poured some hot water over a sprig of rosemary and added a slice of lemon, placing them in front of her little sister, who looked up at her woefully.

'That's the first time I've been sick. Will I be sick again today?'

'Sometimes. Or not again at all. Everyone's different.'

Paddy sipped on the water. 'How did you know?'

'You know. Been there, done that.' She took a sip of her tea and wondered how to proceed. She wanted to tell her her own news. They could celebrate together, but this was clearly at the root of her distress. 'So let's have it. What's wrong? I honestly thought you'd be happy to be pregnant, but I don't ever think I've seen you so miserable.'

Nibbling on the biscuit and sipping her drink Paddy began to detail the fake wedding that turned out to be real, the one-night stand that ended in pregnancy and her being the cause of a cancelled wedding.

She looked across at Ari. 'I'm so sorry to have let you down. I'm so ashamed.'

Ariana recoiled in her chair and looked at her sister in alarm. Dashing around the table she gave Paddy a huge hug. 'Don't ever say anything so horrible to me ever again. You cannot, have not and never will, let me down.'

Now Paddy was crying as Ari continued, 'and how can you be ashamed of a baby? And your baby will be the bonniest happiest baby that it will be the world's honour to meet.' Passing Paddy a napkin, she wiped her eyes and waited until she was a bit calmer. 'Seriously. Why are you ashamed?'

'Because I've ruined the wedding of two people who were in love. She called me a slut. He thinks I'm not worth the dirt on his feet and everyone was staring at me when she hit me.'

Ari had been nodding along making gentle sympathetic noises, but now she was on full guard dog mode. 'Back up! Did you just say she hit you?'

Paddy revealed that horrible little scene as well. As she did so, Ari had jumped up and was grabbing her bag, keys and coat.

'Right, in the car. Let's go get an ultrasound and make sure baby wasn't bounced around in there.'

'But I'm fine. I feel, we feel fine.' She gave Ari a small smile; it was the first time she had said 'we' and a wave of rightness settled over her. 'Honestly, we're fine.'

Ariana stopped and looked at Paddy, remembering in the past how Paddy would fight with her sisters, squeeze body lotion in their hair, burp into their milk, scream like a banshee, laugh like a fool, and now here she sat with a little serene smile of a Madonna. Still, Ari wasn't going to take no for an answer.

'Do you know what? You are probably right. You are going to learn to trust your body over the next few months. You and Baby are on an incredible journey that neither of you have been on before, and it's going to be amazing. But please, please would you humour your big sis?'

Paddy waggled her head but agreed, and soon the girls were driving into the new medical centre in the nearby town.

***

Waiting in reception, Ari seemed to know everyone and was proudly introducing her sister to all and sundry. Paddy charmed the room with her wild red hair and beaming smile. As the nurse came out, she nodded as she saw the two women chatting together.

'Well it's easy to tell you two are sisters.' Both girls laughed saying they weren't that ugly, and joshing each other, they made it through to the treatment room.

As she settled down on the couch Paddy felt worried. What if the fall had damaged the baby and, in her naïveté, she hadn't even realised? She couldn't bear the thought that she might have let the little one down.

The nurse gave her hand a squeeze and smiled at her.

'Come on then let's have a look. How far along are you?'

As the nurse asked her lots of questions, Paddy had to focus on the answers until the nurse exclaimed, 'Hello, little one.'

Paddy stared at the screen in wonder. What had been an abstract concept was now sleeping on the screen in front of her. She had no words but placed her fingers on the monitor. Letting out a big sigh she wished with all her might that Hal could be here with her so that they could see their child together for the first time. Maybe she should ask for a screen grab that she could give to him. God, he might not even want to know. Trying to distract herself from such an awful thought, she began focussing on the image again. Pointing at the screen Paddy asked if that meant the baby was a boy.

The nurse laughed. 'That's their arm! Do you want me to see if I can tell the sex?'

'No!' said Paddy in alarm.

Typical Paddy, thought Ari. She always loved surprises. Nick would have wanted to know immediately. Aster would somehow already know. The idea of Clem as a mother was too baffling to contemplate, and whilst she herself had wanted a surprise, Greg had asked the nurse, and then told Ari despite her telling him she didn't want to know.

'Why are you sighing?' asked Paddy. 'What's wrong?' Her voice began to rise in alarm. 'Is something wrong?'

'No sorry. Just me, thinking dumb thoughts.'

A shadow passed over Paddy's face.

'I know. I wish Mum was here too.'

Paddy squeezed Ari's hand and then, recovering themselves, they thanked the nurse, who promptly gave Paddy a list as long as her arm and asked if she was registered at the practice.

'Do you know I haven't even thought that far ahead.'

'Where are you registered then? I'll add this visit to your notes.'

There was a silence as Paddy panicked. 'Nowhere? I just, I mean, it's all been so sudden.' Overwhelmed by fear she tailed off.

The nurse paused, ready to chide her and then looked at how bereft she was and stopped. This wasn't a naïve teenager, this was a terrified young woman who was not yet facing reality.

'Was this your first scan?'

Paddy nodded.

'Right then. Let's do it properly and take some measurements. May as well do it all now and put your mind at rest. We'll also take some bloods. But from where I'm standing, both mother and baby look to be doing fine. Doesn't hurt to have it in writing though, does it?'

Paddy felt limp with relief. In her heart she knew she had been avoiding the issue but she had been at a loss as to what to do. She had been desperate to be a mother. Growing up, she was the sister surrounded by dollies and tea parties. Reality was not proving to be as simple. And dammit, she hadn't foreseen being single.

'When will I start looking pregnant? I still look really flat; I'm about fourteen weeks, I thought I'd be showing by now?'

The nurse looked at her notes. 'Well, you're tall and baby is in a tilted position which means you may be flat for quite a while yet, maybe even until you give birth. Trust me. You don't want to be in any hurry for the baby to shift. I looked like a whale from month four.'

Ari nodded. 'Do you remember I looked like I was a sumo wrestler?'

'As if,' joshed Paddy, 'besides you were having twins. Oh God,' she turned to the nurse, her eyes wide.

'No, you're fine. There was just the one in there but now I know there are twins in the family I'll have another look.'

The nurse started with her second examination and started to chat to Paddy about the local maternity provisions and told her to investigate the Cornish options as well. 'I've heard they have great facilities down there, so wherever you decide to have this little one, you'll be in very safe hands.'

'Isn't it a bit soon to start thinking about it?' Paddy said doubtfully.

'Hardly. You are pregnant now. You may want help during your pregnancy, plus you can join some of the antenatal classes if you want to meet other women in the same stage. Lots of new mums find this a great way to find new friends and support.'

Paddy looked concerned. She didn't have a great opinion of social services. Ante-natal classes just sounded like a way for people to snoop on her and judge her. She still remembered with terror, the day Clem and Ari barricaded the house to prevent the Social removing the girls into foster care.

'I think I can manage on my own.'

The nurse looked at her. 'Well, you'd better start thinking about it. Baby is on a timetable and you need to be ready, one way or the other.'

Finally, once she was happy, she had got all the measurements she could, she told Paddy she would fast track the bloods and phone her with the results. As they got into the car Paddy burst into tears, and Ari passed her a tissue as she drove out of the car park.

'I think for me, the worst of it was the mood swings, even though I was vomiting all the time. I hated the sudden surge of fury or weeping for no apparent reason.'

They drove on in silence until Paddy had stopped crying and was leaning her head on the window, looking at the passing countryside.

'Paddy?'

'Yes?'

'Don't worry about the Social,' Ari's voice broke as her throat choked up. 'They can't touch us now.'

Suddenly both girls were crying and Ari had to pull over as they hugged each other. The fear and pain of the teenage girls bubbled again to the surface.

'We got through that together, we'll get through this.'

Sensing a conversation about pregnancy and motherhood, and whether or not the father was going to be involved, might overwhelm Paddy at this point, Ari changed the topic.

'So what about you? You went down to Cornwall to think about your career. Have you had a chance to think about it or have events overtaken you?'

'I don't know. You know I love photography and I've been doing loads of that down there. But something Nick said on the phone, though, made sense. Kensey House is an under-used resource. I don't need to live anywhere that big, even if I have a hundred children.'

Ari snorted. 'It's not that big!'

'No, positively a cottage compared to your place or Clem's. But I wonder if we couldn't turn it into a sort of holiday home for charities. City kids, hospice release, stuff like that? We could charge just enough to cover our costs. Heating, lighting, staff et cetera, but other than that the charity could use it for free for the week? Maybe set ten weeks aside for full paying business retreats, corporate awaydays. Maybe a week or two for the family? But otherwise let people who might properly benefit from it use it? What do you think?'

Ari smiled at Paddy. 'Let me run it past the others but I can't see a problem. I think it's a lovely idea.'

Since becoming the Countess of Hiverton, Ariana had run her estate with a light touch. She was gradually bringing the whole business into the twenty-first century whilst maintaining family control. She was making few major changes until she got used to the mantle but she enjoyed discussing things with her sisters. All of them were stepping out into new territories and were aware of the massive financial responsibilities on their shoulders. How many people relied on them and how much influence they wielded.

Privately Ari thought that in another decade or two, if she handled things properly, they could be incredibly influential as a family. But for now she just needed to ensure that no one and nothing bankrupted the estate. Listening to Sebastian and his tales of upper-class woes had made her laugh, but she discovered that overnight you could lose the lot, just like if you were poor.

'Now look, I have a suggestion, why don't you move in here with us? At least until the baby arrives and you are back on your feet? You can run the Cornish project remotely?'

Paddy looked around the Norfolk countryside. She was so tempted, it was lovely here and she loved being with her family. 'How about this? I'll spend a bit more time here then head back to Cornwall and get on with the project. Then at seven months, I'll come back. Would that be okay? I really want to make a success of Cornwall. I think it has loads of potential and the idea of being able to help out people who are desperate for a break is something that would make me very happy.'

Ari was thrilled. It sounded like a brilliant solution. It gave time for Paddy to prove to herself that she could successfully transition away from being a model and then Ari would have her nearby as things became tougher. She couldn't bear to think of Paddy bringing up a baby on her own at the other end of the country.

'What are you going to do about the marriage?' Ari asked tentatively and watched with concern as her sister's face clouded with pain again.

'I have no idea, I asked Duncan to forward the paperwork to Cornwall, so I'll just sign it when I get back there. It's not like we can get annulled now,' she said smiling sadly as she placed her hand over her tummy, 'so I suppose we'll have to arrange a divorce instead. Look, forget it for now. I just want to focus on Baby and happy thoughts.'

Ari looked thoughtfully at Paddy, she seemed in no rush to terminate this marriage and Ari wondered what that might signify.

'What does Duncan say?'

'I don't know. I can't bring myself to speak to him. I just asked him to give me some space and I've blocked his texts.'

'That's extreme?' said Ari carefully.

'I know but I'm just so embarrassed.' Tears began to well up again and she sniffed miserably.

Deciding that now was not the time for further interrogations she gave her sister a hug and a big grin.

'You're on! Let's go and have some fizzy water to celebrate. I have some news as well.'

Paddy looked at her questioningly and Ari couldn't keep it a secret any longer.

'I'm pregnant as well!'

Laughing both girls hugged again and Paddy knew she had made the right choice in coming home.

Chapter Twenty-Six

Grabbing the morning post, Hal headed to the local station and jumped on a train to London. There was a landholders association meeting and whilst it was a long way to go it was important that he kept up to date and start to build contacts across the country. He couldn't rely on his father's contacts, he needed new blood and new ideas. He himself was going to be a father and it was about time he grew up and started planning for the future.

One of the envelopes was handwritten and based on the premise that they are always the most interesting, he left it 'til last. The other was a confirmation of the cancelled honeymoon. He had spoken to Bianca the day after the charity function and had warned her against doing anything stupid like running to the press about Paddy. God knows there wasn't much he could do to make amends to the two women, but he could protect Paddy's privacy and he could stop Bianca by paying her. He had asked if she would be prepared to sign a non-disclosure agreement. In return he would transfer £10K to her account. It wiped out all his savings but it was worth it to make amends to Paddy. Bianca agreed instantly and again he wondered what he had narrowly missed.

He opened the next envelope and found a letter and a sonogram inside. He had never looked at one before but he knew he was looking at an image of his child. He touched the child's face with his finger and stared at it in wonder. Carefully he placed it back in the envelope, then moved his coffee cup onto a table on the other side of the carriage. Only then did he take the picture out again; this time he also read the brief note from Paddy.

> *Dear Hal,*
>
> *I wanted to take the time to apologise for leaving your event so abruptly and to apologise for everything really. I am staying with my sister in Norfolk and am well. I wasn't sure if you would be interested but I am including a scan of Baby. The nurse says they are fine and all is progressing well. I know you have your own life to lead but I want you to know that whilst I don't require anything from you, I will never stop you from seeing your child. Should you wish.*
>
> *I hope you and Bianca were able to patch things up and I wish you both well. Once again, I am sorry for my part in your problems.*
>
> *I shall let you know when the baby is born, but other than that there is no more to say.*
>
> *Yours sincerely,*
> *Paddy*

Hal folded the letter carefully away into the envelope and continued to look at his child. Well, its mother may not want him, she had made that perfectly clear, but he'd make sure his child always wanted him and that he would always be there. He wondered if he had a son or a daughter but he didn't care. He had a child and he needed to get his life in gear. He had a purpose.

As the train pulled into Paddington, Hal had formulated a few ideas and set off ready to put the first into action.

***

'Excuse me.' Getting no response Hal bobbed down to the hunched-over figure. 'Hello, excuse me.'

The young man looked up at him warily.

'Ah yes. Hello, it is you. Last time you had a dog? Good. Um. A friend of mine shared some Burger Kings with you a few weeks back. She had red hair. I wonder if I could share mine with you?'

The lad's face broke into a smile. 'The good-looking one? Yes. Here, have a bit of cardboard. For the pavement. You don't want a wet backside. Trust me.'

Hal sat down alongside what he now decided was a youth, little past his childhood. In fact Hal thought he might still be a teenager. God, to think when he first saw him, he had thought he was an old man. With his back leaning against the wall he started to pull items out of the fast-food bag.

'Now, I had no idea what to order but I picked out various things and I thought that if I've over ordered you might have some friends you'd like to share it with? Mind you, it will be a bit cold. I don't know what they do to their chips but, they can go from burning hot to stone cold if you so much as take your eyes off them.'

'Best eat them hot then.'

For a few minutes the two ate in happy silence. It was an odd view of the world sitting down here. No one paid him any attention and if they did, he didn't notice as they were so far above him. He was busy watching the view on the other side of the road.

'You see a lot more down here, don't you?'

'Like you wouldn't believe. You see a lot more kids too. It's like we are all existing on our own planes. Walking around you are looking above everything, or directly at it. The amount of times I see kids getting their faces bashed by other people's shopping bags is ridiculous. But the kids see me. I think they envy me. Sitting down, not being dragged from shop to shop. Sometimes they wave.' He looked sad. 'But then they get yanked along by some terrified parent. Sometimes I wonder if they think I have rabies or maybe just fleas.'

Looking across he saw Hal recoil. 'Nah mate, don't worry. I don't.'

Hal grimaced. 'God no. I was just trying to work out how to ask how you cope with it. I was trying not to be rude and I managed to cause offence anyway.'

'Seriously. Offence is the least of my concerns. If you live like this what is the point in worrying what someone thinks of you. Trust me, you've got much bigger fish to fry.' Licking the salt off his fingers he grinned at Hal. 'So tell me? How do you know that gorgeous girl? An ugly mug like you?'

Realising Hal was being teased he relaxed into the banter. 'That sir, is no girl, that sir, was my wife.'

'How's that?'

'Actually it's a bit of a mess but we got married by accident and then it turns out we weren't.'

'You jammy bastard. I swear to God, anyone who ever tries to tell me that the rich aren't born lucky needs their head examining. How the hell d'you get married by accident?'

Hal began to explain, until the lad was almost crying with laughter.

'No wonder she hates your guts. You get her pregnant when you're engaged to another woman. Man! What are you going to do about it? You're going to be a dad. Mate, you've got to step up.'

Hal was prepared to take offence and then felt the air deflate out of his response. The simple fact of the matter was that he did indeed have to step up.

'I don't suppose she told you where she lives when you were chatting?'

'Yeah, hold on it's in my address book!' Leaning over the boy patted a worn and dirty rucksack. 'It's in here somewhere next to my fountain pen and family silver.' He laughed. 'And I thought I had problems. At least I'm not an idiot.'

Hal raised his coffee in acknowledgement of an insult well landed.

'All right, your turn then. How did you end up here?'

Sam shrugged and shrank a bit. 'Usual story. Family problems. Got thrown out. Came to seek my fame and fortune. Ended up living on the streets. Game over.'

Hal took another bite of the burger that, like the chips, had also gone cold. The chill from the hard pavement was radiating through his body and a light drizzle had begun to form. He couldn't even begin to work out his problems but he knew beyond a shadow of a doubt that he could fix some of Sam's. Sitting here with a total stranger seemed entirely natural to him. As a captain in the army he was used to leading groups of young men. Sitting with them and making sure they worked as a team, as well as seeing how they ticked as individuals. It was a talent of his and he was surprised and pleased to see it hadn't been something that had been left behind on the battlefield.

'Can I help? I mean I know I can. But will you accept it?'

Sam looked at him warily. Did this burger come with a price tag?

'What I had in mind was this: I live in Cornwall. I can offer you employment and accommodation. It will be labouring work until we figure out what your skills and talents are but you'd be paid the national average and until you are on your feet, your accommodation would be rent free.'

'Why would you do that?' Sam's suspicions hadn't lessened one jot. He had got a safe vibe from this bloke, but now he wasn't so sure.

'Because I've got the money and it would be easy. A better person than me showed me how to be a human. It's not a solution to poverty or homelessness or anything else like that, but it could help you. What do you say?'

Sam raised a knowing eyebrow and Hal recoiled in alarm.

'Christ no, you don't owe me anything.' Hal paused, clearly he hadn't thought this through and this lad had no reason to trust him. 'Look, I imagine over the last few years you've had few options. So I'm going to leave this in your hands. Give me a minute.'

Sam watched as Hal clambered to his feet and then headed off down the street. It had been an odd event, but his life was full of odd events these days. At least this one had included hot food and an enjoyable conversation. For the umpteenth time he wondered if he should get a dog; people always gave food to a dog and he'd have someone to talk to. He'd taken care of Old Tom's dog the other day and he'd loved it. The rescue centres would never give him a dog, but sometimes people on the streets would give their dogs away if they went into hospital or rehab. Or, if they passed away, their dog would move onto a new owner, He'd seen enough dogs pass hands that way. Tom's dog was a lurcher-lab cross who had now passed through six or seven hands, and had developed something of a bad reputation for outliving his owner. Sam thought it was hardly the dog's fault. Only the weakest now wanted him, so inevitably they didn't last long anyway. Sam thought he may go and have a word with Tom. Maybe he'd let him know that he'd be happy to take care of him whenever.

'Hello again.' Sam jumped. He'd been so lost in thought and he wasn't used to people sitting down next to him.

'Here.' Hal handed him a piece of paper with his name, address and phone number on it and £200 in cash. 'This is for you. Do what you want with it. But if you use it to get a train to Cornwall, there'll be a house and a job waiting for you, with no strings attached. If it doesn't work out, move on. It's your money, spend it how you want. When you get to Cornwall, call me or just turn up.'

Shaking the lad's hand, Hal stood up and walked away wondering if he would ever see him again.

***

James looked up in surprise as his son bounded into the study. He wasn't certain when he had last seen him this energised. There was no tell-tale shadow of pain. No glimpse of sorrow.

'Father, I know what I'm going to do!'

James raised an eyebrow. For the past year Hal had drifted in and out of schemes with partial interest. He knew his son had wanted to do more around the estate but if he was honest, James resented Hal's interference. When Hal had returned from the army, James had been grateful for his help. A minor heart scare had caused him to slow down and things had begun to pile up on him. Now he was annoyed by all the changes. The old ways were best because they worked. Why fix what wasn't broken? It had caused friction between them and, whilst one day all this would be Hal's, it wasn't yet. James was relieved he was finally going to have the young lion out from under his feet.

He had thought marriage might be the solution, but on meeting his future daughter-in-law he wasn't convinced. If anything Hal had seemed happier after the end of the engagement. He had come back from London a week ago and Odette had mentioned that Hal was brewing something.

Now, opening his laptop on the table, Hal began to pull up various projections and spreadsheets, explaining his idea for a new charity. He was going to help the young homeless. The charity would give them a permanent roof over their heads and a mentoring scheme and he was going to get them working. They would each have a mentor who would get them back on their feet. It was going to be financed by backers but he hoped his father would consider renting Mellowstone Grange for small breaks or a week's holiday, when the youths were resettled.

James raised his eyebrows. 'I'm not sure you've thought this through, m'boy. They're on the streets for a reason. If their parents didn't want them and no one will give them a job, you have to ask yourself why.'

Inwardly, Hal groaned. He knew he was going to face this sort of prejudice; better that he started to learn his arguments now, here at home, before he began to talk to backers and fundraisers. Hal went on to explain his meeting with Sam and his upbringing, but James remained unconvinced. He tried again.

'What these young people need is a support system. Some will need a lot of support, some only need the smallest bit of intervention to get them back on their feet. Whatever the need, we will provide it. It will be labour intensive and it won't be cheap but it will be worth it.'

'I don't know, Hal. It still sounds like you are rewarding laziness.' James leant back on his chair. It was a new treat to himself, a leather Chesterfield that tilted backwards. It was pricey but he loved the comfort it provided. What was the point of having money if you couldn't treat yourself now and then? He returned to his line of thought. 'And what about you? You experienced a terrible event. Worst thing that can ever happen to a boy. And yet you picked yourself up, got into Sandhurst and went on to serve your country.'

James's voice was tinged with self-reflected pride and Hal wondered if he would ever be able to make his father see the world from someone else's point of view.

'Look, Dad, when I was in the army, we often saw young recruits who were there because they had no one and nowhere else to go. For some of them it was a complete saviour. You could see them grow physically and emotionally, as they found somewhere to belong. To be where they were wanted and valued. But the army isn't the right place for everyone, and there were those who should never have been admitted. They experienced horrors heaped onto immature psyches, that had already witnessed huge traumas in their childhood. Those individuals leave the army even worse than when they went in.'

'I can see you mean well...'

Hal was beginning to lose his patience. 'And losing a mother is not the worst thing that can happen to a boy. Not by a long shot. What I saw whilst I was on service and what I have researched over the past few weeks has shown me that for all my grief, I was actually lucky.'

James rocked forward on his chair, furious at Hal's thoughtless words. 'Lucky! How can you dare to sit there and say to me that you were lucky that your mother died!?' Leaning forward he jabbed his finger in Hal's direction. But Hal was used to his father's temper. An easy-going man until anything or anyone disagreed with him and then it was all fury and bluster.

'Yes, I was lucky. I was lucky because I still had a father who loved me and helped me. Because I still had a home. Because I still had food. Because no one abused me, or beat me, or sold me. And if you ask me, I reckon Mum would be one hundred per cent behind me on this.'

James's fury deflated. The idea of his child facing any of those injustices made him feel sick. But still, the idea of using Mellowstone was ridiculous. He would humour his son and wait for him to tire of the idea. It wouldn't do for Hal to start poking around in the family finances right now.

Chapter Twenty-Seven

Hugo Laing was urging the London taxi to make it through the traffic. His flight from Mogadishu had been delayed first by weather, then by disputes and finally by scheduling and now here he was skidding into London forty-eight hours late and at a very serious risk of missing his friend's wedding. He knew Hal would forgive him, but he didn't want to let his best friend down.

Hugo had spent the last three months in Somalia working for the BBC. He and his fellow cameramen were tracking down rare black boubous and had been totally cut off from the outside world. Now, because of his delay he hadn't been able to make the stag do, catch up with his friends or even grab his morning suit. His battery was flat and he hadn't even been able to text any of the gang. A quick shower and a change of clothes was the best he could manage. Finally, he made it to Chelsea and was appalled to see he was only just ahead of the bride. Bianca would never forgive him if he upstaged her. Giving Bianca a big wave and a thumbs up he ran past her with his luggage slung over his back and slid into one of the back pews and paused to catch his breath.

The organ started up and as he scrambled to free himself from his luggage he stood up with the rest of the congregation. He looked around for familiar faces; most of his friends would be at the front. Oddly the church was only half full, which surprised him, but maybe they had wanted to keep the numbers down? Craning his neck he tried to spot Hal and Jamie but maybe they were sitting or kneeling? Normally that pair towered over everyone else in the room. As he looked at all the bobbing hats and feathers he wondered why he didn't recognise anyone.

Now Bianca walked past him on her father's arm. God, she really had a cracking figure but what an extraordinary dress. Hugo grinned and could only imagine what dear Eleanor would have said as she saw her daughter-in-law to be walking up the aisle. Generous and as loving as the day was long, she would no doubt have made some supportive comment about *modern girls being wonderfully daring*, but Hugo was not certain if buckles and straps on a dress didn't ever so slightly scream bondage. The dress was so super slinky it was very clear to every man in the room what was on offer. Knowing Bianca he was sure this was the height of fashion; what did he know? In the pew in front of him two women frantically whispered back and forth at each other, smothering sniggers.

'I didn't know Ann Summers did wedding dresses.'

'Apparently it's a McQueen.'

'That is NOT an Alexander McQueen. Who does she think she's fooling? McQueen wannabe. My god is that a zip?'

Hugo didn't care much for Bianca himself but Hal did and that was all that mattered. He knew some of the girls in their group were even more opposed to her than he was but then girls could be very tricky. It was always best to not get involved. Bianca resolutely ignored him as she walked past but he could hardly blame her, he had nearly knocked her over in his rush to get in ahead of her.

Now the bridesmaids walked past and he had to bite his knuckle. They looked like Oompa-Loompas. Their dresses were appalling, even he could see that, and the fake tans seemed to have gone a little orange. Thank God Vix wasn't a maid of honour; she'd never live it down. It was a shame, really, he'd have been able to tease her for years. Once more he regretted arriving late. He wanted to be sitting at the front with his old friends.

As the bride reached the front she knelt down and was joined by Hal. Hugo wished he could get a better view and considered shuffling forward a few pews but he was a bit worried about drawing attention to himself. Damn, why weren't the bride and groom standing? Something looked wrong with Hal, was he ill? God, he wished he had his contacts in but flying always dried his eyes out. As the fuggy air and the long flight caught up with him he was beginning to nod off. Voices mumbled from the front, the priest droned on, the congregation sang and Hugo had to keep shaking himself to wake up. How on earth was he going to stay awake through the reception? He needed to catch up with the others. They would keep him on his toes and bring him up to speed on all the gossip. The animal hierarchies of the Somalian jungles had nothing on the social twists and turns of his friends' loves and lives. As he was about to drift off again the organ crashed awake, filling the church with sound. The congregation stood up as the bride and groom made their way down the aisle.

Looking up, something seemed awry with Hal. He appeared to have shrunk and with every step Hugo saw that something was very wrong indeed. That was not Hal. It was some short-looking foreigner. Bloody hell, was he at the wrong wedding? He looked at Bianca again, who was beaming with pride and joy. No, that was unmistakably Bianca. What the hell? As the congregation passed him, he didn't recognise a single face. Rummaging around his luggage he found a travel battery for his dead phone and plugged it in. After a few minutes the phone beeped and he dialled Victoria.

'Vix, darling, it's Hugo. I'm at Hal's wedding. Where the hell is he? What's going on?'

There was a pause and then the hallowed halls of St Barnabus winced to the echoes of Hugo's profanities. Apologising to anyone who could hear him, he got up and headed out of the church, trying to make sense of Vix's call. Hal may or may not have got some girl pregnant, no one was certain on the point. He had definitely called the wedding off. And now it seemed that Bianca had definitely gone ahead with it. With someone else. Vix knew nothing about that part and had been horrified. The whole thing was a mess, and Hugo was heading to Cornwall. He didn't know if he could actually do anything but this was when friends stood together.

***

Hal took in a huge breath. It had been five weeks since Paddy had run out of his life and his only contact from her had been a letter to his home stating her desire to be left alone for a while and a copy of the sonograph of their child. Every day since then he had looked at that picture, and kept it in his wallet along with a picture of Paddy he had found in a copy of *Vogue*. He found he had suddenly taken great delight in leafing through Odette's old magazines looking for pictures of Paddy.

Everything seemed better after a long walk. The sun was beginning to go down and he was very glad that the day was nearly done. Today was supposed to be his wedding day, but instead, if he was honest with himself, he was hiding. He had no wish to make small talk today, or to try and avoid sympathetic glances or condemnatory ones. No, he was to blame for his shameful behaviour; he had let two women down appallingly and yet if he had proceeded, he would have done an even greater harm. This was of little comfort when he thought how Bianca must be suffering. He knew she was quite a determined character and he was certain she would recover, but even so.

As he walked across the lawn he spotted an unfamiliar car in the driveway. His father was at home, he could take care of whoever it was; instead he turned around and headed down to the estate offices. His father was still dragging his feet about the use of Mellowstone, and Hal was beginning to think he might have to find another property. It seemed a waste as Mellowstone stood empty. As he walked away, he heard the front door open and a familiar voice called out.

'Spotty!'

Hal turned, only two people in the world called him Spotty.

'Hugo! Is it possible?' Walking towards Hugo, he gave him a massive bear hug. 'Have you actually got uglier *and* fatter?!' This is what he needed, an uncomplicated friendship. 'What the hell are you doing in England? I thought you were annoying warthogs in Africa. Did they *all* turn you down?'

Hal and Hugo had first met in boarding school. Both had excelled at cross-country and were constant rivals for first place. They had only been united when Jamie had arrived in the second year. The boy was so fast, that all the pair saw of him were his heels, as he overtook them. Never one to hold grudges, the three had rapidly become best friends and did all they could to wind each other up and support each other in equal measure. They were the scourge of the lower fourth, and whilst Jamie was regularly considered the sobering influence by their tutors, Hugo and Hal knew he was just as likely to pull pranks as the other two. If he could get away with it.

As schoolboys, Hugo and Hal knew Jamie's home life was severe. Their way of helping him through it was to create mayhem. And create mayhem they did. Who could forget the time at prize day when the podium was full of visiting dignitaries? The school choir stood up to sing 'There is a Green Hill Far Away,' a poignant hymn based on the painful and noble sacrifice of Christ, and as they got to the end of the line, 'He died to save us all', someone in the audience called out, 'For he's a jolly good fellow', which was taken up by the rest of the lower fourth.

The staff were furiously trying to work out the ringleaders, but the Headmaster knew instantly. Earlier he had had to inform Jamie that he was being asked to stay as a boarder over summer, rather than go home. His father was off on holiday with his latest girlfriend. If he could have given those boys a medal then and there, he would have. Instead he scowled severely at the upper sixth and reminded them that this wasn't the time for high jinks.

Now over a decade later, two of the unholy trio wandered down to the estate office. Hal was delighted to see his old school friend; life had been so complicated but here with Hugo, life seemed simple and uncluttered again.

'Come on, let's go inside. So what the hell are you doing in the UK? How's it all going?'

Hugo looked at his friend. He was looking tired and worn out. He knew he had struggled after his discharge and had hoped his marriage might get him back on his feet, but after the disaster he witnessed this morning, things had clearly gone very wrong.

'Honestly? I was here for a wedding.'

Hal stared at him and then groaned in horror. God he was a fool; in the joy and excitement he had completely forgotten that rather salient detail. 'Christ yes. Oh God, Hugo, I did send word but obviously it missed you in transit. Well I suppose you know the worst of it. I've been an idiot and ruined everything. I know I did the right thing but God I feel so guilty about Bianca.'

'Why?' Hugo was wrong-footed; why was Hal feeling guilty? Hurt, jilted, heartbroken, yes. But guilty, that didn't make sense.

'Well for calling off the engagement. And so close to the wedding.'

'Yes… But…' Hugo paused. He'd assumed Hal must have found out Bianca was cheating. It made more sense than some random pregnancy. Hal didn't fool around. What on earth was going on?

'Look, Hal,' Hugo plucked at invisible threads on his jacket, 'the thing is I've just come from the church. My plane was late and I didn't have time to talk to anyone. So I headed straight there.'

Hal turned and looked at his friend, wincing. 'Oh hell, I can imagine you gate-crashing a total stranger's wedding, I'm so sorry.'

'Well that's the thing. It wasn't a complete stranger's wedding.'

Hal looked up with amused interest as his friend trailed off. 'You knew them? Bloody hell, what are the chances?'

So Hal didn't know Bianca had gone ahead with the wedding. This was going to be ugly. 'The thing is, Hal, the bride was Bianca.'

Hal paused and looked at Hugo. 'What? Did you say the bride was,' he paused trying to manage his disbelief, 'Bianca?'

Hugo nodded.

'Today? On our wedding day. In the church we booked?'

Hugo nodded each time. This was mortifying. 'Yes. She was marrying some Italian-looking fellow.'

'Short? Looked like an actor?'

'That's the chap.'

'Bloody hell, she even brought him here for the fundraiser. Dear God. Married.' And then he startled Hugo by laughing. 'Right, get in the car. Pub time!'

Hal drove and booked a taxi for the return journey. Waving at the landlord he explained that he'd be leaving his car in the car park overnight. Sitting in the Queen's Arms, Hal raised a glass. 'Let's drown our sorrows and thank our lucky stars for narrow escapes.'

Enjoying his first decent drink in months, Hugo took a long draught and then sighed in satisfaction. 'Right, what the hell has been going on?'

Over the next few hours, some pies and some more pints, Hal began to bring his friend up to date. Vix had already told Hugo over the phone about the mysterious Paddy, but when Hugo mentioned her, Hal was curt and said he didn't want to discuss her. Hugo decided to leave it for now; instead they discussed Hal's plans for the new charity, which Hugo thought sounded invaluable.

As the evening went on Hugo wondered about this mysterious Paddy. He didn't know much but he had a feeling that she was extremely important and not just because she was pregnant. Hal was very defensive about her and shielding her from even being discussed. He was being incredibly protective and Hugo was certain there was more to come. This girl seemed to be the key to Hal's future. He wondered if Hal was even aware of it.

The following morning Hugo had to head back up to London to work on some edits and was then heading straight out again. He didn't like the idea of Hal being by himself. Of course they were all grown-ups now, but he, Hal and Jamie had always had each other's back when the chips were down.

According to Hal, when he'd cancelled the wedding Jamie had decided to cancel his leave. He was nearly at the end of a term of service and wanted to spend as much time in the field as he could. He would be back in the UK in a few months' time and Hugo hoped the three of them would be able to catch up then. Hugo also suggested they all head to Courchevel for a spot of skiing and Hal agreed eagerly; it would be fun to have a few things to look forward to.

For now, though, he gave his school friend a quick hug and set off, hoping that by the time they did all meet again,

Hal and his girl would be together, and his friend would be smiling again.

Chapter Twenty-Eight

The sisters were sitting in the solar, with the fire burning. It was June and the heating was off but a sudden cold snap had encouraged Seb to light a fire for the girls. He was naturally protective of Ari at the best of times, but now she was carrying his child he was permanently on tenterhooks. He was also concerned about Paddy; when she had come back from the doctors the previous month, she had looked so broken he thought she must have lost the baby. Ari filled him in about her fears and once again he was amazed at what his wife had gone through to keep her family together. Paddy had been shaky for a few weeks but over the last few days she had begun to perk up and he hoped she was through the worst of her fears and self-doubt. As Paddy recovered, Ari started to regain her happiness as well. Now she was flicking through the latest edition of *Hello!*

'Oh dear. I'm not convinced by her choice of bridesmaids' dresses, are you? It's a definite sort of woman who chooses to make herself look better by making her apparent best friends look worse.'

Leaning over she showed Paddy the photograph of a beautiful bride surrounded by three friends that were desperately trying to overcome their turquoise ruffles. A perfectly fine look on a bikini in the Bahamas or an 80s theme party but rather harder to pull off on a full-length taffeta bridesmaid gown.

Paddy stared at the image in horror.

Oblivious to Paddy's reaction, Ari continued, 'I bet she's the sort of bride that issues her guests with instructions. And would you look at her dress! I must be getting old.'

Surprised by her sister's lack of response she looked at her, as Paddy's face lost all its colour.

'Oh God, are you going to be sick? Hang on.'

Ariana ran out of the room in search of a bucket. Paddy took one final look at Bianca's smug face beaming in victory and threw the magazine on the fire. A huge wave of nausea overtook her that had nothing to do with her pregnancy and she retched into the pretty wastepaper bin. Upset that Ari would be furious, she couldn't stop crying and then threw up again as Ari came in with a bucket.

'I'm so sorry. I've ruined your bin.' Paddy started to sob. 'I ruin everything. My life is such a mess.'

Consoling her sister, Ari chided herself for being a fool. What sort of an insensitive idiot would show wedding photos to someone who desperately wanted her own happily ever after?

***

That evening, Seb came back from his meetings and asked Ari how the day had been. After she had filled him in, Seb could see Ari had once again lost her sparkle. She was the same when the boys were ill. She hated it when she couldn't fix a problem. Grain yields, planning applications, legal disputes, these things were child's play to his indomitable wife, but a bruised knee or a broken heart completely destroyed her. He was amazed she hadn't shaken the father's name out of Paddy and said so.

244

'And what good would that do? Could I insist that he make an honourable woman of her? What would that solve? Just heap on more misery, why not. I can't believe I was so stupid as to show her wedding pictures.'

Seb was about to point out that snapping at him wouldn't fix anything either, but he bit his tongue. He could see his wife was utterly strung out.

'Sorry. I didn't mean to snap. I've been thinking about it all day and I think I'm going to invite her to move in with us. Not just for Christmas. What do you think? Tregiskey seems to be ticking along just fine and I think I've probably asked too much of Paddy. She always was the dreamer amongst us and the least able to handle bad news. Now with the baby, I want her amongst family.' She looked at Seb, who was smiling.

'I think it's a super idea and was going to suggest the same thing. But if she continues to play Mahler at top volume maybe we could offer her the Summer Cottage?'

***

Ari was out in the gardens enjoying the sunshine. She'd picked some flowers for the house and was now inspecting the greenhouse to see if she could rustle up some fruit for this evening's pudding. She was thoroughly enjoying Norfolk in the summer. She and Paddy had gone on lots of excursions with the boys and had enjoyed exploring the county. They had played in Norwich Castle dropping pennies down the well, visited the seals on the north coast and gone kayaking on the Broads. However, in amongst that she had to balance the fun with her job. In a minute she'd need to return to the office to carry on with the paperwork, but for now this was a little stolen moment of pleasure. As she stood up from the strawberry beds she saw Paddy approach her with a large smile on her face.

'Ari. I think I need to go back to Cornwall. I need to set up a few things to get the project running. The change of use has been granted and there's stuff to do. Plus, I'm also missing it. And I guess I need to speak to Baby's father.'

Ari watched as her sister leant against the frame of the greenhouse. She wanted to get these planning development forms off, but she'd been waiting for this moment for weeks and she wasn't about to put it off for something as tedious as paperwork.

'Come on, let's go for a walk. We can stop for lunch along the way as well.'

Paddy had had to give up breakfast completely, even the lemon water was making her sick. Handing the flowers and fruit over to one of the gardeners, Ari linked her arm through Paddy's and the pair made their way down to one of the lower footpaths.

'Right, let's hear all about it. Where do you want to start? How much you love him and how miserable that's making you? Or how you are planning to live when Baby arrives?'

'Bloody hell, Ari. Don't bother pulling any punches, will you?'

'Well, okay. Does he want the baby? Is he going to support you?'

'Don't know. Don't suppose his wife will allow that.'

Ari was confused. 'But you're his wife?'

Paddy sighed. She had managed to come to terms with it over the past forty-eight hours, although it had shaken her to her core. She had completely misjudged Hal.

'He got married last week. I saw it in one of your magazines. They must have decided to go ahead with it anyway. He obviously hopes I'll just fade away into the background. I was going to sign the divorce papers when I got back to Cornwall but I guess he just decided to jump the gun.'

Ari looked appalled. 'But that's illegal! Is he mad? He can't do that. And you're having his child for God's sake. What sort of a man is he!? I'll call the police!'

Looking over at her sister, Paddy looked tired and miserable, her smile slipping into the strawberry beds.

'Oh I'm sorry. But honestly, you are so much better off without him. Trust me.' She linked her arm through her sister's and continued on through the fields. 'Come on, tell me what your plans are.'

***

'Ari, did you hear that?!'

Ari looked up; she was trying to wipe baked beans off Leo's face, feed the dogs, and round up all the various bags for school. Thursdays always seemed to require more kit than a Sherpa could manage. Now William remembered that they needed eggs for science, with Leo contradicting him, and saying it wasn't eggs. They didn't need anything for science but they did need something round for art. It was the final days of the summer term and the boys were looking forward to their holidays. It was getting increasingly harder to keep them focussed on the tasks ahead.

'No sorry, must have missed that. Something else must have been on my mind.'

Seb knew when his wife was having a dig and jumped up, heading in search of eggs and tennis balls.

'Harringtons has gone into liquidation.'

'Need more clues,' she called out as she pulled out some tennis balls that Dragon liked to hide under the kitchen units.

'Harrington's. It's a big private bank. Like Coutts? But older.'

'Really? How does a bank run out of money?' she paused. 'Isn't that the whole point of banks.'

'No idea. Look do you mind taking the children in this morning? I'm going to change my plans and speak to Geoffrey.'

Ari finally caught up with Seb's worried tone.

'Is this going to affect your family?'

'No idea. And look I'm sure Hiverton is okay, but you will need to speak to Nick as well to see if you are safe.'

'Safe?' Seb's level of worry was infectious.

'I've seen people lose their entire fortunes and estates when a bank collapses. Remember the Lloyd's Names?'

Ariana looked alarmed. 'No. What does that mean?'

'Darling, I don't mean to alarm you, but this is serious. There will be people out there who have just lost everything.'

***

Ari dropped the children in the playground giving each a quick hug and a kiss, reminding them not to drop the eggs and hurried back to the car. Sitting in the car park she tried to get through to Nick, but the line was engaged. She drove through the countryside getting increasingly alarmed, when her phone finally rang, she heard Nick in business mode.

'Are you driving? Pull over. Everything's okay but I need to talk it through with you.'

Ari quickly found a spot by a field gate and switched off her engine, pulling out her notepad and pen as Nick started talking.

'Have you heard of Harrington? Good. First things first, we had no direct money or investments with them. I moved our money out when we first inherited. Didn't like their systems. Far too much trust. A gentleman's word and all that bollocks. But some of our other investments are impacted.'

Nick went on to explain how she had been feeling twitchy for the last few days and had started to move money quite dramatically. Sometimes at a loss. 'I didn't catch everything but I would say we've been impacted about five per cent through knock-on investments. There's going to be some massive reverberations over the next few days and I want your blessing to move large amounts of money hard and fast without running it past you first.'

Promising to update her that evening, she hung up and Ari stared out the window at the wide green fields. Getting out of the car, she stretched and looked around. She had become so used to having money that the thought of losing it all made her feel quite giddy. Only Nick's words had made it seem real.

Thank God she had moved the money out. Once again, she threw up a little word of thanks that she had such clever sisters. Her sense of panic had lessened but she had no idea who Seb's family banked with and hoped they were going to be okay. With a shock she realised they hadn't even discussed Paddy.

As she got home, she headed out to the offices. Her uncle had renovated a nearby stables and they now worked as the Estate offices. Seb was on the phone, all his screens were open and his hair was a mess. Making a coffee for the pair of them she waited until he had finished listening to the other end and then with a 'will do' he hung up and looked at his wife.

'Not great news. I think we've lost about a quarter of our estate; Geoffrey is beside himself. He's blaming himself for our losses. I've never heard him so upset. He just doesn't do emotions. Father's blaming the government, the EU, the Chinese, the bankers, anyone. Thank God, you're okay.'

'How do you know?' asked Ari, handing Seb his coffee.

'Nick apparently called Geoffrey at the beginning of the week. She wasn't happy about a small deal that a subsidiary of Harrington's was making, so she asked his opinion on it.' Seb sighed and sipped his drink. 'Turns out she's never rated Harrington's and removed all your money as soon as she took over. Geoff trusts your sister's instincts, says she has no veneer clouding her eyesight. Anyway, he started to investigate her concerns, agreed that potentially there was an issue. He moved all our liquid assets, but the long-term investments were locked. He surrendered those that he could, at a loss. But like I said there was about twenty-five per cent he couldn't touch.' He sighed again. 'And it looks like that has gone. Uninsured losses.'

'Oh, I'm so sorry, darling.' Going over to Seb she wrapped her arms around him and gave him a huge hug and kissed him on the head. Then she pulled out a chair. 'Let's start planning and see what is going to affect us and what we can do to help your folks.'

Seb leant over and picked up her hand kissing her fingers. 'It's silly but even with this loss I still feel blessed to have you. Even if I'd lost the whole bloody lot, I'd still have you. Some poor buggers though are waking up to find they have nothing left at all.'

Chapter Twenty-Nine

'All of it? How can we have lost all of it?' Hal looked at his father in cold horror.

'Well, we took out a few loans and made a few investments. And now the investments have failed and they are calling in the loans. We are pretty much wiped out. They are almost certainly going to increase the mortgage as well.'

Hal's jaw dropped. 'What mortgage? Don't tell me you took out a loan on the house?'

'I did on Mellowstone Grange. We'll have to sell that as well.'

'But that's…' Hal's voice had trailed off; what was the point? His father knew his plans for the charity. The row had got louder until James had slammed out of the house and Hal started to look through the accounts.

Now Hal had spent an appalling morning sending out e-mails, letters and making calls cancelling subscriptions. With every cancellation he chided himself for a fool. He had never thought to question where the money had come from. Certainly his family had grown up comfortably, but during his childhood there had been few acquisitions. If pressed to explain the newfound abundance of wealth he had assumed that the money came from Odette. He had always lived with money, more money didn't strike him as suspicious. When his father had built him a physiotherapy pool to help with his ACL injury, he had simply accepted it with gratitude.

Telling his father he would fix everything, he was slightly alarmed at the alacrity with which James handed over all the passwords to all the accounts. Over the next few days, James took to walking out over the fields of his estate. Each morning he headed out with the dogs, only returning in the evening. Hal thought he was saying goodbye to the place and gearing up for the inevitable loss of the family home. Hal was determined that that would not happen, but for a while it was going to be hairy. He went off in search of his father whilst trying to avoid Odette. An earlier conversation with her had been difficult and he winced recalling her admonishment and his sharp reply.

'You mustn't blame your father.'

'Odette, I don't. Of course I don't, but please don't interfere. It's clear that he overextended in an attempt to flatter his new bride. When we are in love we do stupid things. He is to blame but how can I be angry at him? Just please don't lecture me right now. I have to try to save this estate. God knows what this is doing to his heart.'

Remembering the poor state of his father's health, he was at a loss as to how to broach the subject. He was trying so hard not to be angry, but if only his father had loosened the reins earlier, Hal might have been able to head off some of the problems. Although, of course, now it was obvious why he hadn't wanted his son further involved; James must have known he was overextended but was refusing to acknowledge it. Now it was here, front and centre and threatening bankruptcy.

He found his father in the gunroom, polishing some of his beloved guns. Hal knew the story behind each gun; he remembered the pride when his father first allowed him to use them. Now he just wondered how much he could sell them for. The problem was that Christie's and all the other major auction houses were about to be flooded with a glut of precious antiques.

'Hello, Dad. I think we're going to have to sell some of the paintings.'

James looked up from his twelve-bore Purdy but didn't reply.

Hal tried again. 'Can we have a look around the house? I was thinking about the little Degas?'

James looked at him in horror. 'Absolutely not, that was my wedding gift to your mother.'

'Then it will have to be the Canaletto.'

If it was possible for James to look even more appalled it was hard to imagine. 'How can you even suggest that? We bought that on our honeymoon.'

Hal tried to keep his temper.

'Dad, if we don't raise some serious funds we are going to lose the entire estate. I've already instructed the agents to put Mellowstone on the market. Tomorrow I'm in London meeting the accountants. You need to be prepared to get rid of stuff that mean a lot to you.'

James returned to his gun, polishing the butt. 'Take what you like then,' he spat at Hal. 'Take the sodding Canaletto, take the Degas. Do what you want.'

Hal sighed and left the room. What the hell was going to become of them?

***

Hal leant against the bridge and watched as the Thames flowed on below him. How blissful it would be to jump on a boat and just sail away from all this mess. He had got engaged to a woman he didn't love. The mother of his child wanted nothing to do with him and so far, he had had no involvement with her pregnancy. He had a barely formed charity about to collapse, a father he couldn't stand to be in the same room as, and he was facing bankruptcy. His meeting with the estate's accountant had been ugly. The man had spent most of the time explaining why he wasn't to blame for any of his own advice over the decades. Hal knew that at the end of the day the decision did rest with his father, but who had been encouraging him to take out those more speculative investments? Who made a profit on those leads? The final slap had been when the man had had the nerve to draw Hal's attention to his outstanding bill. Hal pointed out that he was part of a long line of people waiting to be paid. Maybe if he'd done his job better, he wouldn't now be standing, cap in hand, along with the others.

Looking back, he knew he'd been harsh and somewhat unfair. Honesty is what he needed right now, not finding people to blame.

'Pretty, isn't it?'

Hal looked up, startled that someone had managed to approach him without him noticing. Looking across he was instantly reminded of Paddy and a massive smile cracked his face, but this girl had short dark hair and his smile softened in remembrance of Paddy and then he shook himself. This wasn't Paddy; this was some girl out on a daily run. Shaking his head he remembered she had asked him a question.

'Pretty?'

'The city. Look at it. Full of people, yet paying them not a single bit of notice. It thrives and moves and we just have to negotiate around it.'

'You make it sound like a living thing in itself.'

'That's how I see it. The buildings are like giant underground volcanic stacks; they grow on hot air, rising higher and higher. Between the buildings, the money flows in shoals, large single predators, small packs easily spooked and decimated. Giant slow-moving leviathans. And there we are, the little plankton, trying to avoid joining the food chain.'

'Poet?'

'The poetical pundit, I like it.' Looking at Hal again she was glad to see a smile on his face. For a moment she had thought he was a jumper, but now she decided he was just a man with a lot on his mind.

'Harrington's?'

'Is it that obvious? God, did you think I was going to jump!' He looked appalled and ran his hand through his hair. 'My life is just about the only thing I've got left, I'm not going to lose that as well. Plus, I need to find a way to launch my charity, which quite frankly, everyone is telling me to ditch.'

'Fancy a coffee? I might be able to help?'

He looked her up and down with a raised eyebrow. 'You don't look like someone who can help, if you don't mind me saying?' She was dressed in lycra and trainers and not at all what he thought of when he imagined a financial analyst.

'Phew,' she dramatically wiped her hands across her brow. 'Let me ask. Your current adviser? Blue pinstriped shirt. White collar. Navy suit. Large heavy gold watch?'

'Do you know Clive?'

'I know all the Clives. And I know how much money they have lost for their clients and nearly brought the whole bloody city to its knees in the past week. Harringtons has made the whole thing completely unstable at the moment.'

Hal looked at the grinning girl. 'Why are you smiling? It's making me feel sick.'

'Partly because I didn't lose anything and partly because this is what I love.' She tucked her earbuds into her pocket. 'Come on. Let's have that coffee and see if I can help. My shout.'

Hal looked out over the river and back to the girl. What else was he going to do? 'I think I can still afford a coffee. But why me?'

'Oh I don't know. Good feeling. Plus that was a bloody lovely smile you gave me when I said hello. I only have one client but I like to help others out now and then.'

'And they haven't lost a penny over this fiasco?'

'A bit, simply because the market has slumped. But we've already clawed that back and are beginning to make some decent investments elsewhere. Everything is in flux. It's fun!'

'You're not very tactful, are you?'

'What's the point? You're not about to top yourself? Tact and deference got you into this mess.'

'You are quite wise, if irritating.'

'So you've given up on tact as well then?'

Hal laughed. 'Do you know, you don't half remind me of someone.'

'Good or bad.'

257

'Oh definitely good.'

'Was that who you thought I was, when you smiled at me?'

'Funnily enough yes.' His face fell then, thinking about yet another area of his life that was a total screw up.

'Mate, don't worry about it. If she stops liking you because you're broke she ain't worth the effort. I'm Nick by the way.'

'Nice to meet you, Nick, but the fact is she didn't like me much before the crash either.'

He was about to spill his woes to another stranger; he must be suffering from verbal diarrhoea. He just wanted to talk about Paddy at any opportunity. Sam had laughed at him and then told him to step up. He imagined this girl would be the same.

'Anyway, enough of that. I'm Henry by the way.' The couple walked off the bridge towards a little coffee shop Nick favoured.

'So, who is your client?' He could see Nick weighing up whether she was going to share that information with him and was about to tell her it didn't matter when she piped up.

'Old English family.'

'With no Harrington connections?'

'Oh sure,' she scoffed, 'there were loads when I took the account on but oh boy, when I started looking into Harrington's I didn't like what I saw, so I pulled them out smartish. Bada boom, bada bing!' She slapped her hands on the table attracting attention from some of the patrons; most smiled and nodded when they saw who it was.

'My God, the bonus you'll get this year will be stupendous,' said Hal.

She shrugged and grinned. 'I guess. Now let's start looking at your problems.'

They were tucked away on a corner table and for the rest of the afternoon she ordered drinks and drilled him and took notes. At the end of the session, she leant back and stretched.

'Right, this afternoon I'll send you an e-mail of what I think you should do. The first being ditch your accountant. I have the name of a few young firms I rate. Check them out but make up your own mind. Investigate all my suggestions. I don't know the ins and outs of your money, but you should. Some of these tips may not work. I'll highlight which I think are riskier. I think you can save the house and most of your land. Selling off the Grange is a good call, as is the pictures. But let your stepmother have her subscription to *Vogue* back. Life's going to be grotty for a few years, let her have her little pleasures.'

She took a glug of water. 'Regarding the charity. Launch it but use your own money. You won't find investors now anyway. You will need to cut to the bone for the charity but it's worthwhile, so do it. Make your money mean something before you lose any more of it. I have an idea for an alternative venue which I think you'll like, but let me get in touch with my sister. Now, this was fun. Thanks for letting me help. I'll mail you later, plus my sister might write in a week or so.'

Hopping up from the table Nick called out to the chap behind the bar that she'd settle the tab later; flexing a bit she

259

then ran off back into Canary Wharf. Hal felt like he'd been run over by a steam train. Could he dare hope?

Chapter Thirty

The door slammed open and Paddy, Leo and William ran into the kitchen and hugged Dickie. Both boys were shouting, claiming victory whilst Paddy exclaimed she had given them a head start. Amongst all the noise, Dickie pointed out that a race into the kitchen was not the safest of ideas. This earnt an apologetic glance and a worried look from the boys; Dickie had lots of weird strict rules, plus she might not give them any biscuits now.

'Why don't the three of you go and put a film on and I'll dig out some biscuits.' The boys cheered and Paddy shooed them out of the kitchen.

'On you go, boys, pick out something with lots of dinosaurs or monsters in it and I'll tell you which ones you smell like!'

The boys laughed and shouted, running off towards the playroom.

Dickie smiled at Paddy. She had been with them almost two months now and was positively blooming. It was lovely when the sisters came to stay, each of them was another slice of their mother, but she felt Paddy was the most like Lily. Kind, romantic and full of self-doubts.

'Go on, go and join them, I'll bring it all through. Nice to see some colour in your cheeks at last.' Everyone now knew Paddy was pregnant and had gone out of their way to ensure she had everything she needed. Even if she was still barely showing, the constant vomiting was a clear sign. The fact that Ari was also pregnant and already far larger than Paddy had irked her no end. She had grumbled to Dickie about it who promptly asked if she would swap that for all of Paddy's vomiting and she laughed and shook her head. Plus, as Dickie pointed out sharply to Ari, Ari was one month further along and this wasn't her first pregnancy. Now she smiled at Paddy. 'Oh and your sister was looking for you; she's probably back in her study. And try to look fat, cheer her up.'

Laughing, she stuck her head into the playroom Paddy told the boys she would be with them shortly. Any disappointment was quickly lost when she told them Dickie was on her way with popcorn. 'And make sure you save me some!'

Paddy headed off in search of Ari, grinning to herself. Life was good. She loved her nephews and was so excited about being able to introduce them to their new little cousin. She could now feel Baby moving around on a regular basis and the moments when she felt that little quiver inside her were the highlights of her day. At six months she was still barely showing and was still able to go running and swimming. She hadn't even had to go up a dress size yet. That had alarmed her but she had started to read loads about it and it turned out to be nothing to worry about. So long as she could feel the little one moving around, things were fine. And she had never felt happier. Her hands constantly strayed down to her tummy and she would often find herself talking out loud to her baby. Ari was right, this was going to be a huge adventure. When she pictured the future, Hal always featured until Paddy banished him from the image. She felt she was getting better at it but it was so hard; every time she thought of the baby she thought of Hal.

She couldn't help but think who Baby would look like. Would they have red hair like her or Hal's wavy blond hair? She had green eyes, Hal's were a stunning bright blue with flecks in them that... Enough! Sighing, she reminded herself to dismiss her daydreams and focus on the things that were, not the things that she wanted. As she got to Ari's office, she knocked on the door and entered.

Ari looked at her puzzled. 'Why did you knock?'

'The door was closed?'

'Fair enough.' Ari put her pen down. 'It's weird, isn't it. I still can't get used to the fact I have a room where people knock before entering. How mad is that?'

'It's all been a bit mad. Like having a title. I can barely bring myself to use it.'

'In the beginning, Dickie made we wear mine every time I went out.' Paddy laughed remembering. 'Any public occasion, she would make all the staff address me formally until no one, and most importantly me, could possibly forget. Surprisingly, it did help. Although thankfully everyone now seems to know who I am, even if I sometimes forget. Anyway, I was trying to find you. You and Nick are doing your twin thing again. She phoned earlier; she knows of a fledgling charity that is looking for somewhere to offer short holidays to homeless young people. What do you think? Would Kensey House be suitable?'

Paddy thought it would be excellent. Given the recent financial turmoil Ari had been looking at the books and felt now was the time to strengthen their assets. The Cornish venture was the most profitable strand of all the estate holdings and the one that was easiest to ramp up as well.

'I also want to green light the holiday cottage renovations. I've been going through the figures and that seems like a smart investment.'

The two sisters started talking it through, until they were interrupted by a knock on the door. A sad looking William stood beside his brother. 'The dinosaurs ate all the popcorn!'

'Not the monsters?' queried their mother.

'Them too,' nodded Leo solemnly.

Paddy turned to Ari. 'Join us? If I'm away tomorrow, let's spend some time together. We have movies, hot chocolate and popcorn lined up although we might need to rustle up some more of the latter.'

Ari laughed, paperwork be blowed, there was always paperwork.

***

Waving goodbye to Seb at Newquay airport, Paddy thought how lovely it was of him to share the drive home with her. She had arrived in Norfolk two months earlier, exhausted and upset and whilst she was feeling a lot better, she hadn't been looking forward to the return drive. She was six months pregnant now and still seemed to be constantly tired. Everyone she asked had a different opinion on when it would pass.

When Seb had insisted he drove down to Cornwall with her and catch a flight home, she hadn't even debated it with him. It had also been decided that if she was going to have the baby in Norfolk, that Seb would fly down and then drive her back up to Norfolk. They had decided she would come up by week thirty-six. If she decided to stay in Cornwall one of the others was going to come and stay with her until it was all done and dusted. Paddy suspected that *all done and dusted* wasn't a very cosy maternal term but at the moment she had no idea what motherhood was going to be like. Especially on her own. Well, not on her own, she apologised to Baby, but on her own in terms of someone else being able to help. Sighing, Paddy reversed the car and then headed back home.

Seb had loved the cottage and asked her if she swam much. She told him about the seal around the corner, and he regretted not packing any swimming trunks. As much as he loved swimming in Norfolk he had to guiltily agree that the coastal waters of Cornwall were exceptional. Those blue green waters glistened like beautiful jewels and he knew that he and his family would probably be spending a week or two here every year for the rest of the children's childhood. Paddy had also shown him around Kensey House and he agreed it would work perfectly as a holiday retreat for various charities, as well as a family bolthole. If only a few of the family came to stay, the beach cottage was perfect; if everyone descended then they could all pile into the big house.

He admired his sister-in-law's confidence; she seemed so optimistic but she seemed awfully under prepared for the reality of motherhood. Her heart had already been broken by one romantic misadventure. He wondered how she would cope when she was exhausted and lonely and the romantic glow of motherhood had been washed away by the tiredness. He agreed with the sisters' assessment that no husband was better than a bad husband, but he was worried for Paddy. It seemed wrong to leave her in a county where she knew no one and was pregnant and all alone. Paddy had laughed and told him it was going to be a great big adventure and he wasn't to be such a worry wart.

His lips twitched remembering that, and yet parenthood was like being hit by a tsunami. He loved Leo and Will and was increasingly thinking of them as his own flesh and blood. But they were draining at times. He wondered if it would be easier if they were his. Then he would look at Ari, the most patient and loving mother in the world, storm out of the room in a fit of temper and he saw that children were simply exhausting. But at least he and Ari had each other, they also had staff that helped with the load and his folk were only a few miles away. The boys sat in the middle of an entire network of love and support. Down here, Paddy's baby would have a network of one. Paddy would be completely on her own.

Sitting waiting for his plane to taxi he sent out a few texts to friends in Cornwall suggesting they may want to extend a few invitations out. He didn't think Paddy would mind and would be likely to say yes to anything that interested her.

***

Pulling back into the drive, having dropped Seb off, Paddy looked around her with a huge smile on her face, she loved it here. The warm July air smelt of the sea and she thought she could detect the hint of a barbeque drifting across from the village. There were some boats out in the bay and Paddy watched as teenagers dived off the sides, shrieking with laughter as they did so. Walking back into the cottage, she picked up the small pile of mail that Michelle had popped through her letterbox. Nick had hired Michelle Fawkes to run the house admin and enterprise and Paddy had seen immediately how good a fit she was. Paddy wasn't sure how she would manage an assistant but she saw the sense of it especially with her pregnancy. Michelle had previous experience in running country house hotels and this was the same sort of feel Paddy wanted for Kensey House.

Looking at the mail, Paddy could see it was mostly invitations and postcards but a heavy white envelope stood out. She turned it over and saw the return address was from the production company. Tears prickled her eyes. She couldn't bring herself to open it. What was the point? Instead she placed it on the mantlepiece and decided to try and shake off the sudden sense of total despair. Placing some Sibelius on her record player she flung open the windows and headed down to the beach.

Following the swim Paddy felt re-invigorated. Yes, her life wasn't going according to plan but so what? She had money, she had family, she had a home and best of all she was pregnant. She and Baby were going to have a wonderful time of it. Flicking on her laptop, she noticed several of her new e-mails were invitations. Typical Seb. How nice to have someone thinking of her and looking out for her. Ari had a good one there. She was worried that accepting these invitations would mean bumping into Hal, but she was going to have to cross that bridge sooner or later. Maybe he was still on honeymoon. Maybe their boat would just sail away and never come back. She was miserable just thinking how much she wanted to see him and also, never see him again.

Damn it. Sink or swim, she had to get on with it. Before she RSVP'd them, she would run them past Jemima. If Jemima still wanted to have anything to do with her. She sent her a quick text saying she was back in Cornwall and did she want to meet up? Now she would discover whether that awful scene at the charity function had sunk her boat. Relieved, the phoned pinged straight back with Jem suggesting a horse ride.

Paddy texted back saying she'd love to but she was a bit pregnant and then laughed when Jem sent a picture of a watermelon and they arranged for Paddy to head over the following day on the single condition that Hal or Bianca were not to be mentioned once. Life was going to be good. She had a new business venture, she had a friend in Jemima and she was pregnant. A whole new life lay before her and she was looking forward to it. Baby gave her a little kick in agreement and Paddy found herself laughing out loud.

Chapter Thirty-One

Sam became aware of the dark skies gradually giving way to daylight. Whilst he was used to the light sleep of the homeless, he was unused to the country noises. Every snuffle or sound jarred him out of his sleep and he would be instantly alert, his eyes straining in the dark for monsters to come looming out of the trees. In truth he had probably had one of his worst night's sleep in months, which was saying something for a lad who had become used to sleeping on the streets of London. Stretching, he swept the leaves and twigs off his new charity shop clothes.

After Henry Ferguson had given him that money, he had spent a few weeks deciding what to do. Eventually he decided to head west. When he arrived in Cornwall he wanted to make a good impression, so he'd also spent some of the money on a room for the night and had showered himself raw, scrubbing at his hands and feet and washing his hair a few times. In the morning, the breakfast servers had teased him for being such a pretty boy and whilst he laughed, he knew that that wasn't necessarily a smart look for a homeless lad in London. Time to hit the road.

He dumped the clothes he had been wearing but was loath to dump his rucksack and other belongings in case this all proved to be a colossal hoax or joke. Or worse. London streets weren't the only places that offered dangers for the vulnerable. For the next two days he wandered the streets looking out for friends he had made along the way giving them tens and twenties until he was down to his last £20 and then he stuck out his thumb and began to hitch west.

The idea of wasting £200 on a train ticket was laughable. Hitching was free and it was wonderful to be able to spread some of his luck out to others. Maybe he was a fool but it had felt good and that was something he hadn't felt often in the past year.

Now here he was sleeping in a ditch. A little warm lump beside him stirred and a wet nose twitched the air around her. Lucky had slept well; so long as she was by her master, life was fine. Sam ruffled her head and began to remove leaves from her coat. This had been the last thing he did as he left London. He had bought her from Old Tom for £30 and renamed her Lucky.

His last hitch had got him to the train station that Hal had recommended and he had started to follow instructions from a local taxi cab as to how to walk to Vollen. But he either got lost or it was further than he expected and the night caught him before he found his destination. He decided to bed down and try again in the morning. It meant he was a bit smellier and dirtier than he had intended but there was nothing he could do about that.

Slinging his rucksack on his back he set off tramping down the road with Lucky by his side, in the hope that he would happen upon his destination. He'd never been to Cornwall before and was surprised by how green it was. Small fields everywhere, lots of trees, tiny roads and seemingly no people. Overhead a large group of birds circled and cawed, moving from field to tree and back again; in another field he saw two deer run out of sight. Everyone was waking up. There was a rumble behind him and an impossibly large tractor was bearing down on them. Waving, the farmer leant out of his cab having switched the engine off. Sam couldn't work out how the tractor was going to pass him without squishing him flat. He'd need to climb up into the hedge.

'You're up early!'

'Them birds are noisier than an alarm clock. Am I on the right road for Vollen?'

The farmer scratched his ear. 'You're a bit off track but I tell you what, I'm dropping off near there after this. Is it the house or the farm you want?'

Sam wasn't sure but he guessed he was after the house. He showed the farmer the card Hal had given him.

'The house it is then. Right, let's get you in the tractor. Walk on down the lane here till you get to the gate. There'll be room then for me to get past you and you can climb up. I'll get you a bit closer and then set you on your path. You might even make it for breakfast.'

A minute later Sam and Lucky had climbed up into the cab of the tractor. As they rumbled down the lanes Sam looked out over the tops of the hedges. The tractor seats were more comfortable than he ever imagined. And heated! Lucky sat in the footwell, excited by all the strange smells. She was used to being cold and hungry and occasionally waking up by bodies that were stiff and smelt wrong. Now she was surrounded by lots of strange smells that made her feel happy and excited. Plus her new companion smelt young and full of energy. Life was good.

The farmer laughed when Sam exclaimed about the seats. All mod cons in this little beauty and he went on at

271

length to tell Sam all the ins and outs of his tractor. A father holding his newborn could not have glowed with greater pride and Sam enjoyed listening to the man talk of things that meant nothing to him. As the tractor pulled up, Sam was almost reluctant to part ways. Warmth was not a thing he was used to. Neither was kindness. Jumping down he thanked the man and he and Lucky set off down a new lane; apparently the turning for the house was half a mile on the right. 'Just look out for the huge granite boulder. The house name is on that and then just head on down the drive. They're a good enough sort there.'

Half an hour later he found himself wandering down a drive lined with big bushes. He was brushing himself down when a massive baying of hounds sounded out and Sam found himself surrounded by five or six very noisy dogs. Lucky cowered around his legs; these smells were a bit scary. Sam could hear a man shouting and the dogs all sat down around him as Hal walked into view.

'Hello?' The man did a double take and Sam was worried that he wouldn't remember him. 'Sam? Hello, you made it!' Striding up he gave Sam a vigorous handshake and apologised for the dogs. 'It's a wall of sound thing, they are more likely to deafen you than anything else. Did you catch the night train?'

When Sam explained he'd hitched Hal laughed but didn't ask what had happened to the money. 'Come along. Help me feed the hounds; we've just had our morning walk as well and then we'll have some breakfast? Yes?'

Suddenly he spotted Lucky.

'Hello! Who's this?' Squatting on his haunches he extended his hand towards Lucky to sniff. 'Good girl. Did my lot scare you? All bluster.' As he scratched her ear she relaxed and began to wag her tail. 'Good girl. Yes you are!'

Standing up he smiled at Sam. 'New addition?' and listened appreciatively as Sam explained Lucky's history.

'Come on then, there's always room for another mouth.'

After a big breakfast he introduced Sam to Brian. He explained that Sam was a new apprentice and asked Brian to put him to work. He would catch up with them later in the day and show Sam his new accommodation. Brian gave Hal a nod and he knew that lad would be in good hands.

Heading towards the house Hal knew he had done the right thing. He had helped Sam, Sam had helped his friends. It all knocked on. There was no way he could abandon his charity when he could see it in action. He needed to raise more money and he knew what he needed to do, although he knew it was going to hurt him.

He went off to the library. He had never thought in his wildest dreams he would sell his mother's Fabergé snowdrops, but seeing Sam had woken him up. There were more important things in the world than possessions. He knew his mother would understand. With the money he could raise from them he would be able to properly launch his charity and help lots of lost souls like Sam.

A few minutes later he left the library calling out for Odette and found her in the long sitting room.

'Where are my mother's snowdrops? I couldn't see them in the library. Have they been moved?'

Odette looked worried and wished James was here. She had already raised her concerns with him, and he had told her categorically to drop the subject. He would talk to Hal about them. Now it was clear that he hadn't.

'They are missing.'

Hal looked at her in horror. 'What do you mean, missing?'

'They disappeared the night you broke off your engagement with Bianca. I went into the library the following day and noticed one of the chairs had been pushed up against the shelves and there was a muddy stiletto print on the seat of the chair. I assumed that Bianca had helped herself.'

'Why the hell didn't you say something? Odette, I'm sorry, but those little flowers aren't just from my mother, they're also rather valuable.'

'Oh Hal, of course I said something. I went to your father straightaway and told him what had happened and he said he would deal with it. That under no circumstance was I to worry you about it.'

Odette looked ready to cry and he felt awful, snapping at the older lady. She had never shown him anything other than love and compassion.

'I'm sorry. Forgive me.' He wiped his hand across his face and sighed. 'Let me speak to Bianca. It's about time I wished her congratulations on her recent wedding.'

He was livid. He couldn't believe Bianca had taken the flowers. He had vowed never to contact her again after Hugo told him about the wedding but this broke that pledge. He had wasted too many nights feeling regret for the way he had treated her. The slate was clean, or at least it would be when he got his mother's flowers back.

Chapter Thirty-Two

Odette had been trying to read her new book with decreasing success over the past half hour. She had been looking forward to this new release for months and had picked it up yesterday from her local bookshop. All she wanted to do was lose herself in the salt marshes of Norfolk and find out what the wonderful archaeologist was going to do next. However, each paragraph was interrupted by raised voices. James and Hal were fighting again. This past month had been nothing but fights. For a while she thought something was going on with Hal. He appeared lighter and more optimistic. Ending his engagement had clearly been a blessing to him; she had watched him relax and laugh and he seemed utterly unconcerned that that wretched baggage had gone and married someone else at their own wedding. She had been mortified for him, but now was delighted to see how little he seemed to care. In fact when she endured the gossipy commiserations, she was able to take a leaf from his book and brush it off as beneath notice. She was also delighted to see his charity unfolding. This morning she had met a lovely young man called Sam who was an absolute treasure.

But the financial mess they were all in, seemed to be having an effect on Hal. He was increasingly becoming morose. She thought things were on the turn when he came back from London with a rescue package for the finances. Certainly they appeared to have stepped back from the edge of bankruptcy and yet something was still troubling him.

Now he was shouting at his father as loudly as James was shouting back at him. This was unusual. Her stepson was always the pacifier; what on earth was going on? She picked up her book again just as the door to the office slammed shut with tremendous force. '*ça alors!*' She muttered to herself as she put her book down, and headed towards the office just as she heard the patio doors in the breakfast room crash against their frame. Changing direction, she headed towards the breakfast room and watched as her stepson stormed off across the garden towards the woods. Gently, she closed the doors properly and hoped all the glass panes were still secure in their wooden frames. The Lord know, they couldn't afford to have them repaired right now.

Deciding it was probably time to interfere she headed back to the study. As she started to open the door James roared 'Get out' and she quickly retreated. Moving around the house she grabbed a toasting fork and a napkin and tied it around the end. Returning to the study, this time she knocked on the door calling his name. As she did so, she opened the door ajar and waved her little white flag. She heard a grunt of laughter and gently entered the office.

The room was in chaos. At some point all the papers on the desk had been swept off onto the floor along with the laptop and lamp shade. The paper basket had been kicked over and the bust of Wellington had been knocked of its pedestal. As James watched Odette survey the damage he saw her mouth twitch at Wellington's distress.

'Your man Napoleon should have taken a leaf out of your book,' he said pointing to her flag. As she bent to pick it up James stopped her. 'This is my mess. I'll fix it. At least I can get that right.' He paused unable to express all that he had got wrong.

Walking to his side Odette knelt down beside him and lay her head on his lap. For a while neither spoke, and Odette prayed Hal didn't return before she understood what the problem was. She knew if he returned now, the fighting would resume and both men might go a step too far. In fact, looking around the room she wondered if that hadn't already happened.

'James, my love, nothing you can say will make me love you any less but it is hurting me to see you in pain. To see you both in pain. Please, what is happening?'

James stroked her hair; he was so ashamed and he had no idea how to resolve things. Maybe the best thing would be to just get it out in the open. Declare himself a fool and see where the chips fell. His son despised him, now it was time for his wife to hear the truth.

'I've betrayed my son.' He felt Odette's body tense but he continued. 'I sold the Fabergé flowers.'

'I thought they had been stolen?'

'As it happens, I think you were right. I do think Bianca stole that set, but that was an insurance copy. Hal didn't know.' He absently stroked his wife's hair and cast his eye vacantly back to the past, to a time when he was once again, out of his depth. 'Donkey's years ago, our insurance company had suggested that if we wanted to display them that we had a copy made and kept the genuine one here in the safe. Hal was only a small boy at the time and he loved picking it up and watching as the little blooms swung on their stalks. So it made sense to have a replica. When his mother died, she specifically

278

named the flowers as going to him. I mean, obviously everything is going to him, but she named these.'

'Did Hal know about the copy?'

'No, it just never came up. It certainly didn't seem important. Not when we were burying Eleanor and after that…' he trailed off, looking out of the window and across the grounds to where a large tree stood in the park land. Eleanor's great-great-grandfather had no doubt had that oak planted just so, so that a future generation could look out and admire it. 'The thing is, all this was in her blood, oh I mean my family did well enough, but Eleanor had all this in her veins. When we married, she joked she was looking forward to just being a wife and mother. It was only when she died that I discovered how much I had relied on her counsel and how much she did behind the scenes. When she had gone, I started to make mistakes. Little things. But then I tried out new things and they mostly didn't work either. Eventually I saw I needed a clean slate financially, so I sold the Fabergé. I was constantly drunk; I wasn't thinking and I sold it.'

'You were still grieving.'

'No excuse.' He took in a deep breath. 'And then I met you. And I never thought I could love again but it, you, were like a tidal wave. I wanted you to notice me and admire me. I began to show off. I hadn't learnt my lesson. I started borrowing money again. I took out a mortgage. I wanted to wine and dine you. In the end all I have done is disgrace myself.'

He sat in silence looking out over the oak tree again waiting for Odette to speak. He felt her move, and as she looked up at him, he could see tears of mascara slowly smudging down her face. He pulled out a handkerchief and dabbed her cheeks. 'I am so sorry, my darling Odette.'

Odette sighed, how to fix this sorry mess? 'Come on, my dear, help me up, I'm not a teenager anymore.' Leaning on his hand she stood up and removed some of the fallen papers from the other armchair. She took a deep breath, careful how to phrase her words.

'James, I love you. Not your beautiful house, or your fine grounds, or your prosperous bank account. I love you. I love your love of the countryside. I love your sense of humour. I love your gallantry. I love your passion. And now I love your honesty as well. That has taken great courage.'

'Didn't you hear what I just said?'

'You've messed up financially and you sold something that wasn't yours to sell. Yes, I heard you. And I still love you.'

James stood up and went over to the decanter to pour himself a whiskey, offering Odette a glass. It was only just after lunch but neither cared.

Now it was James's turn to take a deep breath. 'So, what do I do now?'

Odette was startled, this was the first time he had ever asked her for help and she realised she may have been remiss in not fully understanding her proud English husband. She always thought he had everything under control and had happily left him to it. All she had done was work to bring father and son back together, and make sure the domestic and social life of the house ran smoothly. It had never occurred to her to enquire after the estate or the business.

'Is it possible to buy back the Fabergé?' James snorted, so she quickly moved on. '*C'est tout*. Maybe instead you step back more and let Hal have the full running of the estate? We could go on a little holiday maybe. Or spend some time at Honfleur?'

After her first husband had died, Odette couldn't bear to sell her home and had kept it. She and James would stay there from time to time and he enjoyed it.

'Hmm, good shooting around there.'

Odette sipped her whiskey. She had said enough. The rest now needed to come from him, but in her mind she was already walking across the French countryside.

***

Hal looked up as James walked into the study. He was about to ask what the latest batch of e-mails were about, but looking at his father he stopped. What was the point? Over the past few weeks James had lost all of his bravado; he looked like a tired old man and Hal was worried for his health. Badgering him about foolish decisions was not going to get them out of this mess. Yesterday's row had been apocalyptical but it hadn't changed anything. At least now he knew the full extent of this situation, and for just how long they had been sailing too close to the wind.

When his father had confessed that he had sold the snowdrops in an attempt to shore up the estate, Hal had been horrified and had exploded. As his father roared back at him the situation had quickly got out of hand and Hal had had to leave the house. Both men had already traded insults and Hal knew he was close to saying things he could never take back. He'd lost his mother; he didn't want to lose his father as well.

Looking at him now Hal was reminded of just how old his father was.

'Can we walk? I want to discuss something with you?' James almost looked humble. Even his demeanour had changed; from a blustering arrogant patriarch he had shrunk to a hesitant apologist. Hal didn't have the time to go for strolls around the estate, he was doing all he could to save it, but what else was he going to say? Pushing his chair back, the two men walked out through the patio windows and down to the flower gardens that Hal's mother had established.

'I'm going to leave.' James waved at his son, 'No, hear me out. I've made a god-awful mess of this, and if I stay, I'll only get in your way. Odette still has her house in Normandy and we are going to move there. Somewhere smaller and more manageable. I've already spoken to the solicitors and have arranged for everything to be signed over to you. The deeds, the accounts, the lot. We'll be leaving next week.'

Hal looked at his father in disbelief. He had screwed it all up and now was running away?

'Are you joking?'

'No of course not. Why would you say that?' Some of James's defensive bluster rose to the surface. 'It's what you've always wanted, now you get to run the estate without interference.'

'Why would I say that?! Are you kidding? I need you here; I can't do this all by myself.'

James softened. 'You'll be fine. I didn't mean to sound so petulant but the truth of the matter is that I've made a mess of all this. If you need me, I'll only be a phone call away. I've even heard that the French have the internet, so we can do that face call thing.'

James pulled out some weeds from around the base of the roses. 'Look, son, the fact of the matter is, I'm proud of you, and I'm ashamed of myself. Selling the Fabergé was so wrong of me, but at the time I was drowning and trying to cover it all up. Everywhere I look at the moment is like a sore wound. And I—' he broke off and tried to clear his throat, his voice breaking. Abruptly, he turned and walked back to the house, leaving Hal standing amongst the flower beds appalled at his father's distress.

Hal sat on the stone bench and remembered chatting with his mother about how she had envisaged the swathes of colours, blooming in soft clouds of pinks and blues. Together they had dug the soil and planted various tubers and seedlings. Now they bloomed and drifted in the breeze, the sweet smell of roses reminding him of better days; but now his mother was dead and his father was leaving. With all his heart he had wanted to sit here with his child and show them the same things but as he struggled daily to get the finances under control he wondered if he was going to have to sell the place off to the highest bidder. His father had let his mother down, he had let his son done. Now Hal saw the parallels all over again. He had let Paddy down but he would not fail his child or his mother. Vollen was theirs and he would fight to save it. Even if he had to sacrifice any work on his charity until the estate was secured.

With a deep sigh he headed back to the house. He would try to convince his father to stay, talk it through with him, but when he got there, his car was gone and he and

Odette must have gone out for the day. He swore out loud. When had his father become such a coward? Hal returned to his spreadsheet and e-mails and continued on. What else was there to do?

Chapter Thirty-Three

Hal put the letter down and looked out of the breakfast window. The contents seemed a gift from heaven and he wanted to pause and take in the enormity of the offer.

His father and Odette walked in and he passed the letter to his father. 'Do you know the de Foixes? The Countess Hiverton?'

James was silent as he read the letter, and Odette poured them both a cup of tea asking Hal what was happening. He was dumbstruck. 'It seems the Hiverton Estate has heard of my charity's situation and have offered Kensey House as a possible venue for respite holidays. According to the letter, if I'm agreeable, I can meet with one of the family to discuss it, a Lady Patricia de Foix. Do you know her?'

Odette shook her head. Growing up in France she had fewer connections with the English titled classes than her predecessor, Eleanor, did. 'Is that where you did that filming back in winter? I don't think I know anyone over on that side of Cornwall. James? Do you know them?'

James looked up. 'Not much; of course Kensey House and Tregiskey village have been in their hands for centuries. It's been run well but remotely and I don't think the last generations had much to do with Cornwall. There was some sort of tragedy or scandal and I remember wondering at the time if the family would flounder, but it seems they had more backbone than I gave them credit for.

Odette turned to Hal. 'So what does this mean?'

Hal took a deep breath, his voice imperceptibly shaking with relief. 'It means that frightened teenagers can sleep in clean beds and play by the seaside. It means they can be safe and restart their lives.' He paused and looked up at Odette, an idiotic grin plastered across his face. 'It's hope, Odette.' Throwing his arms around her he lifted her up and spun her around laughing. 'It means hope!'

***

Paddy nervously tugged on her skirt. This was her second official role representing the family and she wanted to make sure she gave a good impersonation, her meeting in the village pub had been shaky. Today, she was going to project confidence and calm. So much had changed in those months and she barely recognised the girl she was back then.

Ari had been coaching her about confidence. 'No one is going to think you're a fraud. Don't be silly. Besides, you are offering something they desperately need. Nick vouched for this chap. Said he was deserving. Doesn't sound like the sort who will look down on you.'

Paddy was nervous and she knew it. Everyone knew Holly McDonald; people wanted her, she was in demand, they knew what to expect and she knew how to behave. Plus she very rarely had to talk. Lady Patricia was a very different creature. She'd called Clem, who was phased by nothing and no one, for advice.

'Be you. One hundred per cent Paddy. Lady Patricia will have to mould herself around you. If you try and do it the other way, you will always feel like an impostor.'

286

'But look at Ari, she's incredible at playing a countess.'

Clem scoffed at her down the phone. 'Seriously, Paddy, when wasn't Ari in charge? When wasn't she the most important person in the room? The title means nothing to her. She could be Empress Ariana. She'd still be the same. And so will you, Paddy. Don't let Lady Patricia be anyone else.'

She began pacing and wanted to go to the loo again. Why had no one told her that being pregnant made you an absolute slave to your bladder? Typically, that was the moment she heard a car pull up into the drive. With a groan she metaphorically crossed her legs and opened the front door and looked out in horror.

***

As Hal drove up towards Kensey he couldn't help but think back to the winter and to Paddy. The drive had been lined with trailers and camera crew, directions were being shouted out in German. The very air had been alive with promise and he had been very hungover. But then he had walked into that chapel and his heart had damn near stopped beating. A ray of light was shining down through the blue stained-glass window on to a vision drinking water. Her face was tipped up into the light and her white gown shone blue. As she looked his way she grinned and put her finger on her lips and hid the bottle in the pleats of her gown. Seconds later a make-up artist walked past her and then tutted and whipped out some lurid lipstick, and retouched her face. The bride had raised her eyebrows at Hal and was then called over to the director. At that moment Hal just wanted to follow her. To the other side of the chapel. To the ends of the earth. To a life together. Well, that hadn't turned out very well, had it? Maybe through his actions he could show her he wasn't the total tool she seemed to think he was.

He parked the car and, grabbing his attaché case with his proposals, he headed towards the front door. As the door opened, time seemed to slow. A young woman stepped out and Hal stared at Paddy in amazement, drinking in the sight of her like a man lost in the desert glimpsing an oasis. Months of longing hit him like a tidal wave, the force of it staggering. Love and yearning and desperation and hope and fear churned inside him, an emotional maelstrom that left him momentarily breathless. It only took a second for him to notice she was staring at him too - but where he was dazzled, she looked horrified. The flicker of hope that had ignited in his chest sputtered out.

'Are you Henry Fawkes. Founder of City and Sea?' Her voice was strained, her expression shuttered.

'Henry Ferguson Yes. I'm here to meet Lady Patricia de Foix?' He managed to get the words out around the lump in his throat. The e-mail had said Fawkes not Ferguson. He saw the confusion that flickered across her face before she collected herself.'

Let's head to the dining room,' she said tightly. He couldn't take his eyes off her as he followed her inside, his mind whirling. Was she a secretary? A personal assistant? Was that why she had been here? But no she was a model, not someone's assistant. Were they friends? Her clothes were loose and he couldn't tell if she was pregnant or not. Had she kept it? Had she lost it? Both options worried him. Was she still pregnant? The questions scalded his throat but he swallowed them back. As they settled down, she broke his train of thought.

'Right, some ground rules. We are here today to discuss you using our home as a location for your charity. That is all we will discuss. I don't wish to hear a single word of your private life. I am very sorry for my role in it, but what's done is done. I'm going to bring up the baby without anything from you. If you want to visit that will be fine, I will not hinder your access in anyway but I will never ask you for anything.' As she spoke, she ticked the points off her fingers.

Hal's whole body slumped in relief, she was still pregnant. He wanted to hug her.

Paddy watched as he relaxed and then smiled at her. How pleased he was to have her make no demands on him. She wanted to scream in pain at him. What had she expected? A declaration of love? A desire to stand by their child's side throughout their life? Clem had told her to be herself, but herself was a romantic idiot with a breaking heart. And as it happened, a full bladder.

'Excuse me. I'll be back in a minute.'

Wiping away her tears she looked at herself in the mirror. She had better get out there and she had better be Lady Patricia; as Ari had suggested, she was going to lean on the role. God, she wished Nick was here. Over the years she had forced herself to lean on her sister less and less, but at times like this she just wanted to run back to the love and safety of her family.

As she came back into the room she saw Hal hadn't sat down yet and was looking at her closely.

'Are you okay? Can I get you anything?' When she shook her head, he carried on. 'So, have I misunderstood? Are you Lady Patricia de Foix, Paddy? I'm sorry if I'm not following things.'

She cleared her throat. 'Yes, I am, but I don't think that's important right now, do you? As we are going to be working together, we shall have to agree to be professional. Yes? Once this is all up and running, I'll be returning to Norfolk and a manager will be running this place.'

'You're not staying?'

She laughed and was bloody proud of herself for being able to. 'No, why would I? There's nothing for me here. Now, let me show you around the house and grounds and you can decide for yourself if you think it's suitable.' She wasn't sure why she had said she wasn't staying, but seeing him again had torn open her broken heart and she realised she had just been kidding herself. She may have had only a one-night stand with him but she had fallen in love. What a stupid cliché. But now she was determined that he wouldn't see just how much he had broken her heart.

Hal had a thousand questions, none of which he could ask if he wanted to respect her wishes. As they walked around the house, he took notes and decided it would be perfect for the charity, although there may be a need to rearrange a few things. He suggested them to Paddy.

'That should be fine. As I said, it's a family home but it doesn't get used much so we thought the idea of it having a dual purpose may work out well. Longer term we were thinking that some of the outer barns might work as additional accommodation. Maybe for courses.'

They were standing now outside the chapel of the house. It was connected to the house by a small private door for the family only. Anyone else visiting the chapel came in through its main outside door.

Hal thought about it and then decided he could ask this question without annoying her.

'May I ask. Why didn't you mention you owned Kensey when we first met?'

'Was it important?' Paddy was looking out over the garden. She had been studiously avoided eye contact for the entire meeting.

'Well no but I rather assumed...'

Typical she thought. East End girl, East End accent, how could she possibly be the owner of Kensey House and a title? Now that he knew, did he like her more? Did it matter? With a curt reply she moved them away from the chapel.

'Yes. Now these lawns might be nice for outdoor games? And there's a large field over there which might be suitable for ball games or barbeques. I don't know. Just ideas.'

'I can see that. I think this will be perfect.' It was clear Paddy wasn't prepared to discuss their situation, so he tried to find out a bit more about her background. 'Tell me. The woman I met in London, Nick Byrne, is she your sister? Is she married? And the Countess Hiverton, is she your mother? I'm sorry. I just don't want to make any more assumptions.'

'Do you want us all in neat little pigeonholes?'

'No. I...'

Paddy shook her head. 'I'm sorry that was rude of me. It is confusing, isn't it?' she gave him a small smile. 'De Foix and Hiverton? Byrne and McDonald? Well let's see. You know about me as Holly McDonald. Byrne is our father's name. There are five of us by the way. Five sisters; Nick is my twin. Our parents died when I was fourteen. When our uncle, on mum's side of the family, died last year, Ari, my eldest sister, inherited the entire estate and became the Countess of Hiverton. Mum's maiden name was de Foix. Some of us girls are still jumping between the names until we decide what we're happiest with. So I'm either Holly McDonald, Paddy Byrne or Lady Patricia de Foix, depending on what I'm doing that day. Happy?'

Happy was the last word Hal would use to describe himself. But what a story and what a change of circumstances. No wonder he hadn't been able to reconcile her in his mind. Confident, shy, happy, timid. But now he was beginning to have a greater understanding of what must have driven her over the past ten years. In a moment of sudden clarity he knew he needed to move slowly. Insisting on making her answer his questions was the wrong way to try and win her around. At least now he knew who she actually was and how to find her. He had time, he could wait. The last few months had been awful but now he had hope. He decided to change tack.

'Where does that drive go to?'

'Private cottage. There won't be any access to that whatsoever. Come on let's look at the front of the house. There's a gate down there that joins the lane down onto the beach and a great pub.'

Paddy's spirits were beginning to flag; every time she found herself enjoying his company, she had to remind herself that he was married to Bianca. The sooner she left Cornwall the better. This was killing her.

'Now, have you seen everything? I don't want to sound rude but I'm tired and want to have a rest.' The words felt like shards of glass in her throat but she forced them out.

Hal was instantly solicitous, concern etching his features. 'Can I get you anything? Make you a cup of tea?' He stepped towards her but she stepped back and he halted.

Declining, Paddy walked with him around to his car, each step heavy with regret. Despite his best intentions he was unable to stop himself from asking after her health and the baby's.

Paddy felt a pang, touched by his concern even as she fought not to read too much into it. 'Baby is very healthy. Mummy keeps throwing up at any time of the day, and peeing constantly, but Baby is just perfect. Thank you for asking.'

Their eyes met and held, the air between them thick with loss and longing. For a suspended moment it felt like they were the only two people in the world, the only two who mattered. Then Paddy tore her gaze away.

With a murmured goodbye, she hurried back indoors so he wouldn't see her tears, closing the door behind her. She leaned back against it, a silent sob racking her body.

Hal walked slowly back to the car, sorrow and disappointment etched into every line of his body. He understood she wanted nothing to do with him, but he was going to show her that he would be the very best father. As he drove off, he dried his cheeks with the palm of his hand, grief a leaden weight in his stomach.

In the rearview mirror, he watched Kensey disappear from view, taking Paddy with it. He imagined her alone in that big house, managing on her own, and it was all he could do not to turn the car around and run back to her. What a sodding mess he had made of everything.

Chapter Thirty-Four

Paddy filled the kettle and then waited for the others to arrive. Yesterday, had been dreadful. She hadn't been expecting to see Hal but felt she had managed her emotions perfectly. Today was going to be a more thorough investigation of the concept and thankfully she wouldn't be alone. Michelle was due any minute and Paddy knew things were going to go well with her in the business. Like Paddy, she was determined it wasn't going to be a corporate getaway or some sort of institutional halfway house. Paddy wanted this to be a country home experience. She wanted people to feel as though they were staying with friends. That they could wander into the kitchen and flick the kettle on. Not stuck in their bedrooms or sat stiffly in an intimidating and uncomfortable sitting room. This was a place to properly relax, not feel out of place.

She remembered staying in a Devon hotel once for a photoshoot. She was suffering from terrible jet-lag and had woken up at four am and restless. Strolling around the large country house, she had stumbled across the night porter, preparing the morning papers and both had jumped. He had dismissed her apologies with a flourish and the two of them headed to the kitchens for a coffee and a bowl of porridge. In the silence of the house he had entertained her with tales of the original family and local folklore. In turn she helped him set out the papers, aware she had certainly disturbed his routine. He should not suffer for his kindness to her. Paddy didn't think for a second his employers would chide him, but she knew his sort. He was proud and rightly so, it was his job to ensure that when people woke up everything was in place and that every resident had slept well. Unaware of all his actions throughout the night.

She wanted people staying in Kensey to have the same sense of care and attention. Whoever they were. In the future, she had plans to develop the outbuildings into further accommodation or work units. Paddy had suggested working weekends where people came to learn a skill: painting, gardening, bookbinding. For that idea to work they would need work rooms. But that was several years in the future. For now Kensey's main function would be to provide rest and relaxation.

The doorbell rang and Michelle welcomed Hal and an older lady, who he had introduced as Andrea, his charity consultant. Andrea informed her she had a lot of experience in the social work field as well as charities. As she did so, Paddy had a feeling that Andrea was about to inform her of a lot of other things as well.

'I'm here to make sure things don't go off half-cocked in rampant overenthusiasm.' She had a tight smile which reminded Paddy of Professor Umbridge and she instantly found her cooling away from the woman. Her little introductory speech also seemed to catch Hal on the hop, as he tried to soften her statement with how grateful he was for all the help and support his new charity was garnering.

Heading into the dining room they all sat down, and Paddy began to outline her vision for Kensey House starting as a simple country house and later to a shared venue for course and corporate bookings. Between these bookings there would be the facility to offer a range of weeks to deserving cases. Either on an individual basis or via a charitable organisation such as 'City and Sea'.

Hal smiled at Paddy; he thought it sounded like a wonderful development for an under-used property. He was about to thank her for her opening comments when Andrea jumped in.

'What compliance steps have you undertaken?' She looked around the large dining room with an air that suggested that nothing she could see was currently compliant with much of anything that she considered suitable.

'Well, our first priority is to make sure this functions as a country house hotel and home?'

'Exactly,' Andrea pounced in. 'Your first priorities are not the same as ours. That's why we have to ensure any facility the charity is connected with meets our standards. We have to do this on behalf of those who aren't in a position to check for themselves.'

It all sounded good but there was just something about the way she said it. Paddy rushed to reassure her. 'Obviously, we have everyone's safety and wellbeing as our highest goal.'

'Excuse me for saying so, but there's nothing obvious about it at all.' Andrea underlined something that she had scribbled in her notepad and continued, 'You'd be surprised by how often people are in the charity business to either make money, hide money or move it about. They have no actual care for the charitable cause itself.'

'Oh, what sad experiences for you.' Paddy tried to be a bit more charitable herself. 'But obviously we need to make money to be able to help charitable causes. This is why our first focus will be corporate events, so that we can then offer a few rooms free of charge to a charity or an individual.'

Andrea jumped in. 'And when you say free of charge? Just how free is it? Reduced rates, word of mouth advertising, requirements that the charity uses the venue for other paid functions, AGMs or the like?'

'Laundry and electrics.'

Andrea floundered. 'What?'

'I would ask the charity to cover the cost of laundry and electrics. We would provide the staff, food and the accommodation.'

'And any other facilities you had? Those stand-up paddle board lessons you were talking about and the like, would they be free of charge or would they only be available to paying guests?'

Michelle jumped in, aware her young boss was getting increasingly flustered. 'Additional services would be on a case-by-case basis. We would need to ensure all proper insurances and liabilities were in place. For an individual we would probably cover that cost; for a larger booking we would discuss this with the charity. As far as our guests are concerned, they will see no differentiation in service.'

Andrea seemed mollified by the bureaucratic language. The meeting went back and forth. Every time Paddy thought they had resolved an issue, a new concern was raised. She was beginning to wonder what she was even doing. This was ridiculous, she was clearly out of her depth and woefully underqualified to attempt such a scheme. What was wrong with her? She wasn't the clever one in the family, she couldn't run meetings, this wasn't her, what was she thinking?

'Shall we break for lunch?' Hal's voice interrupted her inner despondency and she gratefully jumped at the suggestion. She found sitting upright for too long had started to become uncomfortable she preferred to move around as much as she could.

'Good idea. I've reserved a table for us down at the Fox and Fish. I'll drive down.'

'How far is it?' asked Andrea.

'Just down the hill but it's a bit of a struggle heading back up.'

'I'll walk then,' pronounced Andrea. 'I don't believe in unnecessary car journeys.'

Hal inwardly groaned. He had only met Andrea the day before and he was already regretting his decision to employ her as a consultant. She had almost no social skills. 'Right, well I shall join you. We can discuss some of the topics raised on the way down.' Turning to Paddy and Michelle he made his excuses. 'Ladies, we'll see you down there. Lady Patricia can't be expected to walk back uphill after sitting still for so long.'

Andrea looked Paddy up and down and then dismissed her. 'Dodgy back, hey? Exercise is best for that.'

'Lady Patricia is six months pregnant,' said Hal, 'I think the hill would be most uncomfortable for her.'

Andrea looked at Paddy sitting in her loose blouse, and for a moment Paddy thought she was actually going to ask her to prove it. When Hal had spoken, Paddy felt a rush of warmth, just the idea that he was concerned about her made her feel safe. Fortified by his comment she got to her feet, and smiled at Andrea, suggesting they headed off now before it got too busy down at the beach.

As Paddy pulled out of the drive she turned to Michelle and asked her if she was wasting her time.

'What? Because of what that interfering jumped-up do-gooder said? I could have swung for her. Jesus, if you'd said we were going to give everyone a free unicorn she'd have asked for a risk assessment on the horn.'

Paddy laughed.

'So you don't think this is going to be a miserable failure?'

'It's my job on the line, so no. It's not going to be a miserable failure. As if.' She flung her arms up. 'Honestly, I've lots of experience in running country house hotels and if, from time to time, a few of our guests are a little less affluent than we are used to, it's hardly going to be a problem. Honestly, the way she was going on you'd think this was Broadmoor by the Sea.'

Paddy grinned in relief. 'Thanks for that. I think what was beginning to make me angry was her assumption that poverty made people either dangerous or stupid. I think I'm probably just hungry. Again. Do you know, recently, I've been craving chips dunked in strawberry yogurt?'

Laughing, they walked into the busy pub. Paul greeted them warmly and made Paddy a Virgin Mary. Since meeting Hal's stepmother, this was another constant craving. She and Michelle took their drinks and made their way to the table, and just when they decided that the others must have got lost, Hal and Andrea came in. Hal's brow was furrowed but he said nothing as he sat down. They made small talk as their order was taken. It was August and the pub was jumping. The beach was packed and Paddy could see some of the overcrowding issues first-hand. She was very grateful Paul had reserved her a space in the car park.

Looking up from her salad Andrea pointed her fork at Paddy. 'You do have planning permission for this, don't you?'

Paddy and Michelle looked at each other in concern. 'Yes. Of course. A proper application went in; the villagers were consulted. No objections were raised and change of use was granted.'

'Ah good,' Andrea continued to talk whilst eating, only occasionally covering her mouth, 'only I asked a few of the residents and they didn't know what I was talking about.'

'Now, that's not quite right,' said Hal. 'The way you phrased it might have given them a different idea of what was being planned.'

'No, I don't think so. I simply asked if they would be welcoming to the homeless or those suffering from social issues. It's important you consider the community in which you are placing these people.'

Michelle looked horrified. 'That's a rather over the top way of describing a week's holiday for the occasional single mum? Or a holiday by the sea for a homeless teenager now and then? I hope you didn't alarm anyone. Lady Patricia has worked hard at this; we don't want it undermined by people getting the wrong end of the stick.'

'No, of course not. But you can hardly blame her ladyship for not being in touch with the working classes. It's very easy to not properly understand things if you aren't at their level. That's why Mr Ferguson has employed me to ensure every step of his charity runs smoothly. Every stakeholder must be accountable to the highest standards. It's the very least we can do for them.'

'Well, I thought I was doing a bit more than the very least,' replied Paddy, bemused by the idea she didn't understand the needs of the working class. What a wretched woman Andrea was. To look at someone and to simply assume you knew all there was to know about them. She would bet her front teeth that Andrea had never put cardboard in her school shoes to try and keep the rain out.

She pushed her soup away, feeling ill. Two locals had come into the bar and were talking in low urgent tones with Paul and all three were looking over at them. 'Mr Ferguson, will you excuse me. I don't feel well and think this is probably a good time to call it a day. If our facilities are still of interest to you, please let me know. It seems they may not be suitable, but please let me know either way. Michelle, would you mind driving? I'm suddenly incredibly tired.'

Hal jumped up. 'Paddy are you okay?'

'Yes fine. This tiredness can catch me out now and then.'

Before Hal could reply Andrea butted in. 'You probably need to exercise more. It's very important when you're pregnant to exercise regularly.'

Paddy leant on the table, staring at her knuckles and counted to ten. Looking up she smiled at Andrea. 'Yes. Well, I'll be sure to do that, thank you.' With a brittle smile she stood up from the table. 'Michelle?'

Smiling at the men at the bar, she and Michelle headed out of the front door.

'What do you think?' asked Michelle worriedly.

'Wait and see, but I think she may have just thrown the project on its arse.'

***

Back in the house, she and Michelle finished off her notes. Paddy felt a bit guilty about claiming illness. She just didn't think she could manage another second in that woman's company. Walking Michelle back to her car she was delighted to see Hal and Andrea walk up the drive. Hal was smiling an evil grin as Andrea panted and wheezed behind him. Visibly sweating, she paused as she leant on Hal's car.

Hal came over to Paddy. 'Are you okay or did you just want to escape? Look I had a word with the landlord and I think I've reassured him, but let's keep an eye on things. I think what you are offering is incredibly generous and I think this is going to be wildly successful. Let me get rid of Andrea and arrange another day to go over finer points.'

Paddy smiled weakly as the two of them drove off. As Michelle got into her car she leant out of the window.

'Well, he's nice. And he seems to like you.'

Paddy raised an eyebrow. 'He's concerned about his charity. That's what he is. Besides he's not available.'

'Well damn. Is he gay? The best-looking ones always seem to be nowadays.'

'No,' sighed Paddy, 'he's married. To a girl.'

'Oh and I bet she's really lovely as well, so you can't even hate her!'

'No, she's a total cow actually. Hate away.' Paddy paused, she was pleased she could mention Hal's marital status without getting upset, but there was no need to be unkind. 'Sorry, that was churlish of me. Time for my afternoon nap I think. God this always sleeping is killing me.'

Chapter Thirty-Five

The following morning Paddy woke up buzzing; she had more energy than she had had in months. Maybe this was the surge that everyone talked about? She certainly felt great. She was delighted with Michelle who was proving to be a proficient pair of hands. Paddy had no idea how she was going to do stuff after the baby, but in the first few weeks at least she knew she'd be unlikely to achieve much of anything. Nick had recommended Kensey House to a few of her contacts and they had a small booking in a few months. One of the villagers had also approached her about a new business development to run non-motorised water sports out from the beach. They wanted to convert one of the old fish sheds for the venture. She personally thought it was a great idea, but would need to consider things like increased visitor numbers. There was nothing to be gained by upsetting the locals. At that moment her phone rang and she saw it was Paul from the pub asking if she was able to pop over.

Getting into her car she was concerned about his tone of voice and remembered the look he gave her as she left the previous day.

As she walked into the pub she saw that, although it wasn't opening time yet, the place was full of villagers. She wiped her palms on her legs and fiddled with her blouse.

'Hello, Paul. You wanted to see me?' Her voice was hesitant. Not one person was smiling at her. This felt like a proper ambush. She smiled and nodded at a few familiar faces, but they just looked awkward; those she didn't recognise just glared at her. 'Is something wrong?'

'Is something wrong she asks,' taunted Bill Hunkin. Paddy's heart sank. 'Did you think we wouldn't find out about your plans?'

'Plans?' She had no sooner opened her mouth than she was drowned out by a barrage of shouts.

'To flood our village with up-country druggies.'

'And ex-convicts. What do they call them, rehabilitation centres.'

'I'm not having it. You can't do this to us.'

'I'm going to have to start locking my door at night. I don't want to live with murderers and rapists roaming down the lane.'

'And what about the beach, what am I supposed to say to my children when they find needles in the sand?'

Paddy stepped back under the onslaught of questions and wanted to run out the door. She tried to speak, but each time she was cut off by another protest. Throwing Paul a look of appeal he slammed his hand on the bar.

'Do you want her to answer or just to shout at her? Give her a bloody chance to explain herself.'

A room of sullen faces stared at her.

'Um hello. Good morning.' She faltered, this was horrible. Why were they all shouting at her? 'I'm afraid I don't know what any of you are talking about. We aren't running a rehabilitation centre.'

'Well you would say that, wouldn't you?' sneered Bill.

'Yes! Because it's true,' pleaded Paddy. 'I have no idea where you got this idea from.'

'Yesterday that woman from the council asked several of us how we'd feel if we had that sort in the village. And I'll tell you how I feel about it. It's not happening. And I don't care if you are our landlord, I say no. I know my rights. I'll go to the papers.'

Paddy couldn't keep track of all the arguments being shouted at her, not one of them made sense. 'You're being ridiculous!'

'Ridiculous! It's all right for you. I bet you won't even be living here. Just take the money and run.'

'What money?'

'I bet the government are paying you a huge grant to do it, aren't they?'

Paddy looked at the hostile faces and saw Beryl looking worried. Here at least was someone she could talk to directly.

'Beryl, I'm not opening a rehabilitation centre. I promise you.'

'I believe you, miss, but the woman yesterday was so convincing. She even asked me what sort of security measures I have in place. I'm like Brenda there, I haven't locked my door in decades.' Paddy was horrified. How could someone be so cruel as to deliberately mislead Beryl? She felt ashamed she had had any part in bringing such a troublemaker into the village. Beryl deserved better.

Apologising to her friend, she turned to the rest of the room and tried again. 'We are planning to run a country house retreat for corporate clients and residential classes. Like I discussed with you already. And every now and then we will offer a free week's holiday to people that need it.'

'To dry out! Upmarket rehab centre!' shouted Bill.

Paddy glared at him. Was he deliberately trying to be nasty?

'Look, I'm sorry you have been given the wrong idea, but that's simply not what we are doing.'

'I'm going to appeal. I'm going to write to planning and tell them you've duped us.'

'I haven't duped anyone!' Realising she was about to start crying, she headed for the door.

'Hey where are you going? You can't just walk out on us!' Bill's voice was sharp with anger, his face red and accusing.

Paddy whirled around, her own temper flaring. 'You aren't listening to me, why should I stay?' she snapped, her voice cracking with emotion. She could feel the burn of tears behind her eyes, the tightness in her throat, but she refused to let them see her cry. With a final glare, she turned on her heel and stormed out of the building, slamming the door behind her with a resounding bang.

Her tyres spat out gravel as she tore up the hill. Her heart pounding and her breath coming in short, sharp gasps. By the time she reached the house, her hands were shaking so badly she could barely get the key in the lock. Inside, the silence felt oppressive, the emptiness mocking. Paddy leaned back against the door, squeezing her eyes shut as the events of the evening replayed in her mind.

The accusations, the anger, the complete and utter lack of understanding - it all swirled inside her, a toxic mix of hurt and frustration and despair. Her stomach churned and her head pounded, the beginnings of a migraine throbbing behind her eyes. She felt like she was going to be sick.

Suddenly, her phone began to buzz in her pocket, the vibration startling in the stillness. Paddy's eyes flew open, dread coiling in her gut. Was it Paul, calling to tell her off for leaving the meeting unresolved? With a shaking hand, she fished her phone out and glanced at the screen.

Hal's name flashed up at her and something inside Paddy snapped. The dread morphed into white-hot fury, the force of it staggering. This was all his fault. All the pain, all the humiliation, all the heartache - it all led back to him.

She jabbed the answer button with a trembling finger. 'You!' she shouted, her voice raw and ragged. 'You have just cost me my whole bloody scheme for here! Everything I was trying to build has been ruined by your bloody woman. The whole bloody village hates me. I hate it here. I hate the people. I hate being pregnant and I want to go home!'

The words poured out of her in a torrent, months of pent-up emotion finally finding release. She was dimly aware of Hal saying something, his voice tinny and distant, but she couldn't make out the words over the roaring in her ears. With a choked sob, she ended the call and hurled her phone across the room.

It hit the wall with a crack and clattered to the floor, but Paddy barely noticed. She was already doubling over, retching, as the stress and the anger and the heartache finally became too much. She vomited onto the slate tiles, her whole body heaving with the force of it.

When it was over, she slumped back against the wall, spent and shaking. The wall was cool against her burning cheek, the floor hard beneath her. Paddy wrapped her arms around herself and let the tears come, great gasping sobs that felt like they were being ripped from her very soul.

She cried for herself, for her baby, for the love she had lost and the future she had been denied. She cried until she had no tears left, until her throat was raw and her eyes were swollen and her heart was a hollow, aching thing in her chest.

In the silence that followed, one thought crystallized in her mind, sharp and clear and undeniable. She couldn't do this anymore. She couldn't stay here, in this place that held nothing but pain for her. She had to leave, had to go somewhere far away where no one knew her name or her story.

Somewhere she could start over, build a new life for herself and her child. A life that didn't include Hal Ferguson.

With a shuddering breath, Paddy pushed herself to her feet, ignoring the way her legs trembled beneath her. She had arrangements to make, plans to put in motion.

But first, she was going for a swim. The sea was her saviour, in its embrace she would calm down and begin to plan. Baby fluttered within and she stroked her stomach, worried that she might have upset the little one. She needed to get her emotions under control and she needed to stop hoping.

***

Two hours later, Paul watched as Henry Ferguson left the pub and felt deeply uneasy. Not because of Henry's behaviour but because of his own. One of Henry's comments about bullying a pregnant woman had touched a nerve. He knew the

310

comment had been directed at Bill, the village troublemaker, rather than him, but he'd failed to intervene.

Shortly after Paddy had fled the pub, he'd received a call from a Mr Henry Ferguson. He'd been in the pub the day before with Paddy and the woman from the council and was involved with one of the charities that the villagers were so concerned about. Mr Ferguson felt there had been a problem with communications and the fault lay with him. Could Paul reconvene the villagers who were available and he'd pop down to run through their concerns? He lived about a half hour's drive away but he would come straight over.

As soon as he'd arrived Paul could see this man was far more practised at public speaking than Paddy was. He was relaxed and interested and listened to everyone's concerns and then spoke at length with passion and eloquence.

'If my desire to help a homeless teenager have a break from it all by the Cornish seaside has ruined it for other charities, then I will withdraw my interest in this property. But please consider who you want to say no to. Lady Patricia is offering a week's break to carers who have been looking after their parents for months without end, with no hope or social life. She was offering holidays to young families where one of the children has leukaemia. She was offering free holidays to residents whose flat burnt down leaving them with nothing but the clothes they fled in. These are the people that now and then, maybe once a month, she wants to help, totally free of charge.' He paused and looked around the room. He could see people nodding along with what he was saying.

'My own charity is aimed at homeless teenagers and young adults. We help them finish a basic education where

311

needed. We find them permanent accommodation so they have an address to apply for jobs from. If any have addictions, we help them get clean. They have one-on-one counsellors that help them with traumas, CVs, bank accounts. Anything that helps get them on their feet. And when they are stable and happy, we would love to give them a week's holiday, eating ice cream and jumping in the waves. And we would never ever send anyone that wasn't one hundred per cent back on their own two feet.'

'Will you tell us when they're coming?' called out a voice belligerently.

'No. Because they are no different to you and I, and deserve their privacy as much as you or I do.'

'Well they must have become homeless for a reason,' sneered the man with the bloodshot nose.

'That's right, blame the homeless,' said a middle-aged woman. 'Bill, you haven't got a brain in your head sometimes, let alone a heart. What would you know about being homeless? I was homeless for six months and I tell you what, it only takes the slightest slip before you fall through the cracks.'

One of the women sitting next to her turned to look at her. 'Jane, I never knew! Homeless, like sleeping on the streets?'

'No, like sleeping in my car, sleeping on friends' sofas.'

'Well it's not the same then, is it,' called Bill.

'It bloody is in here,' Jane said, tapping her temple. 'What if I was fifteen and didn't have any mates or a car? What would I have done then? We need more people like him there,' she gestured towards Hal, 'than people like you.' Now she addressed Hal directly, 'You give your young people a holiday here if you want. There'll be no objection from me.'

Gradually the mood had changed; through Hal's eloquence and Jane's passion, the villagers began to be swayed.

'But what about that woman you brought down yesterday? Telling us we were going to be surrounded by druggies and criminals?'

'Yes. I released her from her contract yesterday, after our site visit. I didn't feel she properly understood the charity or had the best skills to develop it. And may I apologise unreservedly for the way she went about causing strife and division. Her behaviour was incredibly unprofessional and caused fear where it was completely unwarranted. I am fully to blame for not properly briefing her and then letting her loose amongst you.'

'Well, what about Lady de Foix storming out of here earlier?' jeered Bill. 'Why would she do that if she didn't have something to hide?'

'I'm guessing she fled, rather than stormed,' said Hal in a cold voice. 'A young pregnant woman, on her own, being shouted at and heckled, for trying to do something nice?!'

'It wasn't like that.'

The others looked at their pints.

'It wasn't,' he protested again, 'but her sort come lording it over us just because she's our landlord.'

'Did she even mention your tenancies?'

'Yes. She did!'

'No, Bill,' said Paul. 'You did, and she said your concerns were her foremost considerations. And you said, 'you would say that'.'

'I tell you what, you're bloody lucky you're not one of my tenants!' snapped Hal.

'Hey, hey!' Bill swung his arms out and appealed to the crowd. 'See that! Lord of the Manor. Do you like to intimidate people because they're your tenants? Hey?'

'No, because I don't have any respect or patience for the sort of man that bullies a pregnant woman!'

Bill tried again but the mood of the pub was now very firmly against him. On the whole they rather liked their new landlady and were used to Bill and his ways. Realising he no longer had the village on his side he stormed out of the pub.

Hal smoothed his hair back and took a deep breath. 'Sorry about that. Now look, I'm going to leave my private contact details behind the bar. Contact me with any concerns you have that you didn't want to raise here or think of later on. I will happily answer all your questions. But please, I beg you, do not derail Lady Patricia's scheme because I hired an unprofessional consultant.' And then he left the pub.

All things considered, Paul thought Lady Patricia's scheme would go through just fine now. He gave Henry the directions to her cottage and hoped she would welcome the good news. He'd have to remember to give her an extra portion of the Yorkshire puddings she loved, to make amends, next time she came in. When it came to Yorkshires, he would swear she had hollow legs.

Chapter Thirty-Six

Following Paul's directions, Hal headed down the second drive he discovered he was heading back down to the sea. According to Paul, Lady Patricia didn't live at Kensey itself, but had chosen to stay in one of the estate's smaller properties. As the car cleared the rhododendron bushes, he saw a whitewashed house sitting above a small cove and Paddy's car sitting behind it. Parking alongside, he opened his door. Classical music was pouring out of the house; Wagner was currently stirring the warm summer air. Heading towards the door he doubted anyone would hear him but he was transfixed by the beautiful cove. It was cut off from Tregiskey Beach by a large protuberance of rocks and gave the occupants of this house total privacy. Looking out to sea Hal was again reminded of how beautiful Cornwall was. The hot August sun shone down and the sea sparkled. Why would anyone want to live anywhere else?

The low walls and porch of the cottage were lined in cockleshells and Hal spotted a bucket of small shells beside the door. Clearly someone was collecting material for repairs. His mind started to drift, wondering about what sort of plaster he would use, to fix them to the walls and shook his head. He wasn't here to play arts and crafts. He walked out onto the terrace overlooking the sea. For a second he thought he had spotted a seal and then he saw it was a swimmer coming into the cove from the right-hand side. As they got closer, Hal saw it was Paddy and then noticed that there was a towelling robe folded over one of the wooden chairs by the lower terrace.

There was a small ladder on the edge leading down into the water and she seemed to be making her way towards that. Hal waved and held up her dressing gown. Siegfried sang out and the gulls replied until Paddy was at the base of the ladder looking up at Hal. She pushed her long hair back off her face and he watched the sea water forming little beads on the tips of her eyelashes. Her freckles were still visible despite her lightly tanned skinned and he couldn't remember her looking more beautiful.

'Hello.' She appeared to have lost her earlier fury. Maybe she liked to swim it out? Leaning over he asked if she needed a hand. He could sense a hesitancy and chided himself. She might be self-conscious, he was after all, fully clothed.

'I'm sorry. Shall I wait by the house?'

'No, but you are in the way and I'm not as graceful getting up these steps as I was.'

Hal stepped back but couldn't resist staying close in case she slipped. As she pulled herself out of the water Hal could clearly see her pregnant frame for the first time. She had obviously decided a bikini was easier to swim in than a costume but he wondered if she wasn't cold? Maybe the baby was cold. The mother of his child, and his child might be cold whilst he stood just gazing at her. The thoughts rushed through his head and he stepped forward to quickly wrap the gown around her.

'Am I that awful to look at?' Her tone was light but her voice trembled. Hal decided she must be cold. It couldn't be doubt; she looked like a goddess rising out of the sea.

'You look amazing. I just thought you might be a bit chilly. Don't you wear a wetsuit?'

316

'Pregnancy wetsuits? They barely make women's wetsuits, let alone for women that decide to go super lumpy. Anyway, neoprene is not the easiest thing to get in and out of at the best of times.' She grinned. 'Once I had to do a photoshoot wearing a neoprene bodysuit for Tim Walker. It took as long to get in and out of it as it did to actually shoot the damn thing. Me and the other girls were practically fainting by the end of it, and covered in axle grease. Glamorous life hey?'

A breeze picked up and now she did give a little shiver. 'Come on, let's go and tell Siegfried to pipe down.'

'Yes, I was going to ask. What's with the music?'

Paddy laughed and explained it was just a little treat to herself. 'The cove amplifies the music and I love being serenaded by a full opera as I swim out to sea. Plus the seals seem to like it.'

Hal raised his eyebrow.

'There's often some seals along the next cove so I tend to sing to them. Don't ask me why. Probably because it doesn't seem to cause them pain and I like an audience. Even if I am rubbish.'

Opening the patio door she invited Hal to come in, and flicking on the kettle she excused herself to go and change.

Hal could smell bleach and vomit and felt a wave of regret stab at him. Was she still throwing up. And had to clean it up on her own? This wasn't the life he wanted for her and yet it was him that was causing this. Hal could see some instant hot chocolate by the kettle; this was clearly a bit of a routine for her. Opening the fridge he found some milk and decided to make her a proper hot chocolate and began to heat it up on

317

the pan. There was also a bar of chocolate in the fridge so he broke off a cube and placed it in the bottom of the mug.

By the time she returned he was pouring her a rich warm cup of hot chocolate. She was wrapped up in a huge dressing gown, with her hair wrapped up in a white towel. She was watching him carefully and Hal was uncertain to proceed. He knew pregnancy caused horrible mood swings but he was anxious not to return to her screaming at him again. No matter how much he deserved it.

'I couldn't find any squirty cream.'

'That's because I would eat an entire cannister in one sitting, so no squirty cream for me! It's bad enough that I have chocolate in the house but I am currently craving Virgin Marys, chocolate, Yorkshire puddings, and chips dipped in strawberry yogurt. By the end of this I will have to change my CV to plus-size model.'

She gently settled herself into a big armchair, and sipped on her drink as Hal passed it to her.

'Oh that's good,' she sighed. 'Sorry, every day seems to be a new adjustment to my shape. Just when I think I've got the measure of my new body, it changes again.'

Hal was desperately trying to respect her wishes in doing this alone but he was so curious and wanted so much to be involved. 'Does it hurt?'

Paddy took another sip and considered his question.

'Yes and no. I'm tired a lot. Like, fall over sleepy. And heels have become difficult to walk in, my back twinges all the time. And I'm not even big yet! God knows what that will be like. In fact the only time I feel good is when I'm swimming. I'm sorry,' she paused. 'I'm babbling on and I haven't even asked why you're here. I suppose it's because I started screaming at you earlier. Sorry about that, my mood swings are also off the chart at the moment. Plus, I really mishandled the meeting at the pub and I was looking to blame someone else.'

As she talked, Hal watched her curl up in the sofa; her feet were tucked up under her and a strand of red hair had escaped from the confines of her towel wrap. A wide smile played across her freckled face as she explained her newfound tribulations. He wanted to go and run her a bath, read to her, ask her her opinions on the crossword puzzle, discuss plans for the weekend, decide which school to send their child to, pick a holiday, take their grandchildren to the zoos. Mostly though, right now, he wanted to hear her sing. He couldn't imagine her doing anything badly.

'Penny for them?'

'I was wondering how bad you sound when you sing?'

She laughed and Hal's heart surged. He couldn't imagine a greater past-time than making Paddy happy.

'Woeful. I couldn't even carry a tune if you gave me a bucket to put it in. At school I was always in charge of handing out the leaflets and putting the chairs away.'

'I find that very hard to believe.'

'Well, I'm not about to sing for you. If you want to hear how badly I sing you'll have to swim to the seals with me.' The thought gave Paddy a tremendous warmth and then she remembered she was flirting with a married man. Technically her husband. But still. She scowled, hurt afresh. Her eyes flicked guiltily to the envelope on the mantelpiece that silently mocked her. She refused to open it. If it were divorce papers, she would sign them when she felt up to it. If it was anything else she didn't want to know.

'So, why are you here?'

For a minute, Hal had been prepared to swim right then and there, but her face clouded over and the warmth of the room evaporated.

'You said earlier you hated it here and wanted to go home.'

Her mood changed again, this time from angry to sad. *Nice going*, thought Hal. Now who was upsetting pregnant women?

'Yes. I just don't think I'm cut out to be a businesswoman. I hate conflict. I know I overreacted earlier. But I honestly hadn't anticipated that people wouldn't like my idea. I didn't have any answers to any of their concerns and I just didn't know how to speak to them to reassure them. I ruined everything. I think I'm going to have to tell Ari I failed.'

Hal recoiled. He knew she must be lonely here, on her own, without her sisters, but he couldn't imagine her moving back to Norfolk. Each time she had said she wouldn't stay he felt panicky.

'Don't do that. You're just tired. Look it's a great idea and any trouble you had with the village was completely my fault, not yours. And, hopefully I fixed that.' And he went on to tell her about his meeting.

By the time he had finished explaining Paddy felt a whole lot better and thanking him she saw him to the door. Spending any length of time in his company hurt and left her feeling conflicted. She felt rude as she made her excuses but she was tired. At the porch he bent down and lifted up a shell.

'New project?'

'Yes! Although I can never find enough.' Paddy was tempted to tell him about the Shell Grotto but then he'd want to see it and it was too small and intimate a space for her to share with him.

'You should collect mussel shells as well. That way you can write this year's date. Their long dark shells will stand out beautifully against the white cockle shells.'

Paddy smiled up at him. 'That's a brilliant idea. I've been imagining repairing the wall with Baby, now I can also add the year of their birth.'

'Well, if you guys ever want a hand with that…' Hal paused and looked out over the beach. How wonderful it would be to be digging in the sand with his child, Paddy beside them looking for shells. He remembered days at the beach with his mother, picking mussels and digging for clams and razorbills, then cooking them on the campfire. Sometimes they would even camp on the beach, waking first thing and running down to the sea shrieking as the cold water woke them up. His father was rarely with them, roughing it wasn't something he enjoyed but his mother had loved it. *The sand between your toes and the wind in your hair, this is what makes you a Cornish boy, that and the vitamin sea.* He would laugh as they rolled down sand dunes and explored rockpools. It was his mother who had taught him to swim and to make a campfire, sometimes after school she would pick him up and they would head to the beach for a barbecue and a swim. Only returning home as the dark fell.

'…I said that would be lovely?'

Hal looked at Paddy in surprise. 'Sorry, I was away with the fairies.' He hoped Paddy hadn't seen the longing in his face and he beat a quick retreat. She had made her feelings clear, he didn't want to burden her with his desires.

After he had left, the sun had come out again and Paddy decided to sunbathe for a bit. The breeze had dropped and the air was warm and soft. Lying on the sunbed she looked out across the patio and to the sea below. The tide was falling and soon it would be a straight drop onto the rocks. She would have to install some sort of barrier along the patio wall. Glass panels would be perfect and would stop any determined toddler falling off; but would the glass survive a big storm? She began to think of various solutions and then paused. So, she was staying, was she? She had meant it earlier when she told Hal she would leave Cornwall and not return, but something, somewhere along the way had changed. She couldn't pinpoint when it was but she realised that every image she had of her with Baby, they were somewhere in Cornwall.

She had adored seeing the change in Leo and William; they were so unfettered it was wonderful and they had clearly taken to country life with ease. In the city, they were constantly being shushed, not to shout, told to walk, told to always be less. The freedom and space to be little boys was bringing out the very best in them and she wanted the same for her little one. And yet every time she pictured it, she and Baby were here in Cornwall not Norfolk, and certainly not in London.

If she was honest, she knew the reason was Hal. Whenever he wasn't around, she would kid herself that it was important that a child should have close access to their father. But as soon as she saw him again, she knew that that was only a tiny reason why she wanted to stay here. It was she who needed to be near Hal. Not just Baby. She knew that that was stupid and she was going to have to work on it; lusting after another woman's husband was repugnant and she felt confident that eventually the attraction would fade; that her heart would stop beating so fast every time she saw him. That she would stop dreaming about him. But for now she would have to endure this bittersweet agony.

***

The next day Paddy got on the phone and began to swing a few things into action. Following some tips from Ari she began to put some ideas in motion to help the villagers. She then got in the car and headed down to the pub. As she drove down, she gave herself a pep talk. As Neil Gaiman said, he liked princesses who rescued themselves. Not that she had objected. In fact she rather loved having a prince to sweep in and save her, but she really did need to fix things herself if she was going to stay here.

Entering the bar she took a deep breath and saw two of the locals sitting at the bar talking to Paul. Calling out to them she went to pull a bar stool over, but Bill had already jumped up and got one for her.

It wasn't the easiest manoeuvre and she was grateful for the fact that she wasn't yet huge. There'd be no bar stool for her then. Ordering a glass of water she began to chat to the three men about the things she had been putting in place.

'Now look, I know you have local councillors and people who do stuff to make sure all the services run properly, but I wonder if I can't help with some things. I was chatting to Beryl last week who was complaining about the poor Wi-Fi signal down here. I agree, it's horribly slow, so I've been calling around to see if we can't get involved in the Cornwall Superfast Broadband roll out. We are exactly the sort of place that needs better communications. But I wondered what else I can help with. I've written a list but I bet there's stuff I haven't even thought of and I'd be grateful if you could get the word out around the village that I'd like to help.'

Bill picked up the list and was surprised to see a suggestion for a bus stop, and a feasibility study for an improved road scheme and new public loos. Practical ideas, not fancy London hare-brained schemes. He was about to speak and then thought better of it; he had won no favours with her the other day and his idea would do better coming from someone else. Like as not, she'd dismiss it out of hand if it came from him.

'Yes?' Paddy smiled at him. 'Go on, what have I missed?'

He was flummoxed by her attention but decided he may as well spit it out and then be proved right. She wasn't going to take on board anything he said.

'Well, it's just the other day, we were talking about a village defibrillator.' Behind the bar, Paul nodded. 'Pricey though.'

Paddy sipped her water. She didn't like this man and she was just waiting for him to trip her up, but she was trying to do better at talking to challenging people. 'So what's a defibrillator? Why do we need it and how much is it?'

As the men started to explain how it worked, Paddy could see it was invaluable. In summer this road was a nightmare to get down and she could envisage an ambulance getting stuck. A portable community defibrillator could be an actual life saver to the villagers or the visitors.

Paddy said she would go home and investigate and then come back and consult with them. She also said she would have a look at the costs involved in adopting the public loos. They had been closed two seasons ago and Paul said it was hampering trade. Bill began to murmur there were enough people in the village as it was. Paul retorted that 'we weren't all retired', some of them needed to make a living.

Spotting this was a sore point and one that would be revisited time and time again, she decided to head home and start putting some of these ideas into action. Besides which it turned out that whilst she could still get up on a bar stool, sitting on one for more than half an hour was torture. As she stepped down, she arched her body and placed her hands on the back of her hips. 'My god, you men don't know how lucky you are.'

Laughing she headed back into the sunlight. That had gone well. She reached for her phone to share the good news with Hal but stopped. As much as she wanted to share her good news with him, she needed to create as much distance as she could. He may be her child's father but he was married to another woman and she needed to remember that. Sighing she focussed on the meeting instead and began to think of other things she could do to make everyone's lives better.

***

Seeing Beryl sitting out on her bench she waved and headed over to pay her respects. By the time she got to the top she was grateful for the metal handrail. 'Do you know, I thought I was fit but this is ridiculous, even this hill is killing me. Are Cornish mothers made of sterner stuff? How do you all manage the hills?'

'Some of us were smart enough not to get pregnant, miss.'

'Ah well, you have the truth of it there. I was not smart.'

Huffing, she plonked herself inelegantly down next to Beryl without waiting to be invited.

Beryl nodded and handed her an apple. 'Can I get you some water?' Nodding, Paddy closed her eyes and leant her head against the whitewashed wall. The sun warmed her eyelids and she listened to the laughing murmur of children on the beach and a radio gently playing Delibes from within the cottage.

'Here you go then, although it seems a shame to disturb you. Your man was in the pub yesterday. Gave some a right dressing-down.'

Paddy breathed out deeply; she loved the idea. 'He's not my man,' she said sadly.

'Hmm. Don't know as he knows that.' Beryl didn't know what was wrong with young people. Life was over so quickly, why did they waste time pussyfooting around?

'Well, he isn't.' Paddy changed the conversation; she didn't want to discuss her private life with anyone. Especially not someone she admired. 'Anyway, I wanted to let you know I'm trying to get a better Wi-Fi signal in the village. I'm also going to turn the other three cottages here into holiday apartments and I want you to be involved in everything. Now, I know you've said you don't have any objections but I want to know the minute you have any concerns. Plus, whatever refurbishments you want in your cottage you can have. New kitchen, new bathroom. Whatever. And if you see the builders doing something in the gardens and you think well, that's nice, let me know and I'll do the same for you. There.'

She had discussed her plans with Ari and Nick and both agreed it was an intelligent investment. These holiday cottages, done to the highest spec, would bring in solid income all year round. When she had mentioned Beryl, she was unsurprised that both sisters had agreed that the old lady should have anything she wanted.

Sighing she bit into her apple and looked out across the water. In the distance the sailing yachts were now sprinting back to shore. The women sat companionably until Paddy made to leave.

'I could do with a new boiler. The old one had to be repaired three times last winter. It would be nice to have hot water as well as heating this year.'

Paddy looked appalled and promised she would get on it. If she achieved nothing else, she could get a boiler fixed. Maybe Hal knew a plumber?

'Ugh.' In annoyance she threw her apple core over the wall and out to sea.

'Are you okay,' asked Beryl in concern.

'I'm fine. Just struggling to keep my thoughts under control. Ignore me. I shall arrange for the estate's plumber to come and sort the boiler.'

With that established, Paddy said goodbye and walked back to the house. Cursing herself as a fool the entire way home.

Chapter Thirty-Seven

It had been a week since her meetings with the villagers and things were proceeding nicely. Paddy walked up slowly from the cottage to the house. There was a site meeting going on with the subcontractors, and whilst Michelle normally handled that for her, she had mentioned that Hal was going to be present and, try as she might, Paddy couldn't stay away. A group of contractors were out by the barns and Michelle seemed to have the whole show in hand. She saw Paddy and gave her a big wave as the men turned to see who was approaching. Hal's face lit up, and the two of them were still smiling at each other when Michelle coughed and introduced the subcontractors. They were discussing some details of the renovations, and Hal excused himself, taking Paddy to one side.

'To be honest. I'm not sure why I'm here. Michelle said she needed my input on something, but when I got here, she said I may as well join in the site inspection. Do you have any idea why she called me?'

Paddy sent her matchmaking manager little daggers and then turned to Hal, artfully declaring that she had no idea. She wasn't supposed to be at the meeting either, she was just on her afternoon walk. If he wanted to join her?

She wanted Hal to see she wasn't going to be difficult. Each time they had met she had worked hard to not mention his wedding or Bianca and keep the topic firmly on Baby. It wasn't easy though. The production company's envelope sat sullen and unopened on her mantlepiece. She kept it in full view, so she wouldn't forget what a fool she was, and that Hal wasn't worth breaking her heart over.

It felt impossible, but if she was going to stay here then she needed to get through this, and learn to talk to Hal without becoming an emotional wreck. 'I thought you should know I've decided to settle in Cornwall. At least for now. There's lots to do in the village and I think Baby will enjoy living by the sea.'

Hal stopped walking, and taking her hand kissed it, beaming at her as though she was a miracle. Alarmed at her surge of emotion she snatched her hand away in case she embarrassed herself. Mortified, he apologised. 'I'm so sorry, that was wrong of me, but that is wonderful news. I can't tell you how happy that makes me. Come on, come back to the car and let me show you what I brought you.'

Her heart was in her mouth, this was hopeless. How could she stay in Cornwall when he made her feel like this? But what else could she do? Morosely, she walked back to the car and looked on curiously as he pulled a large wetsuit from out of the boot.

'It's Dad's old suit. I wondered if you could have it cut down around the arms and legs to fit you. There are some great workshops on the north coast that might be able to do something with it. I was just thinking you and he have the same sort of girth at the moment.'

Paddy laughed. She wasn't sure if this was wonderful or insulting. But it was thoughtful.

'I could drive you over there. Why are you laughing? Oh God, is this really rude of me? I was just thinking of you getting cold and there are jellyfish in the water at the mo, and I didn't want you to get stung.'

'No, I don't want to get stung either but the problem with any wetsuit, no matter how 'fancy',' she waved at the suit that looked like it might have come from the ark, 'is putting the damn things on and then getting them off again. My levels of flexibility are diminishing daily. I fear I might put it on and then end up giving birth in it because I could never get out again.'

He returned the suit to the boot of his car and promised her he would think of a solution. Michelle and the contractors came around to the front of the house and reluctantly Paddy called out to them. As the meeting came to a close Hal looked as if he was about to speak, but then paused and, saying goodbye to all, he drove off followed by the two contractors.

'Well, that went well,' beamed Michelle.

'Oh good, when can they start?'

'I mean you two, all smiles and you kept looking at each other when the other had turned away.'

Paddy bit her lip; she didn't want to sound cross but this wouldn't do.

'Please don't try to matchmake. You know he's married.'

'Are you sure?' From what she had seen Hal behaved nothing like a newly married man.

'One hundred per cent,' Paddy snapped, then realising she was taking it out on the wrong person, she smiled and apologised. 'Now, show me these workshops.'

Chapter Thirty-Eight

Paddy was looking forward to the day ahead. She had a parcel to collect from the house and then she was heading over to Jem's for lunch, before heading out to a dinner later on. The dinner was an awards ceremony for Cornish charities, and Paddy had received an invitation from the organisers, no doubt at Seb's instigation. She'd called Jem about it, who said she was also going with a friend who ran a moorland ponies' sanctuary. It was agreed that Paddy should join their table and she was looking forward to it. If she was honest, she was also hoping Hal might be there, even if it meant that she would almost certainly meet Bianca.

Walking up to the house she was feeling the heat; even though it was September, the fact she was now seven months pregnant hung heavily on her. Her type of pregnancy meant she wasn't huge with Baby sitting against her backbone, but she could still feel the impact of the little one. Her flexibility was poor, her bladder was buggered, she was always short of breath and her clothes no longer sat on her frame properly. Her tummy had swelled but not as much as her chest and she found the entire thing disconcerting. Unless she was in something close-fitting no one seemed to notice she was pregnant. She found she was getting looks suggesting she was lazy for always puffing about and sitting down.

In a sense, she was disappointed she didn't look more pregnant. When she had gone out with Jemima to Padstow, she noticed how attentive everyone was to Jem. People were so thoughtful and kind that Paddy had looked on in wonder.

When she mentioned it to Jem the girl had groaned and said she would swap their pregnancies in a heartbeat. If Paddy wanted swollen ankles, stretch marks and a belly the size of the moon she was welcome to it. Paddy thought her backache was enough to be going on with, so laughed and paid for the ice creams instead.

She walked into Kensey and headed towards Michelle's office. Their first guests were due in a few days and the whole thing was running smoothly. Michelle was proving to be a godsend, and she was loving her job and looking forward to her first guests: a group of bankers that Nick had booked in. They were paying reduced rates to act as guinea pigs, so that Michelle could get the staff and systems running smoothly. Now she looked up and smiled as Paddy came in. Paddy went over some details with her, approving some of her suggestions and then, taking her parcel, she headed back down to the cottage. As far as she was concerned that was her exercise for the day. She was glad she had got her swim in first, there were no hills in the sea and it was impossible to overheat.

Running a glass of water she turned the limp parcel over in her hands. She guessed it was clothing but whatever it was it was heavy. Maybe one of the designers had sent her something? She was excited; she was enjoying Cornish life but there were elements she missed, like all the lovely new clothes. Not that anything would currently fit her. She wondered who had sent her this. Opening the package she saw there was a card and she opened that first. Inside was a little handwritten note from Hal.

'For my shivery mermaid.'

She opened the package and pulled out a two-piece full-length neoprene swim set designed for pregnant women. They were not as warm as a normal suit as they weren't as close-fitting. But they would keep her skin covered, sparing her from rashes, jellyfish stings and sunburn. Plus, they would be very easy to get on and off. She checked her watch, she didn't have time to try it out yet. She had spent too much time going through issues with Michelle and was now running late to meet Jemima. Sending Hal a quick text thanking him for his thoughtful gift, she smiled and for the millionth time, wished things were different.

***

Heading over to Jem's, she couldn't wait to catch up. Jem had bought a new pregnancy outfit for tonight's do and wanted Paddy's opinion on how to make her look less like a whale in a tent and more like a goddess. Pulling up she ignored the geese and noticed the new lad Jem had been telling her about was raking leaves on the lawn. There was something familiar about him, but she just couldn't place him. He was the first 'graduate' from Hal's charity, although not official. Angus had been talking to Hal, saying he was concerned that Jem was on her own a lot. As they were close neighbours could Hal keep an eye out for her? He did one better and suggested he had a lad who was looking for some manual work.

They had met and Sam thought the geese were hilarious and fell in love with the donkeys; Jem and Angus hired him on the spot. As they only lived five miles apart Sam would cycle over each day and apparently it was all working out.

Giving him a friendly nod she headed towards the house and called out as she entered. Jem was sitting in the back garden, a little suntrap of late summer blooms and absolutely no geese.

'I thought we could have lunch out here before the weather turns. I think this is the last gasp of sunshine for a few days.'

Paddy had got used to looking at the clouds, like Beryl had suggested, but honestly, she was still at the stage of pronouncing it would likely rain soon, based on the sole fact that it was always likely to rain soon. It was certainly a lot wetter than London, but it seemed to be a small price to pay, because when it wasn't raining, it was God-given, glorious.

Jem agreed it was a lovely garden; sheltered by a tall stone wall, it trapped all the sunshine and kept out the breeze. A small gate on one side led around to the front, and Paddy could see this was going to be a wonderful space for a little one to wander and explore. It was funny; she found herself regularly looking at places with fresh eyes these days. She had spoken to Ari about it, who had laughed and said that it didn't matter how much you planned, it was never enough. The sound of a mower from the front started up and no doubt the front lawn was being given a tidy up before the rain started.

'Sam will be mowing around here in a minute, when he does, we'll move inside if that's okay? You can tell me what you think of my new dress.' Jem speared a piece of ham and added it to her melon. 'Do you know, all this healthy eating is killing me. How's your yogurt and chips diet going?' Laughing, the girls chatted about their cravings and then moved on to what both was currently reading. Jem also worked as a virtual PA and was able to help authors with their website, reviews and mailing lists. She was also a blogger in her own right, posting reviews and content across the web. 'I love it. It means I can do what I love from home and get paid.' Paddy was used to influencers in the fashion world, but she hadn't known they existed in the book world as well and it explained why Jem was always lending her great books.

They were in the middle of discussing who was the best literary detective, when the side gate rattled and Sam came through with the mower.

Paddy began to stack the plates when Sam smiled directly at her and said hello. She smiled and said hello and carried on stacking the plates. He tried again.

'You don't remember me, do you?'

Paddy looked at Jem for guidance but she just shrugged looking quizzical.

'Sorry, I'm fairly new around here,' she tipped her head to one side staring at him closely. 'I don't think we've met?' There was something about him that rang a bell, but for the life of her she couldn't place him.

'We met in London. You bought me a Burger King?'

Paddy peered at him and then jumped up, running over to give him a hug. 'My god! Look at you! What are you doing here? This is incredible!!' She was so excited that the geese came running around squawking their heads off, and Jem had to shoo them back out. She was determined to have one place free of goose shit.

'This is incredible. I'm so sorry I didn't recognise you. How did you end up in Cornwall?'

Sam was laughing now at her enthusiasm and he explained how her simple gesture had prompted Hal to do the same and that that had grown into a bit of a snowball. 'Honestly, when I saw you get out of the car just now, I couldn't believe it; mind, you look a bit different now.' He pretended to stagger like a heavily pregnant woman and both Jem and Paddy laughed. He was not a convincing actor. 'So did you and Hal get it together then, if you're down here as well?'

Paddy shrugged refusing to let the question spoil her good mood. 'He's married, so no, we are not an item.'

Sam looked at Jemima confused. 'He's not married, is he, Jem?'

Both Sam and Jem now looked at Paddy in confusion.

'No, absolutely not. Paddy, we're talking about Hal, Henry Ferguson.'

'Yes, I know,' said Paddy equally confused, 'but he is married. I saw the wedding photos of Bianca in that horrible dress with her awful bridesmaids.'

'No, that's— wow.' Jem paused trying to work out how Paddy could have got it so wrong. 'Hal didn't marry her; she went ahead with the wedding but married some bit on the side she'd been seeing. It was a huge scandal. Didn't you know?' Alarmed by Paddy's lack of response she told Sam to go and put the kettle on and made Paddy sit down.

'But I thought he was married. When I left the party, he went off to fix things with Bianca?'

'He dumped Bianca. You saw that.'

'But I thought he was going to go back and sort things out...'

'No, not a bit of it. He told us all there and then the wedding was off. Only it turns out she'd been two-timing Hal with some super rich polo player, so she just went ahead with the wedding but with a different groom. It was incredible. Same church, same photographer, same reception. Everything. And when she told Hal that she was pregnant and that she lost the baby, that was a lie too, just to get him to propose.' Jem placed her hand on her stomach, instinctively warding off bad thoughts.

Sam came back with two cups and a pot of tea and told Jem that he'd sweep down the stables instead. Saying goodbye to a thunderstruck Paddy, he grinned, 'It's brilliant to see you again but you seriously need to get yourself over to Vollen, that bloke is besotted with you. All he did in London was talk about you. Plus you know, that's his baby in there!'

'Oh my god!' said Jem. 'I wondered, but I didn't dare ask. Paddy, that's amazing.'

Paddy watched Sam's retreating back and then turned to Jem. 'Besotted?'

'That sounds about right. He never stops talking about you.'

'What!?'

'All the bloody time. He always manages to find a way to bring any conversation back to you and always asks after you.'

'Well, that's just because of the baby.'

Jem poured them both a cup of tea. 'No, it's really not. But I don't understand your interest. You've always asked me not to talk about him. I thought you couldn't stand him?'

'Because he was married,' wailed Paddy. 'It was too painful to talk about him, because he was married.'

Jem grinned. 'But he's not married.'

Paddy couldn't believe it. She tried to replay every conversation they had had and realised everything was coloured by the fact she had insisted they didn't discuss anything personal. Oh God, she was a fool.

'Are you alright? You've gone a very funny colour.'

'Shock I think.' She needed to sit down and have a proper conversation with Hal and try and sort everything out. 'Oh my god, Jem, this is brilliant.'

Jem was beaming from ear to ear. 'He's at tonight's award ceremony. What are you going to wear?'

It dawned on Paddy that she had nothing special to wear, and hugging Jem she said she had to get home and start getting her hair ready. Giggling, she felt like the first night she had met him. What if he wasn't actually besotted with her? What if he was only interested in the baby? Too many questions! She wanted a bath and to shave her legs and look as good as she could possibly get at seven months pregnant.

As she drove home the heavens opened and she had to battle the wind as she made her way there. Throwing open the door she tried to run up the stairs and managed a lumbering shuffle instead. She ran the taps and then went through her wardrobe. The dress she had been planning to wear was now totally out of order. The problem was she didn't have a great deal of options at the moment.

Eventually, she settled on a pink satin dress that was cut on the bias. Clem had sent it down to her, saying she could do with some nice things to wear while she was twisting into new shapes. It showed her small bump off nicely whilst still looking really attractive. She had dismissed it earlier as being too eye-catching but now she didn't care who saw her, so long as Hal did. Laughing she filled the bath with bubbles and texted Jem that she would meet her at the venue.

Chapter Thirty-Nine

Hal felt his phone buzzing and pulled it out. He had been expecting a call from his father. James and Odette had taken a holiday to the West Indies, staying with friends, but bad weather had forced them to catch an emergency flight home. They were waiting to catch a flight out of Freeport and they were going to let him know when they were safe. Hal was sorry that Odette had had her holiday spoilt, but he couldn't help feeling vindicated that his father was not having the time of his life.

Every day Hal was having to deal with tenants who were facing rent rises and customers who were having their accounts closed. Each time he called his father for clarification on a loan or a new demand, James would brush him off and say he couldn't remember the details of that particular issue. Remarkably, he had rung Hal and asked him to ship out some of his guns. He had then roared down the phone at his son when he discovered they had been auctioned off. That call had ended in both men slamming down their phones.

Odette had called Hal soon after, apologising for James. Since moving to France he had become more and more irascible; he refused to speak French and complained constantly about the food. She was worried he wasn't quite himself. Hal didn't know what to suggest; on a previous call James had suggested that Hal had evicted him. Now he was demanding things he knew Hal had sold. He wondered if the shock of the near bankruptcy had addled his mind. Or worse, was this simply more symptoms of an undiagnosed dementia?

Had his profligate spending been a sign of illness rather than wanton stupidity. It never rained but it poured.

Looking at his phone, Hal's heart leapt when he saw it was Paddy calling. The wetsuit had worked better than he could have hoped. Maybe she too had been trying to think of a solution to their problems. Just the thought made him smile as he excused himself from the table and stepped into the hotel foyer.

But as he answered the call, his smile faded, replaced by a growing sense of alarm. Paddy's voice was barely audible over the howling wind and driving rain, her words jumbled and broken by the poor reception. He strained to make out what she was saying, his pulse pounding in his ears.

'Crash... dying...' The words hit him like a punch to the gut, his blood running cold.

'Paddy? Paddy, where are you?' he shouted, his voice rising in panic. 'Paddy, can you hear me?'

The line went dead, the sudden silence deafening. Hal stared at his phone in disbelief, his hand shaking. Then it pinged with a location, the sound unnaturally loud in the quiet of the foyer. He tried to call her back but it just rang out, each unanswered ring ratcheting up his fear.

As he hung up, her final words echoed in his mind, searing themselves into his memory. 'I need you.'

The function room was a serene oasis of gentle chatter and the clink of crystal and china, a jarring contrast to the chaos inside him. Hal ran his hands through his hair, his eyes wild as he scanned the room for the one person who could help. Finally, he spotted Jamie, looking politely bored at a table at the far end of the room. Hal practically sprinted over, his heart in his throat.

'Jamie,' he gasped, tapping his friend on the shoulder.

Jamie took one look at Hal's face and was on his feet in an instant, his soldier's instincts kicking in. In the lobby, Hal explained the situation in a rush of words, his voice tight with barely suppressed panic.

'Paddy's had a car crash. She's in a bad way. I need to get to her but I might need backup...'

Jamie frowned. The situation seemed serious but not life-threatening. Yet Hal was wound tighter than a coiled spring, his agitation palpable.

'Okay, let's take your car,' Jamie said calmly, trying to project a sense of control. 'You get her to safety and I'll handle the car, whether that means driving it back or getting it towed. Okay?'

Hal sagged in relief, grateful beyond words for his friend's steadying presence. They headed out into the night, the wind howling like a wounded animal. Rain lashed the windshield, the wipers struggling to keep up. Twigs and leaves battered the car, the impacts making Hal flinch.

Jamie muttered something about the bloody awful weather but Hal barely heard him. All he could think about was Paddy, alone and hurt somewhere in this godforsaken storm. He pictured her trapped in her crumpled car, broken and bleeding, and terror clawed at his throat.

He pushed down harder on the accelerator, the car surging forward into the darkness. Hold on, Paddy, he thought desperately. I'm coming. Just hold on.

But even as he raced through the night, a small, insidious voice whispered in the back of his mind that he might already be too late. That this time, love might not be enough to save them.

Hal gritted his teeth and drove faster, refusing to listen. He would get to her in time. He had to. Losing her was not an option.

Not now, not ever.

***

As they approached the location Paddy had sent, the road began to narrow and twist. Hal had to slam on the brakes to avoid driving into the back of a car that was sticking out across the road, its bonnet crunched against the Cornish hedge. Jumping out both men ran to the car. Hal got there first but it was empty. Alarmed, he looked around and saw a lump in the road ahead illuminated by the headlights. He could see a deer carcass in the road and Paddy hunched over it. As the light swept over her Paddy stood up and staggered towards him. She was covered from head to toe in blood. Hal ran towards her, his dress shoes slipping on the leaves, Jamie shouting at him. As Hal reached Paddy, he grabbed her to him. He was breathing heavily, all that blood. How was she able to stand?

'Where are you hurt?!' he shouted over the wind.

Paddy's eyes were wild; her hair had twigs and leaves in it and blood and mud was smeared across her pale face. Her dress was torn and soaked in blood and rain.

'It's his leg I think, and there's blood coming out of his mouth as well. I can't stop it.'

344

'HAL!'

Henry looked back in confusion as Jamie caught up with him. 'It's not her blood.'

'What?'

'The blood. I think it's the deer's.'

'Yes!' cried Paddy. 'The deer, I can't stop the blood. I tried pressing on the wound and I wrapped my jacket around it but it's not stopping. I also tried to pull him to the side of the road so no one else would hit him.'

Both men looked at the deer's eyes, already dull in the light of the car's headlamps and knew that the animal had died.

'Paddy. It's dead. I'm sure you did everything you could.'

'I killed it!' Paddy started crying loudly.

'No, well yes,' Jamie stepped forward trying to calm her down, 'but look, deer are forever jumping out onto roads, they are a bloody menace. It's really not your fault. What we need to do now is see if you are alright?' Turning to Hal for support he was surprised by how shocked he seemed to be. God knows they had both experienced worse overseas.

'Hal, if you could maybe put the poor girl down and we can see if she's hurt herself. I've had a look at the car and it's not too bad. Easily mended. Were you wearing a belt? Have you hit your head?'

Paddy was shaking but this man with the calm voice and sensible question was helping her to get a grip. Plus standing in the shelter of Hal's arms was making her feel wonderfully safe and sleepy.

'Miss! Miss, can you hear me? Hal, what did you say her name was?' What was wrong with his friend? He seemed to have completely fallen apart. Admittedly as Paddy had walked towards them covered in blood it had been a fleeting shock, but she was fine. 'Paddy, listen to me. You might be in shock. Perfectly natural, but I need you to stay awake.'

Paddy shook her head. 'Yes sorry, it's a bit overwhelming, I drifted off there a bit. Oh God.' Paddy's wits came flooding back. 'The baby. Oh God, Hal! What if I've hurt the baby?'

Jamie looked back at the car. 'I didn't see a car seat?'

'Oh God,' said Hal as he stepped back from Paddy to look at her. 'She's pregnant. How the hell could I have forgotten that?'

Jamie looked at the pair of them. The way they were looking at each other, he may have well been on another planet. It seemed Hal had a story to tell but that would have to wait. The stakes had just rocketed.

'Okay. Change of plan. Hal drive Paddy here to the hospital. No ifs or buts. Get going. I'll stay here and arrange everything. Now!'

Startled into action, Hal was ridiculously grateful for Jamie's presence. The sight of Paddy covered in blood had scared the living daylights out of him. He hadn't even thought of the baby; all he cared about was Paddy. But Jamie was right, Paddy might be fine, but there was no way of knowing if the baby was.

***

Screeching into the ambulance bay he threw his keys, , to a group of paramedics having a quick fag break shouting an apology and carried Paddy in through the doors. The staff took one look at the tall man in a dinner jacket carrying a woman covered in blood and ran to fetch a gurney.

'She's been in a car crash. The blood belongs to the deer, but she's pregnant!' As he was speaking a team of staff rushed around and soon had Paddy lying down in a small cubicle.

'Sir, can you let go of her hand a minute, we need to take her blood pressure.'

Hal glared at the nurse, who promptly moved to the other side and took the pressure from there. As she did so one of her colleagues turned to Hal.

'If you get in our way, we can't help her. Please sir, we've got her.'

Hal looked at the nurse but Paddy gripped his hand tighter and began to cry. Hal felt his heart break.

'It's okay, darling, they just want to help.'

'Don't leave me!'

He gripped her hand tighter and turned back to the nurse. 'Sorry. You'll have to work around me.'

Nodding, the nurse agreed; it would be a mild inconvenience for them but there was little point in agitating the pregnant woman further. As they waited for the ultrasound to arrive, they established the blood wasn't hers and nothing was broken. She was tender where the seatbelt had snapped her back and Paddy was terrified that it may have hurt the baby. 'I can't feel Baby move!' she wailed. 'Why isn't Baby moving?'

The nurse knew better than to speculate but the mother needed to calm down. She held her other hand and patted it maternally. 'Baby's had a shock, just like you. If it was me, I'd be hunkered down waiting for the storm to pass. That's probably what Baby is doing.' Another nurse chimed in, 'If he's like my boy he's probably fast asleep.' The women laughed, and some of the fear left Paddy's face. 'The best thing you can do for Baby right now, is calm down. All that adrenaline in your blood is probably going to make Baby feel queasy.' As the women made small talk, Hal ignored them; he was staring at Paddy and thinking he had never loved her more. He stroked her hair and removed leaves and twigs as she looked at him. She wanted someone to promise her the baby was okay. Nothing else mattered; Hal was here. Now she needed to know their child was safe as well. Finally, the ultrasound arrived and Paddy wept with relief as they watched the trace of a strong heartbeat and saw tiny limbs gently twitch.

'What do you know. Fast asleep! Now, how about Mum does the same?'

'Can I go home?' Paddy asked in relief.

The doctor looked at her and whilst everything was fine, she had had a massive shock and the father seemed to be in no fit state to drive either. 'Let's admit you for the night. We can keep an eye on you and then you can go home first thing. How does that sound?'

Paddy was about to protest, but the cottage would be cold and dark. She was going to have to face being alone when things got tough but tonight, she just wanted to sleep.

'Before you go, can you phone Nick for me and let her know what's happened?'

Hal pulled his phone out of his pocket and then registered what Paddy had said.

'I'm not going anywhere. Let me step out and call your sister but then I'm back here. Okay? I am not leaving you. Ever.'

As he stepped out Paddy stared after him. What did he mean?

'You've got a good one there,' said one of the nurses. 'Now let's find you a gown. What is this, deer's blood? They're a bloody nuisance; you'd be surprised, well probably not now, by how many people come in here after crashing into a deer.'

As they chatted, she was swapped over to the care of two porters who started to move her to a ward for the night. Alarmed, Paddy called out for Hal.

'He's outside. Better phone reception. I'll send him up to you. Now go to sleep.'

As the trolley bed trundled down the corridors Paddy felt herself dozing off, voices drifted across her head and then a warm hand wrapped itself around hers, as she felt a kiss on her forehead and she fell fast asleep.

Chapter Forty

Paddy woke to hear two voices arguing in the corridor and opened her eyes. Hal's friend was sitting by the foot of her bed and he gave her a warm smile.

'Good morning. How are you feeling?'

Paddy's voice was a bit croaky and her shoulder felt sore, but a flutter inside her told her the baby was fine, and she smiled widely. 'Okay now. Is that Nick and Hal arguing out there? What's going on?'

Jamie shrugged. 'Two scared people establishing a turf war. Your twin is quite fierce, isn't she? She called your phone last night, so I answered it. You'd left it in your car. I tried to explain I was waiting with your car whilst Hal took you to hospital and she went off the deep end a bit. Here it is by the way. Oh and I'm Jamie.' He handed her phone over to her and when she said it could have waited, Jamie shrugged. 'That's not what your sister said. She was quite vocal on that, and many other points. Look I know it's not my place to ask, but is the baby Hal's? I've never seen him how he was last night.'

Paddy nodded, the joy of the morning rapidly dissolving. For some reason two of the people she loved most in the world were shouting at each other.

'Yes, but it's complicated,' she said weakly.

Jamie poured her some water and helped her to sit up. 'People say that but it's usually not. The way I see it, you love him, he loves you, you're pregnant and it's his. Seems pretty simple to me.'

She was about to reply but the door swung open and Nick burst in, her face a mask of worry and anger. She ran to Paddy's side and engulfed her in a fierce hug.

'Oh my god, I was so scared,' Nick cried, her voice breaking. 'Never ever scare me like that again. I had to cope with some stranger on your phone jabbering a load of nonsense about you being in hospital but he couldn't tell me anything.'

Jamie didn't think he'd been jabbering, but decided discretion was the better part of valour at this stage. He was still reeling from the tongue-lashing Nick had given him at seven this morning when he'd handed the phone over.

'I drove through the night to find this snake by your side,' Nick spat, glaring daggers at Hal.

'Nick, I'm fine,' Paddy insisted. 'This isn't like you. And the baby just moved as well. So Baby's fine too.' She turned to Hal, her eyes shining. 'The baby moved, Hal. Baby's okay!'

Hal's face softened, a tentative smile touching his lips. 'Are you sure? Shall I fetch a nurse?' he asked gently, ignoring Nick's hostility. 'May I feel?'

Nick's head whipped around, her eyes blazing. 'Paddy, do you want me to ask security to get rid of him?' she demanded.

Paddy sat up further in bed, confusion marring her features. She scowled, trying to make sense of the situation. 'Why are you calling him a snake?'

'This piece of work,' Nick snarled, jabbing a finger at Hal, 'is the one I 'bumped into' in London. The one who had a charity in trouble. But clearly, he staged the entire thing to stalk you. I'm going to call the police as soon as we're out of here.'

Hal paced the small room, his hands clenched into fists at his sides. He glared at Nick, barely restraining himself. 'For the umpteenth time, that was a bizarre coincidence,' he ground out. 'And I smiled at you like that because you reminded me of Paddy. Which makes sense seeing as you're her bloody twin.'

Nick rounded on Paddy, her expression incredulous. 'This is him, isn't it?' she demanded. 'He says he's the father?'

Paddy nodded hesitantly. 'Yes?'

'The bastard who got you pregnant and then went and married someone else?' Nick's voice was rising, her face flushed with anger.

Paddy sighed, exhaustion pulling at her. 'Yes, but as it happens, no.'

Hal froze, his eyes widening. 'No wait, what? Why does your sister think I'm married?'

'Because I thought you were,' Paddy said simply.

'Who did you think I was married to?' Hal asked, bewildered.

'Bianca.'

'Why on earth did you think that?'

'I saw the wedding photos in Hello! magazine,' Paddy explained. 'But Jem explained them to me yesterday.' She turned to Nick. 'I just found out he wasn't actually married.'

Paddy looked at Hal, hope flaring inside her, then dying as she saw the pain in his face. What was wrong with her? He must have been humiliated by Bianca; not only had she been

352

cheating on him, but she'd also replaced him at his own wedding.

'Right. You two out.' Nick stood up and pointed at the door, her tone brooking no argument. 'If you want to help, call a doctor to sign her release, otherwise leave us.'

Hal looked to Paddy, reluctant to leave her side but she had started to cry and he wasn't sure why. 'I'll call for a nurse but I'm staying here,' he said firmly.

Jamie looked at the three of them; the tension in the room was miserable and whatever was going on wasn't helping Paddy. 'Hal, let's get a coffee and we can sort the car out while we're at it,' he suggested, trying to defuse the situation.

'Yes, that's right,' sneered Nick. 'Sort out the car. Priorities and all that.'

Paddy frowned at her sister, confusion and hurt warring on her face. 'Nick, what is wrong with you?' she asked. 'I wouldn't be here without them.'

'No, you certainly wouldn't be in this position, would you?' Nick retorted. She turned and scowled at the men. 'What are you two waiting for? You're not needed.'

As they closed the door behind them, Nick collapsed into the chair beside Paddy, all the fight draining out of her. 'Oh Christ, Paddy, I have simply never been so scared in my life,' she choked out between sobs. 'I've called the girls and told them you're in hospital. Expect a few phone calls in the next few hours.' She tossed a shredded hankie in the bin and pulled out another from her pocket as she started to unwind from her mad midnight drive from London to Cornwall.

***

Jamie sat down in front of Hal and slid him a coffee. 'Do you want to talk about it?'

Hal drank his coffee and tried to think where to start. 'It's complicated.'

Jamie smiled inwardly, these two wallies were singing from the same song sheet. 'No, it really isn't complicated. You love her, she loves you. That's clear for anyone to see. And she's carrying your child. Honestly, I don't think it gets simpler than that. This world can be short and brutal. You know that. For God's sake, man, get a ring on that gorgeous girl's finger and marry her.'

'But that's why it's complicated. She doesn't even like me. She thinks I'm a spoilt, lazy, entitled jumped-up toff.'

Jamie laughed. 'Well, it's a wise woman who knows her man!'

Hal laughed but inwardly both he and Jamie knew there was a lot of truth in those statements. Jamie had watched his friend and had marvelled at how he was wasting his life. At the same time he had envied him his blissful existence. He loved spending time with him; it was like living in a warm bubble, everything was perfect. The past year had proved to be something of a crucible for Hal, and Jamie wondered how he was going to rise to the challenge. The past week as he had listened to how Hal was working to save the estate and set up a charity, Jamie saw that Hal was exceeding his potential. Now he thought he might know the cause of that.

'Tell her you love her. What's the worst that can happen?'

'She can tell me she doesn't. Which she clearly doesn't, by the way.'

Jamie had no time for self-pitying. Even from a man who was at rock bottom. 'Well, then you'll know. Get a grip for God's sake. You're going to be a father. Stand up and be counted, soldier!'

Hal looked at Jamie in gratitude. This was no time for maudlin introspection. 'Right then. Come on,' he said pushing his coffee cup away.

Jamie looked at him quizzically. 'Don't think you need me for this, old boy.'

'Are you kidding,' said Hal grinning at his childhood friend, 'you'll need to get rid of the sister. Come on, soldier. Stand up!' Laughing the two men headed back up to the ward.

***

Jamie convinced Nick that Hal and Paddy needed a bit of time together and he ushered her out of the room. The door clicked behind them, and Hal came and sat on the other side of the bed.

'Have you really thought I was married all this time?' Paddy nodded mutely. 'Christ, you must have hated me?'

'Slightly.'

'I think I might owe you a thousand apologies.'

'I shouldn't have jumped to conclusions. It's just incredible she continued with the wedding. That must have been horrible for you?'

'Honestly? Not really. I mean it was a bit embarrassing.' He dropped his head into his hands and pulled his hair with his fingers. 'Scratch that, enormously embarrassing. But each time I was embarrassed, I was also overwhelmed with relief.'

He looked up and stared into her eyes. 'To think that I had nearly married someone out of a misplaced sense of duty. And all this time I've been in love with you. Knowing that you didn't love me was what was making me so wretched.'

'But I do!' Paddy looked at him in amazement.

'Do what?'

Paddy started laughing and then started crying again, until Hal swung his legs over to her side of the bed and hugged him to her. 'You love me?'

'Yes,' she sobbed through her giggles.

'Well that's okay then,' he echoed her laugh. 'So we actually love each other?'

'Yes!'

The pair of them were now both laughing. And then Hal caught his breath and gently held Paddy's face between his hands and looked at her in wonder. 'I love you Paddy, I am never going to leave your side again, if that's okay with you?'

Paddy nodded. Tears filled her eyes and she was certain that if she tried to speak, she would start sobbing instead. She ran her hands through his hair and then gave him a light kiss on the lips, wincing from the bruises as she leant forwards. The pain helped her calm down her emotions.

'That sounds heavenly.' She smiled at him, still reeling from the shock that he apparently loved her as much she did him. 'Come on, let's go home and figure this all out. Jamie said it's not complicated, so let's try and prove him right.'

Paddy looked around her bed. 'I think my house keys are in my bag. We'll need to go to the car to get it?'

Hal looked at her trying to understand what she was saying and then informed her in no uncertain terms was she heading back to the beach house. He had wasted seven months of his life apart from her, he wasn't going to tolerate another single day.

'I'd move in with you but I need to be at Vollen, it's such a mess right now. But I don't want to spend another day without you.'

'Is this because of the baby?' doubt flooded Paddy's voice.

'No. How can you ask? Last night when I saw you standing in the road covered in blood, I thought I was going to die. The estate, the charity, everything I am working for, it means nothing if I can't share it with you.' He placed his hand gingerly on her stomach. 'I want this little one, but it's you that I love.'

Chapter Forty-One

The following morning Hal and Paddy waved goodbye to Jamie and Nick. Nick had been reluctant to go, but Paddy needed to do this without her twin hovering around her anxiously. Quite frankly she was freaking her out. She was so used to Nick being calm and quiet, this highly strung, emotional version was exhausting her. She and Hal were tiptoeing around each other and she needed to be alone with him to work things out.

'Right, come on inside and let's sort out what we do next.' They walked back in through the large hallway and headed down a corridor to a sitting room where a fire had been laid out but not yet lit. Settling down in an armchair Paddy looked around her suddenly uncomfortable and awkward.

'Do you like your room?' Hal asked.

Oh God, thought Paddy, *small talk*. 'It's very nice, thank you. But my things—'

'Shall we get your things—?'

Both spoke at the same time and broke off laughing.

'Right. Come on then,' said Hal decisively, as he picked up his keys. Helping Paddy up into the seat of the Range Rover she apologised again, awkward by her pregnancy and the intimacy between them. As she pulled on the seatbelt she winced as it dug into the bruising from the crash.

'Maybe this isn't a good idea? I wanted to get my things but I'm not sure if I can wear a belt?'

Hal paused, he wasn't driving her anywhere without her being safe, but he also knew how important it was for her to feel comfortable at Vollen. Having her own things around her would help with that. Telling her to hang on, he ran back in the house and came back with a couple of pillows. Tucking them gently around her, he leant across her to fasten the belt. As he did, he smelled the shampoo from her morning shower. She was practically in his arms and he very carefully leant forward and kissed her. She leant forward to kiss him back and then hissed as her sore shoulder dug into the belt. Immediately, he pulled away, much to Paddy's annoyance; she had been enjoying that. They both looked at each other sheepishly as he apologised for leaping on her and rearranged the pillow under the belt.

As they drove off Paddy said she had rather enjoyed the leaping and the two of them grinned at each other. Another silence fell between them and Paddy didn't know how to break it. She was so happy and so tired she was content to just look across at him and smile. As they drove though, the silence was constantly interrupted by phone calls.

Ari wanted to know if the baby was okay. When she heard that Paddy was in a car you could hear the pursed lips half a country away. She was only reassured when Paddy told her about the pillows. Asking if she would be up for a visit, Paddy said she was and then hung up telling her she would send directions to Vollen. As she did Ari told her to call Aster.

Clem then rang telling her to take care of herself. Calling out *Hello* to Hal, she welcomed him to the family and hoped he was up to it. Then she reminded Paddy to call Aster and hung up.

Her sisters were doing a better job of breaking the ice than she was. Rolling her eyes Nick's name came up, and she asked to speak to Hal instead. Paddy explained he was driving, so she put her on speakerphone.

'Hal, I know you're brassic, but I've spotted a new company I think is worth investing in. Would you like me to buy some shares on your behalf?' As he agreed she told Paddy she loved her and hung up.

'That's more like it. Yesterday's Nick was not the normal version of herself by a long shot. It sounds like she's forgiven you. Not that there's anything to forgive,' said Paddy quickly.

'I think I have a lot of ground to make up. Anyway, that's three calls. Why do you have to call Aster? She's your youngest sister, isn't she?'

'Probably because she won't call, she's— oh my mistake,' Paddy broke off as her phone rang again.

'Hi, sis are you okay?'

Hal watched his wife's face light up every time she spoke to one of her sisters, and he was looking forward to meeting them. But now as he listened, this conversation was going wrong as she sought to console her little sister; it was clear that whoever was on the other end of the line was crying and now Paddy was as well. Indicating, Hal pulled over to the side of the road and asked if he could speak to Aster.

As he said hello there was silence at the other end of the phone, but he knew from the hitched breath that someone was listening.

'Your sister is fine. The hospital was prepared to let her out last night and they wouldn't have done that if they had any alarms. It was my fault she stayed in. I insisted she slept there. Belt and braces sort of thing. But she and the baby are fine; they were scanned and tested from this way to Sunday and they're fine.' He paused, waiting for any questions but the silence continued. 'I love your sister very much and cannot tell you how happy I am that she is in my life. I know it's corny but it feels like a fairy tale and that—'

'Okay,' a small voice cut him off, 'put my sister back on, please.'

Bemused, he listened as the two girls finished their conversation, and by the sounds of it, Aster was also on her way to stay for a bit.

'She and I can stay at the cottage if you'd prefer?'

'If you want. But I'd love to meet your family and they are all welcome. I want you to feel Vollen is your home as well but I know this is all happening a bit quickly. Your call.'

'Honestly, I don't want to spend another day away from you. Vollen it is. And Aster is unlikely to stay long. That was very unlike her.'

'Being upset that her sister was hurt? Seems a normal reaction?'

'I suppose so; she hates being out of control. She's like Nick in that regard and she was only ten when our parents died. When you got mushy and she told you to stop, that was more like Aster.'

Paddy laughed apologetically and then beamed as Hal insisted it did feel like a fairy tale, and he didn't care how soppy that made him sound. By now they had arrived at the cottage, and Hal ran around the place picking up bits that Paddy asked for. Smiling, she looked at her new wetsuit.

'I haven't even tried that on yet. Next week when the bruising dies down, I'm coming back for a swim.' Hal agreed and thought that that sounded like a nice routine. Obviously, he would be swimming with her.

'Remember your promise? You'll have to sing for me!'

Paddy groaned. 'Be prepared to be horrified.'

As he passed the mantlepiece he noticed the envelope from the production company. He picked it up and saw that it was unopened. Turning, he looked at her curiously.

'Do you know, it took me days to open this letter. I just didn't want to read it. Even then I knew I wanted to be married to you. Every time I thought about it, it made me so happy, although the fact that you clearly loathed me was a bit disheartening.' He chuckled apologetically. 'I just couldn't help myself. I had to cancel my engagement to Bianca. I just didn't know how to proceed. Then of course I opened the letter and well, you know...'

Paddy sat watching him. His revelation that being married to her made him happy was making her feel wonderful. It took her a moment to register his final sentence.

'What do you mean, *'well you know'*.'

'About the marriage not being valid after all. No need for any further paperwork or annulments or divorces.'

Paddy stared at him in horror. 'We're not married?'

'What? No, didn't your agent tell you what was in it? Is that why you didn't open it?'

'I didn't open it because I didn't want to face what was in it. I kept torturing myself with it knowing I should sign the divorce papers or whatever was in there. Then you went and got married anyway...' her voice trailed away.

'Except I didn't.' He came over and sat down on the sofa beside her. 'I couldn't marry her when I was in love with you. I was devastated when those production company lawyers told me we weren't married. At that moment I knew I couldn't proceed with my marriage to Bianca.' He leant forward placing his head in his hands remembering how Bianca refused to return any of his calls that week.

'So you're not married to anyone!'

He laughed and shook his head. 'Absolutely no one.'

'But why was she at the party at your house?'

'She wasn't talking to me. When I discovered you were pregnant, I was so thrown that I forgot to meet her for lunch and went straight home. She was livid. So the first time I saw her was at the party.'

'I still don't understand, if she was so cross with you why did she come to the party?'

'Appearances. I think she had been punishing me, and was expecting I was going to be all apologetic at the party.'

'Instead you told her you'd slept with me…'

Hal groaned and Paddy took pity on him. 'Looks like we've both been screwing up. You were trying to fix the mess and I was running away from it.'

Hal sat back on the sofa and smiled gently at Paddy and placed his arm around her shoulder as she leant into him. 'We're as bad as each other,' he said and rested his head on hers. 'Come on, let's get going, whilst you get your head around the fact that you aren't actually married.'

Locking up, they headed up to the big house and called in to let Michelle know of the change of plans. She smirked, glad to have been proven right and reassured Paddy that everything was under control. Just as they were about to drive off Paddy had an overwhelming urge to visit the chapel. This is where it had all started and she wanted to go and sit there and tell her parents what had happened. As they walked in, she contrasted the serenity of the space to the noise and bustle of the film shoot. So much had happened since then, and it had been months of massive ups and downs. She had avoided the chapel since she had become pregnant. At the time it evoked too many powerful memories. Baby gave a little somersault, making Paddy laugh and she placed her hand over her tummy. 'I know. It is lovely here.'

'I didn't say anything,' said Hal, confused.

Paddy smiled at him. 'Sorry, you'll have to get used to that. I was chatting to Baby. I do that a lot. I was just thinking that it all started here.'

'That's just what I was thinking. I was so hungover, everyone was speaking German and I walked in here and saw an angel sitting on a pew. The light was on your face and I didn't think I had ever seen anything so beautiful in all my life. I was completely blown over and knew I wanted to spend the rest of my life with you by my side. I found myself wishing the wedding was for real and then wondering if I'd lost my marbles.'

Paddy laughed.

'I'm sorry. This is awkward,' said Hal, making Paddy laugh even more.

'Do you think…?' Hal paused and started again. Paddy was currently sitting on the front pew, and Hal moved away from her and knelt on the stone floor in front of her. Putting his hand in his jacket pocket he pulled out an old leather ring case. Paddy looked at him in wonder as he opened the box. Nestled in the dark blue satin lining was a large ruby edged with smaller diamonds sitting in a pretty platinum band. 'My grandmother said I should only give this to the girl I couldn't imagine living without. And now I have. So, 'Not Actually Mrs Ferguson', will you be my wife?'

Smiling, Paddy stretched her hand out and looked at the beautiful ring Hal slipped on her finger.

'Did Bianca…' she paused, doubt and uncertainty choking off her sentence.

Hal looked at her confused and then understood her question. 'I didn't even show this ring to Bianca, she picked one out from Boodles. So, enough of her.' He picked up Paddy's hand and kissed her fingers. 'I believe I asked a question? Will you be my wife?'

A smile bright enough to dim the sun shone across Paddy's face as tears of joy poured down her face.

'I will. I do.' Her breath hitched as she laughed, 'Yes please!'

Sitting back beside her, Hal wrapped his arms around Paddy and kissed her promising he would never let her down, that he would spend every day of his life being the perfect husband and father.

Paddy leant into him. Comforted by the presence of her parents and sisters, she felt Baby give an approving somersault and she kissed her soon-to-be husband-again, back.

Bonus Scene:

Do you want to know want happened to Bianca? Enjoy this epilogue and find out what happened to her and the Fabergé snowdrops. Follow this link to find out.

https://dl.bookfunnel.com/vxicv38tes

Author's Letter:

Hello again and welcome back to the de Foix sisters. I imagine you are beginning to get a real sense of who they all are now and I hope you like them as much as I do. It's important to me that they all get their own individual stories, trust me, sisters can only share so much. However, it's impossible to tell their stories without the other four turning up throughout the tale, and I enjoy it when they drop in.

Thank you for reading all the way to this section, I really appreciate the fact that you have liked the book. If you ever want to ask me anything about the story, I'm on Facebook and Instagram and I'd love to chat.

I can hear the other sisters shouting for their own stories, so I had best get back to the keyboard. Once again, thank you for your support.

To keep up to date with all my news sign up to my newsletter.

Cheers,

Liz

www.lizhurleywrites.com

Now, turn the page to read the first chapter of book four, **From Ireland With Love** to discover Nick's story.

Acknowledgements

I should like to thank the following for their input and advise on various matters. Any mistakes are absolutely my own. Obviously, they know what they are talking about and I'm an author trying to weave a story around the facts, some of those facts may have been nudged through my own ignorance. With that said I would like to thank Clare Williams and Caroline Lawrence for their help on land matters, Debbie Hext for all things equine, both in this book and the last. (Dickie Trant for matter military) tbc and Anita Gupta from Transform Housing & Support for her input into homeless issues.

I am particularly grateful to Fr Richard Tuset for his advice on the legal issues surrounding church weddings. He and his colleagues had a lot of fun with this and helped save the day.

I am also hugely grateful to Al and Steve for reading the various rough drafts of this book, and always being positive in the face of my narcissistic pleadings for reassurance. And to my editor Keshini, who always spotted the right areas to develop or drop.

I have really enjoyed getting to know Paddy, she's a much softer character than Ari and it was fun writing about her. Once again, I hope this is a light-hearted and happy story but I am dealing with a few genuinely difficult topics in this book and if you'd like to know more, I recommend the following two charities. Both are small, but like most small charities they are tireless and deserving of greater recognition and support.

Transform Housing & Support
https://www.transformhousing.org.uk

Battling-On
https://www.battling-on.com

From Ireland With Love

CHAPTER ONE

The wind began to pick up in earnest as the walkers headed briskly across the field to Hiverton Manor.

'Do you think we'll get ahead of the rain?' laughed Ari.

Hal turned back to her with a grin on his face and Will on his shoulders. 'If we were in Cornwall, we'd already be wet! They're not called April showers for nothing.' He tugged on the boot of his little rider. 'One last charge at Daddy and Leo before we get inside?'

Will roared out, pumping his fist in the air, and Hal pretended to be a mighty war horse as he galloped over to Seb, who had Leo up on his shoulders. The two men ran in small circles whilst the six-year-olds tried to hit each other.

Pointing to the child in her sling, Ari called back to Rory. 'You know, as soon as Hector is big enough, he'll require a battle horse as well. Are you up for it?'

'Lassie, I've been a donkey, a dragon and even the Loch Ness Monster for my brother's lads. It will be my pleasure. If my back hasn't completely died by then.'

As she looked at Rory, Nick couldn't imagine such a vital man ever having a bad back. Tiny Clem had fallen in love with a giant of a man. He looked the sort that could probably pull up a tree by its roots. Of the three men, he was definitely the broadest, clearly a very hands-on sort of farmer.

Paddy and Clem were bringing up the rear of the group. 'Are you looking forward to when Eleanor will be demanding shoulder rides?' said Nick to Paddy.

Paddy smiled at her tiredly. 'Yes and no. I love being with her like this.'

Like Ari, Paddy had her baby strapped to her in a sling – country living made a mockery of prams. At five and six months old, the two little cousins were the apple of every one's eyes and Paddy and Ari weren't short of willing volunteers to pitch in and help.

'Although at the moment I could do with a rest,' said Paddy. 'We were up all night with her crying. I don't know where Hal finds the energy.'

Nick watched as her other two brothers-in-laws pretended to be horses, their little charges shouting with excitement from their shoulders. Like Rory they were good-looking and tall if not quite so broad, but it wasn't any of their looks that appealed to Nick. It was how the three men seemed to enjoy each other's company and how well they had joined the family. She had always feared one of her sisters marrying a man she didn't like, and indeed when Ari married Greg, her first husband, all the sisters had been appalled. Poor Ari, unexpectedly pregnant, said yes when Greg proposed. On reflection Nick felt a tiny bit sorry for Greg as well – after all, he had done the decent thing. It was just that the decent thing was also the wrong thing, once again proving that the road to hell was paved with good intentions. His sudden death had been a blessing for all. Well, nearly all.

'Why are you laughing?' asked Paddy.

'Bad thoughts. Ignore me. Here, can I carry Eleanor? Give you a rest.'

Paddy thought about it which surprised Nick – for her to contemplate it Paddy must be really tired, because she knew Nick wasn't a baby person. Pets and children were the very pinnacle of chaos.

'No, I'm grand. We're nearly there anyway.'

Looking ahead Ari, Clem and Aster had already reached the back door and were chatting to Dickie.

'By the time we join them, everyone will have their boots and coats off, the fire will be lit, the kettle will be on and we can just sweep in and put our feet up.'

'The Queens of Sheba!'

Nick stopped and curtsied towards Paddy, who grinned and began to curtsey back, but Eleanor began to grizzle. Nick put her hand out and gently held Eleanor's little chubby fist.

'I meant you as well, little one. We three shall all be the Queens of Sheba.'

As they got closer to the back of the house it began to rain. Paddy tried to keep Eleanor protected from the elements, but the heavens had properly opened. Everyone else had now disappeared inside but a back door opened, and Hal came running out towards them carrying two umbrellas. He had already taken his coat and boots off and was now getting his socks wet as he ran across the lawn towards them.

Laughing and gasping from the sudden downpour, they all piled into the house. Hal peeled his socks off and then grumbled about the cold flagstones. As he went off to grab another pair of socks, Nick and Paddy laughed as they heard him shout to Seb that he needed to install underfloor heating.

Rory then shouted back that he needed to stop being a great southern Jessie. He might have got away with the jest but for the disembodied voice of Clem who reminded him that he had just installed a heated driveway. As the ribbing and the conversation continued loudly across many rooms, the twins headed towards the large sitting room where a fire was blazing, and the other three sisters were already enjoying hot drinks and were cuddled down into various armchairs and sofas.

Hector was sat on the rug in front of Ari, waving a teething rattle and gurling contentedly but other than that the room was still and quiet. Nick smiled and relaxed.

'I know,' said Aster, 'a moment of calm. Isn't it lovely?'

'Enjoy it while you can,' said Ari. 'Seb is washing down the dogs, Dickie is feeding the boys and Rory is getting changed, I think.' Rory had been playing tug of war with Leo and Will and had somehow managed to lose and fall in a muddy puddle – to the boys' great entertainment.

'You know, I think he fell in the mud deliberately?' Ari smiled as she shook her head and continued trying to account for where everyone was. 'What's Hal up to?'

'Changing Eleanor and then they'll come and join us. He might see if she'll sleep,' replied Paddy hopefully.

The door opened and the girls smiled as Dickie came in. She was the only other person who had known their mother and they would regularly plague her for tales of her as a young girl.

'Ariana, I've taken the boys to bed. Their heads were nodding as they drank their milk.'

Ari looked at her wristwatch. It was three o'clock now, they would probably sleep for an hour which suited her perfectly. They rarely napped in the afternoon but with all the family staying they were totally and utterly over stimulated. She had every day to spend with her children but opportunities to spend time with her sisters all together were few and far between. It was only because Aster was about to go travelling that they had all found a free weekend before she left. Ari couldn't help being uncomfortable that Aster was going so far away for so long. Seb pointed out the time would fly by, and that she would do better being worried for the countries that Aster visited.

'You know, Aster,' Ari addressed her little sister, 'you could always get a secondment to work with some of Nick's contacts. They're always looking for computer whizz-kids.'

Aster groaned. 'It's not going to work, Ari. I'm serious, I just want to play and explore. I want a change.'

Aster had got a first-class Honours degree in Classics from Cambridge. It came as barely a surprise when they discovered that she had also been taking a degree in computing sciences and got a first in that as well. Aster was the brainbox in the family. She didn't get bored as such, but everything interested her, and she always wanted to know more.

'I plan to really sink my teeth into Greece and Italy. Imagine the triremes sailing out of Ostia, picture Plato striding around the Agora. I might call in on Otto and Louis.'

'You'll need to be quick; I think they're planning a trip to India before they return to Scotland for the summer,' said Clem, who had first encountered Otto in Scotland, running the family castle. Both women were creative geniuses who knew their own minds, they were both stubborn and had clashed almost immediately. It wasn't until Otto was reunited with the love of her life that she had begun to mellow and enjoy life.

For the past year Otto had been living something of a peripatetic life and hadn't yet decided where it was she wanted to settle. *So long as Louis is by my side, what do I care where I am?* The woman was a nightmare, but Clem missed her when she was away.

Nick sat and watched her sisters chat, gently mocking Ari for trying to divert Aster. She wriggled her toes in front of the crackling logs and enjoyed the moment. After all that they had been through, these moments were more precious to her than any portfolio or asset. The girls had grown up with next to nothing, just the love of their family, and when their parents had died even that was destroyed. It had been a gruelling childhood, but they had got through it together and now life was good.

The door opened and Seb walked in with Dragon and George at his feet – they promptly rolled over Hector's wooden tower. Seb leant across and gave Ari a small kiss, then sat on the floor with the little one and started to rebuild the tower as he laughed in delight at the chaos the dogs had created. The two dogs were scolded and told to settle down in the corner. The problem was that Hector had the best spot in front of the fire guard.

'Dragon, away,' and Ari pointed her finger to the other side of the room. Both dogs stood up and headed over to the far side. Dragon looked over her shoulder to see if Ari had changed her mind and then realising she hadn't, decided to make the most of the warm spot by the radiator. She looked at Ari reproachfully as she discovered it was cold, but Ari didn't appear to be paying attention, so the dog sighed and lay down, George had been better trained or less indulged and just lay where she was told but Dragon always had to push her luck.

A moment later Rory – carrying Eleanor – and Hal joined them bearing a teapot and a cafetière and refilled everyone's cups. Nick shook her head, so much for peace and quiet.

'What was that look, Letta?'

The others all looked over at her as Aster asked her question.

'Do you know, I miss hearing Letta,' said Ari.

Rory was sitting on one of the armchairs drinking a cup of Darjeeling, trying to decide if he liked Clem's latest fad. He wasn't convinced. He glanced across at the sisters.

'Who's Letta?'

'Nick is,' said Aster. 'Her full name is Nicoletta. Da used to call her Nick and Mum would call her Letta. I don't have many memories of them, but I do remember that and how they would sing the two names. *Nick knack paddy whack* and *Alouette, gentille alouette.*'

The sisters laughed, remembering the songs, and joined in. Dragon took her moment and slunk quietly closer towards the fire.

'Anyway,' shrugged Aster, 'I don't hear Letta enough so I like to use that name whenever I can. You don't mind, do you?'

'Not in the slightest. I like it as well. It was just you know, being called Nick in the financial market's never hurt.

It's a lazy and sexist stereotype but one I was happy to use to my advantage. Still, people seem to find other people having more than one name confusing.'

'It is a bit, though, isn't it?' said Rory again. 'I mean, all of you have multiple names. I know women often change their surnames when they get married but you five are also Byrne or de Foix as well as Hiverton.'

'Strictly speaking,' said Seb, 'only Ari is Hiverton. The others are of the Hiverton family. Like the Duke of Norfolk, there is only one person that could be called Norfolk. It's a title as much as a name and only one person can have it.'

'Yes, and that's bossy pants over there,' teased Aster.

'Okay, but you all also have various forenames. Paddy is also Holly McDonald.'

'That's just a work thing.'

'Nick here is either Nick or Letta.'

'Both diminutives.'

'Clem is Clem, Clemmie or Clementine.'

'You forgot "Bloody Hell, Clem".'

'That's not so much a name as a daily cry.'

Clem threw a cushion at Rory which made the dogs look up in readiness for a pillow fight. One stern look from Ari and they lowered their heads again. Now that Ari had noticed Dragon, she had to move back to the cold radiator.

'Anyway, you can talk, Rory,' said Clem. 'One day you'll be Invershee, just like Ari is Hiverton. Plus you call me Bo.'

'I know, it's just you all have so many names it gets confusing.'

Aster poured a cup of coffee and brought it over to Rory.

'Here,' she said handing him the cup, 'and if it helps, I'm just Aster. Short, sweet and uncomplicated.'

That caused everyone to laugh so hard that both dogs jumped up barking. Eleanor, surprised by the sudden noise, began to cry.

Nick smiled to herself; Eleanor was a child after her own heart. She decided that now was probably a good moment to try and calm everyone down.

'That magazine article came out yesterday, by the way.' She rummaged in the bag. 'They've actually written a lot more about the family than I wanted, so I've got you all a copy.' She handed each sister her own copy of *Financial Focus*, the City's leading financial journal. Cressida was the editor and a friend of Nick's. She had asked if Nick would be happy to feature in an article, given her recent rise in profile. Nick had reluctantly agreed, and a particularly hopeless reporter had come over to interview her.

Now the article was published Nick vowed never to be interviewed again. In fairness, it wasn't appalling but she had been hoping for something that focussed on her business and the family's charitable enterprise – which it did, but at least a quarter of the copy focussed on the rags-to-riches aspect of their family and the sisters' private lives. Frankly, she was embarrassed to have allowed this breach into their privacy.

'Oh my God, Nick, where did they get this photo from?' shrieked Paddy in delight. 'You look like some ball-breaking dominatrix.'

When Nick had first started, she'd had a professional head shot done. She wore thick, black-rimmed glasses; her then short hair had been slicked back and she wore a pin-striped suit. She liked the photo a lot, it portrayed confidence. She looked like every other stockbroker and most importantly, if you saw her in the flesh, you wouldn't recognise her. She knew she came across as a dry old stick but that didn't really bother her. Growing up with her more flamboyant sisters she never felt the need to sparkle. It looked too much like hard work. She'd rather just beaver away in the background.

'I like this bit,' said Ari reading it out loud. 'De Foix Investments also caters to a different sort of investor. In Byrne's own words, "I felt that the stock market can seem too off-putting for a large sector of the community. For those that didn't grow up with money or for people within certain social groups, it really seems like it is for the rich only. I wanted to reach out to people from all walks of life." That really sums up your ethos.'

'I guess,' shrugged Nick. 'I just wish she had reported more about the charity as well.'

The Five Sisters Charity helped people into jobs or to set up their own business. It also offered support and advice for those struggling with the welfare services, and recently had started to help small community ventures. This was definitely a passion project and one Nick could talk about for hours.

'Instead, it just keeps harping on about how I brought down the Bank of Harrington's which everyone knows I didn't.' She waved the magazine in Seb's direction, drawing him into the conversation. 'Even your brother didn't actually do it. Harringtons were responsible for their own failure. Geoffrey and I merely asked a few questions.'

'And the financial industry is all the better for it,' replied Seb. 'No one needed another run on the stock market. Even if it did cause a few issues for those of us that had invested in Harrington's.'

Hal winced. His was one of the families that had almost gone under, but he agreed with Seb, none of that was Nick's fault. He raised his cup in her direction.

'This bit is good as well,' called out Paddy. '"Of course there are risks everywhere but I wanted to get away from the idea that various socio-economical groups don't like risk. They do – they're human after all. They just didn't know how to get in. So I set up a small company that offered business services, financial advice and money growth. All on a microscale, but I loved it. This is what money is for. It's about changing lives. It's about feeding ideas and watching businesses grow."'

'That is so you!' continued Paddy. 'Why don't you like this article? It seems really well balanced and ever so positive?'

Nick winced. They hadn't got to the part where the article wandered off into their private lives. 'Carry on reading.'

'Hang on,' said Clem in an outraged voice. 'Paddy, have you read this bit? It's completely unfair. *Abandoned by her muse just as her career began to take off.* You never abandoned me. I have NEVER felt that way. Who wrote this drivel? Nick, you didn't say that, did you?'

'Of course she didn't, Clem,' said Paddy. 'Stop being so touchy. Journalists will write any old tosh. You know that.'

'Oh dear,' said Ari. 'They do love this from-a-city-estate-of-broken-bottles-to-a-country-estate-with-a-title angle.'

'We grew up on a terrace street. Hardly an estate,' said Aster.

'Not as sexy though, is it?'

'Oh, and look the journalist has trotted out the rich-girl-falls-for-penniless-Irish-student. *A hospital porter, doing the best he could for his family. Did Lady Elizabeth ever regret her decision?* Bloody hell, that's a bit rich.'

'Don't they mention Da's work as an artist?' demanded Clem. 'Nick, why didn't you tell her how talented Da was?'

Nick sighed; it was all this sort of guff that had really wound her up when she'd first read the article. The sisters knew the truth of their upbringing and it really wasn't anyone else's business. Especially if they were going to misinterpret it.

'Of course I did. I even showed her shots of some of his pictures on my phone.'

'Well, she hasn't mentioned them?'

'And?'

'Well, all I'm saying is maybe you forgot. Maybe you didn't think it was that important.'

'This shit again!' Nick put her cup down. Maybe it was time to go. She had been really disappointed by the article and now Clem was winding her up with the old you-only-care-about-money crap.

'I don't know what's wrong with you sometimes, Clem,' admonished Ari. 'You know damn well that Nick would have been singing Da's praises to the rafters.'

'Has it never crossed your mind how proud I am of your talents?' snapped Nick, slapping her magazine on the coffee table. 'You and Da always had that in common. But oh no. You have to trot out the whole money-grubbing Nick routine.'

'That's not fair. I didn't say that.'

'As good as,' Aster joined in.

'But that wasn't what I meant.'

'So what did you mean when you said *I didn't think it was as important?*' challenged Nick.

'Maybe she meant not important in the context of an interview about your business achievements,' said Aster and Clem pounced.

'That was exactly what I meant. I know if I was talking about my business, it would take me ages to say how important your skills were to the company. And they are. They are essential. I'm really sorry, Nick.' Clem jumped up from her sofa and came and settled herself down by Nick. 'I didn't mean to make you feel bad. I'm a stupid idiot. Forgive me?'

Nick glared at her briefly then nodded curtly. She knew she was genuinely contrite and was acting from a position of deep insecurity. Honestly, Nick sometimes felt that she was the big sister, not Clem. The awkward moment passed, and they finished browsing through the article.

The three men looked at each other, Rory casting his eyes to heaven. All of the men had found it was safer to step back when the sisters were having a spat. Any time they had tried to get involved, the girls had rounded on them and then the row just escalated and spread out. Rory came from a large family and was used to sibling blowouts. Those same fights tended to make Seb yearn for the rare moments when he and his brother and sister were all in the same country at the same time. Hal, however, as a single child, found them deeply unsettling and Paddy would have to regularly convince him that the family wasn't, despite all appearances to the contrary, tearing itself apart.

Eventually the clock chimed the hour and Nick sighed. It was time to go.

'Okay. That's me.'

'Do you really have to go? You were the last to arrive on Friday.'

'Sorry, Ari, there's a lot going on in the markets at the moment and I have a 4 a.m. call tomorrow morning.'

'Ouch, poor you,' said Seb sympathetically. His brother, Geoffrey, was also a city trader and ran his own investment company. Seb knew how hard his brother worked but like Nick, he thrived off the adrenaline and odd hours.

'Why don't you stay for supper,' tried Ari again, 'then head off?'

'Because then I won't have an early night. And I'll be groggy all day tomorrow and you know I don't like to start the week groggy. You know me, plan to succeed.'

The girls all laughed at Nick's self-deprecating joke. Nick was a stickler for planning ahead. She regularly had to deal with their gentle mockery, but life was so much easier if she didn't have to think about what to wear or what to eat. Every day, all the mundane stuff had been planned out and laid down the night before so that she could focus on work instead. She knew the efficiency could sometimes make her seem a bit boring, but she didn't care – she just wanted to spend time thinking about stuff she enjoyed. And that was her job. Popping the magazine back in her bag she asked if anyone could run her to the train station.

'Me!' said all four of her sisters, and a lovely warm feeling hugged her. She loved them all so much and wished she had been able to spend more time with them. But loving them also meant looking after them and running De Foix Investments properly. Nick looked across at Paddy, who kept glancing anxiously over at Eleanor on Hal's lap, and made her mind up. Her twin needed a break, even a tiny one, and she hadn't spent much time at all with Paddy since Eleanor arrived.

'Come on, Padster, what say you and I have a tiny road trip?'

Paddy beamed excitedly and stood up and smiled at Hal. 'I'll be about an hour; can you hold the fort with Eleanor until then?'

'I think I can manage a baby,' drawled Hal.

Which was precisely the moment that poor Eleanor began violently throwing up. Paddy ran across the room and was now using her pashmina to try and clean up Eleanor's face but as the baby threw up again, she and Hal rushed out to the bathroom. The dogs ran forward excitedly until Ari barked at them and sent them to their beds. Nick looked on in horror.

'Were the dogs about to eat the vomit? This is definitely my cue to leave.'

'And mine,' declared Clem with the same look of disgust on her face. 'Come on, I'll drive, and I can apologise again for being a thin-skinned eejit.'

To Read On - Order Now:
From Ireland with Love

384

Printed in Great Britain
by Amazon